Reunion at Fort Worden

By Joyce Anne Taylor

Kestrel Arts publishing

A Kestrel Arts book
Published by Kestrel Arts, Oregon

Copyright ©2018 by Kestrel Arts
Cover Design by Christopher Taylor

Printed in the United States of America
Trade Paperback Edition

Reunion At Fort Worden/Joyce Anne Taylor

ISBN 978-0-9838176-4-2

First Edition

In memory of my beloved Robert

To

Colleen, Kevin, Rhonda, Terry, Rebecca and Jeffrey

Six joys of my life

Chapter I

Seattle, that gem of the Pacific Northwest, rises on hills above Puget Sound. Not so long ago it was a town of muddy streets--one of them the original Skid Road along which logs were skidded to their destination--an adolescent town with gambling joints, cheap saloons, and gaudy dance halls where those bound for Alaskan gold or back to spend it gathered to talk and dance and laugh the night and their gold away. Now more sophisticated it has a big university, a large airport, the Space Needle built for the 1962 World's Fair, an art museum, tall modern buildings, a maze of highways, ships from exotic ports in Elliot Bay. Seattle, with its wet green winters, framed by mountains, east and west, blessed by lush growth of bushes, trees, flowers, home to people from many lands, with its houseboat community, it's Russian and Irish and other national neighborhoods, is home to many people who live and work and sleep in the city among the hills and trees and flowers.

Alan Metlow and his wife, Anna, both native to Washington, had reared their family in Seattle; now two of their daughters lived there still. On a cool day in May, when the city was in leaf and flower, one of the Metlow girls, sat in her kitchen tapping her teeth with a pencil. She'd discarded the Metlow name and seldom thought of herself as one of the Metlow girls any more. Missily Metlow had a strange sound now she'd been Missily Adamsen for so long.

On the table before her lay a notebook with a list of names written in it. She was trying to think whether she'd forgotten anyone. Feeling pleasantly lazy because she was alone and at leisure for a change, she was loath to move to find her address book and check to see if she'd missed any names. It was her turn to plan the family reunion that had been, until the last three times, held every year even though not everyone could come each time. As the children had grown and begun to have other interests the reunion changed to every three years. That way, more came because they could visit other relatives or take other trips in the free years. Now, some of the older people were no longer around. None of her grandparents were alive and only Mikell's Granny Ellen, who was eighty-eight, remained of that generation.

Missily had to smile as she thought of Granny Ellen. She was such an individual; outspoken but more tolerant of her great grandchildren than their own parents were. They all loved her, from her children to her

1

youngest descendant. At the moment, Missily couldn't remember who that was, a grandniece or something like that.

There would be one new member this year, at least. Suz's daughter, Alexis, was to be married in late fall and Missily would have to remember to invite Jon Craig, Alexis' fiancé. Kitten would probably bring a friend with her. It was interesting to see her guests. She was the only one of the five Metlow sisters who had not married and she generally brought a woman friend with her. She'd brought a man once but she'd written Missily later that she would never do so again because all anyone could think about was marriage and she and Tad had just been friends; he'd been *very* disgusted. Missily laughed as she remembered his reaction to the children's questions, all perfectly innocent. He'd been somewhat of a snob but then Kitten was a snob herself.

She was the third of the sisters, a tall, thin woman of forty-one, who played cello in the Philadelphia Symphony Orchestra, taught cello lessons at home and in one of the conservatories and played with different groups around the country. Her full name was Victoria Theodosia and, as Erin remarked, that was enough to give anyone airs, but her family called her Kitten from the time she was a child and slept all curled up like a cat, even making a kind of purring noise. She hated the name but they'd used it too many years to change now though her nephews and nieces weren't allowed by their parents to call her that. Besides, her family had an amused tolerance of her snobbery, all but Missily who was only irritated by it, and it was part of that amusement to call her Kitten instead of the more grand sounding Victoria, though her father still used that when he was vexed with her.

With a little sigh, Missily arose to cross the room to take her address book out of the drawer of the big buffet standing against the wall. It didn't match the dining set but most of the furniture in the house was hand-me-down, someone's cast-offs, and Missily seldom thought of it. They couldn't afford to buy new furniture, never had been able to, and she didn't let it bother her even though she enjoyed looking at beautiful rooms in magazines and dreaming vague dreams of fixing the house up some day.

As she shut the drawer her eyes fell on a picture of herself and her four sisters taken at the last reunion. That time they'd gone to New Mexico, where Erin and Thor lived and the beautiful blue sky was behind them. Missily never quite got over the blue of the Rocky Mountain skies. She'd lived in Washington all her life and hadn't been anywhere else except Oregon until Erin was married and moved with Thor to Santa Fe where Thor published a magazine for artists, musicians, and writers in the area. That last reunion they'd gone to a guest ranch where one of the artists lived with her husband.

Missily picked up the picture. There was some family resemblance but unless one knew they were sisters it was hard to tell the five of them were from the same family. Her father had always liked to tease his wife about bringing the wrong babies home from the hospital. Then he'd add that at least she'd learned by the time the last two came along.

2

Rose was the oldest. Missily smiled as she thought of their names. Her mother had been determined not to name any of them common names. She'd never liked her own name, Anna, and didn't want any of the girls to have it but their father had insisted that the first girl had to have at least one of her names and since she disliked Margaret, her second name, even more than Anna, the first baby had been named Rosemond Anna though she'd always been called Rose except by her mother who used all of their full first names without fail. That was confusing to anyone who didn't know them because when the second daughter came along a little over a year later she was named Edita Suzanne but Allan Metlow said Edita was no name for a baby and called her Suz. When Anna wanted to know why, he replied he knew she would never approve of Sue because it was too common and though Anna sniffed, Suz had stuck so that the only one using Edita was her mother. Even in school Suz managed to get them to use her nickname even though her mother insisted every year until Suz reached junior high that she was to be called Edita.

Rose, who was passed in height by all her sisters, was now stout as well as short. Her brown hair, which she had done every week at the beauty parlor, was short and always combed neatly in place. She and Graham lived several miles from Missily and Mikell. Graham was a quiet man, with graying dark hair, not much taller than his wife though more spare, and he managed a drug store. They had no children.

It hadn't been Rose, however, who had married first. Suz had managed that by eloping at seventeen. She'd always been restless, in trouble one way or another, and now was divorced for the third time. Missily sighed. It was hard to know how to act around Suz sometimes. She was pretty still with her long, dark blond hair, tall and slender and graceful. But there was a hardness about her now. Though she'd been given both her son and daughter after the divorce - she'd taken them with her when she left Diccon - both had left her as soon as they were old enough. Nigel was living with his father while Alexis was living with the man she was engaged to marry, a man she had met in college.

Missily went back to the table to look at his name. Jon Craig. She wondered what he was like. She'd received just a short note from Suz telling her Alexis was engaged to a man named Jon Craig and little else. Suz was always full of herself and her doings. She had another man friend in tow and would probably bring him to the reunion.

Kitten was third in the picture since they'd stood in order of age, dressed in expensive slacks and a beautiful long-sleeved blouse but Kitten never looked casual. Missily stood next to Kitten. She was almost as tall, in fact she could never remember whether she was as tall or taller. Kitten usually wore high heels while Missily preferred lower heeled shoes or flats. Kitten's hair was darker but quite short while Missily's lovely chestnut brown hair fell to her shoulders. She always looked neat but she had never paid attention to styles like Kitten and Rose did. They had repeatedly told her she would improve in looks if she were more particular in her dress and make-up. Missily smiled but never answered. Mikell liked her the way she was and told her so convincingly.

3

The fifth daughter, Erin Marie, was the fair-haired, blue-eyed one, like her mother. She played golf with her friends and with Thor, skied in winter, worked with local charities, belonged to clubs and was more sports-minded than her sisters. She'd been a cheerleader in high school, in gymnastics, popular, and fun to be with. She jogged every morning, played tennis as well as all her other activities along with chauffeuring her three daughters to their various activities. Now that Celeste was old enough to drive, though, Erin had written earlier in the year, she didn't have so much of that to do.

Missily put the picture back down. They were all so different. She loved every one of them but she wasn't as close to them as she was to Mikell's sisters and sisters-in-law; Eva, Lorna, Jean, and Molly. She and Rose were probably the closest in her own family, which may have been only because they lived in the same town. They went shopping together once in a while and the families went out to dinner together occasionally and had picnics together in the summer along with their parents. Graham and Mikell got along but weren't particularly close.

"He's so boring," Mikell said once to Missily as they were preparing for bed after one of the picnics. "I don't mean just his monotone voice, though that's bad enough, but he talks about the same thing every time I see him; the weather, how terrible the government is and why doesn't it stay out of other people's business, and how big a shipment of this or that he got. You'd think he'd bore himself to death. Remember that time someone tried to rob the store and that young clerk threw a milk shake in the robber's face? When I asked Graham about it after I heard it on the radio he just said, 'What? Oh yes. I'm glad he didn't get anything' and that was it."

Missily, who was sitting on the bed cross-legged rolling her heavy hair in curlers, grinned. "Not everyone can be a gifted story teller like you, you know," she answered.

And Mikell, good spirits restored, grinned back. "Oh sure, I'm the greatest. He's a great guy, really. Just boring. And there *are* worse things than that."

The door slammed as Missily set the picture down and Sean, a junior in high school, ran into the room throwing his coat over one of the dining-room chairs and dumping his books on the table, "Hi, Mom. What's to eat?" He went over to kiss her cheek and whirl her around. Though he ate enough for two, he was tall and skinny.

"I made some brownies today and there's a plate of veggies in the refrigerator. Do you have homework?"

"Yes, worse luck. I've got a Science test coming up. What've you been doing?"

"Trying to make a list for the family reunion."

"That's this year? Neato. Where're we going? I wish we could go to a ranch like we did at Aunt Erin's."

"So do I but we voted then and the majority want to change each time, do something different. Your father and I thought we'd find out about getting some of the officer's houses at Fort Worden. I have to find out how many we'd need."

"You mean at that State Park near Port Townsend?"

"Yes," Missily sat back down with her list. Her son had two brownies and looked over her shoulder as he ate them.

"Isn't Uncle Diccon coming?" he asked with his mouth full.

"Manners," she reminded him. "Don't I have Diccon down?"

He swallowed noisily. "No. You have Nigel but not him."

Missily wrote Diccon's name on the list wondering how she could have forgotten him. They all loved him and Suz had never minded his coming to the reunions though she scarcely paid any attention to him. She seemed so cold-hearted to Missily. She treated him like someone she'd met once, a casual acquaintance, instead of like a man she'd been married to for ten years, bearing him two children. But she did that with all the men she married and divorced, treated them like a discarded dress and forgot about them. Of course, mused Missily, I have no idea what it's like to divorce someone and think I love more than one man.

The problem was that all Suz's men were attractive men, interesting, outgoing, and lovable. Certainly not boring like Graham was. No one could understand Suz. She had thrown over Diccon, who was tall with curly black hair and sparkling dark eyes, for Owen Stillnecker who was in TV, a dashing blond giant, then discarded him for Auden Springer, a suave, good-looking man in advertising. And now she'd deserted Auden. Missily wondered if either Auden or Owen had taken her desertion as hard as Diccon had. She was pretty sure he still loved Suz though Missily often wondered what there was to love in her sister. She was attractive certainly, even her personality, but what was it in her that made her leave one man after another? She'd been married three times but they all knew there had been other men she'd lived with without the benefit of marriage. Suz made no secret about that. Did she think that someday she would find a man who would satisfy that restless spirit?

"Who's Aunt Vicky bringing?" Sean asked as he sat down across from her at the table. "Not that Tad, I hope."

"Do you still remember him? You couldn't have been more than ten. That was six years ago."

"He was strange. He couldn't do anything because of his constitution." Sean mimicked Tad so exactly that Missily laughed.

The door opened again to let in the fragrance of rain and the waking earth. Missily's two daughters came in, much more alike than she and her own sisters were. All her children had dark hair and eyes, except for Myles, the oldest who, at eighteen, was attending college in Tacoma. His eyes were gray like his mother's and his hair closer to her hair's chestnut shade than Mikell's darker brown, so dark it almost looked black. Mikell's hair had a slight wave, which both girls had inherited and in Candace it was close to a natural curl.

"Brownies! Goody." Gretchen kissed her mother. "Did you get my new skirt finished?"

"All but the hem. Get something to eat and we'll go measure it." Missily rose to put away the list and her address book. She could hear Sean telling the girls they might get to go to Fort Worden and stay in one of the officer's houses for the family reunion.

5

"Who cares about officer's houses?" asked Candace crunching a carrot stick. She was on a self-imposed diet though there probably wasn't an extra ounce on her slim young body. "I want to go to a ranch."

"So do I," Sean answered, "but Mom said they voted last time and most of them want to do something different each reunion."

"You mean we won't ever get to go to a ranch *again*?" asked Candace for whom life was often tragic.

"Oh, I imagine Uncle Thor and Aunt Erin will get the place on the ranch when it's their turn again," her mother answered. "Sean, I need some more wood before you start your homework."

"Okay." He grinned as he stood. "I can take a hint."

Gretchen and her mother went down the hall to the back bedroom. The house was an older one and had been added on to whichever way took an earlier owner's fancy so that the rooms were on different levels and there were extra halls. They had four bedrooms but only one bath, which was more difficult, now there were teenagers, than it had been when the children were younger. Their parents had finally set a time limit for the boys as well as the girls, managed to get full-length mirrors, one for the two boys and one for the girls. It had helped some, though they had problems finding outlets for hair dryers. Mikell grumbled at all the "primping' his sons did with their hair.

"Why can't they just comb it like I did mine? Why all the fancy stuff? Or doesn't my hair look nice enough?" He'd complain and Missily would just smile.

Missily was philosophical about it all and worked around the problems in the house but Mikell worried. He felt he should be a better provider. Missily teased him gently, "By whose standards, darling? We're wealthy compared to a large percentage of the world."

"But we don't live there. We live in the United States," Mikell would answer, not mollified, "and you are used to better things."

She usually gave up and let him stew since he didn't stay unhappy long but she'd suggested only once she might get a job and had almost gotten her head bit off. *His* wife was not going out to work. She had enough on her hands as it was. *He'd* take another job if they needed more money. Missily didn't want to work out of her home. She enjoyed her freedom and caring for her family. She made most of their clothes, cooked, baked, canned, froze fruit and vegetables as well as gardened. She also made sure she had some time to read every day, not only because it was the way she relaxed but also because it kept her mind exercised. She was reading the Russian novelists and also still reading Greek which she'd done since her father had taught her years ago. And she scoffed at anyone who even so much as hinted she was a slave to her family. "A slave," she would pontificate, "is forced to do what he has to do. *I* choose my occupation."

Missily watched Gretchen take off her dress and slip the skirt over her head, thinking how much skinnier she'd been at that age. Both the girls were bigger than she'd been. "It must be all those vitamins," she said as she knelt down to measure the skirt for a hem.

"What must be?" Gretchen wanted to know.

6

"I was thinking how much skinnier I was than you girls are."

Candace, who had come into the room, sat down on the edge of her bed. "See, I told you I was fat."

"Oh, Candace! Don't be foolish," Missily answered around the pins in her mouth. "I was talking about how skinny I was. If you're fat than I'm a horse."

"Mother!" Candace slipped off her shoes to lie across the bottom of the bed. "Is Alexis bringing her boy friend to the gathering?"

"Her fiancé, Candace. There *is* a difference," Gretchen said.

"I don't know," Missily answered. "I haven't sent the letters yet. I have an invitation for him."

"Celeste says he's good-looking. Alexis sent her a picture. He's tall and real dark. I mean even his skin is darker than ours."

"Maybe that's just the picture," said Gretchen, turning patiently for her mother.

"No. Alexis says his mother was Greek or Turk or something. I can't remember what Celeste said."

"Greeks don't have dark skin," her sister said.

"Maybe it's olive. That could be any of the Mediterranean countries," put in Missily. "Is he from there?"

"No. He was born in Utah where his parents still live. I don't think he's a Mormon though."

"Not everyone in Utah is a Mormon," Gretchen protested. "Thanks, Mom. I'll put the hem in."

Missily stood and stretched. "Must be getting old. It's not so easy to get up and down as it used to be."

At supper that night the family talked about Fort Worden.

"What's there to do there?" Sean wanted to know. "On the ranch we had horses."

"It's right on the Sound. Or rather on the Straight and Admiralty Inlet," his father said. "A ferry goes across to Whidbey Island. You remember that, I'm sure. We've gone that way before and then the Olympics are there so there's plenty to do."

"I'd like to hike into the wilderness area on the beach," Missily said. "It's something I've always wanted to do and have never gotten to."

"You a Washingtonian, too," Mikell answered. "This is good, by the way," he added reaching for another piece of pizza.

She smiled. He'd always complimented her cooking. He wasn't a demonstrative person, particularly in public, though he took her hand once in a while, or put his arm across her shoulders, but he showed his love for her in a hundred other small ways that made her feel beautiful and wanted. She'd made pizza for dinner, starting from scratch as she always did, generally making three big ones and she had this time though Myles wasn't there. No matter how much she fixed it disappeared. After Myles had gone to college she'd made the same amount of everything as she had before and it was still eaten with seldom any leftovers until one day Mikell asked if food prices had gone up. She'd said some but not much and asked why. He'd

7

answered that he noticed the food bill was the same now as it had been when Myles was home.

"I knew Sean ate a lot," he'd added, "but I did think Myles ate something."

"Oh, that's because this family seems to have some kind of law that everything on the table has to be eaten; that there must be no leftovers. I have to adjust and cook less and I haven't learned how much yet." But she'd been more aware of it since then and had cut down and no one complained. She'd hoped there'd be some of tonight's pizza left over for her lunch the next day and sighed as she saw the last piece disappearing.

"We'll just have to get together some of the hikers and go into the wilderness. When you write, tell them that. Then they'll come prepared," Mikell told her.

"Okay." she smiled again and he knew by the expression in her clear gray eyes, fringed by long dark lashes, that she was excited. Her eyes were what had drawn her to him from the first time he's seen her.

"Do you children know," he said, casually, as he set his cup down after taking a drink, "that your mother is the most beautifullest person on earth?"

"Daddy," Gretchen said, "beautifullest isn't a word."

"It expresses what I mean, though," he answered and reached over to give her hair a tug. "Are you going to be a school teacher? But that wasn't what I asked."

"I think she's pretty but there are other people pretty, too," Candace said.

"Granted." Mikell looked suddenly at Missily who had her eyes on her plate. She'd always felt the family mouse and Mikell had, from the beginning, made her feel like a queen. Now he said, "But I didn't say pretty. Sweetheart, look at me."

Missily looked up, her eyes bright with unshed tears and Mikell reached over to put his hand on hers. "You see," he told the others, "she has this strange idea she has four sisters far more attractive than she is."

"Mom! Why would you think that?" Sean asked as he devoured that last piece of pizza. "Golly, you're a lot prettier than any of them, even Aunt Vicky."

"Even Aunt Vicky!" Candace exclaimed. "Aunt Erin is prettier than Aunt Vicky."

"I think Aunt Rose is pretty," said Gretchen. "She always looks so nice."

"Yes, like you'd better not touch her or you'll get your hands slapped," said Sean.

Missily and Mikell laughed. It was such a perfect picture of Rose as she'd been with them when they were small children. Their hands always had to be examined, as well as their shoes, before they could go into her house. That had been sometime ago and she'd changed over the years but her bandbox appearance and her spotless house still gave the impression she would not put up with a smudge anywhere.

"Do you suppose," mused Missily, "That Myles would think Suz the prettiest of his aunts? We seem to have three different votes here."

8

"I hope not," Mikell answered. "He's too sensible for that."

"Is any man sensible about Suz?"

"I hope I am!" he bristled.

Missily shook her head, "I mean no man seems to be neutral. They seem either to love her or..."

"Leave her," supplied Sean.

His father laughed. "Could be. Though I'm not sure it's the men who leave."

"You know it isn't, Daddy," said Gretchen. "May I be excused? I have some homework."

"Get the Bible first," he answered. "Then you help your mother clean up, you and Candace. Sean, you and I will get some more wood cut."

They'd bought a wood burning stove to help with heating costs and had never been sorry. Mikell could get wood in the mountains during the summertime from someone he'd known for years at far less than they could buy it in town, even counting the cost of gas to haul it down. Missily liked the heater because it was so much warmer than the baseboard electric heat. That was all they'd had before, which had made Mikell worry about his organ.

The organ took up a great deal of space in their living-room but it didn't worry any of them even though they were cramped for space when they had guests over or one of the family birthday get togethers. The organ was so much a part of their life that no one would have thought of doing without it. Mikell was one of the organists at church and practiced at home. Missily's favorite time of day was in the evening when she sat down with mending or crocheting or a book and listened to him. He had always done it so that their children had gone to sleep to the sound of the organ as others did to radio or stereo or TV. Myles had written not long after he went to college to half seriously ask for a tape of his father playing. Said he couldn't get to sleep very well and maybe it would drown out some of the noise.

As they sat together later on in the evening, Mikell was restless and though he was sitting in his chair skimming the newspaper, his foot was moving nervously on his knee. Missily was about to ask him if something was wrong when the sound of arguing from the girls' room grew louder and Mikell yelled in that stentorian voice he could muster, "Pipe down, you two."

"Maybe I'd better go see what's wrong," Missily said, starting to put her counted cross-stitch away.

"I'll do it. Sit still." He strode out of the room just as he heard Gretchen say, "That's stupid, Candace Bryanne!" and he almost collided with her coming out of her room with a pillow and an afghan.

"What's up?" Mikell asked.

"I'm going to sleep in Myles' room. I don't even want to be around her," his daughter answered fiercely.

Mikell put his arm around her shoulders and guided her back into the room. She flopped rebelliously on her bed while he leaned against the highboy. "Let's have it."

"She's making a mountain out of a mole hill," Candace answered.

"I am not!" Gretchen sat up, looking quite pretty in her pink nightgown, her cheeks flushed. It was hard to remember she was already fourteen. "Daddy, I don't think it was nice of her to answer you the way she did at the table. Mamma *is* beautiful."

"In your eyes, Gretchen Jill," Candace said nastily. "Beauty is in the eye of the beholder."

"Hold on," Mikell folded his arms. "Gretchen, Candace doesn't have to think her mother is beautiful though I think she's probably a bit blind."

Gretchen tried not to smile but her eyes sparkled. Candace said loftily, "She *could* be *if* she wore more make-up and got her hair styled. She looks so--so--"

"Original," her father supplied.

"No. Originality's okay but Mamma's just--plain." Candace said. Her nightgown was a garish mixture of colors that Mikell had never liked.

"Would you like it if she were more like your Aunt Erin or Aunt Vicky?"

"Well, at least they dress stylishly."

"I've never seen anything to complain about in your mother." Mikell's voice was dangerously calm.

Candace looked at him doubtfully. She was never sure whether or not she should say anything when he sounded that way. "Well, but love is blind."

"Oh, stop it! All she does is quote these stupid clichés and she doesn't know anything about it," snapped Gretchen.

"I suppose you do?" asked her sister tartly. "You're *so* much older."

"Girls, that's enough." Mikell stood away from the chest ."Candace, when we were talking at the table and I told your mother to write to the others about the hike she was excited and her eyes get very dark then. Perhaps you should look a little deeper than just the surface. You seem to be bothered by the wrong things."

"But you don't let us dress like the other kids. That's surface."

"The 'other kids' don't all dress alike. What I dislike is trying to keep up with the latest fad--which might mean long jeans, frayed at the cuffs, and long unkempt hair like 'the other kids' wore when Myles was your age, to mini skirts so short you might as well be wearing one of my T shirts, to whatever the latest craze is. Dressing neatly, modestly and in good taste, even though you can't afford the new styles every season, is difficult, Candace. It takes a wise woman who can tell what will be faddish for a season or two and what will wear well. And I think if you talked to your aunts you would find that they are not the kind that go out and buy every new thing that comes along. They may be able to buy more expensive clothes, but I bet you anything that they buy clothes that last and wear well. Your mother is always beautifully dressed and don't you forget it, young woman. Many a woman would envy her ability to make clothes *in style* on the budget she has. Now, no more arguing."

Back in the living room Missily looked up as her husband came into the room, a question in her eyes. As he crossed the room to his chair he looked at her--the beautifully fringed gray eyes, straight nose, generous mouth, the heavy chestnut colored hair catching the evening light laying on her shoulders-- and his heart cramped. She was so beautiful and he wished he could afford a wonderful house for her and money to buy clothes, though he wasn't sure she would use it that way. She wasn't vain and certainly she wasn't plain even though she might irritate her sisters because she refused to use a lot of make-up. She knew what suited her best and wore her clothes well.

"I hope Candace isn't going to be a difficult teen-ager. She's far too prone to want to be like everyone else, whomever that may be."

"Only in the outward things," Missily answered with a smile. "She's embarrassed by us because we don't look the way she thinks we should. She'll outgrow it. Poor darling; she'll be miserable until she does."

Mikell bent over to give her a quick, hard kiss. "I never have to ask why I married you. Everything you do proves me right."

"Are you going to play the organ tonight?"

"Yes, but I want to talk to you about something first. Want some tea?"

"Yes, please. There are brownies in the cookie jar. I hope. I made some today. I don't think Sean's had opportunity to get away with them all."

When Mikell came back with their drinks and a brownie each he sank down in his chair and leaned back to close his eyes. "Jedidah, I've decided to try it on my own. I think I have enough customers and I've accumulated enough tools."

Missily didn't reply. Mikell repaired and rebuilt organs, working for another man, but had wanted to be on his own for some time. The last time he'd mentioned it she'd been so afraid he wouldn't make enough to pay bills she'd not let it rest until he gave up the idea. She'd had time to think since then and realized that she needed to let him do what he thought best. It still scared her because she'd always paid bills on time, but she kept her fear to herself this time.

"I thought I'd wait until the first of the month because I have to give my notice and it will be two weeks next Monday until the first. Kurt won't like it but I've talked to others and they do better on their own. You know how I dislike the dishonest way Kurt treats his customers and I don't want to be part of it any more." He sat up to take his mug of tea in his hands. "I know it won't be easy for you, at least until we see how I'll do but we have that nest egg in the bank. It's not big, but it will help if we need it and you are good at economizing. I'll have another organ built ready to sell soon."

"Oh! I forgot. The Good Shepherd Baptist Church called. That diapason is acting up again."

"They need a new organ. It's getting hard to find parts for the one they have. I've told them that. It's ancient."

"Maybe they'll buy the one you're making."

"You know churches won't buy mine," Mikell said without rancor.

"Why not? Have you ever tried selling them one. They're as good as the ones they do buy."

He smiled. "My greatest fan."

"I'm serious, Mikell. Why don't you find out? You shouldn't sell it cheap but there's no middle man so that should cut costs some."

"I'll have to think about it. One thing Good Shepherd won't like is that I'll set a fee when I go out on my own. After all the other churches have to pay full price."

"You mean you haven't been charging them the same price as the other churches? Why not?"

He grinned a little sheepishly. "Scott asked me if I'd look at it once and I did, then fixed it and they gave me something. If I remember it didn't cover costs of material. After that I did charge the price of the parts. But I won't get anywhere if I do favors for everyone."

"But Scott isn't everyone. He's our neighbor and friend."

"I know but I don't' know his church people except vaguely. Can't you see what would happen if it got around I did favors for friends?"

"Well, don't you?"

"Yes, but not that kind. Churches are bad for that kind of thing. Trying to get things for little or nothing."

"Now you sound cynical, Mikell," she said, snipping off a piece of thread. "Churches aren't exactly alone in that."

"No. But I expect more from them."

Sean slipped through the room on his way to the kitchen and Missily said, "Two's enough, Sean. I need them for lunches."

He came back to the door grinning. "She has special antenna or ESP."

"Just years of experience," his mother answered.

"But they're so good. You're the best cook in the world." He grinned engagingly.

"And you'll be the biggest man around--in more ways than one--if you don't stop eating so many sweets."

He crossed the room to kiss her cheek, knelt down beside her. "What are you making this time?"

"A picture for Grandma Deborah--a Victorian garden. Her birthday's next month."

After he'd gone back to his bedroom with a glass of milk and a couple of brownies Mikell said, "You haven't said what you think, Jedidah."

"I think you should do what you want," she answered, her eyes on her stitching. She heard him let out a sigh and then he was on his knees before her, taking away her cross-stitching.

"Thank you, darling," he said, holding her hands. "If you hadn't wanted me to try it alone I would have stayed with Kurt."

"I know," she whispered. How many years ago had he wanted to go on his own before and she had ruined that? He'd never reproached her but she'd seen day after day how difficult is was for him. "I'm sorry I was so selfish before."

"I never thought you were selfish," he replied loosing her hands to caress her hair. "Just careful for all of us. And that may not have been a good time."

"What will you do for a shop?"

"I'll work from home, at least at first. I'll have to get a phone for the van. Will you mind being my secretary?"

"Oh, Kell, will you really work from here? Will I get to see you more often?"

"That I can't tell you," he said with a laugh. "Are you sure you want me around more?"

"If you only knew how much I want that," she said.

He pulled her close for a kiss, then stood up and went to the organ. She'd learned that playing it was one way he expressed his emotions. She settled back in her chair, curled her legs under her and sat freehanded to watch him and listen.

Chapter II

Jedidah. Only Mikell called her by that name though most of the time he shortened it to Jeddie. The first time she'd met him she'd been working in an office as a receptionist-secretary undecided what she wanted to do with her life. She'd tried college for a couple of years but she wasn't learning much beyond what her father had taught her and she was bored as she'd been all through school. She could have been a straight A student like Kitten but she didn't care. When she wrote an essay there were few of her teachers who appreciated her originality. It had angered Allan and if there had been a good private school close of which he approved he would have sent her to it. Missily had been glad there wasn't because she thought the students in those schools would be snobs and she enjoyed her friends. She'd loved studying with her father and when she'd reached her middle teens he'd taken her to lectures, to gatherings with others who were reading and met to discuss the Great Books of the Western World.

Allan wanted her to go on through college, get her Ph.D., and become a professor but she'd told him she wanted time off and looked for a job. He thought she'd demeaned herself and she'd told him to write it off as experience. She'd settle down when she decided what she wanted to do with her life. Meanwhile she enjoyed her work and her fellow workers in a superficial way, dated several young men and spent time with Erin, three years her junior and a high school senior.

One day Mikell had come to the office to see one of the men. After she took his name, which he'd had to spell--the emphasis was on the Kell, he'd said, with a short syllable before it--he'd sat down to wait and watched her. He'd been back a couple of times and then one day when he came he asked her name. She told him and spelled it for him as she usually did when someone who hadn't heard it before asked. That made a bond between them right away.

"Missily. Where'd a name like that originate?" He wanted to know.

"With my mother. She made it up. If anyone else has it I've never heard it."

"The same with mine. First name. My middle name is Sheldon, my mother's maiden name. What's yours?"

"I don't have one. Mother didn't like anything with Missily."

"Hmm-m-m. " He rubbed his chin. "We'll have to remedy that. I'll find one for you."

14

Which he had. He came at quitting time one day in time to escort her to her car, find out where she lived, and ask her if he could come out to meet her family. It was so novel she was taken by surprise. Usually men just asked her out. Her parents hadn't met all of them; they told her they trusted her judgment. He did ask her out after he'd come to the house more than once. Missily had never enjoyed a date more, though she couldn't have said why. They went to the theater to see a stage play after they'd dined and later sat together on a hillside in Lincoln Park overlooking Puget Sound as they talked. It was past midnight when Mikell glanced at his watch and stood up with an exclamation, reaching down to pull her to her feet.

"I'm sorry, Missily. I wasn't paying any attention to the time."

She brushed off her skirt, "What time is it?"

"Almost twelve thirty." They walked down the hill to the car where he opened the door for her.

"That's not so late," she said as he slipped into the driver's seat. "Mother and Daddy don't wait up for me."

"You have to work tomorrow, don't you?" he asked.

"Yes." She didn't add that she'd gotten in much later many times.

"Then that's reason enough."

It was fun and exciting to be with him but strange. He wasn't like anyone she'd met before. It wasn't just that he was a little older than most of those she dated--he was twenty-seven--but she was never sure whether she'd hear from him again or not and that in itself intrigued her because she'd always been popular and she'd always been the one to turn down dates and quit going with someone if she found one of them boring or they kept trying intimacies she wasn't interested in. All her sisters had been popular, also. It would have been strange if they hadn't wrangled over who got the bathroom first--the house they grew up in had two--what to wear, who got the phone first. The Metlow house seldom had a dull moment though Missily's parents were stricter than many of the girls' school chums' parents were. Until they were out of high school they had to be home by midnight. After they graduated the only rules they were given were those that affected the family: to call ahead of time if they wouldn't be home for dinner and, until they turned twenty, they were expected to bring their dates home before they began to go out with them. Only Suz had rebelled against rules and she and Diccon had eloped the year she was seventeen as soon as she graduated from high school.

Missily knew her father worried more about their daughters than her mother did. She'd come home more than once close to two o'clock to find him in his chair reading. He never said anything but she was aware of his disapproval and, in fact, he made a remark at supper table one evening after she started dating Mikell, that at least he kept decent hours and it was too bad more young men weren't like him. Since Erin was the only other one of the girls at home then, both she and Missily knew the remark was aimed at Erin. She'd been too late getting home more than once and she was still under the midnight rule. Though Allan Metlow never said anything that Missily could use for proof she was aware that he wasn't in full agreement with the rule her mother had made about not having to report in at midnight after they were twenty. She'd often wondered if there had been any discussion between the two. They had never argued in front of their daughters.

One Friday Mikell called to find out if Missily could spend Saturday with him and when he picked her up the next day he took her out to his parent's place. His father owned a fish hatchery some thirty miles east of Seattle. The day was warm and Missily, who loved the country, was feeling content as they drove toward the Cascade Mountains. It was one of those days when the mountains, looking breathtakingly high, were clear and she kept looking north to south loath to miss any of the high peaks.

"You love them, too," Mikell said.

She turned to look at him. He had a striking profile, his nose long and straight, his chin firm and distinct. He was quite good-looking, she decided. She'd been attracted to his dark hair from the beginning; neatly combed back from his forehead, parted on the right side, it lay beautifully against his head.

"I grew up where we can see, on clear days, a panorama from the top of the hill behind the house," he went on. "I've always thought I couldn't live somewhere there weren't any mountains."

"I don't know whether I could either. I can just see them from my bedroom window between the trees."

"Jedidah," he said in a different tone than he'd ever used before. She didn't answer. He swung the car into a different lane. "We're here. I'll tell you later about Jedidah."

Missily had liked Mikell's mother, Deborah Adamsen, from the minute she first met her. Mikell looked a great deal like her, more than he did his father whom she met later. They all sat around the table for lunch. All Mikell's family was home during the summer except for Mikell, who lived in Seattle, and his brother Max, just younger than he who owned an apple orchard not too far distant. Perry, who was twenty-one, was taking business courses at college but working on the place during the summer. He and Mikell resembled each other though Missily decided Mikell was the most handsome. Perry was cheerful, easy to talk to. Eva at sixteen, was a lovely young lady, much nicer than too many of the teen-age girls Missily had met. She seemed so unspoiled. Lorna was not far from being a baby. She was six but seemed younger. Missily could tell she was loved greatly.

"She's our caboose," Deborah explained. "We didn't expect her at all and she's a treasure."

Missily, standing with Mikell's mother at the big picture window then, watched Mikell who was outside talking to his father, Lorna leaning against him or tugging his arm.

"I hope we don't spoil her but she has a delightful nature and, of course, she's our baby." Later she said, as Missily and Mikell were leaving, "Come again, Missily. It's been lovely having you here."

Ahead, as they drove toward Seattle, they could see the Olympic Mountains, a bit misty, on the other side of the Sound. Missily sat silent. She had enjoyed her visit but there was something different about Mikell and his family that evaded her. She'd been uncomfortable only once and

16

that was when Gabriel Adamsen prayed before the meal. Missily had been brought up in church but she'd never before heard a prayer that sounded so natural, as though Gabriel were talking to someone he knew and it wasn't a form of any kind. She wondered what kind of religious people Mikell's parents were. There'd been a big Bible on the coffee table but she'd also seen two others, well worn, beside chairs in the living room. There was also one plaque on the wall, which she thought might have been a quotation from the Bible. She'd been in homes before of girls from school where'd there had been such plaques, but she'd avoided going back because they'd tried to make her believe what they did and she thought that was in poor taste. Religious beliefs were personal and private.

"Are you curious about Jedidah?" Mikell's voice interrupted her thoughts.

"Yes. Do you mean you're going to explain?" she asked lightly. She'd forgotten about the word.

"Partly," he said enigmatically. "At least partly today." He swung the car off the road into a place where there were picnic tables and room for camping. "Let's go see the river."

Sitting side by side on the bank, while Mikell broke twigs and threw them into the river, they watched the water. "Do you remember *Winnie-the-Pooh*? I can't remember who was with him but whenever I throw sticks into the water like that I remember the part where they watch them come out from under the bridge. Was it Piglet or Christopher Robin or both?"

"Oh dear, it's been so long since I've read those books I don't remember."

"I'll ask Lorna. She will. Do you remember," he asked changing the subject, "when I asked you about your name and told you I'd find a middle one for you?"

Missily hesitated. Did he remember everything they'd done?

"That day you spelled Missily for me and we found both our mother's had made up our names," he prompted.

"Oh, I remember now."

"That's what Jedidah is. Missily Jedidah. Jedidah was the mother of a king, in fact, one of the best kings of Judah. He began to reign when he was only eight and set about reforming the country." He threw the last twig in his hand into the water and clasped his hands around his knees. "Strange. Judah was under Assyria at the time and King Josiah was killed opposing the King of Egypt who intended to help the Assyrians against Babylon. Today what was Assyria is called Iraq and they're still fighting over there. King Josiah lived in the seventh century before Christ. That's over twenty-six hundred years ago."

Missily was laughing. "Mikell. What do you do? Spend all your time reading history? We've had wars since cave men hit each other over the head but we're learning. Now we're sophisticated enough to make weapons to destroy the world, we're learning to live together better."

He turned to look at her. "We are? Is that why we're all afraid to breathe for fear Washington or Moscow will push the button that will send us into oblivion? And why the Communist crush everyone who tries to gain

17

any freedom if they can? Come on, Missily. We're no different than we ever were."

"You can't say we haven't made great strides in technology and medicine. No one would have believed anyone would even think of sending a satellite into space not long ago."

"Many people would have thought it impossible, but all our technology hasn't wiped out greed and hatred and all the things that cause war. Then too, some of our progress in both technology and medicine have brought more problems plus questions about the value of human life. All most people can think about is a quick fix so we won't have to suffer pain."

"Well, do you want to have some horrible disease and die in agony?" She stood up. "Let's go. I don't like the way you think."

And it was then that he touched her for the first time other than a friendly hand to guide her or help her up. He was on his feet immediately and turning her around to face him, his hands firm but gentle on her arms. "Jedidah, forgive me. I don't want to upset you. Life has enough problems as it is."

She searched his face uncertainly, her gray eyes wide and he let her go with an exclamation. He walked back to the edge of the water and she heard him say, "Will you go to church with me tomorrow morning?"

"To church?" she echoed blankly.

"Yes. I'll come by to get you."

"But--" To church? she thought. Her parents went regularly and her mother belonged to the more than one lady's committee and did things like crochet slippers for missions but she hadn't been to church since high school. "I don't really like church, Mikell. It's so boring. Mom and Dad go every Sunday and Erin has to go with them at least until she graduates. I guess Rose and Graham go, too, but I haven't gone for years."

He turned, "Would you try it once with me?"

He was so handsome, standing there in the evening light, his beautiful dark hair falling onto his forehead and as she looked at him he gave his head a toss so the hair went back into place, but soon fell down again so that he pushed it back impatiently. He *was* handsome. It might be fun to be the girl he took with him. Did he go often? He said," I spent a lot of time looking for a middle name for you. To me it fits you."

"Why?"

He came back slowly to her and took her hands in his, holding them lightly in his to look down at them, their nails pink with polish, her fingers straight, tapered, soft. His eyes came to hers. "I like the sound of it with Missily. And, it just suits." It wasn't until much later in their relationship that she learned it was Hebrew for beloved; that he'd searched for it on purpose. She said to him then, "But Mikell, that was way back at the beginning. We hardly knew each other," and smiling, he'd replied, "I knew you, I've always known you."

But now he didn't explain further. "Don't you like it?"

Missily tried it. "Missily Jedidah. Yes, I think I do."

"I'm glad," he said. "Shall we go find something to eat? I'm hungry. Do you like Chinese food?"

She didn't so they went to a restaurant where she could have a salad and it was while they were waiting for their food that she told him she'd go with him in the mornings. "I'm not promising any more than that," she warned him.

He smiled and she noted, as she had before, that his eyes smiled too, with attractive lights in them. They were so dark they almost seemed more black than brown at times. "Oh," he became serious again. "There is one thing. I play the organ. That means I can't sit with you all the service but Mom and the family will be there. They'd love to have you sit with them and I'll come down when I don't have to play."

"You're the organist? That's a very good reason to go. You didn't tell me you played the organ."

"I guess I just assumed you knew I did because I repair them."

"Do all repair men play?"

"I suppose," he mused.

Sunday morning she sat next to Eva, who was excited to find Missily there with Mikell and who promised Lorna she could sit next to their guest the next time she came. They sat where they could watch Mikell play. It wasn't a large church but they did have a pipe organ which Missily had heard all her years at church as a child. Mikell was good. She could tell that though she didn't have the knowledge to judge exactly how well he played. She loved music though she'd had no particular training. Now she watched him as he changed the stops and played as effortlessly with his feet as his hands. She was so fascinated by his playing that she didn't try to sing though she held the hymnal with Eva. During the prayer the minister prayed, which seemed unreasonably long to her, she watched Mikell from under her lashes. He gave her a special smile when he came to sit down beside her.

She settled back to think of him. Sermons always bored her. Too many times she'd heard a poor rehash of some recent book, often one she and her father had read and discussed, or else something along the lines of pop psychology or some political harangue. Her mother nearly always remarked on how good the sermons made her feel. She said she knew she was adding something to the world by following the golden rule and Doctor--whatever their current minister's name was--knew what he was talking about. Missily often wondered when she was younger, if her father listened to the sermon at all and asked him once. He'd smiled. "In a way. It's interesting to see how one of the books I've read will be explained. But I'm afraid my mind wanders."

Missily also thought the golden rule rather selfish. It was just another way to get what you wanted out of someone. She began to feel uncomfortable now, though, as Mikell took a Bible from the pew and turned to where the pastor directed them, holding it so Missily could read along. Horrors, she thought. Is this one of those Bible thumping, fanatical churches? Somehow it didn't fit her image of Mikell and his family. He kept the Bible opened as the minister began his sermon. Missily began to be more confused than she'd ever been before in her young life. She'd never heard anyone preach about Christ as anything more than an example of how

19

self-sacrificing and high humanity can reach, a good example to follow, but now Christ seemed threatening to her as she listened to the story of his raising Lazarus from the dead. She stole a look at Mikell. Surely he was too intelligent to believe it was anything but a story, a myth of primitive people who had no modern scientific knowledge. However, he and his family were listening quietly, even little Lorna, or at least she was drawing pictures and not fidgeting.

There was so much Missily couldn't understand. Words like grace and mercy and justification didn't sound the same as they did in her world, the real world, she told herself hastily. But the main figure, the Christ of Galilee, came across as more than a man; he was someone with authority, someone in control, someone much more real than the Christ she'd heard about occasionally, much nearer. It was unsettling and she made herself sit still and not fidget. She forgot to criticize the strangeness of these people who obviously believed the Bible literally and tried to get away from the hold this Christ seemed to have on her. How could He give her life? And what did He mean by life? She was already alive. She didn't want to listen and yet felt compelled to. By the time the sermon was over she wanted to bolt and run away. The offering was taken while Mikell played and the music soothed her so that after the benediction she listened to him play the postlude and felt almost normal again.

Mikell took her home at her request right after the service. He didn't ask her how she liked it or if she'd go again. He pleasantly answered her questions about when he'd studied organ and why he hadn't gone onto the concert stage instead of into repair. "I'm not good enough for that," he said. When he stopped at her home he turned to her. "Thank you for coming, Missily. It was a treat to have you there to sit beside."

She smiled as she got out of the car. "It was great to hear you play. I enjoyed it," she answered. "I won't keep you. You probably have things to do. Bye." She ran up the stairs, turned to wave and went into the house. Her parents and Erin weren't back from church yet so she changed into something casual and comfortable before she fixed dinner.

As they ate it later, her mother wanted to know what she thought of church that morning. "Oh, it was all right," Missily answered and was vague about where it was and what kind. For some reason she didn't want them knowing Mikell was like the people they'd all made fun of so often. "You know how I feel about church. But it was fun getting to see and hear Mikell play the organ."

"He plays the organ? How wonderful," Anna said. "I thought you said he repaired them."

"He does and rebuilds them. In fact, he also builds them. But that doesn't preclude playing, does it?"

"No, I suppose not. What kind of organ was it? I mean type, not make."

"It's a pipe organ. The church isn't as big as where you go but they do have a pipe organ. How was your morning?"

"Wonderful," her mother answered and Missily glanced at her father who winked at her. "Dr. Kingly gave an excellent address on human rights. It's about time the world wakes up to these things."

Anna was often lavish with her praise but vague about what was said. The phone rang and Erin ran to answer it coming back to say it was Julie, her girl friend, who was coming to get her. They were going down to the docks to look around, did Missily want to come, too? Missily did and their mother told them to go ahead, she'd clean up.

After that Sunday Missily had an excuse whenever Mikell called. She was going out almost every night with men she'd dated before she met Mikell and had dropped. Or else she and Erin went together to shop or to a friend's house. Since they were only three years apart in age they'd always spent a lot of time together and that came in handy now.

"Missily," her mother said one day, "don't you think you should take time out to rest once in a while? For over a month you've been out almost every night. That will tell on your work if you keep it up."

"Oh, Mother! I'm young. I'm enjoying myself."

"Well," her mother said doubtfully and her father looked around his newspaper to ask, "What happened to Mikell? He out of town?"

"Not that I know of. Why?"

Allan Metlow put his paper down. "Did you have a fight?"

"Daddy! Of course not. I'm not ready to be tied to one man yet."

He picked up his paper. "I like him. He's a decent young man."

Missily was tempted to tell them that he was also a religious fanatic but kept her mouth shut. She didn't want to be reminded of Mikell. She missed him terribly and she'd never liked anyone as much as she had him. They'd spent so much time talking about their childhood, their likes and dislikes, their ideas, so many hours in companionable activities: walking along the Lake shore, going to the University of Washington Arboretum, wandering through the shops on the waterfront, spending time at Shorey Bookstore or just sitting on a hillside watching the activity on the Sound. And the only way she could forget him was to fill her hours after work so she had no time to think. She *was* tired but that was because she wasn't sleeping well. Since she found it difficult to fall asleep she would read until she dropped off only to wake up later and face what she was trying so hard to forget. She was frightened. What if what Mikell's preacher said was right and her life was truly devoid of meaning, of hope, of any of the lasting things that made life worthwhile? Then she would argue with her own thoughts. Hadn't she learned from her father that it didn't matter whether life was meaningless or not. What mattered was that it be met with courage in the face of that meaninglessness.

She wished she had never heard about Christ the way that man had preached. He loomed too large on the horizon of her days and nights now. He wouldn't go away. Where was that safe, gentle, man who'd always seemed a bit weak? After all couldn't He have kept His mouth shut or escaped so they wouldn't have crucified Him? It was so meaningless to die like that. Wasn't it? Night after night she lay awake hoping morning would come, trying everything she knew, from counting sheep to naming the states,

21

to designing clothes but inevitably her mind wandered back to Mikell. She cried a great deal in those hours. Cried because she wanted to see Mikell and because she was afraid to. Why did Christ seem alive? He was dead. Had died two thousand years ago, she'd tell herself.

She loved to talk to her father but she not only did not want him knowing about Mikell's beliefs, she also already knew what he would say. He had taught her well and she'd read his favorites: Nietzsche, Sartre, Camus as well as the Greek philosophers. How could she be thrown by something she knew was only one among many religious beliefs that men created to give answer to things they didn't understand or that frightened them? Eventually, in the early morning hours she would drift off and sleep two or three hours before her alarm rang.

Eva called one day to ask if she and Erin would like to go sailing. They had a friend with a sailboat who was going to take them out—Perry, she and Lorna. They'd like it if Missily and Erin could go, too. Mikell couldn't be there since he was up north working on an organ. Missily accepted and stood on the deck, her lovely chestnut hair blowing back, reveling in the feel of the wind and waves while Erin and Eva talked. Perry had brought a girl with him named Bonnie and Lorna had brought a girl friend her own age. It was a lovely day and gave Missily some rest from the torment she had been going through. The owner of the boat flirted shamelessly with her which she enjoyed, asking him questions about his boat, how to run it, and taking her turn at trying to sail it. That night she sat at the window watching the moon as it made its way across the night sky and cried because Mikell hadn't been there. She slept hardly any that night, fell asleep when the daylight came and slept until ten that morning. It was Sunday and when she woke the family was gone. She got up to fix herself some breakfast, sat down with the newspaper reading paragraphs over and over, none of them making any sense, turning to the comics then pushing them aside to sit with her head in her hand drinking black coffee. That afternoon she went to bed and slept four hours.

However, she didn't sleep well that night again and for the first time in her life she understood why people committed suicide. Except, she thought, what if—what if? No! No! It wasn't true. It was all just men's ideas made to make themselves feel better or to manipulate others. People didn't need a crutch any more. They had come of age. No one, in this modern day and age, no truly intelligent person, needed foolish religious beliefs. But Mikell seemed intelligent. Then why did he believe all that? Or did he? Maybe he just went to church so he could play the organ. Instinctively, though, Missily knew that wasn't true. Mikell had too much integrity to pretend something for the sake of getting to play an instrument. And there were plenty of churches where he could play that weren't like the one he was attending.

The next day she sat at her desk, wan and pale. Her boss asked if she were ill. She shook her head. "Had a bad night."

He grunted and went into his office. It was a little before noon when she looked up to find Mikell standing there. She hadn't heard him come in and now she just stared at him. He looked terrible. His face was drawn and tired and he had dark circles around his eyes.

22

"Missily," he said quietly, "Will you come out to dinner with me tonight? I need to talk to you."

All caution fled. She forgot everything but how glad she was to see him while her heart pounded and she found it hard to breathe so she just nodded, still not speaking.

He relaxed a little, as though he'd been holding his breath. "I'll come back at closing time and get you. Is that okay?"

"Yes," she whispered.

He gave her a long look, opened his mouth, then shut it and left.

Chapter III

The day after she'd made her list for the reunion Missily decided to drive over to see Rose and talk over the coming event with her since her older sister was practical and an organizer. They'd spent the afternoon making lists, planning meals and who should bring what. Mikell had phoned Fort Worden and reserved places for them to stay. It wasn't until Missily was preparing to go home that Rose told her, with a quiver in her voice, that Graham had been to the doctor and was told he had cancer in his mouth.

"Rose!" Missily could say nothing else as she stared at her sister.

Rose straightened the dining-room tablecloth as she talked though it didn't need it. The doctor was hopeful; he thought that an operation would get it all. Missily was aware that Rose knew as well as she did that the doctor couldn't know anything for certain. She went to Rose and put her arms around her. Rose wasn't one who liked demonstrations of affection but she let Missily hold her a moment. "I'll be praying," Missily told her and Rose said, "Thank you" even though Missily knew her sister didn't believe much in prayer.

As she drove home through the traffic Missily thought of Mikell and how she'd feel if it were him. What would Rose do if something happened to Graham? They'd been together for twenty-four years and there were no children. And what about Graham? She remembered Mikell's remark about his being boring. But he'd always been kind and he was a lovable person. From the beginning he'd filled the place of a brother for her and the other girls and her parents depended on him. Missily began to cry. She didn't want anything to happen to Graham. What if he didn't get well? What if he died? As far as she knew he had only a vague belief in God and she thought he was Unitarian in his beliefs. He wasn't an atheist but he'd always said religion was a private thing. She swerved her car suddenly as she almost ran into another car when she changed lanes. Trying to blink the tears out of her eyes just made everything a blur so she pulled over to the shoulder. A policeman would most likely be there right away; they were faithful at patrolling the busy thoroughfares, but she couldn't drive until she could see. Digging into her purse for some tissue to dry her eyes, she was startled by a tap on the window and looked up. At first she just stared. Then she whispered, "Mikell."

"Something wrong with the car?" His voice was sharp, as it always was when he was nervous.

"No." She shook her head and the tears started again.

"Darling girl, what is it?" His voice was no longer sharp. "Will the car go?"

At her nod he added, "Follow me to the next exit."

Just having him there helped and she rolled up the window and followed him back into the traffic. He drove off at the next exit and continued until he found a quiet street where he pulled his van over to the curb, got out and walked back to her. She climbed out of her car.

"Tell me," he said.

"Graham has cancer," she said and began to sob.

And Mikell, who seldom even held her hand in public, reached out to enfold her in his arms. "How bad?"

"I don't know. It's in his mouth."

"That darn pipe," he said.

"Do you think that's what it is?"

"Probably. Were you at Rose's?"

"Yes, we were planning the reunion. She didn't tell me until I was leaving. The doctor says he thinks they can get it all by operation." She looked up at him, "How can they know?"

He dried her cheeks with his hand. "They can't but what else can they say? They'll try. Let's hope they can."

"Mikell, what would I do if it were you?" she asked and now she was shaking.

"I don't know, but, Jeddie, we have Someone to turn to. We're never alone. They are."

"I know," she whispered. "I thought of that. I'm so glad I met you or I'd still be just like them."

He kissed her, then grinned. "Now you know better than that. I was the tool God used but He didn't have to use me."

"No, but He did, so He ordained it that way."

"You're right, of course. I have to get going." He glanced at his watch. "I'm supposed to be on the other side of Lake Washington. Are you going to be all right or would you rather come with me? We'll think of someone to call to come pick you up and come get the car. I want you home safe." His voice broke then and he pulled her close for a hard hug and a kiss.

"I'll be fine now. God is so good to me. I wonder how many times you've been there just when I needed you most. I was thinking about that Monday when you came down to the office after I'd been avoiding you." She reached up to smooth back his hair and put her hand against his cheek. "Remember?"

"Yes, Very well. I'd put in some pretty miserable days. Take care, my love." As he drove off he waved to her when he turned the corner, his mind going back to that Monday. The month after he'd taken her to church had been agony. He hadn't known how much he loved her until he realized she was purposely avoiding him. He knew the church service had bothered her because they had planned to spend the day together and instead she'd ask

25

him to take her home. After that day she was busy whenever he called. He'd decided he'd lost her the day Erin answered the phone, went to get Missily only to come back to tell him she thought Missily was home but she must have gone somewhere, that she'd tell her he'd called. He'd had a feeling Missily was still home because it had taken so long for Erin to get back to him. Missily had never called back. He began to spend hours praying for her, begging God to help her understand, to know that without Him life was useless, to open her heart to the truth and as he did so he realized that he had never cared so much for those who were unbelievers before, never understood their darkness, their hopelessness. During the day he was quiet, pre-occupied and then he began to worry. Every time he saw an accident on his drives across Seattle or to the surrounding communities he thought of Missily driving every day and prayed she would be kept safe. He even began to have nightmares about something happening to her.

One Saturday afternoon, when he was at his parent's place hoping for some kind of peace from the agony he was suffering, he was so absentminded that his mother, who had taken him out to see her flower beds which he'd helped her plan and plant years ago, said, "Mikell, is there something wrong?"

He didn't answer right away but stood looking across the valley.. Finally with a sigh he said, "Mom, Missily's been avoiding me since she came to church that Sunday. She always has some excuse or she's not home. Now she's not even coming to the phone."

"Did the sermon bother her?"

"I don't know. I think she was uncomfortable because she asked me to take her home right after and we'd planned to spend the day together. It's strange. You can hear all you life about hell and until—" he stopped abruptly.

"Do you love her, Mikell?" Deborah asked gently.

Mikell turned to her and leaned over to lay his head against her shoulder. "I can't stand the thought of her being lost. I keep imagining her in all kinds of accidents where she gets killed."

Deborah's arms went around him and she held him, this first born son of hers. She'd liked Missily but she didn't want Mikell to marry her. She knew him well enough to know that it would be terribly hard for him to have a wife who wasn't a believer but she wisely said nothing. Eventually he straightened and turned away from her to wipe his face. They didn't talk of Missily any more that day but when he left his mother told him, holding his hands in hers, "We'll be praying."

It was after that day that Deborah suggested to Eva she might invite Missily along when the rest went sailing some Saturday.

"Do you think she'd go? I'd *love* to have her. She's super."

"You can ask her. And hasn't she a sister your age?"

"Erin. She's two years older than I. I'd like to meet her. Missily says she's pretty. In the picture of Missily's sisters she looked blonder than the others. Missily says she looks like their mother."

Mikell knew they were going and that they'd asked Missily and Erin who'd accepted the invitations. He wouldn't have gone even if he hadn't had

26

a job to do that day. It would be too much like playing a trick on Missily to show up when she didn't know he would be there and he knew that she wouldn't go if she knew ahead of time he was going also. He was a little surprised that she accepted at all but with Erin there too she may have felt safe. However, he worried all day for fear the boat would capsize for some reason. He knew he was being irrational but he seemed to have lost the power of being rational where Missily was concerned. By Sunday night he knew he had to see her and talk to her and even then, after he'd gone by the office Monday at noon, though she'd promised to go with him that night, he was afraid she would change her mind and go home after all. When he turned into the parking lot where her car was and saw her standing by it he had the first ray of hope he'd had since he'd dropped her off at her home after that Sunday service. He swung out of his van.

"Do you mind going with a working man?" he asked for he was still dressed in jeans and a short sleeved sport shirt open at the neck.

She shrugged. "Why should I? You look fine. Want to leave that van here and take my car? You can drive."

"Sure. That, at least, I can do for you. Service vans aren't very--well, not like a coach and four or ro--" but he cut off the romantic. They didn't have a romance.

"I don't mind the van. It might be fun," she said with a grin. "But I know you'd rather take the car. You've said so before. Here."

He took the keys from her. How could he bear never to see her again? Her gray eyes had haunted him for a month and that darling grin she gave when she joshed him. They didn't talk much until they were settled at the table Mikell had called to reserve. From the window they could see the boats and ships on the Sound. They'd been here together before and Missily watched as Mikell ordered for them. She wasn't sure she could eat. What was she going to do? She was sure now she loved Mikell though she had no idea how he felt about her. But even if he did care how could she bear to live with someone so religious?

And yet that was what puzzled her. He didn't act like a couple of the girls at the office who tried to convert her regularly and only succeeded in irritating her. He'd never told her all the things he couldn't do because he was a Christian like they did. He didn't try to push what he believed on her, though talking about God or what he believed never embarrassed him. It was hard to pin down what made him so different from the other young men she'd dated. He didn't smoke but a lot of people were giving up smoking now. If he didn't drink he'd never said anything about it though he never ordered anything alcoholic. He'd taken her to movies though he'd balked at dancing because he said he'd feel like a fool acting the way those guys did but he hadn't sounded as though he thought it was a horrible thing to do. All the things that the girls at the office, and others she had met at school, made so much fuss about he accepted as normal activities. That was, she supposed, one reason his being so comfortable with and part of that particular church service had taken her by surprise. Now he looked up and when he found her watching him he caught his breath and turned to look out the window. She saw his jaw move and tighten. The silence was becoming

27

uncomfortable by the time their soup arrived and with a sigh of relief Missily picked up her spoon. Conversation became general. He asked about her job, her family and she asked about his. He told her about his mother's flowers and wanted to know if she had enjoyed the day sailing with Eva and saw her gray eyes light up for the first time that day as she answered, "Very much."

She had to take more than half her meal with her because she couldn't eat much. Mikell was so dear but he didn't look well and it worried her. Did he have something wrong with him? Was that why he wanted to talk to her? He ate, but it looked automatic, as though he weren't even aware of what he was eating. They rose and left the restaurant, the restraint back again and both were silent as he drove into a park they'd found was usually less occupied than others in the city. There they began to walk along one of the paths side by side. Eventually Mikell began to speak.

"Missily, that Saturday I took you to see my folks and we stopped by the river afterward, I didn't mean to sound so cynical about life. It was rather rude. I guess I was too sensitive. I wanted you to like the name I picked and it was so interesting to me to compare the lands of then and now, how they're still fighting as they were thousands of years ago. I'd found the history when I looked for the name but that was no excuse to be rude."

"Mikell, do you think I--" she hesitated, walking beside him silently a few steps before continuing, "that I quit going out with you because of that?"

"I don't know." He broke off a dead twig from a bush as he passed and began to break it into smaller pieces. "I can't imagine your letting it bother you that way but I don't know the things that might upset you. I had also thought of church. That something there might have made you realize that we are—we are too different to continue any kind of relationship, especially one that seemed to me, at least, to be getting serious."

Missily had stopped abruptly and he turned to look at her. Her eyes were wide and she was biting her lower lip. "Mikell," she burst out, "I'm afraid. I can't sleep. I can't make it go away no matter what I do. Please help me."

He took her hands. "You can't make what go away, my darling?" he asked gently.

"That Sunday your preacher--he made it seem like Christ was real. I mean alive. Right here, now, with authority no man could have. He made me feel my life had no meaning, that I had no hope, and I'm afraid. What's wrong with my life? I don't go to church all the time but I'm a decent person, aren't I? I have a good job. I pay my way. I respect my parents. What does He want of me? Why is He so terrifying? I thought He was good and meek and gentle." Her voice had risen and she was crying.

Mikell, who had told himself he must never hold her unless she became a believer because he wasn't sure of his ability to leave her once he had her close to him, forgot all that now and reached out to gather her into his arms, holding her gently. "Missily," he whispered, "all this month I haven't been able to sleep because I've been so afraid for you. Every accident I saw, every time I heard of someone being killed or dying, all I could think about was you. I can't stand it if you go to hell. I-I can't imagine what heaven would be like without you. Just a month without you has been torment enough."

"But," her voice was muffled against his shoulder. Why should it seem so right, so natural to be in his arms, close to him? "But why would you think I-I would go--would go—to, well, wouldn't go to heaven? How do you know there is such a place? How do you know God even exists?"

"Let's find a spot to sit down," he said. "I'll try to explain." After they were seated on the grass overlooking Lake Washington, hands linked, he said, "I'm not going to prove God exists. I could give you some philosophical arguments. You've probably heard of some of them. Did you read Thomas Aquinas when you were reading the Great Books?"

"Yes. Though all I can remember about him is that he believed ants came from the dust."

Mikell grinned. "He wasn't a scientist, that's for sure, but he didn't intend to be. He has some arguments for the existence of God but instead of talking about those or others I want to try to give you a picture of the whole Bible. One of the problems is that we hear parts or pieces of it and don't get the whole picture. Taken out of context it can seem pretty strange and even superstitious to modern ears. The truth is that it is way ahead of anything modern man can dream up. I don't mean it teaches technological advances or modern medical discoveries. What I mean is that it goes beyond that to the deep questions of life. Questions of how the world got here, why there is evil and if there is any answer to it, what is the meaning of life and about people--what their place is here. And the answer ultimately is in Christ Jesus. I think that's why He seems so terrifying to you. You're not used to thinking of Him as anything except, perhaps, a crusader for a cause like Gandhi or Martin Luther King. To think of Him as the God of the universe is something quite different.

"We have to start where God's own revelation starts. With the fact that He created the world and He created it good. He also created one man and one woman from whom the human race came. You know, Missily, we talk a lot about environment and education and science being the answer to the world's ills. It's interesting that Adam and Eve had a perfect environment, were being educated by the Creator of the universe, and were given a mandate to do what scientists do now--classify and name the animals and plants and the world we live in and care for it and yet when Eve was tempted she decided she didn't have enough. Together they chose evil instead of good."

Missily, who had been leaning against Mikell's shoulder sat up and looked at him, half-amused. "Mikell, you don't really believe those myths, do you?"

"Sh-h-h, baby," he said, as if to a child, and pulled her against him again so that she sat in the circle of his arm. "Because of their disobedience sin entered into the world and has been here ever since. But God, who would have been perfectly just in destroying them, was merciful instead and provided a substitute to die in their place. Centuries passed, men increasingly got away from any belief in the true God, made themselves idols

29

and even decided man was the measure of all things. That's when God confused their language so they couldn't communicate any more.

"He wasn't through with the human race, though, even when he sent the flood to destroy all but one family. Eventually he chose a people for his name, gave them laws--moral, religious, civil, practical--covering every area of life. They had become a nation of slaves and out of them God made a nation of people with laws governing society, which were the foundation of many nations and are still in effect today."

Missily pulled away completely this time. "Mikell, if you'd done any reading on comparative religions you'd know that these people weren't the only ones that had good laws."

Mikell sat with his arms around his knees gazing out across the lake. "Suppose," he said, "a thousand years from now, someone reads about the American dream of freedom, the Revolution, the desire for equality for all and at the same time someone somewhere else was reading about another nation that had followed American ideals and someone somewhere else was reading about another nation doing the same and one day they all got together to discuss and quite an argument issued. Each one is sure that the nation they've been reading about had the original idea. Would the fact that others have tried what American stands for cancel out the fact it was the first nation under the particular form of government we have with the freedom for all written into our constitution--even if we don't follow it in practice perfectly?"

"But there are documents to prove America's claim. You can hardly say that about a religious belief," Missily said.

Mikell looked at her briefly then continued his contemplation of the scene before him. "That's exactly what we do have. The Bible gives us the true story. Others aren't as infallible."

"Really, Mikell that's a very narrow position to take. I can't see how what you're saying answers my questions. Perhaps we'd better change the subject."

"Do you want to hear my story? What about Christ?" he asked quietly.

"Oh, all right," she said ungraciously but she didn't sit close to him again. Instead she sat pulling at the grass as he talked.

"Where was I? Oh, I know. But before I go on I do want to add that God put his moral laws into the heart of man from the beginning. That's why so many peoples have them. For hundreds of years God was patient with those he had chosen while all but a few continued to go their own way. Finally, to punish them, God let them be taken as slaves, and then, after a while brought the Jews back to their land. There is a silence of four hundred years after that--as least as far as Scripture is concerned though historically there are records, of course, of that period. As far as the revelation of the Bible, which is about God's redemptive acts in history, it is silent until Christ comes. He was promised in the Old Testament but He doesn't come like the Jewish people expect. He's born in a stable of a virgin and grows up as a carpenter's son. Then for three years He walks the land teaching, healing, raising the dead, working miracles. But He tangles with the established religion of the day. The Jewish religious leaders had added rules on top of

30

rules so they were safely hedged about. Jesus ignored these man made rules, called the religious leaders to account and they hated him and finally managed to arrest him and he was crucified."

Missily had gotten up and was wondering around but she wasn't leaving and she was listening. Mikell, who had rehearsed it over and over for weeks, felt he was doing a miserable job but he continued.

"I don't mean just that He was hung on the cross. There was a reason; a reason ordained from before the world was created. God the Son, the Lord Jesus Christ came to live the perfect life required of you and of me and to die the death we deserve. I mean he took all the wrath of God against sin on himself. He suffered hell there on the cross for sinners."

"Mikell, why are you going through all this?" Missily interrupted, stopping in front of him. "Christ was a weakling or he wouldn't have been killed. He didn't have to let them arrest Him. Even your preacher said that. It's stupid and senseless and I don't want to hear any more." Her voice was sharp.

Mikell looked up at her. "I didn't know you were a Greek," he said mildly.

"What do you mean? I'm not."

"But the Bible says that the preaching of the cross is foolishness to the Greeks."

Missily stared at him. Then she said, "Then they were right. It *is* foolish. How can what a man did 2,000 years ago have any effect on me or have anything to do with my life?"

"If you let me finish my story I'd tell you that."

"Mikell, this is superstitious nonsense." She came to sit near him, facing him. "You're too sensible a person to be caught up in believing such childish fables. Where did you go to college? Haven't you ever read anything besides the Bible or do you just accept what your parents have told you? Don't you think for yourself?" Her voice was kind, as though she were trying to convince a rather dull child.

Mikell smiled. "Too bad my parents aren't here to answer the questions about thinking for myself. I went through a pretty rebellious period intellectually, in high school and after. Mom and Dad require all of us, if we want to go to college, to go the first two years to a Christian college. I went to one you've probably never heard of before."

He was rocking gently where he sat and Missily watching him, wished there were someway she could make him see how foolish his ideas were. The more she was with him the more attractive she found him. Now he stretched out on his back on the grass. The sky was clean with that pale blue Northwest skies have and the air was cool but comfortable. The sound of the city hummed behind them while overhead a jet made a white trail across the sky, which caught a faint pink from the evening sun slipping behind the Olympic Mountains.

"I wasn't sure whether I believed in God or not, then. I had a lot of doubts. I didn't want to go to a Christian college. I'd gone to Christian schools all my life but my father was paying the bills, most of them, and I

31

respected them too much to rebel completely. It's a good college. I wish I'd paid more attention when I was there." He turned his head to look at her.

"Anyway, I went there two years, came back home and finished up here in Washington. Went two years to Pacific Lutheran University in Tacoma and got my Master's at Washington U."

"Did you major in music?"

"No, in philosophy."

Missily was silent. She was afraid to ask him anything else. She'd grown up on Aristotle and Plato and Hume and Kant and Marx and others. She knew what a Master's degree in philosophy meant.

Mikell didn't seem bothered by her silence. He put his hands behind his head. "The only problem was that after I had my degree I couldn't decide what to do with my education and I still loved organs. Dad and I put one together from a kit when I was teen-ager. So I tossed my degree aside and learned to repair and rebuild and build organs. I've never been sorry."

"But I don't understand," said Missily, "how you can believe what educated people know are myths after that kind of an education."

He sat up, pulled a long stem of grass and stuck it between his teeth. "It was strange, Missily. When I went to the University here in Seattle and sat under teachers who believed all kinds of things, I began to be aware of how the great men of the ages thought alike in many areas and yet how irrational their belief systems were. Suddenly my Christianity made sense in a way it never had before. We all pick and choose what and whom we want to believe. I don't know which educated people you refer to but I do know that there are Christians every bit as educated as those who either reject Christian beliefs or believe Christianity is just one of many religions equally as valid."

"But you can be a Christian and not have to believe the Bible is factual in every detail."

"Can you?" His dark eyes suddenly met her gray ones. "Don't you think it strange that just anyone can decide which part of the Bible he or she would believe is--factual? The Bible itself defines a Christian and what one has to believe if he or she is one."

"But, Mikell, you know people interpret things differently. Some people interpret the Bible very literally, while others realize that it has great teachings but it's not necessary to believe in miracles, for instance. We now know, through science, that many of those things were natural phenomena."

"Like a volcano on Sodom and Gomorrah?"

"Yes, that could be one though I don't know the story."

"It *could* have been a volcano. I have no problem with that. But after all I have no problem with the fact that God uses His creation exactly where and when He wishes, even in judgment."

"I didn't mean God did it. I meant a volcano could have been erupted and the story was then concocted that people were so bad they had to be punished. I suppose that is what you mean by judgment but how is that different than any pagan god, than the Greek and Roman gods and goddesses, for instance, taking vengeance?"

"Missily, have you read the Bible?"

32

"Some. We had it in literature classes, parts of it. And I suppose I learned the stories when I was a child at Sunday School. I don't remember much of that. Mom and Dad never required us to go."

"But you haven't read it for yourself? You're an intelligent person. I'm sure you believe that something should be examined before it's condemned. That's a little what you meant when you asked if I read anything other than the Bible, isn't it?"

"I suppose so."

"If I gave you a Bible would you read it? Read it and compare it with the myths of the pagan gods and goddesses?"

She wanted to ask why she should read the Bible at all but she had set her own trap. He would have a perfect right to point out that he'd read many of the great minds of the world before he made up his own mind. She was more confused than ever. She loved her father and respected his knowledge and yet Mikell seemed to believe just the opposite of what Allan Metlow did and Missily wasn't willing to say Mikell was uninformed or stupid.

"Do you think I'm not a Christian because I don't go to church?" she decided on attack.

"Going to church itself doesn't make one a Christian, though Christians will want to worship with others who believe as they do and churches are a great help."

"Well, I don't go on wild parties or sleep around. I'm not on drugs; I respect my parents. I try to live a decent, clean life."

"Why?"

"Why? What do you mean 'why'?" She frowned. Every time she thought she had a subject they could discuss, he asked something that made her feel unsure of herself, a feeling to which she was unaccustomed.

"Why do you live a decent life?"

"Don't you think I ought to?"

Mikell lay down on his stomach. He wanted very much to reach for her hand, which was nervously pulling at the grass again. "But why ought you? Do you believe there is a day of reckoning coming when we'll have to answer to Almighty God for how we've lived?"

"Why does everything have to go back to religion? Can't I live decently just because I want to?"

"But if you don't have a reason for what you do, how do you know you'll continue to live that way if something happens to make you wonder if it's necessary? Say you fall in love, for instance and the guy wants you to sleep with him."

"Well, if I fall in love there'd be nothing wrong in sleeping with the man I love."

"Before marriage?"

"Well--what difference does it make?"

"Suppose he gets tired of you and finds another girl?"

"I wouldn't like it, perhaps, but I couldn't do much about it, could I?"

"Not about his leaving you, no, but what about giving yourself to a man who is unfaithful?"

"But that can happen in marriage, too."

"That's true. Do you feel it would be the same then as if he took off when you were living together without being married?"

"Mikell, why are you grilling me like this? Are you thinking of asking me to sleep with you?" Missily was angry and made no attempt to hide it.

Mikell sat up suddenly. "Tell me you don't mean that," he said, his voice shaken.

She had the grace to drop her eyes and say, "I'm sorry. I didn't. I-I'm just angry. I can't understand why you are badgering me."

"Is that what it feels like?" he asked gently. "Missily, look at me."

She complied slowly. He wanted to kiss her drooping lips she looked so adorable.

"I thought we were having a conversation. I was trying to get you to see that if we don't have solid reasons for what we do and believe, it's too easy to throw them aside when something happens that makes them seem senseless. We need foundations for why we do what we do."

"Mikell, could we drop all of this? We're getting nowhere and--frankly, I'm bored," she ended though she knew that was not the truth. He was confusing her and she didn't like it.

He studied her a long moment before he rose. "Let's go down to the water and see what's down there." He didn't mention the subjects they'd been discussing again, but pointed out the different kinds of ducks on the water, told her what they ate, how they caught their food. He amused her with stories from his work and told her about his brother's and his pranks when they were young. Walking her to the door when he took her home he said, "Thank you for a most wonderful evening, Missily. Being with you is special."

She smiled up at him, waiting for him to kiss her but he didn't. He never had. He added, "See you," and left her standing on the porch though he waited in his car until she went in.

Chapter IV

The week following that Monday was harder than the month before. Missily began to think she would lose her mind. Her work suffered. She had quit going out every evening and turned down dates again but when Mikell had come over the following night late in the evening on his way home from work, after he'd greeted the family and spent some time talking to her father, he and Missily went for a walk in the neighborhood and now it was Missily who was full of questions. How did Mikell *know* there was a God who cared about them? Or even a God at all? How did he know the Bible was true? Why did he believe in miracles? Why was he so different from the girls at the office who also believed the Bible was truc but wouldn't go to movies, dance, and one wouldn't even wear make-up?

Mikell answered patiently, elated that she was thinking about what he'd said and asking questions. He stopped by every day and they'd either walk slowly around the neighborhood, which was built on hills, or drive somewhere for a milkshake or lemonade or iced tea.

One day Missily approached her father before Mikell came. "Daddy, do you ever read the Bible?"

He looked up from the book he had in his hands. "Occasionally. I like to read parts of it once in a while."

"Do you believe it?"

"What do you mean by believe?"

"Well, do you--there are girls who work where I do who say it's true, all of it."

"It certainly isn't lies. I'd have to know what they mean by true."

"Take, for instance, the miracles. They believe they literally happened."

"You know my thoughts on that, Missily. We've discussed that kind of phenomena many times."

"Yes. I know." She sighed as she sat down on the arm of his chair. Two beloved men. How did she know who was right?

"Do they upset you with their ideas?"

"No. They turn me off, frankly. But I know there are a lot of intelligent people who do believe what the Bible says. Literally, I mean."

"Of course, but we all have vestiges of superstition left. We haven't quite escaped that yet. For instance, the fact that motels and hotels skip the number thirteen says a lot about our society. Anyone who thinks know that the thirteenth room is still the thirteenth even if the number on the door is fourteen."

"Why do you go to church, Daddy?" Missily sat with her head resting against her father's heavy head of hair so like her own.

35

"It's good for business for one thing. I meet people there and it gives me a good image. It's also a decent place to find mutual friends. And, of course, your mother likes it."

"Would you go if she didn't?"

Allan Metlow thought for a moment before answering. "I don't know. Maybe not. But I don't mind going for her."

"I think it's boring. Doctor Branton isn't even as interesting as some of my teachers were. Why do we still have churches when we don't need religion?"

Allan laughed. "We're creature of habit, I guess. And we're social creatures, too. Maybe someday we'll find something to replace them. Meanwhile a church like ours isn't hurting anyone. It's not trying to force a set of beliefs on people. It's trying to make the world a better place to live."

"But aren't we still forcing our beliefs on people?"

"I don't think so," her father replied. "No one has to agree with what we believe."

"But if it doesn't matter what others believe why do we get so disgusted with what they do believe?"

"Sometimes," he said, smiling up at her because she'd sat up to ask the last question, "I'm not sure I was wise to teach you to learn to think for yourself."

She grinned. "I just have so many questions. None of us seem consistent."

"Missily," Erin called from the door, "Mikell's here."

"Tell him to come on in," said Allan as Missily rose from the chair arm.

Mikell came in and spent an hour or so discussing the weather, the headlines, the passage of the Federal Aid Highway Act for the first interstate highway system.

"More road work and detours, I suppose," remarked Allan.

"Sure to be. But it sounds as though it may be a good idea. At least the highway system for cross-country travel would be more even. Some states aren't that good about taking care of their highways," Mikell answered.

Missily had brought them some iced coffee, which Allan preferred to iced tea, and snickerdoodle cookies her mother had baked and now sat on the couch across from both of them. They got along so well together, she thought. What would her father think if he knew Mikell's religious beliefs? Would he be as tolerant as he'd always taught them to be?

That night as she and Mikell sat in Lincoln Park watching the sun go down over the Olympics, Missily began to ask him about all the things the church had done: the inquisition, witch hunts, the crusades. How could he defend people who'd done such things?

"I don't," he answered, to her surprise. "I don't condone any kind of evil action no matter who does it. I know people do strange things in the name of Christ out of a desire to see the right done but that doesn't excuse man's inhumanity to man, ever. Missily, Christians aren't perfect people. They still sin and they are finite. We don't even know what's right many times even when we try to understand. We're all children of our culture and that's one of the things we have to learn: to distinguish between culture and

36

God's way. Don't look at Christians--or those who claim to be Christians since not all who call themselves Christians are--to see whether they are wonderful and good and kind. They aren't always. Look at Christ. We are freed from sin so we don't *have* to sin any more but we still do."

"You said one day you didn't want me to--to--" she stopped. It seemed so ridiculous even to talk about a place she didn't believe existed.

"Go to hell?"

"Yes. Do you think I'm so evil then?"

"We're all condemned and on the way to hell unless we're rescued. It doesn't have anything to do with the *degree* of our sinfulness. It has to do with the fact, first, that when Adam our representative fell, we fell in him and are guilty before God. And we sin because we're sinners by nature. We aren't sinners because we sin."

"Mikell, you keep talking about sin as if that were something intelligent men believe in. But we're formed by our environment, by our parents, by our experiences, and evil is relative. In some places it's considered an act of bravery to eat your enemy. In our society we condemn cannibalism. But each society has it's own taboos. You know that."

Mikell sat silent a while, trying to think how to answer. There were so many things he could say. The sun slipped completely behind the Olympic Mountains and shafts of light shot high in the sky as if the sun were making a final declaration before disappearing in the night's darkness. It was cooler, with a breeze off the Sound and though sirens could be heard in the distance it was hushed and quiet around them so her words hung in the air. Mikell, stretched out on his back, watching the color fade from a few wisps of clouds above him, said, "This is one of my favorite times of the day. Everything seems so peaceful. Wouldn't it be lovely, Missily, if there were peace everywhere?"

Missily, geared for an argument, was nonplused. She would have liked to be stretched out next to him, holding his hand, watching the stars come out but he made no move toward being romantic in any way. Maybe all he wanted to do was convert her but even as she had the thought she knew it was unfair. He'd never done anything but discuss subjects with her, never pushed his religion on her like the girls at the office did. He was always ready to listen to her side.

"Jedidah," he startled her by saying because he hadn't used the name since she'd begun to avoid him after she'd gone to church with him, "the only way anyone can be right with God, no matter what kind of life he or she has lived, is to be perfect exactly as God is perfect. And, of course, not one of us can do that. Only one man was perfect in that way and He lived that way for sinners such as you and I. You said once Jesus was weak for letting them crucify him but I don't think you meant that. Surely not even an insane person would choose that kind of death and Jesus knew what a crucifixion was like. It was a common type of capitol punishment in His day. He'd probably seen men on a cross. Can you imagine the love it took to be willing to die that way? And even then, though that seems horrible enough to us, He was willing to take the whole weight of God's wrath, which was far worse than any physical torment."

37

Missily rose. "We're not getting anywhere, Mikell. I'm not even sure there is a God. How do you expect me to swallow the rest of what you're saying? And I'm getting cold."

"Missily, I'm sorry!" He jumped to his feet and brushed off his slacks. "Come on. Let's get something to drink. What'll you have?"

"How about a glass of wine?" she asked, trying to provoke him.

"Okay, if that's what you want," he answered cheerfully and took her where she could get her wine while he drank coffee. He grinned at her. "Everyone will think I'm on the wagon."

"Don't you drink at all?"

"Can't stand the stuff. I tried it."

"You have to get used to the flavor," Missily said. "Or at least some people do. I've always liked wine."

"I drank enough when I was in college to know I didn't want any more. Why should I get used to it? It's not something I have to drink like I have to eat spinach."

She laughed. "Oh, Mikell! Don't you like spinach?"

"Well--" he took a spoon and began to stir his coffee, "actually," he looked up and grinned, "yes. There aren't many vegetables I don't like."

Her heart rocked. Darn! Why did he have to be so attractive? "You don't seem finicky at all," she said sipping slowly at her wine. Her hands were small, the nails polished a pale pink and she wore rings on both hands.

Mikell looked down at his coffee. She was so beautiful it was hard to remember she couldn't be his. But how could he even think of asking her to marry him when they differed so on the most important part of life? "No," he said. "I guess I like almost every kind of food. Except," he looked up with that smile that made crinkles at the corner of his eyes, "clams."

"You don't like clams?"

"No ma'am! Can't stand them. Or oysters or scallops."

"But you miss out on some of the most delicious dishes of our area."

"Do you like them?"

She giggled. "No. Except clam chowder."

He laughed with her. "I ate them at home because we had to clean our plates and Mom's a good cook, but I still don't like them."

"I don't like a lot of things. Vegetables cooked. Ugh! I don't know one vegetable I really like cooked. They're too mushy."

"Hmm-m. Have you ever tried them stir fried or steamed?"

"I hate Chinese food," she replied.

"What *do* you like besides hamburgers?"

She had to laugh because she usually ordered a hamburger when they went out. "Oh, I like potatoes and most pasta and sea food."

"I'll have to get you out to Mom's. You just might like her vegetables. They aren't mushy."

"Do you cook?" Missily had been in more than one of her boy friend's apartments where they'd cooked meals together. She couldn't understand Mikell. She knew he had an apartment but he'd never invited her over.

"Yes. We all learned at home. In fact, I like to when I have the time. How about you?"

"I don't know a lot about it. Mother always does the cooking. I fix something easy on the rare occasion when I do make a meal. Mother doesn't like anyone else in her kitchen." He hadn't taken the cue. She couldn't remember any other man not taking her up and saying, "Come on over and I'll fix you something." She didn't always do so but at least she was invited.

"Do you like classical music?" Mikell wanted to know.

"Yes. I cut my teeth on Bach, Brahms, and Beethoven. Daddy's favorite three."

"Would you like to go hear the Seattle Symphony Friday night? I have tickets for the performance."

"I'd love to."

"Good. How about having dinner before? May I pick you up at the office?"

"Yes and this time I'll have Erin take me down so we won't have to worry about my car."

"I won't get to see you tomorrow," he said sadly. "I have a worship committee meeting at the church and I've no idea how late it'll last."

"Does it matter that you won't see me one night?" she teased.

His eyes were very dark. He wanted to say he would rather they go home together every day. Instead he said simply, "Yes."

"So you like to come see me?" she asked, piqued because he wouldn't be drawn.

"I wouldn't come unless I did," he answered and she could have screamed. How many of her men friends would have let an opportunity like that pass and not said something like, "You know you're my favorite girl" or "You think I can stay away from anyone as fascinating as you?" And yet how many times had she responded to their remarks with pleasure only to wonder how many others they said the same things to. There was something so open, so honest, about Mikell it was almost disconcerting. She felt uncomfortable, wondering if he could see through her fishing. So she asked him about the worship committee and what they did.

Friday she took one of her most becoming dresses to the office with her and changed into it, brushing her hair until it gleamed, sweeping it back into a French roll. She'd bought higher heels than she wore to work because Mikell was so tall she felt quite short next to him and hoped the heels would help. Though she was over five foot five he was over six-foot. She knew that because he was taller than her father was who was just six foot. As much as she wanted to date Mikell there was something about him that made her feel uncomfortable and she hoped the advantage of more height would help.

They talked lazily over dinner. Mikell was relaxed and let her do most of the talking while he watched the play of light in her eyes and hair. The restaurant they'd chosen was one where dinner was served by candlelight and Missily sparkled in her dark rose dress with it's low round neckline. She was wearing a set of crystals for a necklace, which also caught the candlelight. Mikell was in a suit, the first she'd seen him wear for even at church he'd worn a shirt and tie but no suit jacket. He wore the suit as easily as he did his more casual clothes. Though he hadn't complimented her, his eyes had flared briefly as she had come out of the office and now every time she looked up they were on her.

They enjoyed the concert and found they had similar tastes in music, plus Missily introduced him to friends during intermission and Mikell did the same for her. He'd asked earlier if she wanted her dessert after the concert since she hadn't wanted it after her meal, so now they sat, he with a dish of vanilla ice cream she with a huge piece of chocolate cake.

"Will you sleep after that?" he wanted to know.

"Probably not." Missily laughed. "We'll have to take a walk so I can walk it off."

And they did, strolling slowly down town, window shopping, talking about the concert, then about books as they stood looking in a bookshop window. And Missily wished they hadn't.

"What kind of books do you like to read?" she asked.

"Theology," he answered promptly.

"Is that all?"

"No, but they're my favorite. I like geography, history--both natural and the kind about people."

"Don't you ever read fiction?"

"Sure. Mysteries. Science Fiction. What about you?"

"I like the classics; the Bronte sister, Jane Austen, Dickens, the Russian authors. I also like to read books on sociology."

"You like people? I mean, reading about how they act and think?"

"Yes. I think cultures are fascinating. That's why, or at least one reason, I don't believe in the old Western idea of sin and converting the 'heathen' so-called. They just have different customs than we do."

"What do you think Christians mean when they talk about converting the heathen?" he asked casually.

"Turning them into good little white, Anglo-Saxon-like people wearing Western clothes, thinking Western thoughts, and so on."

"Hmm-m." He was still using that casual tone so that what he said next caught her off guard. She had determined *this* time they would not get started on his religious beliefs. "And what would you say if I told you I consider you just as much a heathen as the man in darkest Africa or the aboriginal?"

"Mikell!"

"Well, what is a heathen?"

"It's someone not civilized."

"And I take it you believe civilization is a desirable thing."

"Yes, of course."

"But doesn't that sound the same as saying they aren't converted if we go by your definition?"

Missily was silent. Why could he get her so confused?

"The dictionary says that a heathen is pagan," he went on, "and a pagan is not a Christian as well, as you say, not civilized in certain places on our planet. Why is it acceptable to want to take civilization to another culture but not Christianity?"

40

"But maybe we're wrong to civilize them. Maybe we should leave them the way they are. They know how to dress for their climate and they have their own culture and religion." Missily said. "I was talking about what I liked for myself."

Mikell stopped walking. They were where they could sit on one of the city benches and he motioned toward one. "Want to sit down?"

She did, glad to get off her feet, and he sat next to her, leaning forward to rest his arms on his legs. "Missily, we've been talking for a week and every night I go home and feel I've done a terrible job of helping you understand what Christianity is. It's very precious to me but it's such a big subject and I get sidetracked in my thoughts."

"What makes you think you understand Christianity and I don't? I've studied it, also, and regardless of what you say, I'm not a pagan. I still have no idea why you think I'm so evil. Is it because I don't agree with you?"

"Whether you agree with me or not doesn't matter. Neither does what I think of you because what I think about you doesn't decide your eternal destiny but I don't think of you as evil, Jedidah. You are a sinner but so am I and everyone else on this planet. You say you lead a decent life and I believe you are morally upright. But there's another way to look at it all." He turned and rested his arm on the bench behind her though he didn't touch her. "We can't tell whether we're acceptable to God by comparing ourselves with others. We do that by comparing ourselves with the Lord Jesus Christ and if we can't say, 'I've been as loving as you, as kind as you, as unselfish as you and I've loved and served God like you, *exactly* like you,' to Him, then we aren't acceptable to God."

"So? What difference does that make? I've told you I'm not even sure I believe there is a God so why should I worry about whether I'm acceptable to him?" She had turned to look at him a bit defiantly and saw him flinch and pale. He removed his arm and sat, his fingers entwined, those beautiful long-fingered hands she loved to watch on the organ. Oh, Mikell, she thought, why do you have to be such a fanatic? As the silence stretched she finally said, "Mikell?"

He turned and smiled briefly "I'm sorry. I just can't think of anything to say." He turned his face to the sky above. "That's the trouble with the city. You can't see the stars." His voice was unsteady and as she watched a tear slid down his cheek.

She stood up. "It's getting late."

Immediately, he stood also. "I'm sorry. I forgot about the time."

The ride to her house was a quiet one. He had turned on the radio and Mendelssohn's Italian Symphony filled the air. When they reached her house, he walked her to the door. Taking courage in hand Missily said, "I don't think we should see each other any more. We are too different in our way of looking at life and I don't enjoy talking religious subjects all the time. I've enjoyed our times together otherwise, but I think it's wiser to part."

He stood speechless, looking at her, saying nothing. If she'd slapped him he couldn't have looked more stunned or hurt. Her heart turned in her. She managed a strangled, "Good-bye", went indoors, ran to her room shutting the door to throw herself on the bed and burst into tears.

Chapter V

Instead of going home immediately after he left Missily, Mikell headed for Max and Molly's place. He knew they liked to watch the late show on Friday night so knew they would be up. Max opened the door to his ring.

"Kell! Come in," Max said, catching the cat just before she slipped out the door. "What are you doing out here this time of night?"

Molly turned off the TV as they came into the family room and got out of her chair to give Mikell a kiss and hug. "Want a cup of coffee?" she asked.

"Sure. Thanks." Mikell sank into one of the chairs.

Max sat back down and the cat jumped up on his lap. "Something's wrong. What is it?" he asked as he stroked the cat. There was only a year's difference in their ages, Max the youngest, and they looked so much alike that when they were children together many people had thought they were twins. Now Mikell's face was a bit finer drawn and he was the taller of the two but they were still much alike in their looks though Max was easier and more philosophical about life. Molly came in with the coffee, curled up on the love seat and the cat left Max to join her.

Mikell picked up his mug and took a sip from it.

"You're all dressed up," Molly said. "Go some place special?"

"To hear the Symphony. I took Missily."

"When are you going to bring her out so we can meet her?"

"Probably never," he replied and sighed. "She just told me it was wiser we didn't see each other any more."

"Mikell! Why?" Molly was instantly not only solicitous but also angry. Why would any girl treat Mikell that way?

Max, watching his brother, knew that Missily meant more to him than any other girl had before.

"Oh, it's probably my fault. I want so badly for her to become a Christian that I didn't let any opportunity slip by, if I could help it, without bringing in what we believe.

"Is that wrong?" Max wanted to know. "I can't imagine you button-holing her and trying to convert her."

"No and a lot of times she asked questions, especially lately. In fact, I guess that's why I thought she was really interested. But tonight she backed off. She's not sure she believes there is a God and her head's full of all the modern ideas about Christ and man. It just seems I could have been wiser. If I'd said things better I wouldn't have turned her off."

"Ah," Max said, drawing it out, "since when are people brought in to the kingdom by wise argument? Aren't you the guy who dinned it into my head that it's not us but the Holy Spirit who convinces people?" He was sitting

43

with his long legs stretched out in front of him, his arms quiet on the arms of his chair.

Mikell looked up with a reluctant grin. "I know, I know. But still, it seems I blundered so badly. I don't think I told her anything that would even give her food for thought."

"What did you tell her?" asked Molly. She was a small girl with a head of short dark curls, right now dressed in a bright one-piece jumpsuit.

Mikell sketched briefly some of the discussions he and Missily had had. He heard a noise and looked up. Max was laughing.

"The poor girl," he said. "No wonder she ran away. You snowed her under."

"But she argued everything I said," Mikell said, a bit piqued by his brother's reaction.

"Of course she argued. She's had a different world and life view all her life. Did you expect her just to believe what you told her without resistance? How would you have felt if your French teacher had given you everything the first month of school?"

Mikell had to grin again but Molly asked, "What's wrong with what Mikell told her?"

"Nothing. I'm just trying to get it through his thick skull that it would be rather unusual for her to change right away. Kell, give her time to think and the Holy Spirit room to work. He does it in His own time, not ours. You don't believe in these instant conversions any more than I do. That's where the modern evangelical church has parted company with the Reformation, remember? There *are* conversions like Paul's, of course, but remember he *knew* the Old Testament. But I don't know why I'm telling you all this. You know it already. Missily has never had any Christian teaching, I would guess, from what you've said about her."

Mikell drove home with a loaf of homemade bread, cookies Molly'd baked that day and in a better frame of mind though the fear that he would never see Missily again wouldn't leave him.

Missily, meanwhile continued to be extremely confused. If Mikell hadn't had the kind of education and mind he had she could have brushed him aside, but she knew he could hold his own with her father whom she'd always thought one of the most intelligent men alive.

One night she sat at her window because she couldn't sleep, her mind exhausted from going around and around. She was rocking gently in the big Boston rocker her mother had rocked all of them in as children. When they were too old to be held she had intended to get rid of it and buy a recliner for herself but Missily protested so loudly her mother gave her the rocker. As she watched the moon climb into the sky she remembered Mikell asking if she'd like to visit it. There'd been a shower and they'd taken refuge in a picnic house, sitting on the table waiting for it to pass over and when it had the moon came out.

"Would you like to go to the moon?" she asked.

"I don't think so. I've thought about it and sometimes I think it would be great to be up there and see what it looks like in the universe from a different view but then I get kind of panicky thinking of going that far," he'd answered and then asked, "Would you?"

"No. There are too many places here on earth I haven't seen yet."

Did he intrigue her so because he had never tried to kiss her, had only held her that one time when he'd told her he couldn't imagine what heaven would be like without her? Was there a heaven? The concept was so bizarre, so unreal. It had always been something others believed in, like the Indian belief in happy hunting grounds in the sky. She hadn't thought much about death and when she had it was in the abstract, not applying to her until the distant future. Slowly she rose and crossed the room to her bed. Crawling under the covers she turned on her bedside lamp and reached for the Bible Mikell had given her over a week ago. It had lain on the bottom shelf of her nightstand under other books but now she opened it to where Mikell had marked it.

"Read the Gospel of John. It starts out 'In the beginning was the Word'. The Greek for Word is logos," he's said, knowing she would be acquainted with the term since she knew Greek philosophers' ideas. "I marked it for you."

She had thanked him, taken it home, put it under some books and forgotten it. Now she picked up the marker as she opened the Bible to where Mikell had placed it. The bookmark was a beautifully hand-painted one with flowers on it: roses, baby breath, and a flower she didn't know. She wondered where he'd gotten it. "Mikell. Mikell," she whispered and started to cry. But soon she reached for a tissue to dry her face and began to read. "In the beginning was the Word and the Word was with God and the Word was God." Who was it that said something like that? She read on and when she came to "all things were made by Him" she put the Bible down. The Greeks. They had thought of the Logos. It was Philo, wasn't it, who said God made the world by the Logos? Was this man John copying Greek philosophy? She picked up the Bible and began to read again. Eventually she jerked awake, turned out the light, after laying aside the Bible, and went to sleep. For several days she was subdued, going to bed early, lying there reading until her eyes burned. Instead of being turned off or explaining away the miracles she read them with interest. Each one seemed to have a purpose and an explanation given by Christ himself. When He healed the blind man He talked about people seeing in a way that sounded as though He meant understand. She became fascinated by Christ's words, by his claims, by the authority, which he seemed to have. During the day she thought about what she'd read and what Mikell had told her. She didn't want to read the Bible and she'd try to get interested in one of the other books she'd started but invariably she'd go back to the Bible. It wasn't easy reading. There were too many concepts that seemed to have an entirely different meaning than what she was used to hearing or reading. Ideas and concepts, too, that she'd never thought of until she met Mikell about which she had no desire to think. The night she came to the story of Lazarus the fear she'd felt the time she'd heard the story from Mikell's minister came back and she fought the desire to call Mikell.

45

Her family noticed her withdrawal, the circles around her eyes, her distraction, but since Mikell didn't come over they thought that there must have been a quarrel and decided it best not to say anything, though Anna Metlow wasn't always as sensitive.

One Saturday Missily left the house early. Taking her car she drove aimlessly about the city, finally stopping at Lincoln Park where she and Mikell had spent so much time. She climbed to their favorite hill and sat watching the people in the park, the clouds over the Olympics, the ferries and other boats on the Sound. She was close to despair. Her world had been shattered, she didn't know anyone to talk to and she felt completely alone. She longed to see Mikell, to talk to him and she wished, as she had so many times, that he loved her while knowing at the same time she couldn't marry someone so at odds with her understanding of life.

As she sat there she idly watched a man coming up the hill who looked as forlorn as she felt. His head was down and he acted as though it were a great effort to put one foot in front of the other. Suddenly she realized it was Mikell. Scrambling to her feet, she fled, running down one of the paths away from the hill then ran pell-mell into another man out jogging. He caught her so she wouldn't fall.

"Hey!" he said. "Angels don't fall from heaven every day. Where're you going? Want to go with me to my place?"

She drew away. "I'm sorry," she panted. "I wasn't watching where I was going."

He reached for her. "Come on, sweetie. We could have fun."

"Oh, leave me alone!" she said crossly and jerked away.

"Okay, okay," he muttered as she ran on.

The next morning Missily decided she would see Mikell one more time and then she'd go back East to visit Kitten on her vacation, due in a week, and try to find a job back there. She would get away from Washington and start over. Putting on a little hat and dark glasses after fixing her hair in a different style, she drove to the church where Mikell had taken her. She arrived just on time on purpose and slipped into the back pew where she could watch Mikell play, then sat crying through the first part of the service though she tried desperately to stop the flow of tears. Mikell had that drawn, tired look he'd had the day he'd come to her office after they hadn't seen each other for a while. She watched him through the singing and prayer. He sat there with his face shaded by his hand during the latter. When the prayer was over he took a great shuddering breath. Missily meant to watch him the whole service. She followed him with her eyes as he took his seat next to Lorna who immediately climbed onto his lap. When the minister read from the Bible her mind was far away from anything he read but as he began to preach it became riveted on what he was saying just as it had that other time. She couldn't believe it. He was explaining the term logos, first from historical backgrounds and then as it was understood in writings other than the New Testament and finally what the New Testament writer meant.

Missily left the service, early, before the doxology was sung, ran to her car and drove to Rose and Graham's house. As often on Sunday, they had a house full of people so she found many ways to occupy her mind, staying on after the others left to help Rose clean up, talking to her about her many activities. Rose was a crusader and generally writing to her Senator or Representative about something, much like her mother, working to get petitions signed, writing letters to the newspapers. It amused Missily and today she was glad for Rose's latest crusade. It helped pass more hours.

Eventually, however, she had to go home and to bed. She took the Bible and put it in her closet under some of the things on the shelf and shut the door resolutely. She would not read any more of it. And as soon as she could she would leave Seattle and start over. The thought was so painful she thought she couldn't do it. She would call Mikell, beg him to be friends but not talk about religion, but even as the thought came she rejected it. She knew instinctively that he wouldn't be the same person without his beliefs though she didn't understand why. No. Best to start anew. Others had gotten over lost loves. So could she.

Her family sighed with relief as she seemed to be herself again though her father missed Mikell. He'd been the most interesting young man any of the girls had brought home. The week until Missily's vacation started was endless to her, filled with confused thoughts and fears while the longing to see Mikell, to walk with him, go to the park together, watch the way his eyes crinkled at the corners when he laughed, see him flip back that errant strand of hair, hear his voice. All haunted her for days. Nights were bearable only because she bought an over the counter sleeping tablet. She hated the way they made her feel the next day but it was better than not sleeping and eventually the time passed and the day came when she told her father and mother good-bye at the airport and walked down the ramp to the plane.

Mikell, meanwhile, was fighting his own battles. He knew this time he couldn't go beg her to come out with him. She had effectively closed the door between them. He fought the terrible sadness that seemed to have left him crippled. Losing Missily had been even harder the second time and he wasn't sure he would ever again meet a girl who would mean as much to him, nor did he want to. He loved her so deeply it was hard to accept that she couldn't be his, that they couldn't have a life together. It was difficult to keep in mind all God's promises, all the things he knew were true, when he hurt so terribly. Then one day Eva told him that Missily was back East, had gone to visit her sister. Eva and Erin had become friends and often did things together so he heard of Missily through his sister.

"To visit?"

"Yes she's on vacation. But Erin thinks she might try to get a job there. She cleaned her room thoroughly before she left, gave Erin some things, and got rid of others."

"Did she say she was going to look for a job?" Mikell tried to keep the question casual as he stood waiting for his turn. He and the others were playing croquet at the Hatchery. Lorna was trying to knock Eva's ball out of the way.

"No. I don't think so. Erin just said that because of the way Missily cleaned out her room before she left. Would you miss her if she did?"

"Good job, Lorna," he hollered as Eva's ball rolled into the flowerbed. "I hardly ever see her," he answered Eva evasively. "Better rescue your ball."

That night he paced the floor. It had been bad enough to have her in the city and not be able to see her but to think that she might move across the country and there would never be any opportunity of even bumping into her accidentally, let alone any kind of reconciliation, was distressing. He knew now he'd pinned his hopes on what Max had said. If he thought it had been hard to do without her when he still had a hope and was just biding time, the pain that filled him now was far worse and he wondered how people lived through losing their mates. He went about his work as though in a fog, starting when someone spoke to him, took long drives after work to go home exhausted and try to sleep. After one of those nights when he couldn't fall asleep until the early morning hours, he slept in Saturday morning and woke up to the ever present, overwhelming misery. It was so pervasive that when the bell to his apartment rang and he went to see who was there, he just stood staring.

"May I come in?" Missily asked timidly.

He stepped back and motioned her in, still speechless. His delight at seeing her was so great he was afraid to touch her. She removed the light jacket she was wearing and he took it to hang in the hall closet, then she proceeded him into the living room. She glanced around, noticing that though it looked lived in it was clean and neat, before she turned to face him. He still hadn't said a word but was standing behind a rocker gripping it so that his knuckles were white.

"You're not angry with me, are you?" she asked.

"Angry?" his voice came out a squeak and he cleared it.

"For coming here." She was beginning to feel miserable and unhappy. Wasn't he glad to see her at all? "I-I'm sorry. If you'd rather, I'll leave," she said unsteadily and started back to the entrance.

"No!" he exclaimed loudly, then more quietly, "Sit down. Do you want something to drink? Coffee? Iced tea?"

"Coffee would be fine."

He went out to the little kitchen, his mind a whirl. Why was she here? He was shaking all over and almost dropped the cups as he took them out of the cupboard. She drank it black like he did, didn't she? "Cream or sugar?" he asked and was surprised at how normal his voice sounded.

"No, just black," she answered.

When he went back into the living room she was seated on the edge of the couch, looking ill at ease but unbelievably beautiful. Setting her cup down on the coffee table he took his to set beside his chair as he sank into it. "Eva told me you were out of town," he said, trying to put her at ease.

"Yes, I went to see Kitten on my vacation. Mikell, please. If you would rather I not be here we can go to the park. It's just—well, I want to tell you something."

"No. Why should I *not* want you here?" And this came out so desperate that he hastened to add. "I just thought you were out of town still."

48

Missily, watching him, saw his hand shake as he raised his cup to his lips and some of the hot liquid slopped down his shirt front. He put the cup down with an exclamation holding the shirt away from his skin. Missily picked up a napkin and went to kneel before him to dab at the wet spot. She looked up to find his eyes very dark. "Missily," he whispered and then she was in his arms in a stranglehold. It poured out--his longing for her, his fear that he wouldn't see her again, the long days and sleepless nights.

Missily, her head against his shoulder, the fragrance of his shaving lotion filling her nose, began to cry and tried desperately not to. She'd been so afraid he would be angry with her for coming to the apartment and the weeks of confusion and fear that had caused her to want to take her life, though both were gone before she'd come to his door, had left her vulnerable. She had not expected anything like this. Nothing had prepared her for the intensity of his words, the fierceness of his hold. She felt his hand on her face, under he chin and then he was kissing her, kissing her as she'd never been kissed before. Suddenly, however, she was free; he had risen and was standing looking out of the window.

"Forgive me, Missily. I had no right," he said unsteadily.

"Will you let me tell you why I came?" she asked, her own voice not quite steady. She was wiping away her tears with the napkin. "Could--would you come sit down? It's important for me to know what you think. Please, Mikell."

He turned to look at her from across the room. The light fell on her face and he saw that, in spite of the tears, there was peace there. She rose and went back to sit on the couch and he crossed the room to sit on it, too, though not close to her.

"I did go away. I thought it would help. After--after that last time I was with you--Mikell, I tried reading the Bible. I read it every night for a while. Then—well--everything was so confusing. My father is an intelligent man and I love him very much. But then I met you and you're intelligent, too, only the two of you believe so differently. I-I didn't care whether I lived or not. It seemed as though everything I'd believed was false--I mean about my father knowing what he was talking about when he told me about religion. If you hadn't had the education you did, I could have just laughed it off as superstition on your part, or a crutch or something like that. But I couldn't after all the talks we had. I didn't know what or whom to believe and it frightened me. I was always so confident that I understood life and people before." Missily stopped to take a drink of coffee. It was difficult to know how to tell her story because she longed to tell him how much she loved him and why it had been so hard for her to know what to do. "I decided to go visit Kitten and while I was there see if I could get a job. It seemed the only answer--to remove myself from here and start over.

"At first it helped. New surroundings and Kitten and I did things together but when she had to work the hours were long even though she teaches in her own apartment, a very large one, I might add. One day I took a walk in the neighborhood. About three blocks away there was a church. I thought it was the same denomination I grew up in and decided to talk to someone there. The pastor was in."

49

Putting down her cup she sat silent a moment, then she reached for Mikell's hand and held on to it tightly because she needed his support. "I found out that the--is it conference or synod?"

"Denomination probably," he said trying not to leap ahead of her in his thoughts.

"Well, anyway, they're different. I mean the one that the church I grew up in and this one. This pastor believes the same way you do. In fact, you talk a lot alike."

She sat looking at him, her fingers against her lips. "Mikell," she said moving her hand nervously against her face, "I-I wanted to see you once more before I went away."

His hand jerked in hers and she frowned. "The---the week before I left I went to church, your church, and sat in the back so I could watch you play. Your preacher--I said I'd been reading the Bible, didn't I?"

"Yes," he said miserably. So she was going away.

"Well, I intended just to watch you because I thought it was the last time I'd see you, but your minister began to talk about the logos. Remember, you told me to read John?"

This time he just nodded.

"So I started--Oh! Who made that beautiful book mark you put in there?"

"My sister-in-law, Molly."

"It's beautiful. Does she do other things?"

"Yes. In fact, she asked me one day when I was going to bring you out?"

"What did you tell her?"

"That was the night--the night of the symphony. I told her probably never and that it was my fault for not letting any opportunity pass without bringing up what I believe. Max told me I'd snowed you under," he said and he wasn't looking at her or he would have seen the tenderness in her eyes. She was still gripping his hand.

"I spent the rest of that day with Rose so I wouldn't have to think--the day after I went to your church I mean." Missily went on. "I was taking sleeping pills to sleep at night. I decided to quit reading the Bible and stuck it on my closet shelf. When I began to talk to the pastor in Philadelphia all the things I'd read and what you and I'd talked about came back to me and I asked him all kinds of questions to try and throw him. He was very patient. He told those who called on the phone he was in conference, took their number to call back, and told anyone who came to the door the same thing.

"You have no idea what effect that had on me. We talked two or three hours. I asked if I could come the next day and he said yes. I went back every day. I couldn't go to church the next Sunday because Kitten had already planned the day but Monday I was back. We talked and talked. He was so patient even when I was sarcastic or angry or cried or even got off on subjects that had nothing to do with religion. Thursday night Kitten had to go to a practice and I told her I'd take the night off and read—we'd been going somewhere ever night since I'd arrived."

50

Missily took a deep breath and smiled at Mikell. He didn't smile back but closed his eyes and laid his head back against the couch. He wondered why she'd taken the time to come tell him all this when she was moving away. To show him he couldn't make her believe?

"Mikell," she said softly, "that night--that night--I don't know how to tell you." She got up and roamed the room, looking out the window and thought how strange that everything should be so normal; cars going past, children playing on the sidewalk, a man mowing his lawn, a woman weeding her flower garden. Slowly she turned and went back to stand in front of him. "I didn't read that night. I wandered over Kitten's apartment and thought and thought and suddenly I realized that instead of arguing against the Bible I was arguing *for* it in my mind. It seemed so clear how it could all be true and I laughed out loud because I'd been so blind. And then--and then I wanted to talk to you. I tried to call you and couldn't get you."

"When?" The question was sharp. His head had come up and his eyes opened when she'd begun to talk about believing.

"Last--day before yesterday."

"I was out driving. I couldn't stand--never mind. Go on."

She sank down on the rug in front of him. "The next day I ran all the way to the church. It was only eight o'clock in the morning but I couldn't wait. I knew he lived next door to the church so I went there when he wasn't in his office. His wife answered the door. They were having breakfast and invited me to join them but I was too excited and I told him what had happened. It was--The hardest part was when he asked me if I believed I was sinner who needed the forgiveness of the Almighty God for what I'd done against Him. I-I still wanted to think I was a decent person. We'd talked about Christ but then he began to show me what kind of a person Jesus was by explaining the law to me and what it meant to be perfect. Mikell, I tried to tell Kitten. She thinks I've gone crazy, I think. But I wanted to tell you so I came here."

"Missily, are you saying that-that you believe there is a God and that the Bible is true?"

"Yes, yes. I believe all you told me," she said eagerly.

He sat forward and reached for her hand. "Jedidah, are you telling me you're a Christian, a believer, too?" he asked, hardly able to take in what she had told him.

She nodded and her gray eyes had never been so beautiful. Mikell put her hands to his forehead as he bowed his head, fighting the desire to weep. "Almighty God," he whispered, "how do I say thank you for this gift?" Lifting his head he kissed her fingers on both hands, rose and went to the window fighting for calmness. From there he said in a shaky voice. "But I don't understand why you want to move back east."

"What?"

"You said you wanted to see me one more time before you went away. Did you--did you find a better job there?" He could barely get the question out his throat was so tight and his chest aching.

"When did I--Oh! I meant before I went the first time. That's why I went to church to see you."

51

"You aren't leaving?"

"No. Why would I? The only reason I was going to before was--" Then suddenly she realized she wasn't sure how he felt about her and she was shy of confessing her desire to get away from him before because she loved him and yet didn't want to marry him. "Mikell, there're are two more things I want to tell you."

He turned to look at her across the room. He wanted more than anything else to sweep her up in his arms and beg her to marry him but he was still trying to assimilate the fact that not only was she not leaving but that the barrier that had been between them was gone. "What's that?" he asked.

"When I was talking to the pastor he said I must have been attending a good church to hear what I had. I told him that you had told me, told him how we'd argued. He looked at me rather strangely and said, 'Mikell Adamsen? You meant Mikell Sheldon Adamsen whose father owns a fish hatchery out in Washington?' And when I managed to answer yes, he said, 'Ask him if he remembers Dizzy Dan.' Do you?"

"Yes." Mikell came back across the room and sat down on the couch. "He was my roommate at college for two years."

"Well, that's who the pastor is."

"Who? What do you mean? What pastor?"

"The one in Philadelphia. His name is Daniel Mendel."

"Missily, you've got to be kidding! Dizzy Dan was the wildest kid on campus. I used to go pick him up from parties so he wouldn't drive back to the dorm drunk."

"He told me." She laughed. "He said you wouldn't believe it. But he said you used to have arguments and he just graduated from seminary last year. He got to thinking about some of the things you said and they made sense to him."

Mikell sat silent. It was all too much to take in. He reached out to lift a strand of Missily's hair and the tears that had gathered in his eyes rolled down his cheeks. He wiped them away with his sleeve. "There--there's just too much to take in. I was crazy about Dan but lost track of him."

"He had to know all about you." Missily sat very still so he wouldn't take his hand away. Then she said, "I asked him about the name Jedidah. He read about it from the Bible to me. Then I asked him what it meant." Her eyes were sweet. "Do you know?" He had been looking at the hair he was caressing, now his eyes came to hers. "Yes," he said. "I hunted for the Hebrew word that means beloved."

"But Mikell, you hardly knew me."

"I've always known you," he said simply.

She gazed at him from her seat on the floor and with an exclamation he reached for her and drew her up into his arms. "You are my beloved. You know that, don't you? I gave myself away when you first came. I wasn't here the other night because I've hardly been alive since—since we parted and I couldn't stand to come here and be alone with the agony of losing you, longing for you. My darling, could you come to care for me? I'd love to have you for my wife."

"But don't you see? That's why I went away. It was the only way I could think of to stay sane. I thought if I went away I could start over and eventually forget you. Now," she sighed happily, "now, I don't have to."

"Missily, you can't mean--" Mikell hesitated. He'd never been sure that she even liked him very well.

"But why not? I've loved you for months," she answered and his mouth came down on hers.

Later, when they had explored all the whys and whens, delighting in being together, Mikell said, "Why don't we give Dan a call? He deserves to be in on this."

"I don't think he'll be surprised. I told him why I decided to leave Washington."

"And why was that?"

"I told you," she said with a grin. "Because I loved you and yet knew it would never work since we thought too differently. Mikell, I want to call Dan and Marie--that's his wife--but first I want you to know I'm glad that what happened when you spilled your coffee, happened. You'd always been so--reserved, I guess is as good a word as any--about showing your feelings that I think I might have felt I wasn't good enough to love before I became a Christian. Now I know that wasn't why you held back."

He closed his eyes and drew her close. "You have no idea how I fought what I wanted. One reason I didn't want you up here--other than the fact that I love you too much to want to do anything to cause anyone to get the wrong idea about us--was because I knew as long as we were in the public I would leave you alone. I wasn't so sure of myself otherwise. You are a very disturbing young woman."

Chapter VI

Thinking back over those days Missily reflected how the time BC, as Mikell dubbed it, seemed flat, uninteresting and unrewarding. When she'd talked to Daniel Mendel he'd helped her examine her life for her goals, ambitions, and the meaning of her days. It was still hard to put into words the difference it made to know that there was a sovereign God who not only created the world but also loved His creation enough to redeem it--all of it, not just lost sinners.

Now she checked the veal birds she was cooking for supper. She'd splurged for once since veal was usually beyond her food budget. She'd wanted something different for supper. The weather had accommodated and stayed cool enough she could use her oven. She called Gretchen in to set the table after glancing at the calendar. Too often she'd called and one of the girls would say, "It's not my turn," then there would be wrangling and arguments, so she'd assigned them a week each. The boys helped with the kitchen work, too, since Missily and Mikell agreed they needed to learn how to care for themselves but they had other jobs like chopping wood and keeping the wood box filled, cleaning the wood stove, shoveling snow if they had any in the winter and doing yard work. The girls took their turn at all the jobs, too, and Missily was amused that they liked the boy's work better than their own and that Sean was a better cook and better at cleaning up after himself than either girl. She and Mikell believed in women's work and men's work but they weren't as strict in the division as their parents had been.

"Mother, what are you thinking about?" Gretchen demanded. "I've asked you three times if we need bread on the table."

"No, not tonight." Missily drained the potatoes to mash them. "I was thinking about when your father and I met and dated."

"Do you believe in love at first sight? Our health teacher told us there wasn't any such thing. That love develops."

"I'll answer that one." It was Mikell, coming in the door with his lunch bucket. "Tell your teacher that your father knows there is love at first sight because he experienced it."

"She says that's just attraction. That you can't love someone you don't know."

"Ah, but I knew your mother. I'd known her all my life. I was just waiting for her to appear." Mikell emptied the lunch bucket and was running water in the thermos to set it to soak. "Tell her I'll come lecture the class if she'd like."

Gretchen laughed and gave him a hug. "She'd probably rather argue with you. Mamma, did you love Daddy at first?"

"No. I found him attractive, though, after I noticed him. That was about the third time he was in the office when he asked my name and we found out that our mothers had both made up our names."

"But Daddy was named after Grandma's brother Michael," Gretchen protested.

"I know. But there were too many Michael's in the family already. She loved the name so coined, I guess you would say, Mikell," her father told his daughter, sitting down in one of the dining room chairs, stretching his legs out on another. "I had to do something," he continued. "I was getting desperate. Your mother hardly noticed me and I'd fallen like a ton of bricks the first time she looked at me with those gorgeous eyes of hers."

"What's it feel like to fall in love?" Gretchen asked, her hands full of knives, spoons, and forks.

"Delicious, fantastic, unbelievable," Mikell answered.

"Daddy! That could describe a lot of things."

"So it could, but so can the word sweet. For instance sugar is sweet, honey is sweet, you are sweet, but not the same way. And love is all those things in a special way you have to experience to understand."

"You're no help," pronounced his daughter and proceeded to set the table.

Missily came to sit on his lap and give him a kiss. "How did you happen to be there when I had to stop?" she asked, running her fingers through his dark waves.

"Providential. I was on the way to another job and thought I was seeing things. I don't remember ever seeing you on the road like that from when we first met."

She laid her head on his shoulder and he encircled her with his arm. "I was so glad to see you."

"How's Rose?"

"Oh, you know her. She won't show anything but she did let me hold her. She'll probably refuse to believe the doctors can't fix things. I don't want anything to happen to Graham."

Candace, who had just run into the dining room because she seldom walked if she could run, came to a sudden stop. "What's wrong with Uncle Graham?"

Missily sat up. "He has cancer."

"Is he going to die?"

"I hope not. It's in his mouth and the doctor is going to operate."

"If he does he'll go to hell. I don't want him to," she said tragically.

Mikell reached out a hand and drew her to them. "Dacey, he's still alive and God can still bring him to himself. Don't jump the gun, child."

"But if he's not elect he will," she insisted.

"Ah, but that's not any of our business. All we're given to do is tell the good news not guess who's elect and who isn't." As Missily rose to check supper he pulled Candace into his arms. "Sugar, don't use election that way. It's a comfort to believers, not something we use to guess God's secrets."

"But it's still true."

"Yes, but Candace, don't forget that people are responsible for their sins and we can't hold God responsible for that. We're all condemned unless God saves us. And we all deserve to go to hell."

"I know but don't you think it's hard to look at Uncle Graham and believe he's not supposed to be saved?"

"But that's exactly what I'm talking about. We can't say that. I can't look at anyone and say he or she's not supposed to be saved. We're to take the gospel to everyone. Maybe this will help Uncle Graham see that he needs someone beside himself. That he needs God."

"Oh. I never thought of that," she answered and he gave her a hug winking at Missily over her head.

As Missily lay in Mikell's arms later that night and listened to him breathe, the thought of his getting cancer and her losing him came back. She tried to pray for Rose and Graham but she couldn't shake the other fear. He had been so much a part of her since that remarkable day nearly twenty years ago in his apartment when she learned about his love for her and her life so different than before she'd run to the church to talk to Daniel Mendel that it was almost as though life had begun for her then. She'd been given two priceless gifts that week that seemed lit by neon lights in her mind.

It hadn't been easy. Mikell and Daniel had both warned her and they had been wise to do so. In her joy and excitement she'd thought she could convince everyone else but she'd come against a brick wall in her family. Erin told her she'd get over being religious when she got used to Mikell. Rose took her aside and gave her an older sister's talk, warning her against fanaticism which Missily thought funny since Rose was quite fanatical about things she believed. Suz just laughed about it and said it was Missily's business, just not to try to convert *her* and Kitten had tried to argue her out of her temporary derangement, as she termed it, with long intellectual arguments in letters to Missily. These Missily showed to Mikell which gave him an opportunity to explain how and why Christians disagreed with Kitten's arguments.

In spite of the opposition at home Missily reveled in what she learned. She loved going to church and started going with Mikell to a Bible study. She even shyly told her co-workers at the office about her conversion and was disconcerted to hear they thought she hadn't heard the truth and was going to what they called a liberal church, which only confused her. Mikell was so disturbed by what they'd said that he'd made an appointment to have lunch with Missily and the other three girls. It proved to be a lively meal. Missily sat listening and, though she understood little, she knew enough to know the girls weren't hearing what Mikell was saying. He'd finally given up but at least was able to make the point that it was what Christ had done they trusted, not themselves and they agreed to that though later Missily had said to Mikell that it didn't sound to her as though they really understood that they didn't have *any* part in saving themselves. Mikell had hugged her in delight.

"You learn fast, my love. You're right. The wonderful thing about God's grace, though, is that even when we don't understand it we are still saved by grace alone."

Missily also found a new kind of love and companionship. She wasn't used to people doing something for her without expecting a return. Even she and her sisters lived that way. If she wanted to borrow something of Erin's she had to promise Erin could borrow something of hers. She wasn't quite sure how to handle it the first time Molly told her she could borrow a book and not to worry about getting it back until she had time to read it. When she'd offered to bring one of hers the next time she was out to see Max and Molly, Molly told her she would enjoy that but Missily wasn't to feel obligated in anyway. Then, besides the precious unselfish love Mikell gave her, a love much different than she'd ever dreamed possible, she found his family took her in. She and Molly spent hours together talking, shopping, cooking, baking, until Mikell complained he never got to see his fiancée.

He'd taken her to meet his pastor the night of the morning she'd come to his apartment. That had been a busy day. After Mikell ate breakfast, which Missily fixed for him while he cleaned up and changed clothes, they had taken his car to buy Missily a ring, and from there had gone first to tell her parents and then his where they stayed to eat dinner with the family. Before he took her back to the apartment to get her car he asked if she'd go with him to meet Pastor Justice and she'd agreed readily. Later Joshua Justice told them that he'd been thinking of leaving the church for another because he'd been so discouraged at the apathy in the one he was pastoring and hearing Missily's story had encouraged him to stay.

Joshua had called his wife to come over to the study so Mikell and Missily could tell her and when she walked in, before Joshua introduced Missily, she said, "Missily! Missily Metlow. I haven't seen you for years."

Joshua asked, looking from one to the other, "Do you two know each other?"

His wife turned. "We went to school together all the way through junior high and high school. I think we had every English class together, didn't we?"

Missily nodded. "And most of our gym classes."

"Klara, I want you to hear what Mikell and Missily were telling me." Joshua got a chair for her. "Sit down, everyone."

So they told their story once again though they hadn't mentioned their decision to get married yet. Before they'd even finished Klara was wiping tears from her eyes.

"Oh, Joshua," she said. He gave her a brilliant smile. Only the night before he'd been terribly depressed even though she'd reminded him that it wasn't results but faithfulness that God asked of them. Now she went to Missily to give her a big hug as Missily stood. "You people don't know this but I've been praying for Missily since high school."

"Klara! And I wasn't even that nice to you." Missily was appalled.

Klara shrugged. "I wasn't much to look at. I thought you and your sisters were so beautiful and you always looked like you stepped out of a storybook."

It was Missily's turn to cry this time. "I was such a snob," she said, wiping the tears away with her hand.

"What matters is now," Mikell said and stood to put his arm around her. "Josh and Klara, Missily has said she'll marry me, warts and all."

They laughed and then congratulated the couple and Klara invited them to stay for supper.

Missily's father puzzled her. He'd said very little when she'd told him about her beliefs, just listened quietly, picked up the book he was reading and went back to it, effectively cutting off any conversation. When Mikell came to tell him he wanted to marry Missily he said only, "Do you? Well, you can take care of her," and that was all. It was baffling and harder to understand than all the rest of the family. However as time drew nearer for their wedding he began a subtle attack on Missily, asking her questions, smiling if she stumbled over her answer and saying, "Well, let it go. It doesn't matter."

However, the seed of doubt had been sown and when she would see Mikell she'd be distant until she'd break down and tell him what her father had said. It wasn't particularly difficult for Mikell to answer her fears and doubts. Her father's arguments were familiar to anyone who had read apologetics, but he was irritated with Allan Metlow. It was an underhanded way to try to shake her faith so one day he confronted the older man in the Metlow library. It was a beautiful room with shelves to the ceiling holding books Allan had collected for years. There were comfortable chairs for reading, a globe, a huge dictionary and rich wine colored drapes at the windows. Allan invited him genially to sit down. They sat across from each other, Allan with his whisky and soda and Mikell with a tall glass of ice water.

"Does your religion forbid you to drink alcoholic beverages?" Allan asked.

"Not at all. It's a personal choice. I don't care for them and see no reason to cultivate the taste."

"I see," Allan replied, though Mikell had the feeling he didn't and might doubt Mikell's response.

"Mr. Metlow," Mikell began.

"Oh, please. Allan. You're going to be part of the family."

The sentence sounded so facile that Mikell wondered if Allan was sincere or if he were imagining things. "Whatever you say," he replied. "I know that you don't profess to believe the Bible as I do but you haven't said anything to me. However, you do say things to Missily. I was wondering if we could talk together about what I believe."

"Missily shouldn't carry tales," said her father genially but Mikell felt his irritation rise. Allan was giving the distinct impression that he didn't think that Mikell was worth the time and effort to spend an evening discussing anything serious, a far different attitude than he had formerly had.

"Why would you think she was doing that?" Mikell asked.

"You wouldn't know we talked unless she did."

"Mr. Metlow," said Mikell, not deliberately but because he felt uncomfortable with the Allan, "perhaps we'd better have some kind of understanding of our ideas of marriage first. To me, it's normal for spouses-

58

-and engaged couples--to talk over things, even what their parents say unless it's said in confidence. I don't intend having secrets from Missily because I believe trust is built that way."

Allan studied Mikell from his big wing-backed chair. He took a leisurely drink before he said, "I can accept that." Then he smiled. "I'll just have to watch what I say."

And Mikell had to laugh. He liked Missily's father. "Will you discuss my beliefs with me?"

"Is there anything to discuss? You believe one way I believe another. We can get along anyway. We'll just stay away from religion."

"But that's just my point. Why should we? That is the most important part of life. If I have a gag on talking about that I'm denying who I am."

"You're young yet. You'll learn tolerance as you grow older. This world would be a far better place if fanatics would learn to listen to others even if they can't agree."

"That is also what I was trying to say. I don't know you well enough to know what you're like but people can be just as fanatical about not talking about religion as they believe others arc about talking about the subject." Mikell didn't add that Allan had a religion, even though he didn't acknowledge it as one, and talked about it constantly.

Allan sipped slowly at his drink. Then he set it down and rose to go to his shelves. Lightly he touched the backs of several books. "Young man, these are written by the wisest minds of all ages. What makes you think that the drivel you believe can stand up to them? Missily might think she wants what you have. She's in love. It's new and exciting now but she'll settle down and what kind of marriage will you have then?"

Mikell rose to cross the room to look at the books Allan had touched: Plato, Aristotle, Thomas Paine, Roseau, Sartre, Kant, Marx, Hegel, Camus, Nietzsche, Beckett--men with whom he was well acquainted. He pulled out the one by Marx and paged through it. Looking up suddenly he asked, "Tell me what you find to agree with in Marx."

Allan Metlow, who had been leaning against the bookcase, stood away from it and strolled down the room, stopping by the big globe to turn it slowly. "I'm not a communist if that's what you mean, but I think he had some valuable insights into the way rich men often oppress those less fortunate than themselves."

"Yes, he did. I imagine you believe that our upbringing has some influence on us."

Allan turned his heard to study Mikell. "Naturally," he said, "that's why I believe you and Missily are not well mated. She's not going to deny all she's learned all her life. She's too intelligent for that and she needs the challenge of someone like-minded."

"Marx had a religious upbringing, as you know," Mikell said quietly though he was angry that Allan had waited so long to put his thoughts into words and at the same time a bit amused that Missily's father would think intelligence had nothing to do with her religious beliefs or at least nothing that would cause her to believe as she professed to believe. "Regardless of what you think of what his father did in changing religions and why, Marx

59

knew his Bible and the prophets spoke out against the injustice of the rich against the poor very strongly. I know you're aware it's not a new problem. Marx's mistake was in believing that economics was the answer to life's problems."

Allan strolled back to pick up his drink, took a swallow and stood with his glass in hand. "Yes, there are interesting things in the Bible, also, just as there are in Marx. How do you, though, excuse the pagan, blood-thirsty god the Old Testament portrays?"

"I don't," Mikell said, putting Marx back in place and walking back to his chair though he didn't sit in it. "I don't have to because that's not the kind of God the Old Testament portrays. It shows us a God of holiness and justice and love and mercy. In other words we are given a revelation of what God really is instead of just what we might imagine."

Allan sat down, indicating that Mikell take his seat also. That night began a series of talks between the two of them. Sometimes Missily would join them, listening in fascination as they sparred and argued. She had never thought anyone could hold their own with her father yet now she saw Mikell disconcerting the older man at times, changing not his mind about what he believed or didn't believe but his preconceived notions of those "Bible thumpers" as he'd always called them.

After one such conversation he said to Missily, "He is different than anyone I've talked to or heard on radio or TV. I suppose it's because he's intelligent. In fact, too intelligent to be an organ repairer."

"Daddy, don't be a snob," Missily said. "He loves organs. He loves to make them sound right. He builds them, too, and rebuilds others, and plays well."

"He builds organs?"

"Yes. He and his father built the first one when he was a teen-ager for a hobby from a kit and he decided to build them, then."

"Does he intend to make that into a business?"

Missily had to smile because she knew the way her father's mind was going. To be the head of an ongoing business was far more acceptable than repairing organs. "I don't think so. He likes to repair them. You probably have about the same idea I had about organ repairers. He's a craftsman and remember he repairs organs for all kinds of places, not just churches. He also gives recitals when a church or some institution buys one. But Daddy, he's not that much different from many of the people with whom I go to church and Bible study. I don't mean all the people are like Mikell. Remember he got his master's degree in philosophy." And here Missily remembered, from the look on her father's face, that he had probably not known that bit of information about his future son-in-law. "But they don't have those strange ways of which we always made fun. They don't think making money is wrong nor do they think everyone should be a missionary or a preacher to amount to something. They believe every decent profession and job is equally important. They do believe things we made fun of but it's not a mystical, airy-fairy kind of belief. It's very solid and intelligent. They believe in using their minds. In fact, the word believe even has a different

60

meaning than I was used to. It holds the connotation of knowledge, also, so that when we believe something we know it's true."

"You can't *know* anything with certainty, Missily. That's a given."

"But I do. It's a very safe place to be. I'm glad that I know that God not only exists but that he is in control." She was shaking as she often did nowadays when confronting her father's ideas. He could make her feel she was on shaky grounds even when she knew she wasn't.

He reached out to hug her. "You've gotten very intense, youngster. Don't you and Mikell ever do anything to enjoy life?"

"Daddy! I've never enjoyed it so much before. You'll have to meet his family. They're great and I love to go see them. We have so much fun just being together. Besides you don't know Mikell very well if you think he's always serious and talking religion or philosophy. We do nutty things like go to the park and slide down the slide, swing, or he pushes me on the merry-go-round and shows off on the monkey bars. We run along the beach just for the fun of it and play tennis and go bicycling."

"All right, all right," her father laughed. "I give up. I do enjoy him."

Missily could have told him that she'd had the same idea about Mikell until the day she knocked on the door of his apartment with a pounding heart. After that he'd courted her in a way any girl would have envied. Flowers were sent to her office as well as to her home. If he were near enough on a job he'd call and they'd meet in the park for lunch, eating in the van if the weather was disagreeable. He brought her candy, books, and things that took his fancy: a delicately carved rose that was a music box, an ivory fan that he found in an antique store. Sometimes he would come by after work to her home with a huge bouquet of flowers from a customer's garden so that Anna, delighted, hunted up vases and the rooms took on the fragrance and beauty of the garden in which they grew. Because Mikell had never tried to kiss her, hold her hand, or find excuses to touch her before they were engaged she was startled and then delighted at the intensity of his passion. Though, for him, caresses were for private, she found that her fears that he might believe sex to be not particularly nice were unfounded. He believed that a man who loved a woman saved the joining for the wedding night and didn't go for heavy petting yet he made it clear that she was very desirable and that was a gift from God, too.

Even though none of her family ever changed their views, they had accepted Mikell and loved him and finally they also accepted the fact that Missily had changed for good, that she wasn't going to back out. They wouldn't have admitted it, either of her parents, but they were glad for the kind of marriage Missily had. There was something between her and Mikell that wasn't in the other girls' marriages even though, except for Suz, they had good marriages. Both Rose and Graham and Erin and Thor were close to their spouses.

Missily sighed. Now that they were middle-aged, she and her sisters and their husbands, it didn't seem so alien that one of them could die. There were too many younger people dying of cancer and heart attacks. She moved closer to Mikell's warm back. What would she do if something happened to him? He moved and turned over, reaching for her.

"Missily? You're not asleep?" he asked drowsily.

"Mikell, what would I do without you?" she asked and began to cry.

He drew her close, his lips in her hair. " Darling, I wonder sometimes about the same thing. It seems I couldn't survive without you. Do you remember the part in Corrie ten Boom's book where she asked her father a question? I can't remember the question but he reminds her that he gives her ticket just before they get on the train and goes on to explain that God does the same for us. I think that's kind of what the Bible means when it says that His grace is sufficient, remember?" He tipped her face up to kiss her. "Aren't you borrowing trouble, Jeddie? We're still together."

"I know. It's just Graham. It makes me wonder what I'd do if you got cancer."

"I can understand that. I still worry about your having to drive in all the traffic. Every time I see a wreck--I see too many of them--I am afraid to look for fear it will be your car. I don't know why that particularly bothers me but it does. How about our Psalm? It helps me." And he went on to say quietly:

> *God is our refuge and strength*
> *A very present help in trouble*
> *Therefore we will not fear*
> *though the earth should change*
> *And though the mountains slip*
> *into the heart of the sea.*

Missily listened to his beloved voice, to the beautiful words and eventually they both slept.

Chapter VII

Erin stood in the doorway of her home taking deep breaths of the fresh, crisp air.

The mountains were white with snow and loomed against the blue sky. She loved this land. Santa Fe sits seven thousand feet above sea level in New Mexico, higher than many of the mountains in her home state. When she and Thor had met at college in California they had wrangled in a friendly manner over mountains. Now they'd seen those in each other's respective birthplaces, Erin from Washington, Thor from New Mexico, they'd learned to appreciate both. It was pretty hard to see Mt. Rainier from different places in Washington without realizing what a massive peak it was even if you discounted all the other high peaks in the Cascade Range. But he hadn't believed her at first when she told him none of the Olympic peaks reached eight thousand feet above sea level. They looked so high, such a mass of peaks, he thought she was joking. It was only after he realized that since they rose from sea level they were about as high above the surrounding country as those in New Mexico where the lowland was from four to seven thousand feet and the highest peak, Wheeler Peak, was just over thirteen thousand feet.

Erin had to learn to love New Mexico. It was an arid land, the plants and trees different, the countryside more open than she was used to, but over the years it had gripped her and now she was glad she had moved there. Erin hadn't been sure at first she would marry Thor, even though she liked him, because he wouldn't leave New Mexico, not even for her. His home was there, his life, and eventually his work. Now she wouldn't live anywhere else.

The mailman came as she stood gazing at the mountains. "Looks like a letter from your sister," he said, "and some junk mail."

She took it with a smile. If he saw her he always told her ahead what she was getting as though he couldn't bear not to be the news bearer. "Oh, Missily," she said as she took the mail from him. "Probably about the family reunion."

He shifted his pack, sorted out the letters for next door. "You had that here once, didn't you? In New Mexico?"

Erin nodded, glancing through the rest of the mail. "Out at the Thomen's ranch. That was three years ago." She looked up. "How's your son?"

"Better. The doctor thinks the leg will heal now."

"Great. That's good news."

She closed her door as he went on his way and sat down to read the letter from Missily. Her house was stucco with a court in the middle and cool. It had that spaciousness that seemed to be part of Southwest homes, at least if one could afford it. Erin had decorated hers with Indian rugs and southwestern colors to reflect the sand, the sky, the gray green sage. A large light turquoise-colored jar stood in one corner filled with pampas grass while a colorful blanket was thrown over the back of the couch and plants hung from the ceiling in front of the sunny window. The room she sat in, their family room, had high ceilings with dark brown beams crossing the white expanse above. There was a sliding door to the court open to the early morning sun. The house, so different from anything she'd known before, was one thing that had drawn her to New Mexico and Thor liked to tease her about marrying him for it.

When Thor came home she told him, "I got a letter from Missily. The reunion's going to be at a fort somewhere in Washington. I don't remember it. She says I've been there. It sounds dull."

He had been holding her, kissing her face and neck as she talked; now he said dryly, "It's never dull around your family," and Erin had to laugh. "Get your map and we'll see what's around there," and when she passed him he gave her a smart slap on her hips. When she turned to glare he winked and she laughed again.

They had the map spread out on the table when their three daughters came home from school. Celeste was driving now so took one of their cars to school, giving both of her sisters a ride, also. She and Stephanie were in high school; Betsy was a seventh grader.

"Are we going on a vacation trip?" Betsy asked, slipping under Thor's arms so she came up between him and the table.

Thor, who adored his girls, kissed the top of her bright hair. "Family reunion this year."

"Oh, good." Celeste plunked her schoolbooks down. "Where're we going this time?"

"To Washington. It's Aunt Missily's turn to plan. We're going to a place called Fort Worden," her father told her.

"A town?" Betsy sounded disgusted.

"It looks like it's near a town," Erin said. "Either near or in Port Townsend. Aunt Missily said Fort Worden up at Port Townsend."

"But who wants to go to a fort?" Celeste asked. "What'll we do? Will there be horses?"

"Here it is," Thor said. "Look, it's right on land's end practically, in the Juan de Fuca Strait. There should be plenty to do around there. I don't know about horses."

Erin was studying the map. "I remember now. I don't remember what it was like but it's not far from Olympic National Park and there are hiking trails there."

"Hey, look!" Betsy pointed to the map. "It's right across from Vancouver, British Columbia. Could we go there? On the ferry?"

"Most likely," her father answered. "Start saving your money. It's been a while since we were in Seattle but there are plenty of things to do there, too."

"Could we go up in the Space Needle again?" Celeste was sitting, chin in hand, looking at the map. She was a very pretty sixteen year old, her gold-blond hair waving naturally, falling halfway down her back.

Betsy's hair was the same color but was cut short and lay shining and straight in a bob. Stephanie, also blond, hadn't taken part in the discussion and her father looked at her

"Stephanie, don't you feel well?" Erin asked suddenly.

Their second daughter, was standing listlessly by the table, her books still under her arms, her face pale. "I have a headache."

Thor looked up quickly. Erin went to take the books from Stephanie's hands. "When did it start? Have you taken anything?"

Stephanie shook her head and then winced.

"Go climb in bed," Thor said. "Mother will bring you something to take? When did it start?"

"Yesterday."

"But Stephanie, you didn't say anything."

"It wasn't very bad and I didn't want to miss my English test."

Erin turned her around and walked her to her bedroom. "You could have made that up. Into bed with you. I'll bring you some aspirin."

Lying in the darkened room Stephanie was very still hoping the pain would go away though she knew it would get worse. She'd been foolish to go to school but she was so tired of missing. She'd started having the headaches about two or three years before and the doctor told them they were migraine and what to do but whatever they did she had to suffer through them. Sometimes they were worse than other times and usually she had an aura as a warning before they started. The voices floated in from the living room where they were still discussing the upcoming reunion. Betsy asked in that whiny voice she sometimes used, "Do we have to go to church?"

Stephanie heard her father's deep voice. She loved to hear him talk and thought he was the dearest person in the world and the handsomest. "You've never had to go to church, Betsy. What do you mean?'

"But Candace always asks me to go with her and I do."

"No one's making you, young lady," Erin said. "If you don't want to go say no. It's as simple as that."

"I think it's fun," put in Celeste. "The kids are nice. I just don't listen to the preacher. He's stupid so why should I?"

"But I get so bored." Betsy said.

"Don't whine, Betsy," Erin said sharply. "You don't have to go so quit complaining."

Stephanie, her eyes closed, thought how nice it would be to be able to go to church. She always liked it when they went with Aunt Missily and her cousins. The music was so beautiful and she liked the stories they learned before they got together in the big part of the church plus she loved to hear her Uncle Mikell play the organ. She wondered if she asked Aunt Missily if she'd tell her about what happened after death. When her headaches made her so ill she'd think it would be nice to die if she knew she could just go to sleep and never wake up. But she wasn't sure that was what happened. Not since the time Gretchen had told her that heaven and hell were real places. She and Gretchen were the same age and did things together whenever they saw each other at the reunions or on vacation. Stephanie loved her Aunt Missily who seemed easier, somehow, to approach than her own mother whom she loved but with whom she wasn't always comfortable. Maybe she'd get the courage this time to ask her aunt. Thinking this she drifted off to sleep.

Thor went into his wife's bedroom that night dressed in a rich, dark maroon, velvet robe. "Erin, I think we should take Stephanie to another doctor for a second opinion."

Erin, who was sitting at her mirror removing her make-up, said, "But you know what they said. Migraines aren't unusual. Plenty of people have them."

"That may be true but I'd like to have another doctor check her. She is missing too much school and having far too many headaches."

"You worry too much. It's painful but not life-threatening and she'll get over it."

Thor stood studying his wife in the mirror. He loved her, thought her beautiful and an asset to his business. She knew how to entertain and probably was responsible for more advertisers in his magazine than he was but her hardness angered him. "Why do you sound so unfeeling? So hard? Don't you care?"

"Of course I care. I just don't think she needs another doctor. How do you know she's not putting on part of the time now she knows she can get out of things and get your sympathy?"

"Erin, why are you jealous of your daughter?"

"I'm not. What a ridiculous idea. Why ever would you say that?"

"Because I can't imagine any other reason for your remarks. You only have to look at Stephanie to know she is ill. Now Betsy's another story. She *does* like attention, but you know Stephanie has never been a shirker. It's one of the reasons she has bad headaches."

"Well, I can't imagine your ever making such a to do if I were like Stephanie. You'd probably be too busy to notice."

Thor stared. "Erin, what in tarnation is wrong with you?" He turned. "I'm going to call the doctor tomorrow and get him to recommend a specialist."

"And now you're going to leave. Well, go on. I can tell when I'm not wanted."

Thor sighed. He never knew what to do when Erin acted as she was doing now. It wasn't often but it always confused him. There never seemed to be any logical reason that he knew or could discern. As usual when she was in that kind of mood, he left her room closing the door between the two rooms sharply behind him. Erin went on with her cleaning, apparently untouched, but inside she had begun to shake. She was so crazy about Thor and so proud of him. He was by far the most handsome man in any crowd with his blond hair, deep blue eyes--like New Mexico skies--and Viking profile. He was also tall and well built. She didn't want to lose him. She wasn't jealous of her daughters because she loved them, too. At least she

66

wasn't jealous often or very much but she wasn't at all sure of the woman Thor had hired as assistant editor. Working together day after day like they did how did she know what Thor thought of her? He seldom spoke of her but when he did it was generally in praise of something she'd done. Erin had met her when she'd given a welcome party for her and her heart had sunk the minute the woman walked in the door. She'd given Thor an intimate smile, then greeted Erin. Impeccably groomed, her glossy dark hair was swept and bound in back emphasizing her high cheekbones. She had a way of lifting her face to talk to a man that made it look intimate. It didn't help Erin that she did it to all the men nor did it help that she was single. Her name was Faith McCall and she'd come to New Mexico from New York where she'd had a lucrative position with a woman's magazine. She and a friend, a woman artist, had bought a beautiful home which Erin had been in a couple of times because the artist belonged to one of the clubs Erin did also.

Erin finished her job, put away her creams and other paraphernalia and finished getting ready for bed. She picked up the book she'd been reading, the most recent best selling novel, and tried to get interested in it. They usually bored her but she tried to keep up so she'd be knowledgeable when others talked about the book. She would rather read history any day but not all of her acquaintances spent much time reading and if they did it was light reading. She and Thor had that in common, at least. They had many things in common, in fact, but Erin had never taken much interest in the business side of Thor's magazine, though she liked to read it.

Putting the book aside, she turned out her light then tossed restlessly. The wind was blowing and made strange noises when it came in gusts against the windowpane. The wind was one element she didn't like about New Mexico. It made her nervous and meant more sand in the house. Erin sighed. She wished again she could hire someone to do the housework but they'd tried that and it hadn't worked out. Erin hadn't known how to handle the Hispanic girl that came and she'd finally sent her on her way. Thor told her she had to be a boss and teased her because she was too softhearted.

"If you don't want to do the work you have to know how to get others to," he'd said grinning at her complaints.

Their girls helped but Erin was a perfectionist, becoming impatient with them even though Thor asked her how they could learn if she kept taking over. She turned on her side now and then back again. Finally, she slipped out of bed and put on her robe to silently open her door and slip down the hall to Stephanie's room. She worried about her, too. Stephanie, however, wasn't in her room. There was a light showing under the door of the bathroom and Erin went down to tap on the door. "Stephanie," she said softly.

The door opened. Stephanie was white and she swayed a little.

"Oh darling, were you sick?" her mother asked.

Stephanie whispered a weak yes and turned back to get the washcloth from under the running water to wash her face. She let her mother help her back to bed and tuck her in. Erin sat down beside the bed, not saying anything, only sitting quietly in the chair until she heard Stephanie

67

breathing evenly in her sleep. She sat a moment longer before she got up to lean over and kiss her daughter then went back to her own room. She stood hesitantly beside the door between hers and Thor's room but she knew she wouldn't sleep the way things were though he was probably sound asleep. Creeping into the room she cast off her robe, slipped into his bed beside him. He was asleep on his side turned away from her so she moved against him and the delight that he was hers swept her as it had so many times through the years.

Many times she had slipped in beside him and he hadn't known it until morning when he would chide her for not waking him. Tonight was one of those nights he turned over. "Stephanie sick?" he asked.

"Yes."

"You worry as much as I do, Babe," he said.

"I know." Erin wished she had the courage to ask him about Faith but she didn't. Let him think it was worry that made her act as she had.

He began to kiss her slowly, his hands cupping her face. "You know I love you?" he whispered and she nodded. She would not, she told herself, get foolish ideas and gave herself to his embraces.

After he left for work the next morning, however, the doubts came back. She dressed quickly and left the house. If she kept busy she wouldn't think of Thor and Faith. She wondered if they should take Stephanie for counseling. She was so quiet and having too many headaches. A counselor might be able to help her handle things. Anyone knew it was hard enough nowadays for kids with the threat of the world being blown apart any time and drugs everywhere. So far none of the girls had shown any interest in drugs. Hopefully they had learned enough about the effects of taking them not to use them. She would ask Thor about counseling tonight and see what he thought.

But he was adamant. "No. She's not crazy, Erin; she's having headaches."

"I know, but migraine headaches come from stress. Maybe she's trying to carry things she doesn't need to."

"Let's take her to the specialist Dr. Moody recommended first and see what he says. I don't think Stephanie's particularly in need of counseling any more than the other girls. She just reacts differently to life."

"Did you call Dr. Moody?" They were sitting together watching the late news on TV.

Thor listened to what the newscaster was saying about the ferment in South Africa before he responded. "I went over there today. I had no intention of letting some nurse take my message and never get back to me," He and Erin grinned at each other. She knew how impatient he could be with people who took messages, whether secretaries or nurses or whatever and usually managed to get to the top. When they'd first met Erin had tried to defend the secretaries then her admiration won out and she asked him how he did it so she could follow suit.

"I can take her to the specialist," she said to him.

"I know you can. You may come along. I hope you will--but I'm going to take her down to Albuquerque. I have some business to take care of there. We have an appointment next Wednesday."

"Wednesday! But you know that's my bowling day. Why did you get it for then? So I couldn't go?"

"Erin, what is all this?" Thor switched off the TV. "I took the appointment they gave me. Otherwise we would have had to wait months to get in. I don't run the doctor's office. Can't you miss bowling once?"

"You know how they depend on me and our league is ahead. I can't miss now."

"Don't you know someone who can fill in?"

"Of course, but I thought you knew that I'm the top bowler on the team. I can hardly expect them to put in a substitute who will probably lose for them."

Thor sat looking at her. "Erin, isn't anything I do right any more?"

"What a stupid question," she said, her insides starting the turmoil again.

"Maybe that's because I'm stupid." His voice had an edge to it. "You used to like some things I did. Now I never seem to please you."

"That's not true. Have you forgotten last night?"

"Oh yes, you can always creep into my bed and we have a good sex session but the rest of my actions aren't so acceptable. I'd like to be something more than a stud."

"Thor! What a thing to say. You liked last night."

"I don't deny that but my idea of a marriage isn't just the marriage bed. You know what you've become? A social butterfly, flitting from one club to another doing your little charity works and having fun. You don't care one iota about your girls or me. Why don't you get a job? Maybe you need something constructive to do." Thor's voice had risen.

"But I sell Avon. I thought you liked it because I was home when the girls came home. You always said so," Erin's voice was very controlled, very reasonable and she had a smile on her face.

"Don't smirk at me. You don't stay home for the girls. That's a lot of garbage. All you want to do is paint your nails and gossip over the latest scandal and then think you're wonderful because you do some good deed. How many nights are you home in time so you'll be here when the girls come?" Thor began to swear at her and, as always when his temper was roused, he swore in Norwegian, his parents' native tongue that he'd also spoken at home as a child.

When he'd first done it Erin had been amused. Now she hated it. She knew she was pushing him too far but she didn't care. If he'd already quit loving her what difference did it make and his accusations rankled. They were unfair. She tried to be a good wife and mother. "I suppose you'd rather I were like Faith McCall."

The name hung in the air between them. For a long moment Thor was silent, staring at her, before he said, "At least she uses her mind."

"If she'd so wonderful, why aren't you with her?"

Thor let out a string of oaths, turned and left the house. Erin heard the screech of tires as he tore off down the street, sitting where he'd left her, shaking, appalled at what she'd said. She hadn't meant to mention Faith at all.

"Why don't you leave?" Celeste was standing in the doorway in her yellow shorty pajamas. "If he doesn't come back I'll never forgive you."

"Celeste, I didn't--it was just an argument," Erin said, rising to cross the room.

"Don't you touch me. Don't you *dare* touch me! I hate you! He's worth ten of you!" she yelled, turned to flee down the hall to her room and slam the door.

Erin stood where she was. How dare Celeste blame her? He was probably with Faith now.

"Where's Daddy?" It was Betsy, half asleep, her hair rumpled. She looked younger than her twelve years.

"He went out. He'll be back."

"I heard you yelling at each other. Why don't you leave him alone?"

"Now Betsy, quarrels take two people. He's just angry."

"Why don't you be nice to him? I don't want you to get a divorce." Betsy was crying.

Erin went to her and turned her around. "Darling, we're not going to get a divorce. All marriages have their ups and downs. Everything will be all right tomorrow. Now go to bed."

After Betsy left for bed, Erin began to pace the floor. She'd tell him she was sorry. It would be fine. He'd been angry before. But even as she told herself that she was frightened. Thor was even-tempered, seldom angry. He'd always been easy to live with. What if he did leave? How could she get along without him? Now Erin was crying, something she didn't often let herself do nor was she aware of doing so now as she walked from one end of the family room to the other. It was a long room, paneled in light wood with Indian rugs on the floor. There was a fireplace in one wall for cold winter nights and a string of red peppers hung near it.

"Mother," Stephanie now stood in the doorway, in her robe, her platinum hair, more like Thor's than the other girls, in two long braids. "What's wrong?"

Erin turned away and hastily dried her cheeks then turned a cheerful face. "I'm trying to make a decision. Daddy and I had a little quarrel. He left to cool off." She went to sit in her chair and reached down for a magazine.

Stephanie came to kneel before her. "Mother, it's not wrong to cry and it must be hard to quarrel with someone you love."

Erin dropped the magazine, her face down. The tears started again. If only there were someone to talk to. Someone who could talk to Thor and make him understand the problem. She would get a job if he wanted her to but that wouldn't change things with Faith. She felt Stephanie's arms go around her, stiffened, and then relaxed.

"I don't want to make him mad, Stephanie. I love him so much. But I get afraid."

70

"What about?" her daughter asked, reaching for a tissue to hand her mother before putting her arms back around her.

"Stephanie, I-I couldn't stand it if he left me."

"I don't think Daddy's going to leave. He loves you, Mother," Stephanie said, hoping she was right.

Erin kissed her cheek. "You'd better go to bed, darling. We don't want another headache. And I'm going, too."

They walked together down the hall and parted a bit awkwardly at Stephanie's door. Erin sat down in front of her dressing table. Tomorrow she would start looking for a job though only heaven knew where she'd find one. She went through a list of her friends mentally to see if there were someone who could help her. Then she thought of Etta who had a dress shop. That would be something she could do. She'd gone through college and gotten a degree in education but she knew she could never handle a classroom full of children. The very idea made her cringe. It would be fun to have more money of her own and she should be able to get beautiful clothes less expensively there. Not that she and Thor were paupers but they weren't rich either. It would be good for the girls to learn to take care of themselves. She wouldn't give Thor any reason to complain about her.

Though it didn't work out the way Erin hoped it would she did get a job in the exclusive boutique Etta ran. Thor made some snide remark about sticking with her buddies when he was finally home one time long enough for her to tell him about getting a job. Most of the time now he was gone from early morning to late night though he didn't repeat his actions of the night of their quarrel. Erin had gone to bed that night and was asleep when he did come home in the early hours of the morning so she didn't see him then. However, he had a hangover the next morning and he didn't stick around for breakfast, then came home late again. Erin had stayed up but he'd told her in vulgar and insulting language not to bother him, he was going to bed. He'd been drinking again but he wasn't drunk this time. Erin had to accept the fact that he wasn't going to be home. When the girls asked about his whereabouts she told them he was working late. Since she was working evenings three nights a week they had to fend for themselves then. Celeste began to spend more time with her friend, Stephanie took over at home and watched over Betsy whose whining had gotten worse since her parents were gone most of the time.

One night Erin decided to go to a local restaurant on the way home from work to get a drink. She smiled at the hostess and started to say she would sit at the bar when a burst of laughter in the room jerked her head around. Thor was sitting at the table with a group of men—men he'd known all his life but had seen only occasionally since his marriage. Was this where he spent his free time? But why? Erin changed her mind and asked for a table in the back, ordering her drink. She was sitting where she could watch Thor. As she sipped her drink she tried to think. Why would Thor look up old friends? Did he spend every night here? Should she say something to him? But what if he made some snide remark like he had been doing so often lately? She finished drink and slipped out quietly. Night after night she went to sit and watch him, giving the girls vague reasons for her absence on the evenings she didn't work.

One night she received a call at work from Betsy who was almost hysterical. Stephanie had fallen and hit her head and Celeste had taken her to the emergency room. Erin tried to calm her but Betsy told her mother it was her own fault and wouldn't quit crying.

"I'm going over to the hospital, Betsy. You go stay with Cindy until I come home." Erin said firmly. "Do you hear?"

"Yes," came the tearful reply.

"I'm going to call Cindy. I'll also call from the hospital as soon as I can."

"Okay." Betsy was still sobbing but not quite as hysterically. Cindy was their next door neighbor, a little older than Erin whose children were all in college or married. The girls had known her all their lives.

Erin told Etta and left the shop trying not to imagine things. Since the night Stephanie had come in and held her as she cried Erin had depended more and more on her daughter. She needed someone because Thor's absence left such a hole. Erin and Thor had always been close; they golfed together every Saturday in warm weather and in winter went skiing. It was unusual for Thor to be away from home unless he had to work late or be away on business. Erin had her clubs and bowling during the day when he was at work. She was at a loss when she tried to understand what had changed him so drastically so that he stayed away from home on purpose most of the time. As soon as she reached the hospital she would call the restaurant she'd seen him in to tell him about Stephanie. Or after she'd seen Stephanie. She ran into the emergency room, her heart in her throat, and saw Celeste sitting stiffly, her hands clasped around her purse. The room was not full as it was most times but there were still several people there.

"Mother." Celeste's voice broke. "It's awful. She had blood all over her face and hair and down her blouse. Should I have called 911?"

"Possibly, but don't worry about it. You got her here," Erin answered.

"But what if she dies?"

"Celeste, you have to lose a lot of blood to die from that. Even a small cut can look like it's bleeding a lot. Where's Stephanie?"

"They took her right back. I didn't know our insurance company."

"All right. I'll go talk to them." When Erin had given them all the information they wanted and found that she and Celeste would have to wait she went to a phone to call the restaurant. But Thor wasn't there. She called his work place. Though he didn't answer the phone after closing she had a signal so she could reach him. When no one answered there she called Faith but Faith had no idea where Thor was, said she tried to forget work when she got home. Desperate, Erin wracked her brain for the names of the men he'd been with. She could remember some of their first names but no last name. When she finally thought of one man he'd talked about often—though she'd never met him—and called he asked her twice who it was she wanted.

"Thor. Thor Nielsen."

"Who is this?" demanded the man at the other end.

"His wife."

"Don't' you keep track of him?" came the sneering question. "What makes you think I'd know where he was?"

"I-I-yours was the only name I could remember of his—his friends he grew up with and—and he was supposed to meet for a boys' night out tonight." Erin replied improvising as she went. "Our daughter is in the emergency room at the hospital. I-I need to tell Thor and I forgot to ask where they would be."

"Sorry lady, you'll have to try someone else."

Erin held the buzzing receiver away from her ear, slammed it down, then went to sit by Celeste.

"Did you call Daddy?"

"I can't get him. He must be out for supper," she said.

"How come he's never home any more? Why are you both gone? This never would have happened if you'd been there." Celeste's clear voice rose in her distress.

"Hush, Celeste. You know better than to air family—doings that way." Erin had started to say problems but she would not admit to her daughter there were any.

"Oh, what difference does it make? Who cares about all that stuff? Don't you care about Stephanie?"

"Of course, I care and I've noticed that it's Stephanie who's been fixing supper the nights I work," her mother responded sharply. "You're not around. How did you happen to be there tonight?"

"I-I went home to change clothes. Tessa and I were going roller-skating. When I went into the house Betsy and Stephanie were fighting. Betsy pushed Stephanie so she fell down the stairs and hit her head on the banister. It was awful. Tessa brought us to the hospital."

"The stairs?"

"Yes. The ones that go down to the family room." The Nielsen home was built on a hillside and was a tri-level with the family room on the lower level at the back where they could go out to the back yard.

It seemed a long time before they called Erin to the desk. She took Celeste with her. Stephanie, she was told, had had seven stitches. She could go home but should be kept quiet. She'd had a concussion and would have a headache. When they brought Stephanie out in a wheel chair and wheeled her to the car she was pale and weak but she smiled at her mother. "I'm sorry," she said.

"Don't talk, baby. You don't have anything to apologize for," her mother told her. As soon as they reached home she put Stephanie to bed, sending Celeste over for Betsy who was sick with worry since Erin had forgotten to call from the hospital. Cindy came with her.

"I fed Betsy. She said they hadn't eaten yet. I didn't realize you were working, Erin. The girls can come to my place in the evenings," Cindy said after Stephanie was settled and Betsy sat reading to her. Celeste had gone to her own room and was talking on the phone, one of her sixteenth birthday gifts from her parents, Thor's idea.

"I don't work every night though we've been busy lately. Thanks, Cindy, but I think the girls are old enough to take care of themselves.

Stephanie has turned out to be quite a good cook. And responsible. More so than Celeste." Erin, who smoked occasionally, had a cigarette in her hand now.

Cindy didn't reply. She'd always thought Stephanie the most reliable and responsible of the girls. "Is Thor working tonight?"

"He's had so much to do lately we hardly see him," Erin replied, putting out her cigarette. "I'd better get something for the girls to eat. I don't feel very hungry."

"We had tamale pie. Why don't I bring over what's left and you can add a salad."

"I'd appreciate that, Cindy. They say Stephanie will be all right but it's hard not to worry. She has so many headaches."

That night she lay down on Thor's bed fully dressed except for shoes and pulled an afghan over her. She had to talk to him, if only to tell him about Stephanie--but she was asleep when he came home. He opened the door cautiously because he could see a light under the bottom of it. Carefully going into the room he saw her, sound asleep, propped against a pillow, a book against her knees. Because she was fully dressed he remembered the remark he'd made about her coming into his bed and it brought back all the memories he was trying to forget. She'd become a nag almost over night, it seemed, after all the years he'd congratulated himself on marrying a woman who wasn't like the rest. He backed out of the room quietly as he'd come and left the house after hesitating a moment in the hall. Best not to risk waking any of the girls.

Erin woke much later, stiff and cold and looked at the clock. It was after two and Thor wasn't there. Anger filled her. What kind of father and husband did he think he was? He was probably with Faith even though Faith had tried to make it sound as though she didn't know where he was.

Going into her own room, she got ready for bed and lay there planning all the ways she could get Thor back and make Faith look a fool, rejecting one after another. She did finally sleep only to wake early with a bad headache. It was Saturday, the day she and Thor had always made especially their own. Usually they would have gone skiing though it was getting a little late in the season for that. How many Saturdays had he been gone now? Erin had lost track. This time, instead of going shopping or to a friend's house, she spent time with Stephanie and Betsy who both wanted to know where their father was. Erin had a strong desire to tell them he was with another woman while at the same time she resisted the impulse because it was too humiliating to think she had lost Thor.

Celeste had left early in the morning for a friend's house or at least Erin supposed that was where she was going. Instead Celeste had gone to the office building. Thor wasn't there so she'd left and gone to one of the shopping centers to look through some shops. Later she went back and this time Faith opened the door and said Thor was there working. Celeste went back to his office and opened the door without knocking. He was sitting at his desk writing and looked up as she came in.

"Celeste! How nice to see you." He got up to get her a chair.

She sat down and waited until he did so also, leaning back in his chair, his hands behind his head. He looked tired. "Daddy, why aren't you ever home any more? Why aren't you and mother doing things together? What happened?"

"Nothing happened that I know of. Erin knows I've been snowed under lately."

"But she couldn't find you last night."

"Last night?" He became very still. "What do you mean?" They couldn't any of them know, surely, unless someone carried tales. No, it was too early for anyone to do that. He and some friends had rounded up some women and taken them to Albuquerque to dinner and dance.

"I know that Mother tried and tried to get you and couldn't. She said you must be out to supper but I watched her and she called three different places."

"Do you always check up on your mother like that?" he demanded.

"Daddy, Stephanie almost got killed last night. We were in the emergency room when Mother called."

"Emergency room? What happened to Stephanie?" The questions were sharp and Thor was sitting upright. His platinum hair was getting a little shaggy and he had on an old T-shirt that had seen better days, not his usual work day attire.

"Betsy pushed her down the stairs and she hit her head on the banister. It was awful," Celeste said, turning pale as she remembered how Stephanie had looked, her hair, so like her father's, bloody and matted, her blouse blood-stained. "She was bleeding all over everything."

"Is she in the hospital?" Thor had risen and taken a jean jacket from the back of his chair.

"No. She's at home. She had seven stitches"

"Did you call emergency?"

Celeste shook her head and looked up, frightened. "I-I couldn't think what to do. Tessa was with me and we took her to the hospital. I'm sorry."

He held out his hand to pull her to her feet when she gave him hers. "As long as you got her there don't worry, sugar." They went out together. "Faith, I've an emergency at home. We'll have to go out to the ranch later, maybe tomorrow."

"I'm tied up tomorrow," Faith answered from where she stood looking through the files.

"Okay. We'll go Monday." He opened the door for Celeste and followed her car in his truck. Celeste was driving the family car so when they reached home and found Erin gone. Betsy explained that Etta had called and said they needed Erin for the sale they were having and Cindy had taken her to work.

"Mother was furious," Betsy said, hanging onto her father's hand, swinging it back and forth in both hers. "She said she might quit work. Etta told her she couldn't get off every time one of her girls fell down. I heard Mother try to explain it was serious but Etta wouldn't listen. Mother said that Etta told her she could make up her mind whether she wanted to keep us tied to her apron strings all her life or act like a mature woman."

75

Thor gave a private sigh of relief. He dreaded seeing Erin. He could hardly explain to himself why he stayed away from home, how could he have anything to tell her? It wasn't that he didn't want to see her at all, but he wasn't going to take all the questions and there would be more now. Stephanie's face brightened as he went into her room.

"Daddy!"

He leaned over to kiss her. "How's my girl?"

"Okay, except for a headache and some dizziness, but it's not as bad as a migraine."

He laughed, sitting on the edge of her bed. "At least you look alive. The way Celeste told it I was sure you would be in a coma."

"You know Celeste never could stand the sight of blood," Stephanie answered, her small hand in her father's warm, large one. "Mother will be sorry she missed you. She didn't want to leave but Cindy said she'd stay with us."

Betsy had come in and now stood in her father's arm her head against his shoulder. "What's this about pushing Stephanie?" He asked her.

There was a silence and then Betsy began to cry.

"Daddy, she's already said she was sorry. Besides we were arguing so it was my fault, too," Stephanie said.

"What was the argument?"

Another silence. Celeste, who had followed Betsy in, said, "Stephanie was trying to get Betsy to set the table for supper."

"Tattle-tale," accused Betsy and began to cry harder.

Her father pulled her around to face him. "Betsy, why would you push Stephanie because she wanted you to set the table for supper?"

"I don't see why we should set the table," she sobbed. "Just Stephanie and I eat. We can eat at the breakfast bar. No one else is ever home." She darted a look at Celeste.

"Your mother isn't gone every night, Betsy, and Celeste is here."

"No, she's not. She's always gone and Mother goes somewhere every night. She hardly ever eats with us."

Thor turned. "Celeste is that true? That you aren't here?"

"Why should I be? If you and Mom can go have fun, why can't I?"

"You know the rules about school nights, young lady."

"So? No one's here to care whether I keep them or not." Celeste's voice was impertinent.

Thor stood up. "Since when do you need someone to police you? Rules are obeyed because they're made for a purpose, not because someone is there to make you do them. I have been busy and the money I make pays for your clothes and the gas you use. Perhaps you'd rather do without any of that for a while."

Celeste's eyes grew large. "What do you mean?"

"If you don't do as you're expected you will not be permitted to drive the car and I certainly will not give you an allowance, nor will your mother when I tell her what I've decided. Since you have to be made to obey, I'll do so."

76

"Daddy!" she wailed. "You wouldn't be so mean. All the kids get to go out on school nights."

"Oh yes, I know. Just like all the kids drive to school and all the kids do this and do that. That's the kind of nonsense I tried to use on my parents. You and Betsy get busy and do some house cleaning. It's a mess in this house."

"But we always have Saturdays off," wailed Betsy.

"I think you've had too many days off. Go get busy. Now."

Both girls left, angry and resentful. Thor turned back to Stephanie. "Tell me about the fall? What happened? What did the doctor say?"

He left before Erin came home. Cindy had come back to find him sitting with Stephanie so she went home until he sent Betsy to get her again before he left.

"Sorry to run off," he told her as he pulled on his jean jacket, "but I've got things that need to be done. The girls have their instructions. Stephanie has the list I gave her. Give it to Erin when she comes and this note," he added, then he was gone.

Chapter VIII

Erin, still angry with Etta and undecided whether to continue working or not, came home to a clean house and dinner almost ready. Etta had dropped her off and she walked to the front door noticing the car was there. Celeste was home then. But she wasn't prepared to find the house neat and the table set. The girls were watching TV and Cindy was with Stephanie. When Erin went into the room her daughter gave her a warm smile and Erin kissed her. "You look better," she said.

"I feel better. Daddy came home for a while."

"He did?" Erin failed to keep the surprise out of her voice.

"Celeste went down to the office and told him I almost got killed." Stephanie giggled a little. "He said I didn't look quite as bad as he thought I would."

Erin looked nervously at Cindy who was watching Stephanie. "Where is he now? Back at work?" Erin asked the question casually though her heart was racing.

"Yes," Cindy answered. "He left this list of things for Celeste and Betsy to do. And he called to ask me to tell you that Celeste was not to go out on school nights any more, that he'd told her so and he thought she'd obey since he's threatened to take away the use of the car and her allowance if she didn't. There's a note to you, also."

Erin took the list and the note. She didn't know whether to be angry or pleased. After Cindy left she went out to check on dinner. Celeste was mashing potatoes. "I didn't know whether we should set a place for Daddy or not. He didn't say when he would be home," she told her mother.

"We can set one if he comes. Celeste, haven't you been staying home on school nights?"

"What difference does it make what I do? You and Daddy don't care any more."

"Celeste, that's not true. Just because we've been busy and gone doesn't mean we've quit loving you or caring about what you do. Many girls your age have never had their parents around as much as you have."

Celeste turned her head away so her mother wouldn't see the sudden tears. "But why do you both have to be gone all of a sudden? Are we in financial trouble?"

"Heaven's no. Why would you think that?" Erin poured herself a cup of coffee and sat at the breakfast bar to drink it.

"Well, you got a job and Daddy's at work day and night."

Erin didn't say Thor wasn't at work at night. As long as she could she would make everything seem the same. "I don't know why he has so much to do but magazines have to meet deadlines and all kinds of things can stall that."

"Why is he going to the ranch with that Faith McCall?"

"What ranch?" Erin's stomach suddenly felt like lead.

"I don't know. He just told her they couldn't go today and when she couldn't go tomorrow he said they'd go Monday."

"Probably has something to do with an article they're writing. Or an advertisement if it's one of the guest ranches."

"I don't like that woman. She gives me the creeps," Celeste said as she forked the chicken out of the skillet.

"That's fried beautifully, Celeste," Erin said. "I'd better go change. I don't want to stay in these clothes."

Celeste turned to watch her mother leave taking the opportunity to wipe the tears from her cheeks. She loved her mother who was fashionable and always looked so young. She never seemed to have to worry about her weight and her hair had a natural curl so only needed to be combed in place. Erin didn't go out that night and she and the girls were lazy the next day. Stephanie was up so they played some games together, made tortillas for dinner, watched an old movie. Tessa called and wanted Celeste to come over so she left.

Life went on. Erin stayed at her job though she didn't like it as well as she'd thought she would. One night she drove out to where Faith lived and waited until past midnight but never saw anyone come or go. She didn't leave home again at night except for the three nights she worked and, though she wasn't at all sure the girls were fooled, kept up the story of Thor working long hours. Sunday he left the house early, before anyone was up, and came home after they were in bed. The girls were too timid to ask him why he was gone. Even Celeste didn't have the courage to go to his office again. They remembered the quarrel and were afraid it was more serious than Erin let on. Thor had never been gone so much before and they were accustomed to their parents going places together, teasing each other, kissing, holding hands, behaving like teen-agers at times. The change was so drastic they were too frightened to even talk about it to each other. They missed Thor, too, because he always spent a great deal of time with them teaching them to ride their bikes, to ride horses, reading to them, playing with them. Stephanie's headaches were more frequent, Celeste spent hours on the phone talking to one friend after another when she wasn't working to bring her grades back up. Betsy cried more easily though the whining had seemed to disappear since Stephanie's fall and her mother had started staying home most nights again. The four of them didn't talk about Thor. Erin began to worry about his health. She didn't feel free to go to his office like she'd always done. She was afraid they would quarrel and she didn't want to give Faith that satisfaction. Every night she lay awake until he came home. He didn't seem to drink as he had that one night and he always came in quietly.

Towards the middle of May Erin had to let Missily know whether they would all be coming to the reunion. She'd written earlier to say they'd be there but now she wasn't sure of Thor. She told herself she had no proof he was with Faith and reminded herself of the times she'd seen him in the restaurant with his old buddies. She missed him terribly but refused to give into tears, which she believed were a weakness. One night she decided she had to find out whether he was going to the reunion or not so she sat up in a chair in her room, dressed in slacks and a blouse, leaving her light out so he wouldn't know she was awake. It was close to one thirty when he finally slipped into his room. With pounding heart Erin went to the door between their rooms, a door that had seldom been closed until after the night of the quarrel. Carefully she turned the knob and slowly opened it. He was facing her, unbuttoning his shirt and his hands stayed arrested when she came in.

"Thor, I want to ask you just one question. I won't bother you long. I need to know if you'll be coming to the reunion."

"Of course. What a stupid question," He said angrily.

Erin looked as though he had slapped her. She blinked and clenched her teeth. She would *not* cry. Turning she left as quietly as she had come.

Thor pulled his shirt off and threw it on the floor furiously swearing as he did so. She'd looked so beautiful, so desirable. He hadn't seen her for over a month and her attraction hit him hard. He almost went to her when he remembered Celeste telling him about her going out at night. What if she had a lover? He *wouldn't* be made a fool of. Get the reunion over and then he'd move out. That way he could have the girls once in a while or even take them from her.

However, he couldn't sleep. Erin, his love, his own treasure. How could she do it to him? What had happened? He would have thought nothing could shake what they'd had. He remembered the first time he'd seen her, she a freshman in college, he a junior. She'd been standing, books in her arms, talking to a friend of his, her hair shining like gold in the sun. He'd gone over to be introduced and she'd smiled up at him. From that moment on he'd never been the same. Remembering the woman he'd taken dancing he felt a despair closing over him. He didn't like her. She was too brash, too forward. She had none of the graces Erin possessed, none of the loveliness of character, none of the quick laughter and ability to weather irritating moments and problems. She was insipid, empty-headed. Why did he take her places? He resolved never to do so again. He wouldn't play Erin's game. He'd stay true to her as long as they were together. Perhaps, some day, there would be someone else he could share his days and nights with. But the very thought was torment and he said Erin's name over and over with longing.

After that night he began to wait in his car on the nights she worked for her to come out of the boutique so he could follow her. The first night he lost her in the traffic but he knew she wasn't going home. She'd headed in the opposite direction. The next night she went home immediately and the same thing happened the next night she worked a couple of days later. After that he drove to their neighborhood at night, parking where he could see if she left their house after she was home from work but she only went once and she had the girls with her. He was confused. There was no way she could know he was checking on her but Celeste had told him she was never home at night. She loved the girls, though, and maybe Stephanie's accident had shaken her. He gave up trying to follow her but spend the days in torment, sure she was going out to rendezvous during the day. He called at odd hours and she answered every time but once. He hung up without saying anything but quit calling when he realized what it might seem like to Erin to get that kind of calls.

One night he sat in the restaurant with the men Erin had seen before, impatient and irritated with all of them, wondering what he'd ever seen in them, longing for Erin and his daughters, bored with the hunting and fishing stories--neither of which he liked to do- repelled by the way they spoke of their wives. One of them, a man called Buddy, with whom he'd been pals years ago, stopped in the middle of a sentence and gave a low whistle. "Hey! Look at that dame," he exclaimed.

They all turned but the woman was obscured by a couple going out when she passed behind Thor, following the hostess.

"Boys, I'm going to get acquainted with her. She's got class," Buddy announced.

Thor turned to look. Instantly he jerked his head back. It was Erin. He would know that walk anywhere, though her bright hair was covered with a hat. There was grace in every line of her. What was she doing here? Would she see him? Was she meeting someone? Buddy stood up but Thor reached over to push him roughly back into his chair. "Leave her alone."

"What do you care?" Buddy's eyes narrowed.

"She's probably here to meet someone. Do you want to tangle with him?"

"Who cares?" Buddy started to rise again when the door opened to let in a group of laughing women who shrieked when they saw the men.

"So this is where you hide out," one of them said, a heavy-set bleached blond, making straight for Buddy.

Another one, a dark-haired, thin woman with hard features, plunked herself in Thor's lap. "You've been avoiding me, handsome," she said in a voice that carried.

Thor stood up hastily, so fast that she would have fallen to the floor if he hadn't caught her. He mumbled something about having to go home, pulled out some money to throw on the table, then left.

Erin, sitting where she could see the whole thing, was trying to sort it all out when Buddy finally made it to her table.

"Hi, doll. Let me buy you a drink."

She just stared at him through the dark glasses she was wearing. When he reached for her hand she threw the rest of her drink in his face, rose gracefully, and walked with dignity to the door while the room behind her rocked with laughter as Buddy mopped his face. Erin didn't know that Thor was still in the parking lot or that he followed her when she started for home. After he saw her reach their house he drove on to his office, opening and locking the door behind him to sit in his chair in the dark still not knowing whether she had a lover or not, in agony because he wanted to go to her and was too proud to do so.

Chapter IX

Suz stretched lazily and yawned widely like a cat, a habit that caused Auden, her third husband, to say she should have been called Kitten instead of her sister. Her long, lovely body, bronzed by the California sun, the envy of girls younger than she, was stretched out in a lounge chair beside a green swimming pool shaped like a kidney bean. A young man, on the diving board, waved at her before executing a perfect back flip into the water. He swam over to her.

"Come on in, Suz."

"I'm too lazy," she said and closed her eyes.

When he threw some water at her, she sat up, pulling off her dark glasses, running to the pool to dive in and chase him. They wrestled with one another, laughing, and finally climbed out to lie on towels on the warm tiles.

"Gosh! You're beautiful!" he said reaching over to run his hand down her arm. "Going to stay here tonight?"

Suz didn't answer right away. They were at his home, a Spanish style house with red-tiled roof. He was the first man she'd had much to do with since her divorce from Auden a couple of years earlier. She'd felt so weary then she didn't care about anything and then one evening there he was at a party she'd gone to; tall, a little stooped to compensate, she supposed, because he topped all the men in the room. His dark hair hung down to his shoulders and he wore a mustache neatly trimmed. He'd been watching her when she looked up and came across the room to be introduced. His name was Shaul Kittam and he was a jazz pianist. Later on she learned he was ten years her junior and divorced also. She'd always married men older than herself so she found it intriguing to be with him.

Now she rolled over on her back and he moved over to kiss her. "Stay with me, baby," he whispered.

Suz traced his eyebrows and down the side of his face, smoothed out the mustache. "Would you like to go to a family reunion with me?"

"Family reunion?" he echoed between kisses he was trailing down her face to her throat.

"Yes. We have one every three years. This year it's going to be in Washington in July. Missily, my sister, asked me if I was bringing anyone. I hadn't met you yet, then, but I haven't answered her."

"What's it like?" He rested on an elbow looking down at her.

82

"I have four sisters. We get together with whatever family members who can come, including in-laws once every three years. Alexis and Jon will be there, and Nigel."

"Your kids?"

"Yes and Alexis' fiancé. And probably my first husband, Diccon. He's usually there." She laughed as she saw his expression. "Don't worry. I got over him years ago. We're friends--sort of. At least we're civilized now on account of the kids."

"You have four sisters? And four brothers-in law? How many nieces and nephews?"

"Just three brothers-in-law. Kitten's never married. She's the one back East."

"The cello player?"

"Yes," she grinned. "Trust you to remember that. Let's see." She counted on her fingers. "Five nieces and two nephews. One sister, my oldest, doesn't have any children; my youngest has three girls and Missily has two boys and two girls. Then Mikell's family--he's Missily's husband-- his family will be there and any of their other in-laws who want to come. Weird, I know, but we've done it for years. Diccon's parents died before I met him, but Mikell's, Graham's, and Thor's parents usually come as well as Granny Ellen, Mikell's grandmother."

"Sounds like a crowd."

"It is. It's kind of fun, though. I can't remember how many nieces and nephews there are on Mikell's side. He came from a family of five like Missily and I. You're dripping on me."

"No, it's my hair," he said and she laughed as he sat up to rub a towel over his head. "But you haven't answered me yet. Are you going to stay tonight?"

"Why should I?" She was drying her hair, too, shaking it loose, running a comb through the long, dark-blond locks.

" What a question," he answered rising to his feet. "Do you like shish kebob?"

"Mmm! Are you coming to the reunion with me?"

"I'll have to check my schedule."

"You can go mountain climbing," she said, knowing his passion.

"Where?"

"I don't know. The North Cascades, Mt. Rainier, the Olympics. All are close enough to where we'll be staying."

His eyes had lit up and he laughed. "You know how to tempt me, don't you? But I *will* have to check my schedule."

"Let's go check it now. I have the dates for the reunion."

He walked ahead of her to open the door to his house and let her in. Following her he took her in his arms. "I'll go to the reunion if I'm free or can get free. Are you going to stay here?"

"I'll try tonight," she said lightly.

"Come on. Let's shower, then I'll get dinner started. This is Brett and Eleanor's night off."

Suz woke before Shaul did the next morning, stretched and then lay watching him sleep. He was an earnest young man, too serious at times. Something about him made her think of Diccon. Not his personality-- Diccon had been lively, almost merry--but they were both dark. She supposed the reunion brought Diccon to mind also. She didn't often think of him or of Auden or Owen, living, instead, one day to the next, not worrying about the past or the future. Auden and Owen had both been wealthy and she had enough money to keep her in style the rest of her life. However, she wrote a gossip column for one of the slick magazines, more for the chance it gave her to meet people than anything else. Every time she went to the family reunion Erin demanded she tell them which celebrities she'd met since they'd last seen her.

Slipping out of bed, she showered, dressed in jeans and a red blouse with flowing sleeves gathered at the wrist and bound her hair back with a matching scarf before she ventured out into the courtyard. The woman and man who worked for Shaul greeted her and asked if she wanted breakfast. She told them she'd wait for Shaul. From the door of the courtyard she could see the blue mountains above the rolling hills. The ennui that had been present for sometime enveloped her. All her life men had given spice to her life and suddenly they didn't seem to matter as much. Nothing did. She didn't feel depressed, just as though life had, like a long uncapped soft drink, gone flat, so that she could still live with laughter and ideas and interest but without zest. She wasn't *that* old, she thought. Did she want to start another affair? The whole thing made her tired. Maybe she needed to get away for a while. It would be fun to see her family, which she seldom visited except at the reunions. Diccon came back to mind. He hadn't married again. She wondered if the religion he'd taken up was against divorced people remarrying. It was strange how Missily had swallowed all that junk whole and never been sorry and then somewhere along the way Diccon had, too, and after him, Nigel. Suz could understand Rose going to church. It fit her personality to be doing charitable works but Missily had been the one who seemed to have their father's brilliant mind, more than Victoria though Kitten put on airs and talked more about intellectual things. It was odd. Missily still used her mind. She and Mikell. They hadn't shut themselves off from the academic world--she remembered they'd been part of a group that discussed the great books of the Western world--and their children were bright. It never made sense to Suz how intelligent people could believe the things part of her family did, but stranger still was the way they lived, at least from what she knew of other kinds of religious people. She'd only been acquainted with the kind of people her father called Bible thumpers until she met Auden who was a Roman Catholic. But the other kind didn't smoke, dance, drink, play cards, go to the movies, and spouted Bible verses at you. She'd met up with them more than once on the beach where they walked in groups talking to people. Of course, neither Mikell nor Missily smoked or drank but that seemed to be a personal choice and not a dictum of their religion. She remembered asking Missily once if she belonged to a new kind of Christian religion and Missily, puzzled, had told her no. When Missily and Mikell asked her what she meant, Suz tried to

84

explain the difference in others she'd met who also said they were Christians. Missily told her that they believed the same basic--what had she called them? It wasn't facts. Oh, yes. Doctrines. She remembered the word because she'd connected it to indoctrinate. Anyway, Missily said she and Mikell believed the same doctrines Christians did, the ones believed from the beginning of the Christian Church. When Suz had protested that she and Mikell went to movies and didn't see anything wrong in drinking and dancing, Missily had answered that wasn't Christianity, that was tradition or personal conviction. That had left Suz more confused than before so she dropped the subject.

Two arms encircled her from behind, startling her out of her reverie and Shaul pulled her back against him. "You left me," he complained.

She turned in his arms. "You were sleeping so nicely."

He freed one hand to run his fingers down her cheek and cup her neck. "I would have liked to be awakened by the Princess," he said. "Brett and Eleanor have breakfast ready. Are you hungry?"

Suz was a tall girl but he was two or three inches over six feet so she had to tip her head a little to look up at him. "Yes. I told them I'd wait for you."

" 'A lovely lady garmented in light from her own beauty'," he quoted softly before he bent his head to kiss her.

They sat across from each other outdoors in the sun at an ornate white metal table covered with a spotless cloth done in intricate embroidery of orange blossoms. "Eleanor's work," he said when Suz asked about it. "Her own design, too." He had only oranges, three of them, a piece of wheat toast and coffee. Suz had always eaten a hearty breakfast and Brett put before her an omelet with green peppers, onions, and cheese folded into it, bacon and toast on the side and a tall, cold frothy glass of orange juice. She watched Shaul's hands as they deftly pealed the orange, beautiful, long-fingered hands, almost like a woman's they were so fine-boned. And he could use them on the piano with skill and feeling just as he had used them last night against her silky skin. He separated the orange sections, cleaning away the white membrane before he took a bite and found her watching him.

It didn't disconcert him. Rather his eyes flamed. "Are you going to come live with me? Was last night good?"

"Definitely, to the last question. I'm not sure about the first. I'm not ready for that yet."

"Was he a scoundrel, a drunkard, a freeloader, or what?" he asked picking up his cup of coffee.

She was fascinated by the beauty of his hands in everything they did. "Who?"

"Your ex-husband."

"No. All of them were quite respectable," Suz answered remembering sitting across a different kind of table from Owen. He'd been as blond as Shaul was dark but big and full of life, vivid, with a big laugh and voice. He'd sung to her instead of quoting poetry, naughty and sometimes bawdy songs he'd picked up over the years.

"What happened or isn't it any of my business? I can't imagine anyone giving you up."

She shrugged. "We just came to the parting of the ways. Bored with each other, I guess."

"I would never become bored with you." He said it quietly but there was passion nevertheless.

"You might, like Auden, get tired of me. I was too lazy, he said," Suz told Shaul without rancor. "He was an energetic, busy man, always going somewhere, doing something."

"And no time to lay beside the pool?"

Her eyes came to his and she laughed. "Exactly."

"Suz, I would never grow tired of you." Shaul said it almost the same way he'd said the other.

Suz busied herself with eating. She was less sure than ever that she wanted to get involved with him. Intense people can be hard to live with. They expect more than one might be able to give.

"I watched you across the room that night. I've never seen any woman before move like music. You were the most glorious thing I'd ever seen and you've become more so every time I see you. I was hurt by my divorce. She left me for another man and I loved her. I was young--we married right out of high school and I thought the sun rose and set on her." He began to peel the third orange deftly. "I was pretty bitter after that and stayed away from women. I just let my piano be my lady." His dark piercing eyes came suddenly to hers. "I'd come out of my shell years ago but there's not been a woman I wanted much until I saw you. You made even Pamela look pale."

"Pamela?"

"My ex."

"Let's not rush things," she said gently. "After three marriages, I'm not in a hurry to get involved again seriously."

"Three?"

"Yes. Take warning. Diccon and I married young, also. He's the father of my children. I left him. I wasn't ready to settle down and act like a mature woman I was supposed to be. My children grew up with an absent mother most of the time though they don't seem any the worse for it. I had a lady come to the house to care for them. She was better at it than I was."

Shaul finished his coffee, then leaned back in his chair. "Suz, I want to marry you but I won't rush you. We don't have to get married, but I would like you to come live with me."

"Give me time, okay?" she asked smiling at him.

"All right. What shall we do today?"

"Don't you have to practice?"

He waved that aside. "One day won't matter."

Suz surveyed him. "Well, I'm sorry but I'm a working girl and I have to get busy."

"What do you mean you're a working girl? You only write that one column, don't you?"

"Yes, but how do you think I get information for it? Not by sitting on my hind side." She stood and stretched. "I've got an interview today and some parties to drop in on."

He stood behind the table rather stiffly and asked, "When will I see you again?"

"Across the crowded room? I don't know. Do you work tonight?"

"Yes. I'm playing at The Blazer this month." He was still stiff, distant.

"Maybe I'll come see you. Thank you for a loverly time." She went around the table to him. "Bend over. I can't kiss you way up there. Are you part giant?"

He didn't smile but bent to kiss her briefly. She smiled, waved, and was gone. It was three nights later that she sat watching him play from a side table where she could see his fingers. His hands stirred her strangely as they had before. He played for what seemed a long time to her, at the end, taking requests and when he finally rose to bow and leave the piano he was immediately surrounded by young women with menus or other pieces of paper for him to autograph. Sitting down at one of the nearby tables he pulled out his pen and Suz watched in fascination. He was charming. What would he do if she went to ask for his autograph? The whimsy amused her. She did, eventually, get up with that lazy grace of hers and make her way to his table. Some of the women had taken the other chairs at the table where he was and others surrounded him. Suz always commanded attention by her presence, though never by design, and the women parted as she approached Shaul. He looked up just as she reached him and his eyes blazed with delight.

Bending to kiss him, she said, "You were wonderful, darling. I've been listening for hours."

The stiffness was gone, as was the distance. He took her hand. "You made it!"

"Yes, finally." Then she put her cheek against his and whispered in his ear, "Come to my place tonight."

He rose, then, bid the others goodnight and followed Suz out. Hours later, on the roof of the apartment building where she lived, they were still sitting, talking, telling each other their life history, laughing together. "Are you coming to the reunion?" she asked.

"Not much else I can do. Three days without you taught me that."

She turned in her chair. "Shaul, don't get too fond of me. I'm fickle. I get bored and leave."

"I thought it was the men who did that," he said casually.

"The last two times we just parted amicably. But you've been hurt once. That's enough. I know."

"Your first husband?"

She rose and walked over to look across the rooftops and up into the night sky decorated by stars. "Yes. I didn't want to stay with him but I didn't want to leave either. We quarreled about where to live for ten years. I finally left."

"Do you still love him?"

"I hardly ever think of him unless I hear about him from one of the kids or see him at the reunions, but I remember the pain of those first years after I left him and you loved your Pamela."

He came to join her, sensing she didn't want to be touched. "I loved her until I met you. Now she seems like someone I imagined or read about. You're real. In a way she never was," he added.

"Real? In what way?"

"It's hard to explain. She was so wrapped up in her work, her world that I felt as though the only time she thought of me was when we were together. She hated my music, my friends, the hours I kept, my way of dressing. She had an idea of how everything should be. She was--rigid, I guess I could say."

"How did you ever get together? If she didn't like your music or anything else?"

"Physical attraction. She was sexy, to be blunt and I was young enough I thought that would satisfy me."

"And you're a marvelous lover," Suz added and heard him catch his breath though he still made no move to touch her. "So the attraction was mutual."

"Yes. But she wanted to make me over into a nice, clean Mr. America after we got married. Suz, I wonder now why I was so hurt. I should have been glad to get rid of her."

She moved close to him and laid her head on his shoulder. "Life's strange. It seems there should be some way of knowing ahead whether you would want to stay married to someone or not. I liked both Auden and Owen at first. I have three sisters happily married. What's wrong with me?"

He had put his arms around her and pulled her against him. Now he said, his lips in her hair, "How do you know? Maybe behind closed doors they aren't at all."

"No, I don't think that's true. Thor and Erin--she's the youngest--were still acting like lovesick teen-agers last reunion and they'd been married fourteen years. Rose and Graham are like people who've lived together forever and are permanently tied. The ones you'll have to watch are Missily and Mikell. He isn't a demonstrative person, not in public at least, though Alexis followed them on one of their walks--they take them alone every day when we get together--and said when they got where no one could see them they did a lot of smooching, her words. But there is something indefinable there. It's almost tangible. I'd like to have what they have."

They walked slowly back to their chairs where Suz picked up a wrap she'd brought up with her and Shaul, their empty glasses.

"Except for one thing," she added in her kitchen as they rinsed the glasses.

"What's that?"

She went into the living room and he followed, sitting down at her feet. The drapes were open on the wide window and from their vantage point on the hillside they could look down on the sleeping city. Suz began to braid his hair. He had wonderful hair, soft and thick, with a natural wave. "Missily is smart," she said after a long silence, which had been comfortable and peaceful. "I mean brainy. She's the one most like Dad. She's read philosophers, poets, the classics, more than any of the rest of us. Kitten puts on but she doesn't know anywhere close to what Missily does or Mikell either, for that matter. But they're religious."

"They don't particularly cancel each other out, do they? Lots of brilliant men have been and are religious. I may not agree with what they believe but I hardly think they're stupid."

"Well, no, I didn't mean it to sound that way. It's just--well, for instance, they believe the Bible is literally true."

"Holy rollers?"

"No. That's what I can't figure out. All the things I knew about people who said they believed the Bible and called themselves Christians don't seem to apply. And don't ask me to explain. Wait and see if you can figure it out. You have beautiful hair," she added, running her fingers through it so the braids came loose and it fell in waves down on his shoulders. "It's almost morning. Shall we go to bed before the sun comes up?"

Suz called Missily late the next day. Shaul was in her tiny kitchen--"How do you turn around?" had been his first comment--fixing Chicken Cordon Bleu. "Hello, sister," she said lazily into the phone.

"Suz!" Missily's voice was clear, cheerful.

"How's rainy Seattle?"

"Sunny at present. Beautiful. How's California?"

"Warm. I called because I'm too lazy to write. I'm bringing a friend to the reunion. We'll only need one room. His name is Shaul Kittam and he plays jazz piano."

"What fun. Mikell will love that. We'll have to find a piano so we can hear him play. I don't know whether there's one at Fort Worden or not. Didn't think of that. What's he like?"

"As a musician or a person?" Suz stretched her long legs and wiggled her toes. She'd had sandals on but kicked them off and lay relaxed on the couch in blue shorts and halter-top.

"Both."

"He's a good pianist but since he's standing here listening I don't know whether I should tell you about him or not. Well, he's not just standing." She grinned at Shaul. "I just got a glare. He's fixing dinner. He's tall, taller than any of our men, I think. A little stooped," and here she laughed as Shaul straightened. "He has long black hair, wonderful and wavy, piercing dark eyes, and the most beautiful hands I've ever seen." Suz, watching Shaul, saw him turn suddenly to look at her and she grinned again. "Is Kitten bringing anyone?"

"I haven't heard yet. Last time she wrote she wasn't even sure she'd make it."

"She has to. What's a reunion without all of the Metlow sisters there?"

"Have you heard from Rose?"

"Not lately. What's new? Is she running for office?" She heard Missily's lovely laugh, which she'd always, envied a little.

"No." Then Missily's voice became serious. "Graham has cancer in his mouth."

89

"Oh no!" Suz sat up suddenly. "How bad?"

"I don't know. You know Rose. She gives the barest information on what you want to know most. He's scheduled for surgery next week."

"Will they be able to come to the reunion?"

"They have every intention of doing so and, of course, Fort Worden isn't far from Seattle."

"That's true. We've been lucky. This is the first cancer in the family. I hope they can get it all. It's a horrible way to die, by slow degrees."

"I know. I've cried a lot since she told me. Rose keeps a stiff upper lip. Do we have English blood in us somewhere?"

"I don't know but mother always said only babies cry."

"I'd forgotten that. Maybe that's why I feel so guilty every time I cry. Hold on a minute."

Suz could hear her talking to someone else then she came back on the phone.

"Sorry. Mikell dropped by. He has a job in Port Angeles and wanted to let me know. He could have called," she added, "but I'm glad he didn't. I think he forgot a tool."

"How's my favorite brother-in-law?"

"Great. Did I tell you he's on his own now?"

"You mean he finally had the courage to quit working for that crook?"

Missily laughed. "It wasn't his fault. I was afraid we couldn't make it if he worked alone so he stayed with Kurt. I get to be his secretary and receptionist--or whatever. I answer the phone for him and relay the messages. He has a phone in the van for that."

When Suz hung up, after a lot of questions about her nieces and nephews and their doings, she rose from the couch to walk into the kitchen. "Need any help?"

"No. This is my meal. So he's your favorite brother-in-law. What's he like?"

Suz perched on one of the kitchen stools munching on a piece of celery, her long legs curled around the legs of the stool. "Mikell?"

"Is that his name?"

"Yes. An adaptation of Michael. You'll see. He plays the organ. In fact he's church organist."

Shaul straightened up from the stove. "And you like him best?"

Suz looked up at his question. "Shaul, don't get the idea that because I've had three husbands I like every man that comes along. Mikell's a love but not for me. Even if I did want him--which I don't--he's never had eyes for anyone but Missily and . . ." She stopped. She'd started to say that he was younger than she but remembered Shaul was and that Mikell was not. He was older than she by a year but she always thought of him as younger because of Missily.

"And?"

"Nothing. Just that I don't want you to get false ideas. I'm glad I like my brother-in-law, and that's as far as it goes."

90

She saw him relax a little. He turned back to the stove where he was stir-frying vegetables. "It will be interesting to meet your family. I can't imagine you a family person."

"Only every three years." She laughed. "It does me until next time."

Chapter X

Victoria hadn't opened her letter from Missily right away. She had a habit of letting mail pile up because she hated to answer letters. Then she'd take a day out of her busy schedule, spend it at her home writing letters, scribbling off short replies, putting them in envelopes, going out to mail them, sometimes late in the evening depending on how many she had, and then going back home to curl up with a good mystery and listen to her records. She had an extensive library of albums all cataloged and shelved in order. This time she'd put off the letters longer than usual because she was getting her students ready for a recital and practicing to play with a string quartet for one of the city's doings.

Now she sat down at her desk, sorted her mail and slit each envelope open before she began the task of reading and answering; one from her mother who always reprimanded her for not writing more often, one from Rose with the usual drivel about the crusade she was currently pursuing. Victoria dismissed Rose's crusades as nosiness. There was a letter from a friend in Virginia and one from Missily among others. Starting with the one from her mother she worked through them, putting Missily's aside since she'd have to check her schedule before she answered it. Whenever it came time for the reunion she was tempted to find something else to do so she'd have an excuse not to go. She lived so far from them all, in more ways than distance, that she was never sure she wanted to see them again. Last reunion at the ranch had been terrible. How anyone could enjoy riding horses or any of the things they did she could not understand. If she hadn't had Sasha with her she would have been bored to tears. And noise! She couldn't sleep at night for all the noise. Diccon had laughed at her but Diccon was a rustic anyway. How Suz could have stayed with him as long as she did Victoria would never know. Auden and Owen had been far more civilized.

She read Missily's letter finally, which was chatty and newsy as usual though Victoria would never admit she liked them and frowned as she read that they would be spending their reunion at Fort Worden but her face relaxed as she read about Port Townsend and the Victorian homes preserved there. She could remember little about Seattle. It was so different than when she'd left there twenty-five years ago to attend college and she'd never been back any more than she could help. Victoria loved the East and thought the West still crude and uncivilized. It was a state of mind no one in her family could change

Mikell, when Missily had been particularly irritated with something condescending Victoria had written, shook his head. "Don't let her get to you, sweet. It shows how narrow-minded she is. It's the same kind of mind that thinks only Paris or England is worth anything, and you can't change her. You could list all the plays and concerts and operas and cultural doings in Seattle on a paper and show her and she'd find some criticism. She'd got blinders on, that's all."

The phone rang and Victoria reached for it.

"Victoria," said a deep voice at the other end.

"Auden! When did you get in?" She leaned back against her chair, smiling.

"About an hour ago. I'll be here three days. Would you like to go out to dinner tonight?"

"Yes, I would. I'm free, too."

"Good. I'll be over about six-thirty. We can talk for a while before we go out."

"Fine. I'll see you then." She put the receiver back and sat a moment in thought before she went back to reading Missily's letter. Opening the side drawer she drew out her appointment book and turned to July. There wasn't anything listed for the week of the reunion though it was busy enough before and after. She never had as many pupils in the summer either and could cancel any lessons that week. Sighing, she put the book away and taking pen in hand, wrote to Missily, telling her she wasn't certain whether she'd make the reunion but would let her know later and also whether she would be bringing a guest. She put the rest of the mail, two letters with some other things, which would have to be done later, into a drawer, and pulling down the roll top locked the desk. One of her pleasures was all the antiques she'd managed to collect over the years and the desk was one of them. As she rose a large silver gray cat that had been sitting in the window, stretched her long, limber body, shook a paw, and jumped to the floor. Victoria stooped to scoop her up and put her face to the cat's.

"Sorry, Danty. I can't spend the evening with you. You be good for me, you hear? I know we were going to have an evening together but circumstances have altered that. I have to change my clothes." She carried the cat with her into her bedroom and set her down on the bed where the cat stood looking at Victoria as if to say this isn't what we usually do, then lay down though Andante wasn't relaxed. She knew Victoria was going out.

As Victoria took clothes out of her drawers and closet she reflected on her friendship with Auden which began when they met at one of the family reunions after Suz and Auden were married. They'd enjoyed each other's company then and since. Victoria was too busy to date much but when she learned Auden flew East often on business trips she'd told him if he ever got to Philadelphia to look her up. He'd done so before his and Suz's divorce and had continued to call her whenever he was in town. She wondered if he'd married again. He hadn't the last time she'd seen him. They always spent an enjoyable evening together, sometimes dining out, other times going to a play or a concert. If he had longer than a day or two she would fit him into her schedule as often as she could when he had the time, also. She couldn't understand why he and Suz had broken up but Auden just dismissed it. "It was one of those things," he told her. "Wasn't meant to last." He didn't seem to have any rancor against Suz, usually asked about

93

her, but neither did he seem to care that they'd parted after a marriage of five years.

He was impeccably dressed as always, his thinning dark hair neatly barbered. Victoria had drinks ready when he came and they sat down to talk over the news of the day, over what he was doing in town and generalities until it was time to leave. He was an expert driver; when she'd remarked on it once he'd said thank you, usually California drivers get insults.

After their meal was ordered Auden sat back to survey her. "Don't you ever age?" he asked and the color rose to her cheeks. He seldom made personal remarks.

"Of course. I have some new wrinkles. It's the candlelight."

"I saw you in your apartment. Busy?"

"Yes. I have a recital in about two weeks and I'm playing in a string quartet in June. A library doing of some kind. Important people are supposed to be there. I sometimes wonder why they have us. The VIP's, most of them, couldn't care less."

"Atmosphere, my dear Victoria. You give it class, of course. What do you hear from your family?"

"Do you mean Suz?"

"No. I don't. If I meant Suz I would have said so. You know that," he said with asperity.

"Sorry. I guess she was on my mind. We're having a reunion this year."

"Are you? I enjoyed those. You have some interesting relatives. I hated losing them more than I did Suz." He tasted the wine the waiter brought and nodded so their glasses were filed.

Victoria moved hers so the candlelight sparkled in the wine. Looking up at him curiously she asked, "Do you mean my father?"

"Him for one. Mikell and Missily. Rose."

"Rose?" Victoria interrupted in surprise then apologized.

"She amused me. She's so earnest. It livened things to get her talking."

"Especially if she and Mother argued, I suppose," said Victoria acidly.

"They're a lot alike," Auden said. "Your problem is that you're too close." He began to eat the soup that had been set before them. Auden who never spilled anything always looked as though he'd just come from his dressing room, something that had irritated Suz but pleased Victoria.

"I supposed so." Victoria paused with her spoon above her bowl. "I've never thought of comparing them."

"You've never learned to enjoy your family. You like them better far away."

Victoria laughed. "You're right. Rose irritates me and I can't stand Graham. I love my parents, of course, although I can take my father longer than I can my mother. Suz--is Suz. She and I never did get along well. It used to drive me crazy that she's so easy going about everything, as though nothing mattered much."

"Lazy," Auden said and there was an edge to his voice. "Bone lazy."

"Do you think so?" Victoria sat with her brow wrinkled, thinking. She was a tall, thin woman, her dark hair cut quite short and worn close to her head but she was attractive. "I don't think Suz is lazy. Just not ruffled

94

easily. Erin was enough younger I never got to know her except as a child. She was a beautiful little girl with her hair and eyes, only twelve when I left home. We get along all right. She thrives on having sisters who are important people. She doesn't realize her own husband knows important people, also, and she entertains them for him. He knows them much better than Suz and I. Missily--" she paused to wipe her mouth with her napkin and then looked up and it was the first time Auden had seen pain in her eyes. "We could have been close. She came out here before she married Mikell, planned to get a job, then talked to a minister down the street and went religious."

"But she and Mikell aren't fanatics," Auden said, nodding at the waiter who took Victoria's bowl and then his.

"Aren't they?" Victoria asked. "You don't know then very well."

"They don't have a lot of nonsensical rules and regulations. At least I've never heard them talk that way and they're certainly not like this new craze that's going around. Even the Catholics are into it. Speaking in tongues and the whole lot."

"It depends on what you mean by rules. Have you ever tried to talk evolution with them, for instance, or education in general? They are quite antiquated and Mikell gets irate about psychiatry and psychology as though they weren't possibly one of our society's greatest helps. And abortion. They are so irrational it's hard to talk to them. I try to leave those subject alone." She cut through her steak, examined it and took a bite.

"I've talked with Mikell about psychology and psychiatry. He feels the same as I do; that there are things in both that have helped people but neither is the answer that too many people think they are and I think you've forgotten that I am Catholic." He smiled. "Perhaps you think I am irrational also, but I've found that there are irrational people on both sides of all these things and also that there are people who try to think them through in a rational manner. I believe that Mikell and Missily are in this class." He didn't add that he thought that she might be in the other.

Victoria ate in silence a while then asked, "Auden, have you married again?"

Auden, who had been carefully buttering a roll, looked up, startled, almost apprehensive. "No. Have you heard I had?"

"No. I just wondered. It seems strange you haven't."

"Well, but you are still single, I presume," he said.

"Happily so, but I've never been married. I'm not the marrying kind."

Auden deliberately finished buttering his roll and put his knife carefully on the plate. "Neither am I. It would have been better never to have married at all."

"Why did you marry Suz?" She asked.

"I'm not sure now. When I met her I knew. Do you know why she and Diccon broke up?"

"No. Why?" Victoria paused in her eating as she asked because she'd always wondered even though she thought them poorly mated.

"I don't know. I thought you did. She still loved him when we married, and that was after Owen. At first, at least, I knew she still loved him. She didn't talk much about him after we'd been married a year or so."

"Was Suz so bad?"

Auden studied her. Though she wasn't beautiful her attraction drew him. There was an aura about her he would have found difficult to explain and he had wondered more than once if he would have been content married to her. "She was lazy," he answered. "I can't abide laziness. I used to tell her she should be called Kitten, not you, the way she loved to lay around and stretch."

"I've never heard or read that cats are lazy," she bristled.

Auden smiled. "I forgot you like cats. I didn't mean to insult Andante. Do you still have her?" The cat had never liked Auden and refused to be in the room where he was.

"Yes, of course, and I don't like her. I love her. In fact, she's probably sulking right now because we were going to spend the evening together."

"Now, Victoria, that cat won't know the difference. You go out many times. Does she always-er-sulk, as you say?"

"No, she doesn't. She knew I was intending to stay home tonight. She knows the difference."

"Whatever you say." And, he thought, he definitely would not be content married to her. "Shall we dance?"

After he had swung her out onto the floor he surveyed her. They were well matched and enjoyed dancing. "Were we quarreling?" he asked with interest. "I don't think we've ever done that before."

She laughed. "No. I don't believe we have, not that I remember, anyway. Tell me why you're in Philadelphia."

It was late when Auden drove her home. "Thank you, Victoria. I always enjoy our evenings. When I come next time you'll have to tell me about the reunion. I'd like to know about the young ones. Are any of them married yet?"

"Alexis is going to be. I can't remember the date."

"Alexis is Suz's girl. I don't remember how old she is."

"Neither do I," answered Victoria. They had been in the elevator. Now they walked down the dark hall quietly. "Want to come in for a drink?" she asked as she opened her door.

"I won't stay. I have an early meeting tomorrow morning and I want a clear head." He stood in her little entrance hall. "How's Stephanie?"

"Stephanie?" Victoria stared at him. "You mean Erin's girl?"

"Yes. The middle one. She was always such a serious child. I often wonder about her. I can't remember all of them."

"I can't either. I haven't any idea how old Stephanie is now."

"And Candace?" he asked. "I always thought it fascinating that they use the other pronunciation of her name instead of the usual one. I can remember her telling me that it rhymes with 'and you see' not with 'and us'."

Victoria laughed. "Yes, she's not a shy child. I'll bring back pictures to show you."

"Good. Take care." He bent to kiss her cheek before he left.

Victoria went to look for Andante who wasn't in any of her favorite hiding places so making sure everything was locked and ready for the night she went to prepare for bed. "Danty, you'll have to stay where you are unless you hurry. I'm going to bed," she said cheerfully as she slipped off her high heels and unzipped her dress. When she came out of the bathroom, her navy blue waltz length nightgown flowing around her, Andante was sitting on the bed glaring at her. Victoria laughed and scooped up the cat. "Silly girl! You know Auden only comes once in a while. I don't know why you dislike him so much." She carried the cat to the window with her and pulled aside the drapes, after turning out the lights, so she could look out on the street below.

Auden had never talked about the family much after his and Suz's divorce. He'd probably done so tonight because she had mentioned the reunion but he seemed more interested in them than she was. Victoria didn't have any reason to complain about her childhood though she'd never liked being the middle child. Though Rose and Suz weren't close, neither were she and Suz. Suz had been apt to get into mischief or trouble too often and Victoria didn't enjoy that kind of attention. She, Missily, and Erin had usually done more things together when they were small and Erin was young enough to do what the other two told her to do. Life was much more enjoyable when she didn't have to think of any of them. Was she an unnatural child? She wasn't even sure she loved her parents. What was love anyway? Andante was cuddled against her shoulder purring contentedly and Victoria rubbed her cheek against the cat's soft fur.

"I'd rather be with you," she said, "but I suppose I'll have to go to the reunion." She sighed. She hated being called Kitten, disliked Seattle and being near Puget Sound, and had never liked all the water. Not that she'd ever analyzed or wondered why. She just knew it frightened her and could remember that during the Second World War she'd been afraid that the Japanese would sail into Elliot Bay and capture the city. One thing was certain, she wouldn't go alone. She'd go crazy without someone from her world. Sasha had moved to Florida so she didn't see her often any more. Crossing the room she put the cat on the bed then climbed in herself. "I'll think of someone then write Missily," she thought as she drifted off to sleep.

Chapter XI

Rose sat by the hospital bed, her knitting needles busy. The doctor had told her they thought they'd gotten all the cancer. Graham would have to come back for tests later then they'd see if they wanted to do further treatment. Graham didn't complain usually so Rose knew the growth had been bothering him when he began to speak of it often. Well, it was out now. She was glad the reunion was close to home this time. Then if Graham needed to go to the doctor they could go to their own. She was also glad Mikell and Missily hadn't chosen one of the mountain lodges though she would have never said so, but neither was she sure she would have gone unless she knew Graham was out of danger. She didn't believe in airing her affairs and worries for all the world to see like people did nowadays. No one seemed to be able to handle their own affairs any more. They wanted someone they called experts to do it for them. She agreed with her mother when she said no one had any spunk these days.

She looked up as Mikell came quietly into the room but bent her head quickly as he kissed her cheek so he wouldn't see her sudden tears. Things always felt better when Mikell was around.

"How are things, Rosie?" he asked, getting a chair to set next to hers. He was always so quiet in all he did. Rose had never been sorry Missily had married him.

"Fine. The doctor thinks they got all of it."

"Good. And you? How are you?"

She looked up then and he reached over to take her hand. "Holding your own, as usual, I suppose," he said and grinned. "You're one in a million, Rose."

Her hand shook a little in his. "I'm doing quite well, " she answered.

He reached over to brush away a tear from her cheek then stood and walked to the window, turning to look at Graham's still form on the bed with the inevitable tubes attached to him. "Isn't it strange how things can seem so safe, so normal, and then suddenly turn so frightening? It reminds me of once when I was a child and Dad was late getting home from Seattle where he'd gone to buy a part for one of the motors. I found mother crying and suddenly realized my father wasn't indestructible. It shook me for quite a while."

Rose was silent. Even to Mikell she would not admit the terrors she felt. Standing in front of the window he was outlined by the light behind him. "Don't forget, Rosie, there is someone who cares. Not just your family but the God who made us."

"Of course," she answered though she didn't believe as he did at all. "Thank you, Mikell. How's Missily?"

"Busy. She must have a dozen lists." He came to sit down again. "We've heard from everyone except Kitten. Suz is bringing a friend, a jazz pianist."

"A man?" Rose's lips pursed in disapproval.

"Yes. We've got to find out if there's a piano at the Fort. I want to hear him play."

"Are they going to--room together?"

"Most likely," said Mikell easily.

"That will make two couples." Rose's voice was quite severe. "I don't see why you and Missily allow that kind of thing. I thought you didn't believe in-in-that kind of thing," she finished lamely.

"We don't agree with what they're doing. It's wrong. But, Rose, I'm hardly in a position to tell them what to do. They know we don't believe it's right but they believe we're fossils. You know that. And it's a family reunion where everyone comes independently. It's not the same thing as my own children or in my own home. Then I would ask them to go according to our rules the same as I do for other things, like foul language, etc." He looked toward the bed where Graham was still under anesthetics. "I'd better get along. I have a job not far from here so thought I'd drop by. Missily said to tell you she'll come this afternoon."

After he left, Rose sat knitting, thinking how strange he and Missily were. They went to church faithfully and she knew they believed the Bible in a way she called literally and yet he hadn't made a fuss out of the fact that both Suz and her daughter were living with men to whom they weren't married. That was *not* something nice people did. How could he just accept it? But her good sense took over eventually after she'd knitted her disapproval for a while. He was right. The reunion wasn't something he controlled as if he were the father of everyone. And Suz and Alexis were adults. She wished, however, that they wouldn't come. It had been embarrassing enough when Kitten had brought that insufferable Tad. They hadn't slept together nor had they even held hands, but no one seemed to know much about Kitten's private life. Nigel had asked once, when he was a teen-ager, if she was someone's mistress which had caused laughter and then a serious answer from Mikell that he didn't know but he'd believe her innocent until proven guilty.

Rose supposed he was right but one never knew about musicians and it was unnatural not to marry. A woman shouldn't be alone in today's world, she added hastily to herself as though she had to explain what she'd thought, for fear someone would get the wrong idea.

Her mother came in and Rose laid aside her knitting, answering the questions again.

"I couldn't find you at first," said Anna fretfully. "I asked one of the nurses. You aren't in the room they gave me."

Confused as to whom 'they' were and who had told Anna where Graham was, Rose almost smiled. It was so typical of Anna. "Graham's not out of anesthetics yet. They'll move him when he is," she answered.

"How can they be sure they got all the cancer? It might be somewhere else and they just haven't found it."

Rose's father came in then and heard the last sentence. "Anna, don't borrow trouble," he said, bent to kiss his daughter and asked how she was doing.

Later, Rose stood in one of the little waiting rooms talking to her father while her mother went to repair her make-up. "Dad, Mikell says Suz is going to bring some man to the reunion. He says they will room together. Doesn't he care about his children?"

"I'm sure he does, but he can hardly run Suz's life. Suz knows how we feel about such arrangements. She just thinks we're old-fashioned. Well, maybe we are. Society's changing."

"But we don't have to believe that it's proper just because society's changing."

Her father stood with his hands in his pockets, rocking from heal to toe as he surveyed her. "I didn't mean that people have changed. What Suz is doing isn't original with today's society. It depends on one's choice, I think. I don't choose that kind of life for myself but who's to say it's wrong? You have to remember a good many ideas our society has came from the Puritans."

"But that's just it," Rose said, as frown on her forehead, "Mikell and Missily *do* believe it's wrong but they don't seem upset."

"I suppose there are a lot of things we do that aren't as right as they should be. However, I hope you won't shun me if I do one of them," he answered reasonably.

"Dad," she said hesitantly, paused, then continued, "what will I do if Graham doesn't live?"

"Doesn't he have life insurance?" asked her practical father.

"I don't mean that. Of course he does and I can work but--" her voice died away and she turned from him.

He pulled her into his arms while she cried. How many years had it been since he'd held his eldest daughter? She was such a fiercely independent little thing, and yet she wasn't that independent if the thought of losing Graham could shake her so. It was a gray day, one of those days when the clouds hung low and threatening without doing anything but blot out the sun. Allan Metlow, as a native of Washington, seldom worried about the weather. It was capricious when one lived by the Sound and there were many cloudy days but holding his daughter he wished it were a little less gray out for her sake. Things might not seem so gloomy if it were sunny.

Later on, when Graham was beginning to feel halfway human again and could talk without discomfort Rose talked the problem of Suz and Alexis over with him. "I would think both of them would have more respect for the rest of us."

"You're such a proper little woman," he said with a twinkle in his eyes. "I don't think they're doing something so horrible. After all Alexis and Jon are going to get married and who's to say you have to wait until the wedding day for sex?"

"Graham!" Rose was horrified.

He held up his hands. "All right, I understand. But you just as well accept we live in a different world than we did when we were younger. Not that it didn't happen then, it was just kept more secret. But Alexis won't be the only one of the nieces and nephews who decide to live with someone without marrying them."

"Do you agree with them?" she demanded.

"Oh, I don't know. Sometimes I wonder what difference a piece of paper makes."

"Graham!" Rose said in distress. "I thought you had some morals anyway."

"I don't agree with the way Suz does it, hopping from one man to another," he said mildly, "but living with the man you intend to marry isn't so bad. After all, the weddings we have are a custom. Other places they just take them into their tent."

"People don't live in tents now. Besides, even if they do they're heathen and we're civilized." She jabbed her needle viciously into the cloth she was embroidering.

"There now, Rosemonde," he said to soothe her. "There's nothing you can do about it so no need to get so upset."

At the Adamsen home Gretchen approached her mother one evening before supper where she was folding clothes. "Mother, may I talk to you? Privately," she added as Candace looked up in interest from the school work she was doing at the big dining-room table where her mother was also folding the laundry.

"Of course. Let me finish this. I'm almost through. Will you take Sean's clothes to his room? Yours, also?"

Gretchen filled her arms with the sweet smelling laundry. Just before she left the room Candace stuck out her tongue at her. Gretchen tossed her head and left. She and Missily went back to Mikell and Missily's bedroom and shut the door. The room wasn't large but Missily had made it beautiful, sewing drapes and a matching spread in lavenders and greens, with an Iris pattern. There wasn't a chair so they perched on the bed.

"Mother, what is wrong--" and here Gretchen stopped, twisting her hair in her fingers. Missily waited. "Please don't get mad."

Missily was taken back. "Do I usually get mad?" she asked.

"No, but I've never asked a question like this before."

"Your father and I have always tried to make you feel comfortable about asking questions, Gretchen," said Missily a little concerned. Had she not been open to something Gretchen had asked before?

"I know, but it's not a comfortable subject," Gretchen said.

Her mother reached over to still the nervous hands. "You'll feel better if you ask, probably."

"Unless--well, you didn't promise not to get mad."

"Gretchen, I can hardly promise something when I have no idea whether there's a reason for that kind of reaction or not. If you told me that you were going to quit school or that you were--well, going to become a prostitute, for instance, I would be mighty upset."

Gretchen laughed. "I guess so. Why is it wrong--" here Gretchen took a deep breath. She let her dark hair fall around her shoulders and clasped her hands together. "Why is it wrong for Alexis and Jon to live together? I mean, they're engaged."

Missily sat thinking. It wasn't a strange question considering the modern ideas of morality but how best to answer it.

"You're not angry, are you?" Gretchen asked anxiously.

"No, darling. Why would you think I'd be angry? I guess I'm surprised. I just took for granted all of you knew why it's wrong."

"But isn't it just custom? I think I read that in some places engaged couples are allowed to be--to be--"

"Sexually active? If they are, and I can't remember my sociology well enough any more to know whether that's true or not, but if it is allowed then--if I remember right--the engagement is as binding as marriage which it definitely is not in our society. In fact, I think we've gotten away from the original meaning of that, too. So much so that I'm not sure I know what it means to most people other than a public announcement of the couple's intentions. It used to be more binding. In fact, young people who were engaged understood it to be that way and quite often would marry even though they changed their minds about whom they wanted to marry. It was a point of honor."

"I never thought about the engagement being broken. I can see why it wouldn't be right then, but if the engagement were binding?"

"The engagement still isn't the wedding."

"I don't see why it's important to get married in front of a lot of people. Marriage is a private thing between two people." Gretchen stretched out on the bottom of the bed, her chin in her hand.

"Parts of marriage are private, but getting married isn't. It's something that's done before God and man. Important vows like that are taken before people and serve a double purpose. Or used to. They let people know the commitment two people have made to each other, and it holds that couple to that commitment. That's why I said used to. Vows taken in that way used to be considered binding. I'm glad I married your father in front of the people at church and our families. I didn't want to hide him. I was proud of him." Missily pulled a pillow out to lean against.

Gretchen grinned. "I don't really think getting married should be private and I want a church wedding if I ever get married. But it's hard to explain to people why I think it's wrong to live together without getting married. I mean, do we need a piece of paper?"

"Gretchen, is there a particular reason you don't want your sister to hear this? I think it would be a good subject to discuss at our family forum tonight. Sean and Candace might both wonder about the same things you do. When I was young most young people thought such arrangements unthinkable--I don't mean there weren't those who lived that way but they were thumbing their noses at society. Of course, now, it's quite common. I wouldn't have even known about such things at your age, I don't think." Then she smiled. "I do remember that I was quite nasty to your father about this very subject. He used it to try to show me that if we don't have a solid foundation for our beliefs they can be overthrown. Then he asked me about living with a man without the benefit of marriage. I didn't think it was right

102

but I knew I didn't have a good reason and so I said that if I loved a man it wouldn't be wrong. Then I asked him if he were asking me to sleep with him."

"Mother! What did he say?"

Missily 's face lost the smile. "I'll never forget. He was lying on the grass with a piece of it in his mouth and he sat up and said, 'Tell me you didn't mean that' in a funny kind of voice; almost as though he could hardly speak."

"Did you?"

"Of course I hadn't. I was just irritated because no matter what I said he had an answer or a question. He was quite persistent."

Gretchen laid her head on her arms. "Mother, do you think I'll ever get married?"

"I don't know why not." Missily smiled. Had she worried at fourteen whether she would marry or not? If she remembered right she and Erin were still designing and making doll clothes then.

"Candace is so much prettier than I am. I know people think we're twins sometimes but she's not fat like I am."

This time Missily controlled her smile though her daughter still had her head down. "You're *not* fat, Gretchen Jill Adamsen."

Missily said it so forcefully Gretchen lifted her head to look at her. "Why did you say it that way?"

"Because I don't want you to get any nonsensical ideas. Candace is bad enough with her diet. I don't need two idiots around the house."

Gretchen grinned reluctantly. "But I am bigger than she is."

"Number one, you're older and you're developing into a young woman. Number two, you are built differently. Candace will probably be like Aunt Suz and Aunt Vicky. Tall and thin."

"Aunt Suz isn't thin. She's slender, maybe, but not thin. I'll probably be dumpy like Aunt Rose."

"Gretchen," her mother protested, though she laughed. "Aren't you already taller than Rose? You could be like me, you know. Am I fat?"

"Mother," Gretchen said, as if that were a stupid remark.

"Tell me. Of all the people you know who are married, how many of them are--fat?"

"They probably got that way after they were married," Gretchen replied, sitting up now, running her finger along the leaves on the bedspread.

"All right, then, think of the girls you know who are or were engaged. What about Cecile?"

"But she's such a darling it doesn't matter."

Her mother's eyebrows went up. "That statement doesn't fit your argument."

"What do you mean?"

"Major premise," Missily announced didactically. "I'm fat. Minor premise: People don't like to marry fat people. Conclusion: No one will want to marry me. All false, by the way."

Gretchen giggled, "Oh, Mother."

Missily grinned and touched Gretchen's head lightly as she rose. "I have to get supper. Do you have any homework?"

"Yes, some."

"Get at it, then. We'll discuss your question tonight." She put the pillow back, straightening the bedspread. "My mother would have a fit if she saw us sitting on the bed," she remarked.

"Mother, why do you always have Daddy answer our questions?"

"Do I? I thought I answered more than one just now." Missily stopped with her hand on the doorknob.

"I mean questions about the Bible."

"Well, he knows a lot more than I do about that."

"I don't think so." Gretchen was putting on her shoes back on.

"He's been a Christian longer."

"Mother! You've been one for at least twenty-two years."

Missily had to smile. "I know, but I always feel he does a better job of explaining. Do you mind his answering?" she asked as they went down the hall together.

"No. I just wondered. You know I think Daddy is super."

That evening after supper was eaten and the kitchen clean, the five of them gathered in the living room. Mikell was relaxed in his chair, a cup of coffee close by and Missily sat in her chair doing some mending, the lamp table between them. Sean was in a bean bag chair playing with one of the kittens they'd gotten from one of Max and Molly's cats' litters. Candace was manicuring her fingernails while Gretchen lay on the couch watching Sean. It was a warm evening, warm enough to have the door open to the fragrance of the evergreens and the blossoming trees that drifted in. The hum of the city was so much a part of their lives that they hardly noticed it, a cacophony of traffic on the highways, planes overhead going to or coming from Seatac, the big airport south of Seattle, sirens in the distance plus the closer laughter and shouts of children.

"Before anyone else brings up a subject," Missily said, "Gretchen and I were talking this afternoon and I thought her question would be a good one for our family forum. Gretchen, I just remembered I didn't ask if you minded, or at least we got side-tracked."

"I don't mind. Not if you think it's important enough."

"Thank you. Gretchen wanted to know why it's wrong for Alexis and Jon to live together since they are engaged."

"That's easy," said Sean. "It's adultery."

"Only if they're sleeping together," put in Candace.

"I thought adultery was when you cheated on your wife or husband," protested Gretchen. "Besides, I already know people say it's adultery but I read somewhere that in other societies the engagement is as binding as the wedding so it's all right to - to sleep together."

"Sleeping together isn't adultery," put in Mikell. "You know I like you to speak definitively. Say making love if the words sexual intercourse or sex bother you. Both are perfectly good words, you know. If a paper I have to fill out asks me which sex I am, I'm not going to have a fit."

"They don't ask that. They say male or female," Gretchen said.

Mikell grinned. "True, at least most of the time, but that's the same thing. They aren't asking what kind of tree I am or what kind of flower."

His offspring laughed. "Daddy!" Gretchen protested even as she giggled.

"I'm only trying to understand why you're using a euphemism when we have a perfectly good--and clear--word for what you mean. But let's go back to adultery. Gretchen is right about it meaning cheating on your spouse. When you're married and have an affair with another person you are adulterous. There is a word for sexual affairs between unmarried men and women. Do you know what it is?"

"Fornication." It was Candace. "We learned it in Sunday School last Sunday."

"Did they tell you the Greek word from which it is derived?" and as she shook her head he went on. "*Porneia.*"

"Hey!" Sean said so suddenly the kitten, which had been asleep on his shoulder, jerked awake and jumped to the floor. Sean retrieved the shaking animal and began to pet it soothingly. "Sorry, Sooty."

"That's not her name," Candace protested.

"It suits her. She's all black,"

"But it's so simple. Anyone could think of that name." Candace argued.

"Time out." Mikell said it mildly but Sean and Candace stopped their bickering. "I'm interested in the 'Hey!' which scared him or her."

"Her. Uncle Max said so. *Porneia* is where we get the word for pornography and words like that," Sean explained.

"You are right," his father said. "Good thinking. Now that distinction between adultery and fornication that we were talking about is made in the dictionary but not so much in the Bible," he went on. "And, in fact, our Lord Christ, when He spoke of adultery, places it where it begins, in our hearts or thought processes. Can any of you remember what any of the catechisms say about the seventh commandment?"

"I remember the Westminster Larger Catechism because it goes on and on," said Sean. "I don't mean I remember all it says, just that there's more than just cheating on your spouse. It even talks about gluttony and drunkenness and dirty books!"

Missily and Mikell laughed. "Good for you, Sean," said his father. "Do you remember why all those things are listed under you shall not commit adultery?"

"Doesn't it have something to do with purity? That we're supposed be pure in all we do?" Gretchen asked.

"A most excellent way of explaining it." Mikell said, pleased with his daughter's insight.

"But that's where I get mixed up. Why is it pure to have--to make love," and here Gretchen looked at her father with a sheepish grin, "after marriage but not before?"

"Perhaps it would help to talk about marriage itself since engagements are preliminary so the couple can get to know one another. A broken engagement is far better than a broken marriage, as you all know," Mikell

105

said. He smiled up at Missily who had gone to get the coffeepot to warm up his coffee. "Thanks, Jeddie."

She leaned down to kiss him before she returned to the kitchen. She loved these evenings when they gathered to talk together although she missed Myles. He was a great deal like Mikell without Mikell's nervous nature. He would be home in a couple of weeks after completing his first year of college though he'd been home off and on through the year since he was attending Pacific Lutheran University in Tacoma. He was still unsure of what he wanted to do with his life. As she put some cookies on a plate and got cups down for hot chocolate, she could hear the others discussing marriage customs. Usually she said little, just sat listening. She'd never quite gotten over the wonder of finding that Mikell, who was one of those "Bible Thumpers" her family always mocked, was intelligent, well-read and well-educated, though she knew by now that thinking because someone believed the Bible he or she was ignorant was an irrational. It gave her great pleasure to listen to him and she wondered again how she could have thought all the ideas her father had were so much wiser than people who believed in a Creator who cared for his creation.

As she went back into the living room Sean jumped up to set a tray for her. "Thanks, Momsie. Just in time. I was beginning to feel hollow."

"Just hot chocolate for me," said Candace.

Her father laughed. "When are you going to come off you high horse and enjoy being human, Dacey? No man will want you all skin and bones. They'll prefer someone like Gretchen who has some nice soft curves."

"Daddy!" said both girls together, Candace in irritation, Gretchen, whose cheeks had turned pink, in embarrassment but pleased also. She avoided her mother's eyes. Missily picked up the kitten and curled up in her chair with it on her lap.

"Go on. I think Gretchen was telling about marriage customs among some native tribes," she said.

"May I ask a question?" asked Sean around a mouth full of cookie. He had his cup of hot chocolate balanced precariously in the beanbag and held a handful of cookies. "Aren't we supposed to get our information on how to act from the Bible and not culture?"

"I know that," Gretchen protested. "I was just telling about some of the customs we've been studying in school. I just want to know *where* the Bible says it's wrong to live together before you're married if you're engaged."

"Gretchen, we already answered that," Candace said. "Can't you hear?"

"Dacey," her father reprimanded gently and she subsided. "The Bible teaches by more ways than just commandments. One is example. Think of the stories in the Bible that might have something to do with the subject. Anyone?"

"Jacob and Rachel," suggested Missily.

"A good one. If you remember it you'll know Laban evidently wanted Leah, who wasn't as pretty, to get married and saw his chance and gave her to Jacob."

"And also because she was the eldest daughter," put in Missily.

"I can't figure out how he did that," said Sean. "Didn't Jacob have eyes?"

Missily had been looking for the story in her Bible, "It probably had something to do with what the marriage customs were then. I haven't looked them up but it sounds as though the father took the bride to the man's tent at night. If she were veiled, and of course, they didn't have electricity--"

"Mother," Candace interrupted in irritation.

Mikell turned to look at her. "Candace, that is quite enough. You will remain quiet the rest of the forum. Go on, Missily."

His wife glanced from him to Candace who was sitting with an angry expression on her face, then she said, "Well, it sounds as if he didn't see her until morning."

"Golly," remarked Sean, "that wouldn't work today. I bet if Jacob lived now he would know what Rachel felt like."

Missily and Mikell, after a moment's silence, looked at each other and laughed.

"I agree. It doesn't sound as if there were much going on before that night or he *would* have known by touch," said Mikell and grinned at Missily, who blushed. "You'll notice that her father gave Leah to Jacob and Rachel wasn't allowed near until he did the same with her. In other words, they cemented the marriage by their sexual joining after they'd gone through the public ceremony. Think, too, of the story of Ruth and Boaz. In the laws God gave Israel there are all kinds of guidelines regarding sex and marriage and punishment for disobedience and the laws point to purity before marriage. That doesn't mean sex is wrong, only that the rightful place for it is within marriage. It's a safeguard, not a punishment of some kind.

"Look, Gretchen. It's something like opening all your birthday presents three or four days ahead of your party, having them wrapped and then opening them again. It's putting the cart before the horse." Mikell stretched his legs out and clasped his hands across his chest. "I don't mean to imply that everyone has a perfect wedding night, but the most intimate joining belongs to marriage, and it is far more precious if you wait. In fact, I can understand the modern question about why does a piece of paper count when they have already consummated their relationship without any public ceremony and have forgotten about the fact that marriage is a covenant."

"There's a place in the Bible I like," said Missily. "I found it before your father and I were married. It's where Paul is writing to the Corinthians and he says, 'For I am jealous for you with a godly jealousy, for I betrothed you to one husband, that to Christ I might present you as a pure virgin.' Even though my parents weren't Christians they still taught us it was right to be a virgin until we were married though I think they may have accepted the double standard and just expected girls to be virgins. They taught us, anyway, to save ourselves for the man we married."

Gretchen had gone across the room to her mother's chair. "Where does it say that? I like that. It makes sense. I mean he wouldn't say that if he didn't know it was right for us to wait for marriage."

The phone rang and Sean jumped up to answer it, knocking over what was left of his hot chocolate. Missily ran to get something to clean up the mess and when she came back Mikell was talking on the phone. He hung up shortly and came back into the room.

"I've got to run over to St. Mark's. The organist has to practice tonight and the organ is acting up. Sorry, kids." He leaned down to kiss Missily who had been looking at him in dismay but she turned her head so the kiss landed somewhere near her ear and she wouldn't look up. Puzzled, Mikell hesitated a moment then went out the door and ran down the stairs to the van.

Sean came with a rag to help Missily clean the rug and beanbag. "What's wrong, Mom?"

"You'd think he was a doctor and organs were sick people the way he runs," she answered irritably.

"He doesn't go unless he has to," Sean answered.

"That's what he says," Missily rose with her rag and went to rinse it out.

Sean looked at his sisters and they shrugged their shoulders.

Chapter XII

There was an uncomfortable silence before Sean swooped up the kitty that was exploring Missily's mending basket. "Come on, Sooty. Let's go outside for a while."

"That's not her name," said Candace as she carefully put away her manicuring set.

"What is it then?"

"I don't know. I haven't thought of one. Neither has Gretchen."

"Well, she's community property so until you find a better one she's Sooty to me," he said as he went out the door.

Gretchen sat down at the organ. She had taken a few lessons but hadn't liked them and her parents finally let it go. She had a good ear and after she quit lessons began to play by ear or make up her own pieces. It irritated Candace who was taking both piano and organ lessons--the later from her father--and was reasonably proficient on both.

"Gretchen, do you have to play that thing?" she asked now.

"Candace, I want you to come to the store with me. I have some shopping to do." Missily had come back into the room.

Candace sighed but followed her mother down the hall to comb her hair. When they were in the car and turned into a small park she knew she was in for a lecture. She set her lips and settled in the seat prepared to listen in silence, or not listen at all, but Missily got out. "Let's walk," she said. "This used to be your father's and my favorite place to sit or wonder around."

Surprised Candace got out, too. They locked arms and began to walk slowly side by side in the warmth of the evening. It was clear so they could see the Olympic Mountains blue against the evening sky across Puget Sound. Missily stopped to look. "I never get tired of them. Do you know, Dacey, after I met your father and learned there truly was a Creator, all this became so much more beautiful. To think it was designed instead of just happening by chance makes so much difference."

"How could anyone believe it happened by chance?" asked Candace, intrigued in spite of her resolve to stay distant.

"I don't know. I believed that once, though--and, of course, your grandparents and the others do still." She pulled Candace's arm through hers again and they went up the path, the one on which she'd run away from Mikell years ago. "Dacey, can you talk about what's bothering you?"

Candace, expecting a lecture, had been disarmed by the earlier conversation and now was shaken. "What do you mean?" she asked, not able to stay cool and distant with her arm linked in her mother's and the use of the name only Missily and Mikell called her.

"You're so irritable lately. Almost like--well, like nothing we do is something you like."

"Do you say that because I didn't say you were beautiful?"

"What?" Missily stopped so suddenly it swung Candace around. "What are you talking about?"

"Well, that night Daddy said you were more beautiful than anyone else I didn't agree."

Missily smiled down at her daughter. She looked so earnest and so young. Reaching up she pushed the dark bangs out of Candace's eyes. She needed to cut them again. "Darling, I don't know of any law that says you have to think I'm the most beautiful person around but," and here she turned Candace so they could walk side by side again, "you have to admit it's pretty nice for me to have my own husband believe so."

"Well, I guess so," Candace admitted, "But why did you ask that question?"

There was a bench beside the path and Missily sat down on it so Candace perched beside her, curling her legs under her.

"Because you are so unhappy with all of us. I know you love us but it's hard to have you snap at us like you've been doing. It's not like my cheerful Candace."

Candace turned to slide her legs from under her and sit on the seat, looking down the path. "Mamma, did you ever feel like no one liked you?"

"Yes. I had four glamorous sisters. Well, I guess you wouldn't call Rose glamorous but she's stylish. I never cared about that but I did feel it made people not like me."

"Oh, Mamma," Candace turned to her mother. "I'm sorry. I didn't mean it when I said you were plain."

"Did you say that? I don't remember. I was talking about how I felt when I was younger. What makes you feel no one likes you? It can't be because you aren't stylish," and she smiled because Candace was the most likely of her four children to follow the latest fad of the day if her parents let her.

Candace got up to walk a little way from the bench, her back to her mother. "Daddy loves Gretchen best and don't tell me he doesn't because he sticks up for her and you know what he told me about--well, I guess he told Gretchen. I can't remember his exact words, but it was something about curves." Candace's voice wobbled.

Missily was silent a moment. "Daddy was joshing, Candace. He knows that's not what makes people love someone. But we neither one believe your dieting like you do is good for you and you don't need it, Dacey. You'll probably have a figure like Aunt Suz. If you quit trying to ruin it," she added dryly.

"There. That's what I mean. You never think I do anything right."

Missily went to take her daughter in her arms and found Candace was crying. "Come sit down, darling," and as Candace did so, Missily sat beside her, giving her a tissue out of her purse. "Candace, you're going through a lot of changes now. We talked about the physical ones before and how that effects how you feel but you're also beginning to think for yourself and you're getting ready for when you'll leave home and have to make decisions for yourself. I hope your father and I will be wise enough to know when not to interfere. But, darling, you are still young and in our care. It's proper for us to try to teach you and if that means we disagree with something you do or say it doesn't mean we don't love you. Don't get confused and think admonition is something horrible. It's part of love." Missily pulled her daughter into her arms. "Your father and I don't have favorites. He wouldn't feel free to joke with you if he didn't love you. I'm sure he had no idea he upset you.

"Would you like to know what your sister said when she asked if I thought she'd ever get married and I said I didn't know why not? She said that you're so much prettier and that I knew how fat she was."

Candace looked up in amazement. "Gretchen said that? Why would she? She's pretty and not fat at all."

"No, but she feels like she is. I don't suppose there are very many people satisfied with the way they look but not one of my children is ugly nor do you have any physical handicap of any kind. God, for some reason, gave us four healthy, beautiful children, but outside beauty doesn't last and it certainly doesn't count where it matters most. I would love a handicapped, plain child as much as I love you four. There's something twisted in just loving someone because we believe they are beautiful, and don't forget that different people have different ideas of what is beautiful."

Candace threw her arms around her mother impulsively. "I feel so much better. It--it just seemed everything I did was wrong. Even Sean doesn't like the name I want for the kitty."

"I thought you didn't have one."

"I don't but he likes Sooty."

"But Candace, each of us has a right to think for ourselves. We aren't clones, you know. Would you like it better if I agreed with you on everything you said, as if one or the other of us didn't have a brain? Sean could, after all, complain that you don't like the name he picked."

"I guess you're right. I never thought of it that way."

"And I know you like to have the freedom to think for yourself. That's why it irritates you when you think Daddy and I aren't letting you. There are areas, however, where we are still responsible to teach you and help you."

"I know. Most of the time I don't care. But sometimes I feel like everything is wrong. School bores me then and I don't know what I want."

"Welcome to the human race," responded Missily with a smile. "That's something we all probably feel sometime or the other. We'd better get the groceries. I'm getting cold."

The sun had gone down while they talked so they ran back to the car hand in hand. Mikell was home when they drove in. Missily got the grocery sacks out and Candace ran to open the door.

Mikell came into the kitchen. "Why didn't you call for help?" he asked perching on the step stool.

"There are hardly any groceries," Missily answered. She put away the milk and bread and fresh vegetables and started to leave the room.

Mikell reached for her as she went by but she avoided him, not looking his way and went to give Gretchen and Sean the candy bars she'd gotten them. Sean had to tell her about the kitty and she stood laughing with him. Mikell frowned. That was the second time she'd avoided him. He tried to think what could be wrong or was he imagining things? She was good-natured most of the time but when something upset her she wouldn't talk to him unless she had to. He wandered into the room where she was talking to Sean who reached out to take the kitten from his mother.

"Sooty needs to be in bed. I'll take her there."

Missily sat down to take up her sewing again. Gretchen and Candace had gone back to their room.

"Missily, is something wrong?" Mikell asked as he took his own chair.

"I wouldn't know. I'm not the one who's always leaving."

"Leaving?" Mikell was puzzled. Why must she talk in riddles. "But *you* just came back. I don't understand."

"Of course, you don't. You don't want to. I don't want to talk about it."

"About what? Missily, I have no idea what is wrong."

"I told you, you wouldn't want to. And I said that I didn't want to talk about it."

"But if I've done something how can I correct it if I don't know what it is?"

She didn't look up or answer but went on putting the hem in the blouse she was making for Candace. He waited but when she stayed silent he rose to go out to the garage where he had his workshop. He had an organ almost finished but he had to stain the cabinet yet. He tried to concentrate on doing that though his heart wasn't in it. They had so few times where there was discord between them that when something did happen it confused him. She'd been all he'd expected and more, a treasure that he loved more and more every year. She was so beautiful inside and out, he thought, giving the wood a swipe with his brush.

It was much later that night, later than he usually went to bed, that he finally ventured in, hoping Missily would be asleep, but she was sitting up in bed reading. Well, at least he'd find out what was wrong even though he dreaded what was ahead. He'd probably say something he'd wish he hadn't and his stomach tightened.

"I'll probably have to give that thing another coat of stain. I'd like you to take a look when you have time and see what you think, if you could." He stood at the foot of the bed, both his hands on the wooden bedstead.

"Did you have a good time with your girlfriend?" Missily asked cattily.

"My girlfriend?" Mikell stared at his wife. "I was out in the garage."

"All any woman has to do," said Missily sarcastically, her eyes on her book, "is wail about her organ and our white knight is off like a flash like a doctor for his patients, only your patients are inanimate objects that could just possibly wait another day."

"Only this time it was Mrs. Stepson. Remember? I've told you about her. She's in her eighties and a superb organist. She has a rehearsal tomorrow with a chorus that is going to sing one of Bach's cantatas Sunday. Tonight was the only time she had to practice and the A key wouldn't work

112

at all," Mikell said, his voice calm, though he felt more like yelling at her. "Missily, you know I don't go at night unless I have to."

"Unless you *think* you have to," she retorted.

He stood looking at her, confused. What could make his usually cheerful and loving Missily begin to act like some sarcastic, catty nag? "That may be true but I try to judge as fairly as I can. Is it because I left in the middle of the forum?"

"What difference does that make? It's not apt to stop you any more than anything else is. Mister high and mighty, now he's his own boss, is having the time of his life."

Mikell choked, turned on his heel and left the room. He went out the back door and walked slowly across the yard where they'd planted conifer and flowering trees. The magnolia blossoms were fragrant in the cool night air. He stood in the grove of conifer, hands in his pockets, looking up at the night sky where banners of clouds floated across the stars, hiding them only to reveal them a moment later. Taking a deep breath he felt a pain in his chest as he fought a desire to weep. He thought their marriage was safe. Now he wondered how many other things he did she disliked. She'd never said anything until tonight about how his going into business for himself had affected her. He was doing well and hoped eventually to buy her a better home. He'd felt grateful he could give her extra money for groceries. But why would she say that about a girl friend? Didn't she know how he felt about her? He heard her call his name from the front door then eventually she came out the back door and called again timidly. He didn't answer. He was still too hurt. It didn't make any sense.

"What's the matter? You lose your hubby?" Jake called from next door.

"You still checking up on your neighbors?" he heard Missily retort and then the back door slammed shut.

Mikell heard Jake chuckle and had to smile himself. Missily and Daylene got along well but Missily couldn't stand Jake. "Why did she marry him?" she'd asked one evening after they came home from a barbecue with their neighbors. Jake loved to tease and was a ham and he'd been in form that night. "I don't see how she can stand all his silliness."

"Maybe she overlooks it in all his good points," he'd answered.

"Which good points?" Missily had asked then laughed. "I'm sorry. He irritates me so much. I'm sure he's okay."

Slowly, now, Mikell walked back to the house, almost afraid to go in. He didn't want to fight with her and he didn't understand her. There seemed a yawning hole in front of him. He'd felt so comfortable and thankful for their relationship. Quietly he went through the dark house to their bedroom, hesitating with his hand on the doorknob, his stomach in knots. She didn't usually close the door when he wasn't there. Missily was kneeling beside the bed weeping.

Mikell stooped to gather her in his arms and sat down on the bed, wishing as he had many times before that they had a chair for the room and that the room was big enough for one. "Jeddie, my beloved, my own," he said holding her tight, "can you tell me what's wrong? I don't understand."

Her sobbing quieted though she clung to him. "Where were you?"

"Out in back," he answered after a pause. He felt her stiffen but held her tightly. "I heard you. I heard Jake, too, but I was so hurt I couldn't answer. I'm sorry. It's just that I--I've felt so content and comfortable since we were married. I've always been grateful for your trust, that I could trust you and that we've been free to make decisions without worrying about one another misunderstanding."

"Oh, Mikell!" she wailed and hid her face against his shoulder. He held her, feeling some of the pain leave now that she was here in his arms. Laying her down on the bed he kicked off his shoes to lie beside her, taking her into his arms again, smoothing her rumpled hair back from her face.

"Please don't be mad at me, Mikell. I'll try to tell you what's wrong but-but--'" and here she sobbed again. "Ever since I've been taking the phone calls and realized how many women call you I've been panicky."

"Missily! Why?"

"I--I--They know so much about organs and I don't and so many times you seem so depressed or something and when someone calls, you go out and come back in a wonderful mood. If I depress you and they make you feel that way then--"

"Oh, my darling! It's not *you* who depresses me. It's this house. I want to be able to get you a beautiful home and matching furniture and we've been married almost twenty years and you still live in a dump with cast offs. I guess when I go away I forget for a while what a failure I am because I can at least fix organs."

"Mikell!" Missily sat up abruptly and turned to face him. "I *love* this house. It's fun and I love my mixed-up furniture. Do you know how bored I get with houses like Rose has or my parents? They have no character."

"Do you really love it here?" Mikell asked her anxiously.

"Yes. I love every crazy corner, the halls that are in the wrong places and the split-level that has nothing to do with any architects design but kind of grew because the hill was there when they added on. I love the back porch where I can stand and watch the rainbows and the storms come in." She stopped for breath.

Mikell gave a great sigh. "I thought you were always just being kind because I didn't make enough to get a better place." He reached for her hand. "Darling, why does it bother you that the women call me?"

"I know you'll think I'm silly," she answered, holding his hand in both hers, turning his wedding band around on his finger, "but for some reason I just thought the minister or one of the deacons, maybe, called from the churches. It was dumb of me not to realize the organist could call and that most of them seem to be women."

"Not dumb," he said with a smile. "That's not a word I'd ever apply to my Missily. Ignorant, possibly, but more likely you just didn't have any occasions to think about it before. And, you're right, the organist isn't always the one who calls. But I'm still puzzled as to why finding it out should make you panicky. I guess--I guess I thought you trusted me."

She looked up. "Oh, it's not you. It's me. I'm so plain and on top of that they can talk your language. It would be normal for you to enjoy their

114

company. I try not to be boring but you're so intelligent and I--well, I'm not ashamed of it--but I'm just a housewife."

Mikell exploded with laughter. "Missily Jedidah, I refuse to believe you think that. Anyone who reads Greek to relax, who keeps me on my toes with questions I've never thought of could never be boring. Come on. Confess. You don't mean that."

"Well---" she said and a reluctant grin came, "maybe not exactly, but I don't know much about music."

"So? I know very little about Greek or some of the books you read. I don't think I bore you, though. Missily, isn't our relationship as challenging, as satisfying to you as it is to me? Have I failed you in some way?" Mikell was serious now, watching her from where he lay, one hand behind his head.

"Yes, it is challenging and satisfying and no, you haven't failed me in anyway. It's just that I can't understand your depression."

"Do you believe my explanation?"

"I guess so, though I feel if you love me as much as you say and as I have always believed you do, then even the house wouldn't depress you because I'm here."

"I suppose that makes sense, but to me it also makes sense that I come home after being in beautiful homes and see what you are and all I can think is that my jewel deserves a better setting."

"Mikell," she whispered and put his hand to her cheek. "That's beautiful!" Then she scrambled off the bed.

"Where're you going?"

"I want to write down what you said before I forget it." She found a pencil and a piece of paper in the nightstand. While she was writing he got up to get ready for bed.

"Missily, will you be all right about the women who call now? Do you believe me when I say I only want you and love you and no one else?" He emptied his pockets into his dresser tray before he began to unbutton his shirt.

Missily came to help him with the buttons. "I believe you. I'll just have to remind myself when they call."

He opened his shirt and pulled her against him capturing her there with his shirt. "You do that. Don't you forget! How dare you question my ability to judge which woman I want."

She looked up laughing, her beautiful dark-fringed eyes sparkling and he caught her mouth that way in a long kiss. Later, when she came back from brushing her teeth and her hair so it lay shining and smooth on her shoulders, she found Mikell in one of the long nightshirts he liked to wear, which she always made for him, standing at the window in the dark with the drapes open. She crossed the room to put her arm through his and laid her head against his shoulder. "Problems?"

His arm went around her waist to draw her against his side.

"When I was at the hospital that first day after Graham had had his operation Rose asked me if Suz and her friend would room together, I think is how she put it, and when I said probably she said she didn't see why we allowed it. I told her they were adults and you and I weren't their parents or something like that, but I do wonder if we shouldn't say something. I don't want our kids to think we approve."

"They know we don't. Even if they hadn't before they would after tonight. She asked me the same thing."

"What did you tell her?"

"That we couldn't expect people who weren't Christians to act as if they were and my children know that."

Mikell threw back his head in a shout of laughter then bent and kissed her hard. "Let's go to bed. I'm going to demonstrate instead of count some of the ways I love you."

Chapter XIII

Myles came home from college taller and broader, stooped to kiss his mother, teasing her about shrinking, gave himself to his father's embrace, Sean's punch to his shoulder, Gretchen's shy hug and Candace's exuberant one.

"I was home Easter time," he reminded them. "What would you do if I were gone for a year or two?"

"Why? Are you going somewhere?" asked Missily, trying to sound casual.

"Not to my knowledge. I just wondered. It's nice to know I'm liked so well."

He stretched out in the big chair by the window. "It's good to be home. What's for supper?"

Missily laughed. "Wait and see. You'll have to take what you get."

"Anything of yours will taste heavenly after college food." He shivered. "Who's coming for the reunion? Anyone interesting?"

"Everyone's coming. At least everyone accepted," answered Gretchen.

"Suz is bringing a jazz pianist," added Sean.

"She is? Anyone we know--I mean, have heard about?"

"No," Mikell answered. "At least, I've never heard of him before. Shaul Kittim. You know him?"

"No. Wait." Myles had caught the kitty and was running his finger down her silky fur as she lay curled in his lap. "I think I've heard of him. One of the guys at college used to talk about him. They're distant cousins so he was quite proud of the fact Kittim was playing in some pretty posh places in California."

"If he's used to that he'll think we're hicks," said Missily from the door. "Except Kitten. And Erin. Come on everyone. Supper's ready. Granny Ellen's coming tomorrow," she added as they gathered in the dining room. "Grandma called this morning. Granny's going to stay a couple of months."

"Goody! Can I stay at Grandma's while she's here?" asked Candace.

"Not the whole time. Maybe over night once in a while. You'll have to find out from Grandma when, but Granny'll be down here. Grandma says she's still driving so they'll let her have one of their cars to use."

"I wonder if I'll be able to drive when I'm in my middle eighties," Mikell mused, taking a couple of biscuits before passing the basket.

"She probably shouldn't be," said Myles. "She scared the pants off me last time she was here. She expects everyone to get out of her way."

"I think it's fun." Candace giggled. "She honked at everyone and just drove on as if nothing had happened when we almost collided with another car."

117

Alarmed, Missily looked at Mikell. He was frowning but didn't say anything although she thought he might to his parents.

"I think it's scary. I don't like to ride with her," said Gretchen.

"Neither do I," agreed Sean, "but how do you say so respectfully?"

"Why not tell her she scares you?" Mikell wanted to know. "After all it's her life, too, besides everyone else's. I don't think you're afraid just for your skin."

"Alexis and Jon are fornicating," said Candace apropos of nothing.

There was a silence before Myles said casually, "Are they? I don't suppose that's unusual."

"Have you ever fornicated?" his sister asked him.

"Candace!" Missily exclaimed while Mikell choked and reached for his glass of water. "That is not a proper question to ask your brother."

"Why? Gretchen asked the other night."

"Gretchen did not ask that question. She wasn't asking a personal question. She was asking one about what is right in the sight of God."

"Besides isn't it just as bad to think about it as it is to do it?" asked Gretchen.

"Well, you were thinking about it," pointed out Candace.

"No, I wasn't. I only asked why it was wrong for people who are engaged to--to sleep together before marriage."

"Well, that's fornicating," insisted her sister.

"It's not either. I wasn't thinking of what they do in graphic pictures, only asking if what they were doing is wrong."

"I meant sleeping together before marriage is fornicating," explained Candace with exaggerated patience.

"But that's exactly what I didn't know."

"Candace, your mother is right. There are certain things we don't talk about so lightly and sin is one of them," Mikell said, struggling to keep his voice calm. He was having a hard time keeping a straight face and he noticed Missily was having the same struggle while Myles had retreated behind his napkin. Sean had left the table and was doubled over with laughter in the living room where Mikell could see him but Candace couldn't.

"I'll answer the question you asked me with a no," said Myles after taking a drink of water and composing his face. "But I think you're jumping to conclusions. No one *knows* whether Alexis and Jon are sleeping together except them, and maybe friends. At least not any of us." Here he glanced at Missily and winked. "We just assume."

"But they're living together," Candace protested.

"That doesn't prove anything, you know. Not all who live together sleep together."

"O course, not," she said. "Like two men and two women but Alexis and Jon are engaged."

"Two men and two women what?" Gretchen asked, confused by Candace's sentence.

"If they live together, two men or two women, they don't sleep together. I mean like forn--well, I mean like if they were married."

118

There was a silence and then Myles asked. "How's Uncle Graham doing?"

Missily smiled at her son as Mikell gave him the latest news. "He seems to be doing pretty well," he added. "They can't seem to find any evidence of there being any more than those two growths they cut out."

"I hope they don't. What a horrible place to have cancer. Not that I'd wish it on anyone any place," he added as he saw Candace ready to pounce.

"No. But I know what you mean," answered his father.

After supper, while Missily and Gretchen did the dishes and Mikell went out to work on his organ, Sean, Candace and Myles drove to town to get some groceries and stopped by to see Rose and Graham. Everyone knew that Myles was Rose's favorite nephew but it never bothered any of them because Myles was too congenial and lovable. She had the door open before they reached it and Candace slipped by her to run to her Uncle Graham while Myles stooped to kiss Rose's cheek.

"Blooming as always," he said, putting an arm around her shoulders as they went into the house, Sean following.

She had to tell him about her present crusade even though she'd already written him plus talked to him when he was home at Easter break. He had never thought her crusades a joke as the other members of the family did, even when he disagreed. When they went back home Missily was out back with Mikell and Gretchen sat reading, looking a little left out. Myles carried the groceries into the kitchen and she followed to help put them away. Candace must have forgotten her diet because she was taking an ice cream bar out of the box and asked the others if they wanted one, which only Sean accepted.

"I'm glad you're home, Myles. It seems right again," said Candace.

"Are you, pigeon?" They were sitting in one of the big chairs together where she'd plunked on his lap after he sat down and was feeding him bites of her ice cream bar. He curled her hair around his finger. "I missed all of you. Play something on the organ, Tetchy," he said.

Gretchen went to sit on the bench. "What?" she asked as she opened the organ and turned it on.

"I don't care. How about 'Zippity Do Dah'? I feel like some show time."

Missily came in later to find Candace and Myles dancing and singing with Gretchen at the organ and Sean using whatever was handy for drums. He'd played in band from the time he was in fifth grade but had dropped out the last year because his schedule was too full. His drums were seldom played any more and he hadn't gotten them now but had one of her pans upside down on a chair and a box of oatmeal between his knees. She stood watching them, the joy of having them together again grabbing at her. She loved them all so much and it was good to see them back at their fun. So many hours they had whiled away putting on shows good enough to have gone public but the thought would have horrified them. Gretchen had gone from "Zippity Do Dah" into "I Wanna Be Like You." Myles had always excelled as a mimic and he was even better now. He and Candace loved to clown around together while Gretchen and Sean preferred to accompany them on instruments. By the time they had sung "Seventy-five Trombones",

119

"Superfragilisticexpialidosious", and "Chin Chin Cheree" Candace had the giggles and Myles collapsed in a chair. Gretchen swung around, her face brighter than it had been for some time. Sean sat back with a contented sigh and Missily thought, "He's always been able to keep things lively and interesting. No wonder we all miss him."

He looked up and caught her wiping away a tear and winked at her.

"Isn't he super, Mom?" Candace asked, taking her mother's hands to swing them back and forth. "No wonder it was so boring around here."

Sean laughed. "So much for us, Gretchen."

Before Candace could retort her mother put her arms around her. "When people go away you quite often find out what's so nice about them, don't you? It is good to have you home, Myles."

"Gretchen plays a mean organ," he said smiling at her where she sat on the organ bench.

"*That* kind of music," said Candace.

"Don't be stuffy, pigeon. All kinds of music have their place. If you don't watch it you'll begin to sound like Aunt Vicky. Would you like to play something for me?"

"Piano or organ?"

"Your choice."

"I'll play my recital piece for you," Candace decided. She sat down at the piano, fussing a little to get the bench just right and then played John Thompson's arrangement of 'Carry Me Back to Old Virginy'. She was an exact player but not particularly impressive. She had none of the natural feel for music that her siblings had. "Like me," Missily had said more than once to Mikell who was musical through and through.

Later Myles wandered out to the shop and perched on a stool. "That's a beauty," he said, watching as Mikell put the second coat of stain on his organ. "That's a new design isn't it? Looks about complete."

"It is. I even have a buyer. A family from one of the churches where I care for the organ."

"I'm taking organ lessons at the U," Myles said casually.

"Myles!" Mikell swung around. "You didn't tell us."

"No. I wanted to see if I could do it. Remember how I hated piano lessons and trumpet and violin?"

Mikell laughed. "Yes. I decided that wasn't your thing. I mean instruments. Your voice has always been good."

"Well, yes. I was going to keep up with voice but one day I was early at the chapel and sat down at the organ, which was open. I couldn't really play, of course, but something happened when I tried some of the stops and fooled around with it. It's--it's a very emotional thing for me. I mean I almost feel I love it. Is that strange?"

"No," Mikell managed though his throat felt closed.

"So I'm going on. I'll play for you later and you can see what you think."

Mikell turned back to his organ more to hide the tears that had sprung to his eyes than because he wanted to work. What he wanted to do was give his son a big hug. When the family finished reading the Bible later, Myles

120

told them he had a little surprise for them, sat down at the organ to play a hymn and, while they sat in stunned silence after he finished trying to think of what to say, he went into a Bach fugue.

Mikell was sitting on the couch, his arm over the back of it behind Missily and holding her hand so tightly it began to ache. He kept swallowing and when she looked at him she saw a tear slide down his cheek. She laid her head on his shoulder trying to forget the last time she'd seen that happened, but could see the bench where they had sat and hear herself telling him she wasn't even sure there was a God. That was the night she'd told him they'd better not have any more to do with each other. The tear had haunted her in the days that followed; it had been disturbing to have someone care that much about what one believed. Mikell pulled her close now.

When Myles finished the Bach piece and turned to look at his father Candace was there beside him. "Myles! Where did you learn to play? I didn't know you could read music."

Sean gave Myles a thumbs up sign and Gretchen went to hug him. She had been crying. Myles smiled at her and dried her face with his hands then said, "Dad?"

Mikell looked away from Missily to his son. "Wonderful." He said it in a whisper.

"Then it's okay? I can play?"

"Yes. It's there, Myles. You're right. It fits you."

Myles let out a sigh then explained to the others about taking lessons.

As she and Mikell lay together that night Missily asked, "Did you know he was taking lessons?"

"No. He just told me out in the shop tonight. He's marvelous, Missily. I don't mean concert material and I don't think he wants that, not professionally anyway, but he's good and some church is going to be glad to get an organist some day."

"But how could he learn so fast?"

"He's had music lessons, remember. He knows how to read it no matter what Candace thinks and he has always, from the beginning, been musical. That's why it puzzled me so that he wasn't interested in learning an instrument. He could play every instrument he tried. He just didn't take to any. He's got Candace beat so far she isn't even in the picture. I wanted him to try organ, remember, but he wasn't even interested enough to fool around on it like all the others have."

"What about Gretchen?"

"Oh, Gretchen," Mikell said fondly. "Who knows. She has potential but she doesn't want to put in the drudgery of practice. Who knows what she'll do. Let her enjoy it. She has at least learned to play by note first, which I believe is the right way, though I know not everyone agrees with me."

He didn't tell her about the other conversation he and Myles had had when he told her son what Missily had said about liking the house. Myles was taking architecture in college though he wasn't sure yet whether he wanted to make it his career.

"I know she loves it," Myles had said when Mikell mentioned his and Missily's conversation about the house, "and I can see what she means. It's an architect's nightmare," he'd laughed, "but it's original, at least, one of a kind. What you can do, Dad, if she wants to stay here--sometimes she talks about moving into the country but I'm not sure whether she would like it. However, if she wants to stay here why don't you do some remodeling? We can do some ourselves and I can help you this summer. You could put another bath in, for instance, refinish the bedrooms at back. The ceilings are horrors--they need replacing--and you could add to the living room, make it roomier for the instruments. Even put a room over the garage, perhaps a master bedroom with bath. Then over a period of time get some new furniture. That way you'd feel better about the place and Mom would still have her home."

"Can you come up with some kind of plan and estimate the expense? I like the idea of a master bedroom over the garage. It would give Missily and I more privacy, the girls could each have a room and maybe we could put windows in the back so your mother could see her favorite view. In the new bedroom, I mean. I don't want to do the work." Mikell added as he cleaned his brush. "I'm not good at that kind of thing. If you can give me some idea of what it would cost, Missily and I will talk it over and decide whether we'd rather fix this place or move out of town."

Chapter XIV

Summer would have been a lonely time for Missily if she'd had time to think about it. She had her children home more when they were going to school. In the summer the boys usually spent most of their time at Max's working in the apple orchards and helping out with work around their uncle's place while Gretchen was at Perry's and Jean's riding stables. There were also guided horseback trips into the mountains. Gretchen loved being stable girl where she got to work with the horses and this year Candace would be there, also. Their cousins, Trudy and Lynette, worked there, too, although Trudy, at sixteen, had graduated to a guide.

Missily had kept the girls home until the summer before they were to start high school. She not only believed they were too young to work summers that way before then, but she wanted to train them in housekeeping, teaching them how to sew, can, freeze, cook and bake, garden, and shop while at the same time making sure their minds didn't become lazy. She read to all her children from the time they were babies and then as they learned to read, guided their choice of books with Mikell's help. She continued to read aloud to them while they did embroidery or knitting or crocheting in the winter evenings and the boys had gotten in on this, while they worked on their models, though they had all tried each other's hobbies so that both sons could either knit or crochet. Myles and Sean had given those up by the time they were in high school. The girls, however, still made models every once in a while. They liked the sailing ships best and their room was rather cluttered with those they'd put together. Mikell often took time to listen while Missily read, also, and did some woodcarving.

This summer Missily had the added task of bookkeeping for Mikell as well as answering the phone. Mikell had made it plain she wasn't to stay home all the time just in case someone called, so had bought an answering machine for the phone to put on when she wasn't there. She tried to schedule things so she would be home in the morning and Mikell let his customers know that was the best time to call or after five since Missily refused to be gone so long she couldn't fix supper.

Her father stopped by one day to see her, a thing he seldom did alone, asked her what she did with her mind since she decided to be a good little mother and housekeeper. They were sitting at the dining-room table drinking coffee and she looked up startled. There had been a note of sarcasm in his voice, which was unusual in her father.

"What do you mean?"

"I'd hoped for more for you, Missily. I trained your mind on purpose. I knew from the time you were a child that you had an exceptionally bright mind and I had great dreams for you. One of them was not that you should

123

turn religious and I was wise. I wish I had known more about Mikell before you got so involved with him. I'd have headed you off. You could be a college professor now instead of cooking for a bunch of kids and waiting on a husband."

Missily stared at her father. It had been years since he had said anything about her marriage to Mikell and her religious beliefs. She'd thought he'd just accepted both and loved Mikell. She took a deep breath, shut her eyes, and tried to think what to say. "Daddy," she began carefully, "one of the things you taught us was that you didn't think it was parent's place to run their children's lives. Guidance, yes, but in the final analysis it had to be we who made the decision about our lives. I'm sorry you are so disappointed in the choices I made. If you remember, I told you years ago that I wasn't sure I wanted to go to college because I didn't think I could learn much more than you had already taught me. I wanted time to find what I wanted to do with my life because I didn't want to go into the academic world. I didn't want to be a teacher. That much I did know. I enjoyed working at the office, though I wouldn't have wanted to make that my life's work. I'm glad that I met Mikell. I love being married to him and I love being a mother. And even though you don't like this it's still true. I would believe what I do now about God and the Bible and Christ Jesus even if I had never met Mikell. He didn't convert me. God did."

"But what are you doing, vegetating here?" he asked in irritation.

"Training young minds to think. Do you know how mindless young people seem now? They don't appear to know how to think or make decisions. Mikell and I are trying to train our children so they can think and not just follow. It's exciting and challenging as any other vocation, and I believe, important."

"You'll never convince me they aren't followers. Those as fanatic about religion as you all are have to be followers. You can't think for yourselves. You can't deny that you have a certain set of doctrines you believe." Her father said this with scarcely veiled contempt.

"That's not limited to religious people, Daddy. You have your own set of beliefs. One of them seems to be that a housewife is in some way demeaning to intelligent women. And you can't convince me, either, that you aren't a follower. Of Darwin, for instance, or John Dewey."

"Missily, there's a great deal of difference between reading men who have done exhaustive research in their field so they know what they're talking about, and just accepting a book written centuries ago and full of contradictions."

Missily sat regarding her father. She'd heard him use the same kind of arguments with Mikell. She wondered why it didn't occur to him to question Darwin and others. "Daddy, just because something is old hardy makes it worthless. You read and appreciate Aristotle and Plato. I've heard you argue things Mikell's said using their arguments. Why are they acceptable and not writers of Scripture?"

An expression of admiration crossed his face and he smiled briefly. "I see you haven't let your mind go stagnant. You and I don't talk much any more. You usually let Mikell do the talking."

"I thought you enjoyed him," Missily poured her father another cup of coffee and warmed her own half-full cup. "In fact, I thought you liked Mikell."

"I do. Enjoy talking to him and like him. In fact, I love him as a son, but I miss talking with you. However, you know, Missily that even though I appreciate Aristotle and Plato, I don't think they are infallible. And you do think that about the Bible."

"Yes, I do. It is unique and different and there is nothing else like it anywhere. But the point I was trying to make was that believing in someone or their thoughts doesn't just apply to Christians. It applies to everyone. We all have presuppositions and apply them to what we read. It's what and whom we believe in that is different, not believing itself. You don't accept the supernatural, I do."

"How you can believe in something that can't be proven is beyond me."

"But evolution isn't proven either. There are scientists who are not Christians who don't accept the hypothesis of evolution. I read an article not too long ago by a biologist who probably doesn't accept the supernatural any more than you did who was very critical of Darwin's theories."

"So you still read people who aren't Christians?" her father asked reaching for one of the cinnamon rolls that Missily had put on the table.

"Of course. Just because they aren't Christians doesn't mean they don't have important and interesting things to say. Daddy, it's too bad we don't talk more often. One thing that you taught us was that to know what the other person believes one should read their writings and listen to them and yet you have refused to read anything that Mikell and I have suggested."

"I don't enjoy religious writings any more than you enjoy, say, books about mechanics or plumbing. It's true that I taught you to read people before you criticize them but I didn't make you read all kinds of books." He sighed. "The older I get the more I miss my girls. It seems so empty at home any more."

"You're welcome here any time. We love to have you. You might even enjoy arguing with your grandchildren, especially Myles and Sean. The girls haven't learned to separate personalities from subjects and get upset arguing."

"I just might do that," he took a sip of coffee and set it down again. "I guess I'll have to come alone. Your mother still has fifteen irons in the fire at once and it's a wonder she takes time to breathe."

Missily laughed at this apt description of her almost frenetic mother. "You'd never know she was nearing seventy. Or is that because I'm older that seventy doesn't seem ancient like I once thought?"

"I suppose so. I certainly don't feel it most of the time. Missily," he hesitated, looking at his hands, clasped together on the table, then up at her, this child of his heart. "Tell me honestly. Do you truly believe all this--this religious nonsense? Or do you just want to keep Mikell?"

"Daddy," she answered gently, "even if I didn't believe it, even if I'd only said so to catch Mikell and told him what I'd done afterwards I wouldn't have lost him. He wouldn't have deserted me."

"You don't know that."

"Yes, I do, because he not only loves me deeply but part of his Christianity is living as well as he can the right way and leaving your wife is not acceptable. Mikell doesn't love me just because I became a Christian. He loved me before, in fact, but was wise enough to know our difference in thinking would not make for a good marriage. He loves me for who I am. But I will answer your other question. I believe with all my heart and mind that God is real, that He created us, that we are sinners and that God also redeemed lost sinners through the work of Christ. And I know," she added with a little smile, "that the Bible doesn't contradict itself."

Allan Metlow sighed. "I'm glad in a way. It would be cheap to pretend to believe something to get a man. At first I thought you were doing that but twenty years is a long time to pretend anything and not have it become apparent. I've never detected anything that even smells of pretense."

Missily let out a sigh of relief. When he had asked his question it had alarmed her. Was she not, then, acting as though she believed what she said she did? Now she knew he hadn't meant that. "You know, don't you, that I want very much for you to become a believer, too?" she asked.

He regarded her, thinking how much he loved this daughter of his, that strange unaccountable love that had been there from the first time he'd held her in his arms. Why Missily, even before she had shown that remarkable mind of hers so young? Why, he didn't know. He only knew it was true. He had never intended to have a favorite, he hoped none of the others knew though he thought Missily might. In spite of her religious beliefs they were still close. "But Missily," he replied, "what difference would it make? Unless you're thinking of an afterlife."

"Not entirely and not primarily."

"Would it make me a better citizen, a better husband, father, business man? I've always tried to be honest, to care for Anna and you girls. I don't chase women or drink to excess or gamble or go to filthy movies or fill my mind with worthless books. I can't see that we live that differently. I go to church, too. If there really is an accounting for our time on earth I think I can stand beside you and say I've done as well as you."

Missily's eyes filled with tears. How familiar the arguments were. It was so hard to believe she'd once thought the same way. She blinked her eyes to clear them. "It isn't me you are compared to, Daddy. It's Christ. But I wasn't talking about a final accounting. There will be one, of course, but I don't live my life in a way to make sure I'll measure up. I know I can't. I want you to know what it's like to know that you aren't on this planet, in this universe, autonomously, that you can have a better life and every area will be different. It's motives, values, reasons for doing things that are different between us, but even more important, you are an enemy of your Creator."

He started to answer when the phone rang. Missily said yes, she would give the message to Mr. Adamsen. No, he wasn't in at present but would check in in fifteen minutes. No, she had no way of getting hold of him right now but he would call back as soon as he could--not long after she told him. Yes, she understood it was urgent and she would make sure he understood, also. Allan Metlow listened to her pleasant, patient voice and smiled. She grinned back as she hung up the phone. He rose.

126

"I'd better be on my way. I promised your mother I'd get some milk and bread."

"Thank you for stopping by, Daddy. Do it more often."

"I just might," he said, bending to kiss her. "Don't worry about me," he added touching her cheek lightly with his hand. "If there is a God he's smart enough to know I live better than most people. He'll take that into account. Tell my grandchildren hello. It would be nice to see them occasionally."

"I know. I'll see if I can get them over. They're busier than we were, I think."

She watched him as he walked to his car, his stride free and his carriage as straight as it had always been. He waved to her before he folded his slender, tall frame into the car and shut the door. Missily turned away from the window with a sigh after waving to him. He was as set as ever and so was her mother. They were both sure they were living good enough lives to count. Even the grandchildren hadn't had any effect on them though her four, when they were small, had been almost embarrassingly direct about their grandparent's fate if they didn't believe.

All four were a busy bunch now. If they weren't working they were at one or the other of their cousin's houses. Since Mikell's family all lived in or outside Seattle the cousins had done things together since they were babies and now six of them were driving, counting her Myles and Sean, they were together more than ever, spending the night wherever convenient. It was feast or famine she thought with a wry smile. Either she was alone most of the day or the house was overrun by energetic young people ranging in ages from nineteen down to twelve year old Kate, Eva's daughter. Eva and her husband, Dundas, had gone into partnership with Percy and Jean and the two families had homes on the land where the stables were, not far from Mikell's folks' place. Other than Kate there were three others near Kate's own age: Kent, Kate's brother was two years her senior and Perry's girls sandwiched him, Trudy at sixteen and Lynette, thirteen. Missily was grateful that the cousins were close. She'd never known any of her cousins very well and it was delightful to know her four children's closest friends were their own cousins. She was also thankful they were Christians though her own had never limited their friendship to just Christians as some church people they knew did. Though she loved her nieces and nephews on her side just as much as on Mikell's, aside from Nigel none of them even attended church. It was a heartache she carried with her every day.

Lorna, Mikell's youngest sister, wasn't married yet at twenty-five and divided her time between her parent's place and the stables, helping out with the bookkeeping as well as acting as a guide. And, of course, Max and Molly had their three sons: Martin, nineteen, just finishing his sophomore year at college back East--she could never remember the name of the school---Adam, Myle's age and at Pacific Lutheran University this year also, and Rex who would graduate from high school in a couple of weeks.

Molly and Max had purposely had their children one right after another hoping for a girl which they'd never had. Molly and Missily spent much of each summer together with Mikell's mother canning and freezing fruits and vegetables and making jelly and pickles and relish. Jean disliked housework of any kind so Missily and the others always put up enough food for her family and in exchange could get a horse any time they wanted one. Eva helped sometimes but she taught English classes for adult immigrants so wasn't always free.

They always tried, Mikell and Missily and their children, to go camping during the summer. Mikell could choose his own days off so it would be easier now, if the others could get the time off. Now that all four were working it might not be as easy. This year's vacation time would be spent at the reunion, at least one week of it.

Kitten had finally written to say she was coming to the reunion and bringing a friend, Imogen Murray, a writer for some esoteric magazine Missily had never heard of before. She groaned. They would probably both be bored. Next reunion it would be Kitten's turn to plan. The last time they had met in Chicago and come to know some of the city which, Missily found to her surprise, fascinated her. She hadn't expected to like it at all. Kitten wasn't fond of outdoor activities so had planned trips to museums and concerts and sightseeing jaunts in the city itself. That had been about ten years ago, before they'd decided to have the reunion every three years instead of every year as they'd done in the past.

Now Missily, who had been sitting perched on the kitchen stool reading as she ate her breakfast after getting everyone off—school wouldn't be out for another week for Sean and the girls but Myles had gone out to Max's to work—closed her book regretfully and climbed down to carry her dishes to the sink. Today she *had* to make a list for groceries for the reunion. She'd been putting if off, loath to get started. She never minded fixing meals for her family but those coming weren't all her family and she'd have to be careful to remember Graham's mother was a diabetic and Thor's father had a heart problem. Both were on strict diets and while she didn't have full responsibility for either she tried to be thoughtful. And then there would be strangers. Mikell always told her they could eat what was put before them or go get their own and not to worry but she did anyway. She had grown up in a family where they were expected to eat what was put before them but she'd never liked many things her mother fixed and it had taken years after her marriage to learn that she could cook what she wanted to and not feel as though her mother were looking over her shoulder making sure she had all the food groups. She'd learned from Deborah Adamsen, Mikell's mother, how to cook vegetables so they were palatable and she'd gone through cook books and magazines until she'd developed a style of her own.

Not that she'd have to do all the cooking but the host family planned the meals. If you were like Kitten you expected everyone to eat out but Missily was far more knowledgeable about the finances of her guests than Kitten would care to be. She'd just sniff and say that was their problem. Why didn't they get better jobs that paid better? It didn't occur to her that caring for a family meant even good salaries didn't stretch as far as it did for one person, especially if your children were in Christian schools as her four and the cousins on Mikell's side of the family were. But then Kitten thought that was ridiculous and even un-American. It didn't do any good to remind her that private and parochial schools had been around for a long time and children of wealthy families quite often went to the private ones. Kitten would counter that they could afford it and when Mikell quizzed her about the un-American bit she replied that part of America had always been that anyone could get to the top with hard work and ingenuity. When he reminded her that her argument had been it was un-American to send children to private schools instead of public ones, not that it was un-American not to be as rich as your neighbor she quit talking to him and changed the subject. It amused Mikell because she was irrational but it irritated Missily.

"She always was a snob and she thinks she'd better educated than we are just because she lives back East."

"Sweetheart, she's hurting herself more than us. What she thinks doesn't matter two whits when she's being foolish," Mikell had told her more than once. It made her smile reluctantly but she still became irritated when Kitten put on airs.

Thinking about that made her realize why she'd been putting off getting groceries. She knew Kitten would turn up her nose at everything and they'd all be told how much better it was back East. Kitten didn't like anything about her home state, but did she like anything other than her cello and her cat? Maybe that was why she could be so disagreeable. If life was that empty for her no wonder she was unhappy and taking heart, Missily began to plan the meals. She still had some of the fruits and vegetables she'd canned and frozen last summer plus some jam and jelly. She and Rose would bake ahead and freeze pies, cakes and cookies. With the hoard of young ones it would take an enormous supply of desserts. She'd counted and if all the cousins on both sides came--and they usually did --there would be sixteen if she started with Nigel who was the oldest at twenty-one. He hadn't been to see them for a while.

Nigel had been in Seattle, or at least near there, more often than Missily was aware. He generally made the trip up from eastern Oregon several times a year, sometimes with Diccon, sometimes alone. It was quite a trip but not bad. Since he hated driving in the traffic, when he came up to eastern Washington he crossed the Columbia River at Maryhill where there was a replica of Stonehenge and a castle of sorts. It is a museum now but had been built by Samuel Hill, son-in-law of railroad magnate James J. Hill. Samuel Hill had been an international peace promoter, a world traveler and a friend of royalty. He had intended to start a Quaker agricultural community on the cliffs above the Columbia River in Washington with Maryhill, his mansion, as his residence but his plans didn't materialize. He turned the building into a museum and later one of his royal friends, Queen Mary of Romania, dedicated the museum to beauty and peace as a symbol of her gratitude to the aid America had given Romania after World War I. The museum has valuable art, part of it Sam Hill's collection of the sculptor Rodin's bronzes, plasters, and sketches Rodin kept in his studio for reference. Missily had been to Maryhill several times when a child with her sisters and parents. Allan Metlow particularly enjoyed the Rodin collection but Missily and her sisters' favorites were the l940 French mannequins and the Queen Marie room. They had never tired of looking at the throne, the coronation gown and other personal belongings of the Queen. It had give Missily a special interest in Romania.

Nigel had gone by it so many times he didn't even look at it consciously, he said. He'd never been in it. Art bored him and even after Missily told him there were things like antique chess sets and American Indian baskets he just shrugged his shoulders and grinned. He liked the outdoors better; his reason for going into the Forest Service.

From Maryhill he had to drive up and over the mountains but he would have chosen the mountains in any weather rather than have to go down I5. He'd had enough traffic in California to last him a lifetime, he said. He went to the stables. Not for the horses but because Lorna was there often and he loved her. She was four years his senior and treated him like a younger brother which was frustrating to Nigel but he didn't give up hope since she was still single and there seemed to be no one else in the wings waiting.

Lorna had developed into a lovely young woman quite unconscious of her beauty. She had an oval face and parted her black hair in the middle, pulling it smoothly back on both sides to clasp in back so that it accented her creamy skin. Her blue eyes were startling with the dark hair. She looked wonderful on horseback, long hair flying, as she raced the horse expertly. She consistently won ribbons and awards in horse shows. Nigel had heard her mother say more than once, rather wryly, that Lorna loved horses, period.

At about the same time that Missily was finally getting the lists for menus and groceries made, Nigel was headed for Perry's place. He had come from Oregon the day before to apply for a job he'd heard was open in the Snoqualmie Forest area. For some time, he'd been watching for an opening in Washington thinking that if he were closer he could see Lorna more and it might make a difference in how she felt about him. Because he'd gone to the stable for years to ride no one thought anything strange when he went there whenever he was in Washington. If Lorna knew he came to see her she didn't let on. He hadn't gotten the courage yet to ask her right out where she was if she weren't at the stables or in the office and he usually hung around until she either came or he found out some way whether she was going to come or not. No one was around when he first drove up this time so he parked and walked to the stables.

Nigel was a great deal like his father: tall, dark curly hair, cheerful. He had left Suz as soon as he was old enough. Why the judge had given Alexis and him to her he could never understand. Diccon had wanted both of them but he hadn't been considered fit. It had, Nigel supposed, something to do with the fact that in those days the mother was considered the best at nurturing while the father supplied the money because Diccon had paid child support until both Alexis and Nigel had left Suz. It never occurred to him to ask either of his parents why they'd been given to their mother. Nigel had gone to college in eastern Oregon, getting a degree in forestry. Alexis had gone to college in Colorado for some reason Nigel had never understood and met Jon Craig there. Nigel wrote to his mother when his father kept after him enough but that wasn't often though she wrote him regularly and called at least once a month.

Nigel wasn't sure how he felt about her. He'd been sure he hated her until he started living with his father and found that though Diccon was saddened by Suz's behavior, he was never bitter nor vindictive and took his share of the blame for their marriage falling apart. It was confusing because Suz had never been vindictive about Diccon either; just kind of off hand and they seemed to be able to get along. Nigel had demanded, at a young eighteen, how Diccon could even be nice to a woman who ran from one man to another.

His father had looked at him and asked gently, "Have you ever wondered what makes her so restless, so dissatisfied? She's not a vicious woman. In fact, she's rather a dear but she is irresponsible. And I don't excuse the men. We can hardly claim to be perfect as if none of the fault was ours."

"But what did *you* do?" Nigel had demanded.

Diccon had shaken his head and he'd turned to gaze out the window. "I don't know, son. I don't know. I was young and not sensitive. Maybe--" He hadn't finished the sentence and when Nigel prompted him he'd changed the subject. When Diccon had tried once to explain to Alexis and Nigel that he should have lived closer to a big city for Suz they had been incensed. It was the wife's place to go with her husband they said.

Nigel had never gotten the courage to ask his father if he still loved Suz. Alexis had tried to get him to ask but he couldn't. "But he's never remarried," she said. "It should be easy enough to start from there and ask."

And Nigel had told his sister, "I can't stand the way he looks when he talks about her. I bet it wasn't his fault."

Nigel's feelings for his mother had changed over the years. He wasn't sure yet he loved her. She'd never abused him; in her own way she loved him, he knew, but he'd found it hard to forget the turmoil of his growing years and as his admiration and love for his father grew his questions did also. Why would his mother leave a man like Diccon? He knew that there were women attracted to him and while Diccon was friendly and kind he never gave himself to any of them. The only woman with whom Nigel had ever seen him completely at ease was Missily; they were like a brother and sister. All Missily's family loved Diccon. It was because of his father, Mikell, and Missily, that Nigel came to understand what it meant to be a Christian and eventually came to faith also. That, of course, had influenced his thoughts about his mother. At first, after he understood what sin was and name for what she'd done he didn't want to own her as his mother. It was his Uncle Mikell, in that easy but direct way he had of seeing through a problem and addressing it, who took him for a walk one day when the family had come to Oregon for a visit, and told him the story of the Samaritan woman and her multitude of husbands, and her live-in, what Christ had done and said, how pervasive sin is in each person so that none can point a judgmental finger at another, how one is acceptable only because of what Christ had accomplished, that he'd begun to think differently so that his bitterness began to fade. But he still wasn't sure he loved her and didn't look forward to seeing her with another man.

Now, as he walked into the stable from outside, it took a moment for his eyes to adjust to the interior. He heard the weeping before he could see Lorna standing with her arms across one of the mare's neck, sobbing. Nigel crossed quickly to her side. "Lorna. Darling. What is it?" he asked urgently.

Startled, she turned, raising a dear wet face. She looked so young and defenseless that Nigel's heart turned over. He reached out to dry her cheek with his hand. "Can you tell me?" he asked gently.

"Patsy's Pride's colt died," she said on a sob.

Nigel gathered her into his arms, holding her close. "I'm sorry, darling. I know how much you love Patsy's Pride. What happened?" But she didn't answer, just went on sobbing. "Lorna, I know it must be terribly disappointing," he said but she interrupted him, pulling away.

"Don't say it! Don't tell me she can have another one! I know that, but she can't have *this* one and it was--Oh! What does it matter. You'd never understand. You don't care two cents about anything but yourself," she went on, knowing that wasn't true but embarrassed that he had caught her crying and shaken by his gentleness and endearments. She'd hoped he'd gotten over his infatuation.

Nigel, stunned, could only stare at her while he remembered how many times he'd cursed the careless hunters who shot for the sport of it, wounding animals and birds then leaving them to take themselves off to die. He remembered particularly weeping over a doe as she tried to stir her fawn to life after it had been killed. There were many hunters he knew and liked, but the careless renegades he had no use for. He'd always loved the wild animals and because of that had understood Lorna's love of horses. Without a word he turned on his heel and left the stable, got into his car and roared out of the yard without looking back.

Lorna ran to the door and called him but if he heard her he didn't turn. She stood watching him drive away far too fast, her heart in her throat. Nigel. Oh, Nigel, be careful, she cried wordlessly. Come back. I didn't mean it. Slowly she went back to Patsy's Pride. Running her hand down the long nose, putting her face against the horse's long, warm one, she stood lost in thought. Was he really that much younger? He was a man, now, not a child. He stood tall and broad and his hands had been warm and tender against her face. Lorna looked at her horse, wonderingly, as though the animal could answer her questions. Turning, she left the stables, walking across the paddock to climb up on a fence and gazed off to the mountains where Nigel would cross. Lorna had never given much thought to loving a man, to marriage--except for one impossible dream--but now it opened before her as a lovely possibility.

Chapter XV

"Uncle Diccon's here!" yelled Candace from the door before she dashed out and ran to be caught in Diccon's arms.

The reunion would start in three days. Granny Ellen, of course, was already at Mikell's folks and there would be others arriving in a couple of days. Missily wondered why Diccon was early. She hoped it didn't mean that he wasn't going to be able to stay. Putting down the lists she had been checking she went to meet Diccon as he came in the door, laughing as Candace tried to tell him everything at once. He swept Missily into his arms for a warm kiss.

"How's my favorite sister?"

"Diccon! It's so good to see you. You're early. You are going to stay, aren't you? I mean you haven't come to say you can't come after all?" Missily, flushed with pleasure, held on to his hand.

He laughed and reached over to muss her hair. "You worry too much. No. I came to help madam in whatever capacity she wished to use me."

"Diccon, you are a love," she said as she gave him another hug. "I could use another head. I've gone over the lists so often I can't tell whether they're complete or not."

"Let me at 'em. Let go, youngster," he said with a grin at Candace who was hanging onto his arm. "We'll have lots of time. Right now your mother needs my help."

"Where's Nigel?" She followed them into the dining room where Missily had the lists on the table.

"He's coming Saturday night. Had to work. I wasn't about to wait when I got a day off early on purpose to come help. "Now, where do we start?"

"Candace, get us some iced tea, will you? I think the sun tea is probably ready." Missily sat down next to Diccon. He was so tall. One forgot between times. He topped Mikell. She was just five foot six so her husband's six foot one was something to look up to, but Diccon topped six foot four and stood slender and straight, his carriage lithe and supple. She wondered, briefly how tall Shaul Kittim was and if Suz had forgotten the height of her former husband. Often, when she saw Diccon again, she wondered what had gotten into Suz that she'd left him. Maybe he was too good for her. Perhaps she wanted someone more worldly, sophisticated, even tainted.

Diccon had taken out a pen and was running down the list of first aid equipment. He was trained in CPR and she knew he had other emergency medical training, he and Nigel. Candace set glasses down with ice in them

133

and poured them both some tea and then a glass for herself. Missily looked up, "You can take yours back to your room while you finish cleaning it."

"But I want to be here. Can't I do it later?"

"Come." Missily took her daughter's arm gently and led her down the hall. In the girls' bedroom she said," You have a choice, Candace. The room has to be cleaned and you do it now and go to Uncle Perry's tomorrow or not do it and stay home and do it then."

"Gretchen got to go," Candace said sulkily.

Missily turned to leave. "Your choice," she said as she went out the door.

Candace's lower lip stuck out and she plopped down on her bed. Gretchen's side of the room was usually clean. Candace wanted to tear everything apart there. She hated to keep the room neat and usually stuck things under her bed out of sight but she knew she had to do what her mother said if she wanted to work at Uncles Perry's so reluctantly she began to put away her paraphernalia now stacked on her bedside table, on the dresser, or on the floor.

"Did you know Graham had an operation? Did I write?" Missily asked Diccon once she was back in the dining room and in the chair next to him.

"No. Something serious?" His head came up and his pen stayed poised.

"Cancer in his mouth. The doctors think they got it all. Rose is glad the reunion is in Washington this year."

"How's Graham?"

"He seems to be fine. He's back at work. I hope he'll not have any more trouble but it's scary. Mikell thinks it's his pipe."

"Could be. I don't know. Cancer's strange. I keep wondering if, in the future, if they find what causes it for certain, we'll laugh at our ideas like we do the ones our grandparents had about things. You haven't an antihistamine of any kind on here. Don't we usually keep some around in case someone gets stung by a bee or wasp?"

"Of course. Thanks. Write it down. I'll get something when I do my last minute shopping." Missily took a drink of her iced tea then said casually, "Suz is coming. Bringing a man friend along."

"Is she?" He didn't look up this time and his voice was so normal Missily couldn't tell whether he was interested or polite. "Who is he?"

"A young jazz pianist, Shaul Kittim. Myles knows his cousin."

"But Suz has never liked jazz," Diccon said.

"No, but she was never especially musical anyway. It irritated Kitten terribly."

Diccon laughed. "Poor Kitten. The world's a hard place for her. I wish she'd loosen up a little."

"She and Suz could divide up a bit," replied Missily. "They're both extreme--though in opposite ways."

"Do you think Suz is extreme?" Diccon asked, leaning back in his chair.

"Yes. She just doesn't let things bother her," Missily said it like her sister always did and Diccon laughed again. "I always wish she'd act as though *something* bothered her, or she liked someone, or didn't like them. Diccon, you know what I mean."

He was silent so long she turned to look at him and caught one glimpse of his eyes, dark with pain and something she couldn't name, before he looked away. "I didn't know her that way," he said briefly and took up his pen, pulling another list toward him, trying not to remember the lovely warm girl he'd held in his arms, her eagerness not only in their physical loving but in all the things they did together. What a delight she'd been, dark blond hair flying, running barefoot on the beach, riding bareback in a race with him and usually winning, climbing the stairs and hills of Seattle, strolling on the piers or walking around the downtown area, curious and convincing him to take her to the original Skid Road.

"Diccon," Missily asked gently, "do you still love her?'

A hand went up to shield his face and his voice was rough. "I'll always love her," he said.

"Yoo hoo," came a voice from the front door. "Anyone home?"

"Lorna! We're in the dining-room."

Lorna came in, her dark hair shimmering with the mist that had settled there. "Forgot my umbrella. Diccon! It's you. I didn't recognize your car."

He turned. "Too bad I don't own a horse and carriage. You'd know my horse." He smiled. "How are you, Lorna?"

"Fine. You're looking fit. I came to lend a hand, Missily, with the packing. I figured your girls would be at the stables."

"Candace isn't today but I'd love the help. She's cleaning her room. Sit down and have some iced tea. When did it start raining? I've been so busy I haven't noticed the weather."

"Just a few minutes ago." Lorna sat down across from them after getting herself a glass and filling it.

"Nigel tells me Patsy's Pride lost her colt, Lorna. I'm sorry," said Diccon.

Lorna had looked up quickly when he said Nigel's name. She wondered where he was but felt self-conscious asking now she no longer thought of him as a kid. "Yes. It's pretty disappointing."

"Was Long Jim the sire?"

"Yes. How did you know?"

"Nigel told me that, too."

"Oh. I don't remember telling him." Then, "Where is he?" she asked, trying to sound casual.

"Working. He'll be here late tomorrow."

"When did Patsy's Pride lose her colt?" Missily asked.

"Last week. I can talk about it now but it was pretty hard at first."

"How did Nigel know?"

"He came to the stables when he was here on business last week."

"Last week? We didn't see him."

"I only saw him a few minutes. I don't think he had much time," Lorna answered and hoped Diccon wouldn't say anything to make that sound wrong. She wasn't prepared to explain why Nigel stopped by the stables so often or even that he did. Since that day she had spent a lot of time thinking

135

and realized that he'd come to see her quite often, or at least come to the stables, though he didn't go riding much and she wondered if he came to see her.

"You're right. He'd heard about a job up here and wanted to see if he could get in here in Washington," Diccon said.

Lorna breathed a sigh of relief. It never occurred to her that neither Missily nor Diccon had any reason to question her since no one knew that Nigel loved her. "Did he get the job?"

"Too early to tell. I'll miss him if he does."

They worked together, the three of them, the rest of the afternoon, Diccon telling Missily not to worry about supper, he'd take them all out for pizza and root beer, including Lorna. And Lorna, who loved Diccon along with the rest of them and had sometimes, when she was a much younger, dreamy teen-ager, dreamed impossible dreams of his falling in love with her even though he was nearly twenty years older than she, realized with a shock that with his son, equally at attractive and lovable, the dream might not be impossible; that this man might even be her father-in-law some day if she knew how to let Nigel know she didn't dislike him or think him too young any longer. The thought was overwhelming and she both dreaded and longed for Nigel to come. She would have to apologize for what she'd said to him. At all these thoughts she grew so quiet that Diccon asked her if she were tired and she blushed and said, no, just thinking and grew even redder. Missily glanced at Diccon and away. He winked but she knew he was as curious as she.

Later that evening Missily and Mikell were in their back yard talking while Mikell checked his roses for aphids and cultivated around them. Diccon and all four of their tribe had gone down to Elliott Bay. Diccon said he wanted to get down to the waterfront so they'd all piled into his jeep, and left. Since the evening was cool Missily had on a sweater but Mikell was working in shirtsleeves.

"I think," he said, as he searched another bush for aphids. He'd cleaned them last week carefully and painstakingly. Missily would have sprayed them but Mikell seldom used spray if he could help it.

`"You think what?" Missily asked since he hadn't continued.

"Hmmm? Oh, that the stupidest thing your sister ever did was leave Diccon. Are you sure she's quite sane?"

Missily laughed. "No." Then she sobered as she remembered her earlier conversation with Diccon.

"And," he went on, "I still wonder if we shouldn't do something about her bringing that guy with her."

"But why? She's not married to Diccon, hasn't been for what? Over fifteen years."

"She's not married to this other guy either," Mikell said. He was on his knees, now, pulling weeds.

Missily usually helped him though she didn't like weeding, but she was weary. "I know but we can't stop her bringing a friend. Kitten's bringing one, too."

Mikell snorted. "Missily mine, you know that's not the same. If Kitten's ever had an affair—which I doubt, she's so proper—she would be or has been very discreet about it. Besides her friend is a woman."

"I know," Missily sighed, "but what can we do?"

"Tell Suz that she can do what she wants in California but not when she's with our kids. After all she wouldn't force them to take drugs or read dirty books."

"But she's not forcing them to do anything, now. And what do we tell Alexis? The same thing?"

Mikell puffed out his cheeks and then blew out a long breath. "Oh blast! I don't know."

"Mikell!" Missily said more out of surprise than anything else. Mikell seldom used strong language of any sort.

He looked up with a sheepish grin. "I'm sorry." He looked so contrite that she had to laugh. "It's just that the thing has been going around and around in my mind since Rose asked me."

"I still don't think we can expect unbelievers to act like believers. Don't you remember you and I had an argument once about my motive for not having an affair. At the time I said it would be all right if I loved a man even though I knew my folks disapproved. Besides we tried telling Suz something like that once about something else and she just defied us and did what she liked. Sometimes I think it amuses her to try to shock us and the less we say the better."

"Probably so. Missily, do we have any of that slug bait left? I can see they've been busy here."

Missily glared at him but he wasn't looking at her. "I don't know. I'll go see," she said stiffly. He liked his roses better than he did her. He couldn't even take time to talk when she hadn't seen him all day. She took the bait out to him, tossed it on the ground near him. "Here! That's all that's left."

"Thanks," he said without looking up.

She walked away, feeling irritated with him and with herself for feeling that way. Why didn't she just join him? She'd learned years ago that it was the best way to keep up the companionship she loved. He was content just to have her in the vicinity but she wanted his attention. She would love to tell Suz not to bring Shaul Kittim but she didn't want to risk the defiance because Suz did all sorts of outrageous things. It was the only way she ever let on that anything bothered her. At least, *if* that were why she did what she did and as she thought of that what Diccon had said earlier came back to her.

"Mikell," she said, leaning against the trunk of their willow. He didn't answer. She knew he'd heard but when he was preoccupied he often forgot to answer. She sighed and realized tears were running down her face. She sniffed and wiped them away with her hand irritably.

"Did you say something?" Mikell asked finally, putting aside the box that held the slug bait.

"No. Why should I interrupt your communing with your darling roses?" Missily asked with contrived cheerfulness.

Mikell got to his feet, dusting off his trouser knees, laughing at her. "Okay, okay. Point well taken, my little cat. I'll put away my tools, then you tell Daddy what's wrong."

"Aren't you mixing your metaphors?"

"Probably. Who cares as long as you get the message?" he answered genially. "Are you pouting?"

Missily had to laugh. He knew her lower lip went out if he upset her. When he finally ducked under the drooping willow branches her irritation was gone.

"You didn't save it for me," he said.

"What?"

"Your pout," he grinned down at her and she blushed knowing he liked to catch her lower lip in a kiss. He bent to kiss her anyway and it was a very nice one indeed. Afterwards he stood, one hand on the trunk behind her, the other in her hair. "What did you say, Jeddie?"

"I only said Mikell but I wanted to tell you about Diccon." She repeated what had happened that afternoon and added, "He told me he'd always love her. She doesn't deserve it. She never did," she ended fiercely.

He gathered her into his arms. "That's a long time to love a fickle woman. He must have seen something I don't."

"You mean we don't. She always was a brat."

"Oh, come now. You've told me a lot of good times you had together."

"I know. It's just--Diccon's so special. I wish he could find a woman who was good enough for him and good to him."

"So do I but love is strange. One isn't often rational about the one you love."

Missily looked up at him. He was gazing up into the tree. "Like me?"

His eyes came to hers. "Like you, beloved. I didn't think I could live without you and I'd never even been married to you."

"Or kissed me for that matter," she said, laughing at him.

"That, too," he agreed.

"Have I ever told you how *much* I love you?" she asked next then answered her own question. "No, because I don't know how to. But I'm not a very gracious person. I'm even jealous of your roses."

"Don't worry. I have my moments, too."

"What do you mean?"

He smiled. "Diccon, for one."

"Diccon?" and as he said nothing, just continued to smile down at her she asked again, "Diccon?" Then, "You aren't jealous of Diccon. You don't mean that." It was a statement.

"But I am. You like each other tremendously."

"Yes. That's true. We have some kind of affinity, but Mikell," there was distress in her voice, in her dark-lashed gray eyes, "I could never love Diccon. Not the way I do you or want to live with him. Not even if I'd never met you."

"I know. My feelings are as irrational as yours. I just wanted you to know I have those moments, too."

She sighed with relief. "I couldn't stand it if you thought there was anyone in my heart but you."

He turned her with his arm around her shoulder, parted the willow branches and walked slowly across the lawn with her. "Did I tell you that we're going to be able to go see Elephant Rock?"

"Mikell! How?"

"Martin knows a young man from the Quinalt tribe and he told Martin he'd take us down."

"How many?"

"Not all of us, but you're going, young lady. No ifs, ands, or buts, you hear?"

She laughed. "I hear, my lord and master."

"How many are coming?" he asked, stopping to turn off the water he'd had running under the rhododendron bushes.

"Last count I made there will be thirty-five, eleven of them under eighteen years, six more under twenty-two."

She sat down on the porch swing and he joined her, linking his fingers with hers. They watched the sun go down, listening to the sleepy night chirping of the birds, watching a lone gull against the gold and pink clouds, breathing in the fragrance of the evergreens, the roses, some newly cut grass somewhere in the neighborhood, sitting with clasped hands as Mikell gently moved the swing. "Nineteen adults should be able to handle that. Then all the in-law parents are coming?"

"Yes. Isn't it strange how they all come every time we have a reunion? I was talking to Tammy at church Sunday and she said we were crazy to include them in a family reunion. I asked her if she didn't think of Henry's folks as family and she said yes, but they wouldn't be at a reunion of her side of the family."

"But ours isn't a family reunion that way. Both our parents come and all the nieces and nephews on both sides. Did you ask my family?"

"Of course I did, Mikell."

"Hey, simmer down. I guess I was asking if they're coming. Sorry to word it wrong. Your temper's showing lately. Nervous?" He let go her hand and drew her into the circle of his arm.

"I guess so. The thing about Suz and Alexis bothers me and Kitten always makes me nervous plus I feel like a--a faded photograph next to them and Erin."

He rocked her in his arms, laughing gently. "Let me put it this way. They attract attention with all their stylishness and jewelry and excess make-up but you go right on shining beautifully even in an old shirt in the middle of a rain storm with your hair every which way."

And she had to laugh because they'd gotten caught in the rain that way once on a trip to the mountains when they were engaged and he'd told her then she was quite breathtakingly beautiful.

"Is my family coming?" he asked then.

"Same excuse as always. They can't leave their work that long. Oh, except Lorna. That makes thirty-six. She quit coming--or rather she didn't come last time so I forget she'd decided to come." Missily laid her head on Mikell's shoulder.

"I can see why Max and Molly would have problems but you'd think either Perry or Eva could come," he said. "Or take turns."

"I asked them to be honest and say whether it was because my family weren't Christians. Eva looked so blank I believed her when she said she'd never thought of that. That she loves my family. They are going to try to come over during the week, but not all on the same day. "

"I guess I wouldn't be good at farming or whatever. I'd hate to be so tied down that way," Mikell said, relaxing, feeling all the tension leave his muscles.

"You'd have to be rich enough to have a big operation and lots of employees. Then you could leave. A while anyway."

He turned his head and ran his lips across her fragrant hair. "I think one reason I picked the job I have is because I'm not tied to a desk, or a fish pond, or anything else."

"Just organs." Missily couldn't resist that and he gave her a little shake.

"Behave yourself, young woman, and be grateful it *is* just organs."

"I am," she said with a contented sigh. "I can compete with them. I'm a lot softer."

Chapter XVI

Erin and Thor were the first to arrive. They drove up Saturday evening in their big RV. Missily and Mikell were sitting out back after spending the day packing. Diccon and the others had gone to Perry's, phoning back to say Nigel was there, too. Mikell heard the front doorbell and ran lightly through the house to open the door while Missily followed as soon as she heard Erin's voice. They hugged each other tight. Then Thor held out his arms for Missily and Mikell reached over to kiss Erin.

"I always forget what a giant you are," Missily said looking up at Thor who laughed down at her. He wasn't taller than Mikell but he was a big man, muscular, broad, and in good shape physically.

"I always forget what a beauty you are," he answered softly and bent to kiss her.

"Oh! It's good to be here," Erin said in a rather strident voice. "I get so tired on long trips. Your house looks lovely, Missily."

Startled, Missily glanced around. "It does?" she asked, thinking of Erin's beautiful home with its matching decor.

"Yes. Do you have something to drink? I'm dying of thirst."

"Iced tea, lemonade, milk, iced coffee. Oh, and orange juice,"

"Lemonade sounds heavenly."

"Mikell and I were out in back on the porch. Why don't we go out there. Where are the girls?"

"I don't know," Thor answered. "I told them to wait until I found out if there was anyone home but they aren't always that obedient."

Missily went to get the lemonade while Thor and Mikell went to look for the girls. They were on the side lawn playing with the kitten, which no longer tumbled over when she tried to run and was now chasing a ribbon Betsy was trailing.

"These are your girls?" Mikell asked in mock horror. "But I thought you had *little* girls."

"Uncle Mikell!" Betsy shrieked and ran to be caught close. "Where's Candace and Gretchen?"

"Out at Perry's. We'll give them a call. Come on, all of you. Let's see," he stood surveying his other nieces and shook his head. "What a miracle three years have wrought. *Viola!* Two beautiful young ladies."

They laughed and went to him for a hug. Mikell looked from one to the other and then at Thor. "Are you sure that ugly man over there is your father?" he asked as they turned to go into the house.

"Uncle Mikell!" Celeste protested. Both the older girls' hair hung long and shining down their backs. Stephanie had had the ribbon around hers but it was now unbound.

"Erin, I do believe your daughters have outgrown you," Mikell said as they stepped into the house.

"All but Betsy. I feel quite the midget any more," she replied.

Diccon and Nigel brought the other four home in two cars. When they joined the rest in the back yard and greetings were over the adults had the young ones compare heights.

"Like we were little kids," grumbled Celeste.

Sean, who was her age and stood close to her, grinned. "To them we probably are. It's fun. At least you're not taller than I like the last time we got together."

"Was I? I don't remember. Let's see. I was thirteen and you were--oh, of course, you were, too." Celeste was now sitting on the grass cross-legged, propping her head in her hand. "Golly, I'm sleepy."

"An hour later back home, babe," Thor said. He was in a lawn chair, his big frame stretched out in comfort.

"Oh, I forget that. But I don't go to bed at nine."

"You don't usually get up at six like we've been doing either," responded her mother. "Which means we got up at five this morning."

Celeste groaned. "No wonder I feel like I haven't been to bed for a week."

Thor laughed. "She can't burn the candle at both ends, anyway. She's a night bird."

Celeste stuck her tongue out at her father then smiled at him. "Like you."

"I think Myles is tallest," remarked Missily still thinking of them lined up together earlier.

"Not taller than Nigel," Candace said.

"I don't know but Nigel's grown up, I think."

"I doubt it," said Thor, understanding Missily confusing statement. "I remember I grew up and out until I was twenty-five or so."

"And from then on just out," said Erin.

Missily looked at her sister. Her voice had an edge to it and Missily had never heard her criticize or make fun of Thor before. She'd always been so adoring it had been embarrassing. "If he did it doesn't show. Was he fat once?" she asked.

"You know he wasn't," Erin replied tartly. "You've seen him as many years as I have."

"But not as regularly. How do I know he didn't do one of those fabulous 'I-lost-x-pound-in-one-week-so-you-can-too' kind of thing?" She grinned at Thor who grinned back, delighted.

"Daddy's *never* been fat," said Betsy heatedly.

"Well, it's not a sin," interposed Mikell mildly. "There's no law that says we have to be skinny even if Twiggy was."

"Daddy! That was for women, not men," protested Candace.

"I'm bored. Let's go to a movie," Celeste said to Sean.

"How can you be bored already?" Stephanie asked. "We just got here. Besides, I thought you were tired."

"I won't feel tired if I have some action."

"Sitting in a movie?"

"Oh hush! You know what I mean."

Nigel wandered over and squatted down between the two sisters. "I won't believe it if you tell me you're arguing. Not since you just came over one thousand miles to see your cousins. I'd be very injured," he said plaintively.

Stephanie laughed. "I don't think I was arguing."

"I'm bored. Who wants to sit around and talk? Is that all we're going to do all week?" Celeste asked petulantly, pulling at the grass.

Nigel looked at his cousin closely. She'd been a sweet child but she wasn't behaving very well right now. He thought of Trudy, who at the same age fit the sweet sixteen image. "You'll probably be so tired by the end of the week you won't want to move for two."

"Why? What's going on?"

"Your choice: swimming, mountain climbing, hiking, shopping, going to concerts, sailing, scuba diving, a trip to Canada--"

"Really?" She perked up. "Who said so?"

"Aunt Missily and Uncle Mikell have made up a program with all the choices. You've come to the golden land of opportunity, young lady. We offer ocean, mountain, desert, valley, waterfall, rain forest, glacier, river, Puget Sound, the big city--" he paused for breath and Betsy, round-eyed, asked, "Do we get to go to all those places?"

"If we have time. Someone will take you along."

"How about a movie, too?" asked Celeste.

"Count me out," said Sean. "If I go out on Saturday night I have a hard time concentrating Sunday morning."

"Sunday? On what?"

"At church," he answered easily.

"Oh. I forgot that." Her lip curled. "Don't you ever have any fun?"

"All the time. Why?" He was grinning at her, enjoying himself. "Do you think people who go to church don't know how to enjoy themselves?"

"But how can you miss Saturday night? That's when all the neat things happen. We go to movies and then ride up into the mountains and in the summer we swim."

"After dark?"

"Sure. It's more fun. One of the ranches has a big swimming pool. Then we go back to town for something to eat and sit and talk until the restaurant people make us get out. After that we drive around to find excitement. I hardly ever go to bed until early Sunday morning."

"Since when, young lady?"

Celeste looked up to find her father towering over her. "Well, I did that one time," she said, her mouth sullen, "and if you and mother weren't so stick-in-the mud parents I could really have a good time."

"Someday, you'll be glad you had stick-in-the-mud parents--whatever that means. No one's going anywhere tonight. At least," he amended, "none of the Nielsen family is. We're going to get some rest tonight so we'll be fit for all the excitement ahead. Stop acting like a spoiled child, Celeste. All you could talk about coming out were your cousins and now all you're doing is showing off and probably impressing no one." Thor's voice was irritated.

Celeste flushed and sat feeling embarrassed. He seldom reprimanded his girls in public. She felt like crawling into a hole. Life was horrible any more. She and Betsy had chattered most of the trip to Oregon to cover the unnatural silences and snide remarks of their parents.

Much later that night, after nearly everyone else was in bed, Diccon stood under the willow where Missily and Mikell had stood talking the night before. He was leaning against the trunk, his head resting against it. Tomorrow. Tomorrow Suz would come. He asked himself why he continued to come to the reunions to open himself up to more pain. The years hadn't changed his love for Suz and part of him felt the old excitement that she'd always brought. She was so beautiful, such a joy to watch. He'd always loved her low, lazy voice, her attractive pleasant laugh.

They'd never lost touch because of Nigel and Alexis. Suz called him almost from the time she'd left him to tell him about his children and to ask advice, even after she married again. Nigel and Alexis had spent every summer with him, or at least July and August, and they were certainly his children in their love of the outdoors. Both had begged to stay and live with him at the end of every summer and when Alexis was in high school she had written, "When I'm through college, Daddy, I'll come live with you and take care of you. I don't ever want to get married." And now, in December, she would be married. He wondered briefly what Jon Craig was like.

However his thoughts soon went back to Suz. He'd learned to treat her as a friend. They didn't have much to say to one another now that their children were grown. If Suz resented it that both had decided they would rather be with Diccon she never let on. When Nigel had left her as soon as he'd graduated from high school and shown up on Diccon's doorstep and Diccon called Suz, she'd said it was natural for a boy to want to be with his father. She'd been between Owen and Auden then, if he remembered right. Odd, but he'd liked both men. He hadn't understood why Suz was attracted to Auden, though he had Owen, who was something like Thor though more gregarious and somewhat brash. What was the jazz pianist like? He knew that there had been other men in Suz's life because of what his children had said, but he'd never encouraged them to talk about that. Variety. Was that what Suz liked? Why she went from man to man? In his young naiveté he had believed in love forever between him and Suz so had been crushed when she left.

He knew one reason she'd left was because she didn't like living out in the forest. They'd had one of the houses in the compound at the ranger station so there were other women there and planned activities but she loved the city. He'd had no education then so worked at whatever he could get. Now he had a degree and was several steps up the ladder from that young callow man of eighteen she'd first married. Twenty-six years ago. It seemed so strange. So much had happened and while he didn't feel like that young man had, he certainly didn't feel as though twenty-six years had gone by since the day she had become his.

He turned and lay his arm around the tree loosely, resting his cheek against the cool trunk. "Oh God," he whispered, "why can't I get over this longing for her, this love? Why can't I love someone else? Please, help me." Tomorrow. Would she have aged much? Changed much? He hadn't seen a picture of her since the ones Mikell had taken of the last reunion. He didn't take any of her. He'd found out years ago that was too painful. Those he had of her were locked away and he never took them out except for one taken the first year of their marriage.

Diccon parted the branches of the willow and walked out to gaze up at the stars. They used to lay on the blanket in the meadow on the softest place they could find and try to name the constellations and the planets. She thought it would be fun to go to one but he couldn't work up interest. There were too many places he wanted to see here on earth. Then she'd make him name all the places he wanted to see and by then she was cuddled close to him, lying still, the long body warm against his. With an exclamation Diccon tried to bring his mind to the present. It never did to dwell on what was gone and he'd done it over and over through the years to his despair. But his mind refused to obey. They'd been married ten years, his stubborn thoughts went on, still in the past, when he'd gotten up one morning to find a note on the table and most of her clothes gone plus Nigel and Alexis and their things. They'd had another bitter quarrel the night before. She wanted to move to Portland or Seattle. He told her he couldn't work in a city. She'd said he was selfish and he'd asked *who* was selfish? Wasn't he supporting her? She'd laughed and asked him if he called the piddling amount he brought home support? The note had said, and he could remember it as if he'd read it just that morning:

> "Diccon,
> I'm a rat but I can't take it any more. I'm going where things are happening.
> I'm taking the kids with me. I won't leave them for you to have to care for.
> I'll keep in touch.
> *Au revoir,*
> Suz

She must have left in the dead of the night because she knew he seldom woke when she got up to take care of the children then even when they were sick. How selfish he'd been! As if they weren't his children, too, and Suz found it hard to care for a sick child. Nigel had been four, Alexis, two. She must have carried them out to the car asleep since they both slept like he did. He'd never asked her how it happened and what she'd done when the children wanted to know where he was. Those first days he'd gone around like a sleepwalker, hardly aware of his surroundings. When the shock wore off enough the terrible pain began and then he'd gone to Mikell and Missily. At the time he wouldn't have been able to say why; he only knew they seemed a refuge. He'd left his job and they kept him there at their place. He and Mikell were about the same age though he'd always felt younger.

Missily had listened hour after hour as he cursed himself for a fool, for a failure, cried for Suz, begged Missily to get her back. Slowly, though, as the weeks passed and Missily gave unfailingly her love and support and Mikell took long walks with him when he was depressed and didn't talk, a measure of healing began. Through it he had, finally, come to the God of his parents, the God Mikell and Missily served. Left in the care of his grandmother when he was only six, then passed from one relative to another after she'd died, he'd had little stability and had grown up undisciplined and immature. Through the months that followed Suz's desertion, while he stayed with Mikell and Missily, he learned through Mikell's thorough teaching about the sovereign God who was his Savior as well as his Creator. Eventually he'd gone to college and graduated with a degree in biology and entered the Forest Service, working nights to get his MA

In the years since then he'd worked up to a good position. He'd almost married again, once, a nice young woman he'd met, pleasant to be with, but it was a year of the reunion and when he saw Suz again, though she was married to Auden then, he knew it wouldn't be fair to any woman to marry her while he still loved Suz as strongly as he did.

"Dad?"

Diccon turned, "Here," he answered. He and Nigel were spending the night in a tent in the backyard. "How was the show?" Nigel had convinced Thor to let him take Celeste to a movie, promising to have her home before midnight.

"Terrible!" Nigel appeared out of the darkness. "Celeste liked it but she says she's gone on Burt Reynolds or something like that. I can't even understand her sometimes. Don't kids talk English any more?"

Diccon laughed. "Probably as much as you did at her age."

"She's changed. She's not the sweet kid she was three years ago. And I don't think it's just because she'd that much older. She seems brash or something."

"I noticed. She's on the defensive. Stephanie hardly said a word, Betsy was acting like, well, like a spoiled brat and Erin and Thor's girls have never been spoiled." They walked together to their tent. "Maybe I'm just used to Gretchen and Candace and Lynette and Kate and the rest here."

"Dad," Nigel said again out of the darkness when they'd been quiet a while, lying in their sleeping bags, "do you dread seeing Mom?"

There was a silence before Diccon answered casually, "No, I don't think so. Do you?"

"Yes. I'm so tired of her and her men. I try to--I'm not sure I love her at all. Alexis think I'm silly. No. She thinks I'm self-righteous. I don't think I am, it's just--" his voice trailed off.

"Love's strange," Diccon answered in that quiet way he had that was so comforting. "One can hate and love someone at the same time and not be sure which it is. I love your mother, Nigel. I guess I always will. I don't like what she does but I know what a beautiful person she is. I was remembering just before you came how we used to lie together under the stars and identify them and try to count them. That's hopeless," Diccon laughed, "and she always ended with the giggles. Someday, son, you'll know what it is to love someone and you'll understand what I mean about your mother. I hate what she's doing to herself." His voice had taken on a rough quality.

"I already know," Nigel's voice was muffled. "Dad, I've loved Lorna for years but she thinks of me as a kid."

"You are younger, aren't you?"

"Four years. But what's four years? I feel older then she." Nigel's voice was now a little belligerent.

Diccon smiled in the dark. How young he sounded? "There is one consolation. I think she still loves horses better than any person. Don't give up hope. She told me she didn't remember telling you the colt was sired by Long Jim. Then she wanted to know where you were yesterday, when she came over to help Missily."

"She told me--oh, it doesn't matter. We'd better get some shut eye or I'll fall asleep in church tomorrow," Nigel said but felt strangely comforted. She had asked about him.

Chapter XVII

The pew in church was full the next morning where Mikell and his family usually sat; though they weren't often all six together since Perry's two girls and Eva's son and daughter attended the same church with their parents and the cousins took turns sitting together. This Sunday, however, all six were there with Nigel, Diccon, Betsy, who'd decided to come with Candace, and Stephanie who'd asked Gretchen if she could come with her. The girls had switched beds so that the two younger girls were in the RV with Erin and Stephanie slept in Candace's bed. Celeste stayed in the RV, also.

She was sleeping in, as were Erin and Thor. She'd been excited about going to the movie with Nigel alone. He was so good-looking and she pretended he was her date, making eyes at him and clinging to his arm. They'd stopped for a coke afterwards at a drive-in and argued about the movie. Nigel thought it terrible, not only the acting and production but the story. Celeste, not accustomed to critiquing what she watched, defended it stoutly though she wasn't sure whether she liked it or not.

When she woke, just before noon, both her parents were gone so she dressed in shorts and a T-shirt and went to find them. They were eating breakfast and she found an apple and a glass of milk and joined them.

"Is that all you're eating?" Thor asked breaking the silence that had been there since he and Erin had sat down.

"It's plenty," she answered.

"Did you enjoy the movie?" he asked next.

"Yes. At least I think I did. Nigel and I stopped for a coke. He'd ruin all movies for me if he pulls them apart like he did that one. He thought the production was poor, the acting terrible and the story immoral without any redeeming--redeeming--" she came to a halt.

"Features?" her father supplied.

"Something like that."

"And you don't agree?"

"I don't know. I just go for fun. I don't pay that much attention to all that. I don't see how he enjoys anything if he always picks it apart."

"Maybe he only does that to films he doesn't like," Thor suggested.

"No," Celeste shook her head, her uncombed hair falling over her forehead so she thrust it back. "He says just watching a film mindlessly isn't sensible. That we should be just as, as particular—he didn't use that word but it's what he meant—what we put in our minds as we should our mouths and stomachs. I asked him if he didn't ever do anything just for fun and he told me that it was fun to—to—well to do what he does with movies. He says he'd be bored otherwise."

"Did you ask him if he ever ate for fun?" Thor asked, enjoying the play of emotions on his daughter's face. She had a tendency to act empty-headed though she had a good mind if she wanted to use it.

"Yes and he said, 'Sure, I just don't eat garbage for fun'."

Thor laughed. Erin glared at him. "I don't see anything funny in that and I don't appreciate his implying my daughter watches trashy movies," she said.

"Oh come on, Erin," Thor protested.

"I think it was funny. We had a good time; he made me think," said Celeste, defensive of Nigel.

"I wish you'd go brush your hair. You know better than to come to the breakfast table that way," Erin said.

"Yes ma'am!" Celeste said insolently and rose. "I can tell when I'm not wanted. I'll take a shower. I was going to anyway after I ate. That's why I didn't comb my hair." She ran out of the house.

"Erin, what was all that? I was enjoying her. Or was that the problem? Do you intend to make the whole damn trip miserable? You've managed to mess it up so far. Missily and Mikell must wonder what's happened to our daughters. Celeste acting like a brat, Betsy like she's been spoiled and Stephanie hardly saying a word. What *is* wrong with you any way?"

Erin gazed out the window. She'd hoped the trip would bring them closer but Thor had been so distant that she'd begun to worry that he was just waiting until after the reunion to tell her he wanted a divorce. She'd seen him more on the trip than she had the two or three months before and she knew that she was just as much in love with him as she'd always been. He hadn't touched her or kissed her for months. She hunched miserably in her chair and didn't answer. What would she say if she did?

Thor got out of his chair with a snort of irritation and left the room to sit down in the living room with the paper. He would definitely move out after the reunion. He supposed she had some man waiting for her back in Santa Fe.

When everyone came back from church, cheerful and noisy, Celeste was blow drying her hair, Thor was still reading the paper and Erin was out wandering around the yard. Nigel and the girls had been invited to Perry's for dinner along with Myles and Sean and they were changing clothes. Missily went in search of Erin and found her under the willow.

She looked up as Missily parted the branches. She'd been crying but now she said, "I can't believe how tall everything is out here. You'd think I'd remember but I always forget until we get back in Washington. We have some pretty big willows but this is wonderful."

"I love it." Missily went to lean against the trunk. "I like to sit in it and read. Do you feel more rested?"

"Oh, so, so. I didn't sleep too well. What is that beautiful bush in the corner over there? I can't remember. You've probably told me before."

"It's a variegated weigelia. Birds love it, particularly the humming birds. See, there are two of them now."

149

Erin peeked through the willow branches to where two tiny birds hovered at the flowers. "What kind are they?"

"I'm not sure. I think one's a ruby-throated but the other one I can't get close enough to identify."

"Remember how mother used to try to get us to make lists of all the birds we saw?"

"Yes. I still do it. Or I guess I should say I do it now. Mikell knows the birds so well and I've been trying to learn them. He can see them in flight and tell what kind it is. I can't. He doesn't know that hummingbird, though. I've looked in books but I can't tell."

"I never cared," Erin said turning back from watching the humming birds. "I hated to make lists of them but I love humming birds. We have a feeder."

"We used to but Mikell wanted to plant things to attract them instead. It's not always as easy to see them that way. The feeder was right outside the dining room window so I could watch them."

"Why didn't you keep it?" Erin asked studying her sister. She was looking particularly attractive in her flowered summer dress she'd worn to church. "Do you do everything Mikell wants?"

Missily looked around at Erin. "No." Then she laughed. "But he's pretty persuasive when he gets an idea and he didn't like giving the birds sugar water. What do you want for dinner?" she asked, not willing to get started on what Erin called her religious submission. She could never make her sister understand that she liked to do what Mikell wanted or that she didn't always follow his wishes. "I've got to get something started if we want to go to get Kitten at the airport with Mikell at four."

"I just ate breakfast and so did Thor so don't worry about us."

"Then I think I'll hunt up some leftovers and we can have a meal later. I wonder what Kitten's friend will be like."

"What did you say her name was?"

"Imogen English."

"Imogene?"

"No, Imogen. I asked Kitten the same thing when she called me. Imogene is a variation."

"Oh, there you are, Mother." Gretchen ran to them. "I just wanted to say 'bye. We'll be at church tonight."

"Have a good time. Don't forget to help Aunt Jean."

"I won't. 'Bye, Aunt Erin."

The others waved from the cars; Myles and Nigel were each taking their own. "We'll have to drive out later so you can see Eva," Missily said as they stood together waving to the young people.

"I told her we'd be out. We still write all the time."

"She told me you did. Sometimes I hear more news about you from her than I do from you."

Erin glanced at Missily but she was smiling as she held the door open. "Isn't it funny how we hit it off? I mean since she's so---"

"So what?" Missily asked because Erin had broken off abruptly.

150

"Well, religious. I don't mean she stuffs it down my throat," Erin added hastily, "but she does believe--what she believes--quite strongly."

"I'm glad you write. I was joking with you, Erin. Mikell," she said as they entered the living room where the two men sat talking, "I'm just going to fix a lunch. We'll have dinner after Kitten gets here."

"Fine," he answered. "Want some help?"

"No. Erin and I can talk while I fix some sandwiches."

"Don't worry about dinner," said Thor. "I'll take you out tonight."

"No you won't," Missily protested. "I've fixed Vichyssoise and we have some smoked salmon. You can take us out later in the week."

"You angel!" Erin gave her a big hug. "I haven't had Vichyssoise since you fixed it last time we were together. Mine never tastes as good as yours."

Missily laughed and went into the kitchen. She heard Thor say, "When do you fix anything any more?" in a sarcastic voice. Then quickly he added, "Sorry. Since she started working she doesn't do much cooking, but I guess it doesn't hurt the girls to learn."

Missily had turned back and saw that Erin was staring at Thor, her face white. The night before, after Erin and Thor had gone out to the RV Missily had said to Mikell, "There's something wrong between those two. They hardly look at each other."

"I noticed," he answered, "and the girls are unhappy." He sighed. "I was hoping their marriage would last. Well, maybe I'm imagining things. Maybe they're just tired."

Missily had shaken her head slowly, removing her shoes and setting them carefully side by side. "No. They aren't acting normal and Stephanie watches both of them."

"It's so fragile," Mikell had answered "Marriage breaks faster than a glass plate. It's frightening. Look at Hub and Marilyn. I thought they were as close as we are and here he had another woman."

Missily had crossed the room to put her arms around his neck. "Let's keep working at ours and praying. I don't think I could live if I lost you."

Now Erin, her voice strident, said, "How do you know? You're never home."

"I know you work."

"Three or four nights a week. I'm home the rest of the time and it was *your* idea that I get a job."

"Not at night. But let's not discuss it now, Erin. Mikell you were going to show me the organ you're working on."

"Yes, but that'll wait," Mikell answered quietly. "For one thing I'd like my sandwich and for another," he added as Missily went to the refrigerator to get the meat loaf she'd save for his sandwiches, "Erin, come sit down." And as Erin sank into the chair Missily usually occupied, Mikell perched on the organ bench. "Look, you two, something's wrong. It sticks out all over all of you. I may be butting in where I've no business but you've had a good marriage for what? Sixteen years?"

"Seventeen," supplied Erin.

"That's a good many years to waste. And the girls are unhappy."

"Ask Erin. She knows what's wrong. I'm sure I don't," said Thor as if bored. He was sitting on the couch with both arms stretched across the back.

"*I* know? How could I know? Mikell, for over three months we've hardly seen him unless one of the girls goes to the office. He leaves early in the morning and gets home after we're asleep. I have hardly laid eyes on him at all. Stephanie fell and cracked her head open and do you suppose I could even find him to tell him? He didn't even come home that night."

"I did so," said Thor and when Erin stared at him, he said, "I suppose it was that night any way," though he knew it was. "You were--Celeste came--" suddenly he stopped, then he blustered, "This is none of your damn business, Mikell. I can take care of my affairs myself."

Missily brought Mikell's sandwich in, put it beside him on a tray with hers and sat down beside him.

"You're not doing a very good job. Please, I want to talk about it," Erin said, the tears threatening to overflow.

"We'll go out back and you can fell free to talk. The kids are gone for the day." Mikell rose but Erin was on her feet.

"No! Don't go. He won't talk if you do. I mean, when I say I've hardly seen him, I saw him once when I made myself stay awake in the dark until he came home so he wouldn't see a light under my door. And once in La Casa where I went to get a drink. He and all the guys he grew up with and some--some floozies."

Thor groaned. So she had seen him.

"That time I threw my drink in one of his friend's face when he tried to proposition me."

"Who?" Thor's question was sharp.

"How would I know? The only one of those--those men you used to run around with I remember a name for is Steele Jason. I called him the night Stephanie fell. He hung up on me."

"Steele? I haven't seen him in years. Why did you call him? I haven't seen him in years," Thor repeated in irritation.

"Because I was trying to find you. I was afraid. I didn't know how badly Stephanie was hurt and I knew you were going out with your old friends."

"How did you know that?" Thor, sitting forward now, seemed to have forgotten Mikell and Missily.

"I stopped at La Casa after I started working and you were there. I--I went back several times and sat and watched you, wondering what you would say if I went up to your table."

"But Erin," Thor's knuckles were white as he gripped his hands together, "Why didn't you? Why were you--I don't understand--Celeste said you were out with some guy?"

"What? Why would she say that?"

"You were never home even in the nights you didn't work."

"That's not true. At least not after Stephanie's fall. I've been home every night except when I have to work. Before that I--I tried to find out where you were."

152

Thor stared at her. "Where did you think I was?"

"I didn't know. But--but I was afraid you were with Faith."

"With Faith?" He echoed as if he'd never heard of her.

"Yes."

"Why would I be with that--" he glanced at Missily and changed what he was going to say. "Erin, are you out of your mind?"

"But you're always telling me how wonderful she is and you went to the ranch together." Erin sank back into the chair because her legs were shaking and threatening to give out.

"Ranch? What ranch?"

"I don't know. Celeste told me you and Faith were going to go that Saturday she came to the office to tell you about Stephanie and then you decided to go the next Monday because Faith couldn't go Sunday."

"Oh. That's that fancy dude ranch I told you about. Faith and I did an article on it."

"See. That's what I mean. She and you have a lot in common and you've been--been distant since she came."

"*I've* been distant? Look, Erin, I don't know when it started but I do know that all of a sudden you became a nag. I swore I'd never marry or live with a woman like that after I saw what it did to my father. I asked you that night I walked out if I never did anything right any more and you told me it was a stupid question, but everything I did you criticized."

"And you told me that I was a social butterfly and liked to gossip and paint my nails," and now Erin was crying in earnest, "and that I didn't care about you and the girls any more. Then you told me that Faith at least uses her mind. But I got a job and it didn't make any difference. You just gave me a sarcastic reply about staying with my buddies. What was I supposed to do? You know I'd never make a teacher and I thought working at Etta's was one thing I could do. You don't care. You only said that to throw me off the track."

"Throw you off the track?" Thor repeated, frowning at Erin but she hardly heard him.

"I know I'm not brilliant and--and decorative like Faith. I don't know anything about magazines. I can hardly write a decent letter but that didn't bother you until she came" she sobbed.

"Damn it, woman! Will you shut up a minute and listen. I don't *want* you to be like Faith. I just want my Erin back again."

"If that's true why didn't you tell me what was wrong and why were you going out with that other woman?"

Thor stood up and began to pace the floor. Mikell and Missily looked at each other and Missily gave a little shrug. She didn't know whether to sneak out or stay. Mikell said, "You two must be sisters."

Arrested, Erin lifted a tear blotched face. "What do you mean?"

Missily went to get a box of tissue to hand to Erin while Mikell explained, "You're worried because this Faith talks 'journalese' while Missily worries because the organists and I have organs in common."

"Missily?" Erin stared at her sister.

"Yes," Missily answered. "I was okay until I started answering the phone for Mikell and found out so many of the callers were women. He brightened up so when he had a call and seemed so depressed around here that I thought he was--was discouraged with me and I was, frankly, jealous and panicky. I thought I was losing him. What was wrong was so far from what I thought I hope it taught me a lesson not to jump to conclusions."

"There," said Thor stopping in his tracks. "Maybe Erin can learn one, too."

"But Mikell wasn't gone all the time, was he?"

"It seemed like it, but no. In fact, I see more of him now that he's on his own then ever did when he was working with Kurt." She crossed the room to sit beside Mikell again, slipping her arm in his.

"Thor, why are you gone all time? He is," she added to Missily and Mikell. "I have seen more of him on this trip than I have in months and so have the girls. The four of us do everything without him, even eat our meals. I have to make all the decisions, take care of all the emergencies. The only thing he does is put a check in the bank and sleep in his bed for a few hours so I have to make it the next day. I've quit cooking his favorite meals; he's never home to eat them. I do his washing even though I never see him, just his dirty clothes. We never spend our Saturdays together like we used to and I know he spends them with Faith because the girls go down to the office and they are the only ones there. Now, you explain that." she said turning back to Thor. "All the way out here I've been terrified to go home because I believe you are going to leave and Faith is waiting."

Thor took two long strides to Erin, lifted her out of the chair and gave her a hard shake. "Damn it all, will you listen to me? Don't you know what kind of woman Faith is? What her relationship to that artist friend of hers is?"

Erin stared at him, her once carefully coifed hair tumbled around her shoulders. She looked very beautiful and fragile, Missily thought, next to her big husband. "What--what do you mean?"

"Erin, you've been in their house; you've seen them together. You're not stupid."

"But I've only been there a couple of times for a party. I don't understand."

"That woman is a lesbian."

"Faith?"

"Faith. You must have seen the kind of art work she has on her walls and the books on her shelves."

There was a long silence so that Missily became aware of the outdoor noises: dogs barking, the traffic on the street in front of the house, sirens wailing in the distance, the air traffic overhead, children yelling down the street.

"Why did you hire her?" Erin asked finally.

"Because she's a darn good journalist."

"But did you know at first she is what she is?"

"Yes, she told me."

154

"And you hired her anyway? Thor you're hurting me," she complained because he was still gripping her arms.

His hold loosened though he didn't let go of her. Right now he never wanted to let go of her ever again. It had been so long--

"Thor?"

"I hired her for her work. What she does in her private life has nothing to do with me. It's putrid but as long as she keeps it at home she works for me. Erin, can't you understand? I don't want *any* other woman. I only want my treasure back again."

Missily felt a lump in her throat and her eyes stung with tears as she remembered what Mikell had said to her, the words she had written down. Mikell put his arm around her as though he, too, remembered.

"Thor," Erin whispered and the transformation in her face was visible to all. Gone was the discontent, the unhappiness. Back again was that adoration almost embarrassing to those watching.

"Come on, woman. Let's go talk this out," Thor pulled her toward the door.

"Catch," called Mikell, tossing the keys of his car to Thor who caught them, grinned, and ushered Erin out.

Mikell and Missily looked at each other, fell into each other's arms, laughing and crying. At least Missily was crying. Then as Mikell got a tissue to dry her face she gasped suddenly.

"Now what?" he asked mildly.

"The car. How are we going to go get Kitten and Imogen?"

Mikell put a hand to his head. "Oh no! We can't use the van for that. Oh well," he relaxed. "If they don't get back in time I'll call Myles and have him go to the airport."

Chapter XVIII

So it was Myles with Celeste, Betsy, and Candace who stood waiting at Seatac for Kitten's plane to land.

"Do you remember that awful man she brought once?" Celeste asked Myles as they stood watching the planes taxi in and take off.

"Tad? Oh yes. He was a snob and a prude if I ever saw one. Wonder what she saw in him?"

"But Aunt Vicky's a snob and a prude, too," Celeste protested.

"A snob, yes. I don't think she'd a prude, though. And maybe prig would suit him better. Aunt Vicky's too modern to be a prude."

"Why didn't Aunt Missily and Uncle Mikell come get her?" Celeste asked next. "I never know what to say to her."

Myles turned to look at his cousin. "You didn't have to come."

"I know but I do know what to say to you and I've hardly seen you. You should have gone to the movie last night."

He grinned, "You mean you weren't satisfied with your handsome escort."

"He's no more handsome than you are. Maybe not even as much," She said giving him a sidelong look.

"I would have done just what Nigel did. That's the only fun in seeing a bad movie--picking it apart. Anyway, to answer your question. Dad gave the keys to his car to Uncle Thor and they aren't back yet. Dad said he didn't think the van was quite the thing to come to get Aunt Vicky and her friend."

"Who's not back? From where?"

"Your mom and dad. They went for a ride together."

Celeste, who had been gazing out the window, looked around quickly. "Mom and Dad did?"

"Yes."

"Oh," she said so strangely that Myles asked. "Why? Is there any reason they shouldn't?"

"No. No, of course not. It's just that--"

"There it is! It's coming in," yelled Betsy.

"Sh-h-h! " Candace glared at her cousin. "You don't have to scream it."

"I didn't," protested Betsy angrily, giving her bright hair a toss.

"Girls. Girls." Myles stepped between them. "It's not as if you see each other every day like sisters. Candace, don't be such a grouch." He gave each of them a hug.

"Betsy, Candace is right. No one's deaf," Celeste said, shaken by the news that her parents had gone for a drive together. What could it mean? They'd fought all the way to Washington when they spoke to each other at all. She began to feel very ill and wanted to cry. She wished Myles would

156

put his arm around her like he was doing with the others. What would she and Stephanie and Betsy do if their parents got a divorce. Didn't they love them any more?

"Celeste, have you left us?" It was Myles, by her side again, while the two younger girls went back to the window.

"No."

"What is it? You don't look--are you sick?"

She shook her head. He reached for her hand. It was icy.

"I'll talk to Aunt Vicky. Don't worry, love. She'll probably do the talking anyway."

"It--it's not that. Myles, did Uncle Mikell say why Mom and Dad went for a ride."

"No. Just said they had the car and weren't back. Would I pick up Aunt Vicky and her friend? Is something wrong?"

She managed a smile. "No. I just wondered. Dad said yesterday he didn't want to drive another mile."

Myles studied her but she wouldn't meet his eyes. She was biting her lip. He started to ask another question when Candace said, "Here they come," as the passengers began to file in from the plane. "They," Celeste and Myles discovered, meant the people, not Aunt Vicky and Imogen but it wasn't long before they saw their Aunt.

"She doesn't look any different than last time," said Celeste.

"It hasn't been that long," said Myles.

"I bet she doesn't know us."

"Well, maybe not, but we were children then. Adults don't change that much in three years, do they?"

"I guess not."

He'd still had her hand and now gave it a squeeze before he let it go. "Betsy, do you know which one is Aunt Vicky?" he asked.

Betsy shook her head. "I can't remember what she looks like."

"She's right there," Candace pointed. "Behind that man with all the white hair. She looks just like her pictures."

Myles captured her hand. "Don't point, chicken. Let's go," he said and led the way to meet their Aunt. She would have walked right past them if Myles hadn't stepped up and said, "Aunt Vicky, over here."

She turned and looked around. A big handbag slung over her shoulder, she was dressed in a dark suit that looked as though she had just put it on. When her eyes focused on him she went slowly forward, "Myles?"

He smiled. "Yes. Mom and Dad don't have their car so Dad asked me to come get you." He reached out to take her in his arms for a hug. She allowed him to hug her rather than to give him one, then stepped back.

"You look very much like your mother," she remarked.

"So they tell me," he said with that easy, relaxed way he had.

"Imogen, this is one of my nephews, Myles. Missily's oldest son. Myles, my friend Imogen English."

Myles took the hand held out to him. He hadn't noticed the tall, thin woman behind their Aunt. "I'm glad to meet you. Welcome to Washington."

157

He turned around and drew Celeste forward. "This is my cousin, Celeste Nielsen and her sister Betsy, and this one is my youngest sister, Candace."

Kitten looked at the girls. She hadn't recognized them at all. "Where's Stephanie?" she asked, remembering that Auden had asked about her.

"She's at Uncle Perry's. We all were there for dinner. I mean the young set. Mom and Dad and Uncle Thor and Aunt Erin didn't come along. In fact, they weren't invited. If you'll give me your baggage checks, I'll go get your things."

Kitten handed the tickets to Myles and turned to the girls. "You have certainly grown since I last saw you. I didn't know you at all."

Betsy and Candace were standing together giggling over something Candace had said and now quickly sobered. "You look just like your picture," Candace said.

"I recognized you," said Celeste. "You don't look any different but it's only been three years and like Myles said, adults don't change as much as children."

"That's true. Have you been in Seattle long?"

"We got here yesterday. We drove in our RV and it's a long way," answered Celeste and thought, "I sound so stupid."

Myles came back to get them and after some discussion, Betsy and Kitten sat in front with Myles and Celeste and Candace in back with Imogen. Myles had his Uncle Perry's station wagon and the younger girls had wanted to sit in the back of the wagon but Myles said no.

"Uncle Perry let's us," Candace protested.

"I'm not Uncle Perry. You know the family rules, Candace. There aren't any seat belts back there."

It was Imogen who said Victoria should sit in front. She'd sit back with the girls and Betsy had slid into the front seat next to Myles. As he drove through the Sunday traffic Celeste politely answered Imogen's questions about her age and what grade she would be in next fall while Candace volunteered the information about herself. At the beginning of the ride they listened to Myles and Kitten who seemed to have no problems talking with each other.

Imogen, however, sitting between the two girls in the back was turning her head from side to side, craning her neck to see out the back. Celeste asked finally, "Would you like to trade seats? You could see better then."

"Oh, that would be lovely," Imogen answered. "It's so beautiful out here. We saw the mountains from the plane. I'd never seen any so high or big before."

You flew over the Rocky Mountains, didn't you?"

"Yes but we were so high I couldn't really see them and it was too smoggy in Denver, Colorado."

Celeste started to say she knew where Denver was when she remembered their guest might not be as familiar with the West as she was and wouldn't know perhaps that one didn't have to add Colorado. "Did you grow up back East?" she asked instead.

"Yes. I've never been West of the Mississippi before."

"I hope you enjoy it out here."

"Oh, I'm sure I will. Victoria is such a wonderful person she must have a wonderful family. I didn't realize there would be so many. She isn't the kind to talk about her family like some people I know. It's so boring, don't you think, when you don't know people, to hear about all the relatives."

It was a statement more than a question but Celeste answered, "I guess so," a little uncertainly. She had been about to ask Imogen about her family.

When Myles drove up at Perry's after leaving Kitten and Imogen at his folks' place, they were surrounded as soon as they got out of the car.

"What's she like?" Lynette demanded.

"Tell us, tell us," echoed Kate excitedly.

"Nothing," said Candace and she and Betsy giggled.

"What do you mean, nothing?" Kate demanded.

"Just that. She's a nothing."

"Candace!" Celeste said. "She is a nice person. She talked to me all the way. She liked the mountains."

"But she hasn't got any color," Candace said.

"That's true," agreed Betsy and added, "Her hair is real light, so are her eyes and her skin and she doesn't look like she has any eyebrows."

Myles thought, that's it. He hadn't even seen her at first. Aloud he said, "She is very fair next to Aunt Vicky."

"And she didn't have on any make-up. Plus she had on a weird dress. She's weird," pronounced Candace.

"She is not. She's nice and friendly," said Celeste. They were standing in the driveway leaning against the station wagon. Betsy, Kate and Lynette were sitting on top looking down at the others. They, with Candace, would be the youngest at the reunion. Lynette was Candace's age while Betsy and Kate were both twelve. When Missily and Mikell had written all their young people down according to age Mikell had groaned.

"Four youngest, all girls. I hope I don't have to sleep anywhere near them."

Missily had wrinkled her nose at him and grinned. He would be the first to spoil them. He was already clay in the hands of his nieces and adored them all.

Perry came out of the house. "Off the car, girls. You know better than to sit there. Come on around back. Jean put out some snacks."

Jean, who had a figure men dream about and two dancing dimples in an otherwise plain face, had already fed them on barbecued beef and potato salad along with fresh homemade bread and garden vegetables. Now her own clam dip, made from the big geoduck clams she and Perry liked to dig from the Hood Canal beach when the tide was out, was on the big picnic table with chips as well as fresh vegetables, more of the bread and a fruit punch made from the blackberries she and her daughters had picked the year before.

Lorna was there now, sitting talking to Eva and Jean. She waved as they came around the house. Nigel was sitting on the grass talking to the men--Max and Molly had come over after dinner with their family--but he was watching Lorna who had, so far, ignored him. He had counted them all, before Max came, and also before Lorna had driven up. Now with them

159

added there were twenty-two. In fact, all but Alexis was there of the younger crowd. She and Jon were supposed to be driving in sometime later in the evening as were Suz and Shaul. Early in the morning some of them would go ahead to Fort Worden, particularly those who were camping. Thor and Erin had had Mikell reserve a place for their RV as had Thor's parents who would arrive from New Mexico on Monday, and Graham's parents who lived in Olympia and traveled regularly with their Air Stream trailer. Most of the younger set would be camping in tents as would Diccon and Nigel, but Missily and Mikell had decided to stay in the officer's quarters with Suz and Shaul, Rose and Graham and Allan and Anna Metlow. Mikell's parents would drive over during the week even though they wouldn't spent the whole week there. But Granny Ellen intended to. She informed her daughter she refused to be cheated out of a stay in an officer's house. Her husband had been in the army but hadn't been an officer and it pleased her to think she would be privileged to eat and sleep in the houses officers had used even if they weren't where she and her husband had been stationed. Granny Ellen was eighty-seven years old so to Gretchen and Sean, who were particularly fascinated by her stories, World War I seemed like ancient history.

Usually the younger set took turns staying in the RV's with the Nielsen's and also with Graham's parents in their Air Stream though they didn't have as much room. From the beginning of the reunions years before, when children started making their appearance, they were taken into the activities with the adults and though they had times when they were with those their age both the older people and the young ones loved each other and were comfortable together.

"I just got a call from Missily," Perry now said to those at his place. "Both the older Nielsen's and Graham's folks are already at Fort Worden. We decided if any of you want to go on over today and set up camp you may."

"Let's," said Celeste. "Let's go over this afternoon." She had brightened considerably since they'd come to Perry's place though, since Myles had told her about her folks going for a drive, she'd been nervous.

"Not 'til after church," said Myles. "Remember?"

"Can't you miss once?" she asked in irritation

"Yep. I can miss it any time I want. I just don't want."

"I thought terrible things happened to you if you didn't go," said Betsy who, with Kate, was dressing Kate's Barbie dolls.

"You did? What kind of things?" Myles wanted to know.

"Oh, I don't know. I mean doesn't the priest make you say a lot of prayers?"

"That's the Roman Catholic Church, dummy," said Celeste. "They're Protestants."

"We don't have priests," volunteered Kate. "We have pastors who preach. We don't have Mass."

"What's Mass?" inquired Betsy.

"It's awful. They do terrible things," Kate told her confidingly.

But Myles, who overheard the question and answer said, "Kate, Mass is their name for what we call communion. They believe differently in what

160

happens and they don't do it the same way we do but they do serve wine and bread like we do. And it's about Jesus' death."

"It is? But I thought they really ate Jesus and drank His blood."

"First, how could they do that? Who told you that?"

"Kent. He was telling me a lot of things about them."

"How does Kent know?" Myles asked. Kent was Kate's brother and two years her senior.

"He reads stuff."

"Hmm-m-m. I'll have to have him show me some of that. It's not completely false but you have to understand what they believe happens. They don't carve up a body and catch the blood. They use bread and wine."

"Oh!" Kate sighed regretfully. "Patty--you know--the girl who lives next door?" (next door being a half a mile down the road.) "She goes to the Catholic Church and she got con-con--something so she can go to Mass now. I thought she was eating somebody. I didn't know whom. But they do believe Jesus is still on the cross. They don't believe in the resurrection."

"Kent again?"

Kate nodded. She was small for her age and had a head of short, curly, dark hair.

"They believe in the resurrection, Kate."

"But they have Jesus on the cross still."

"So do the Lutherans. That's a reminder of what He did. It's not because they don't believe He is alive today. They believe that the wine and bread turn into the body and blood of Christ at Mass. But, Kate, Roman Catholics--many of them--believe in the virgin birth, Jesus death, resurrection and ascension like we do. They just add a lot of other things to that. Like all denominations do. Whenever we add anything to Scripture as truth or are in error in our interpretation of Scripture than we are wrong whether we are Roman Catholic or Protestant. Please don't misunderstand me. The Roman Catholics are wrong in many areas and I would never encourage anyone to go to their services. I just don't want you to get false ideas about where they are wrong." Myles was now stretched out on his stomach, a long stem of grass between his teeth, watching the two girls dress their dolls. "Where in the world do you get all those clothes?"

"Make them. Lynette and I do," Kate answered. "Mother and Aunt Eva give us scraps of material to use. Why aren't we Catholic if they're okay? They were here first. Patty told me that. She said the Protestant Church left the Catholic Church."

"Well-l-l, not exactly. They were kicked out is more like what happened. Luther and Calvin didn't intend to start new denominations, just reform the Church from within. Kate, you know the word catholic means universal, don't you?"

"Yes. When we say the Apostles' Creed it does."

"That's why I usually say Roman Catholic to identify the denomination and they are just one among many even if they want to think they're the true church. They weren't here first. None of the denominations were. From the beginning there has always been only one true Church even though there are differences among the people." Myles sat up, idly picking up one of the

161

dolls, turning it around to look at the slack outfit it was wearing. "Did you make this?"

Kate glanced up. "Lynette did. But Patty told me there weren't denominations until the Protestants broke up the Church."

"What's she trying to do? Convert you? Have you talked this over with your parents?" He laid the doll down again and began to pick grass and stack it carefully.

"No. I forgot until Betsy said that about terrible things happening if we don't go to church."

"How'm I supposed to know?" Betsy protested. "We don't go to church."

"You could," Kate said.

"I don't want to. It's boring."

"Betsy, Kate doesn't know about the Roman Catholic beliefs. None of us know about things we've never learned. That's why it's good to ask questions and not jump to conclusions." Myles flicked his grass stack and rose to his feet. "Who's for a horseback ride? I'm tired of sitting."

Before anyone answered they heard a shout from the front and Myles said, "I'll go see," to Perry and ran easily around the house.

"He gets taller and more good-looking every year," Eva said.

"I know," answered Celeste, who had just refilled her plate with snacks. "Too bad we're cousins. He is better looking than all the guys back home." Then she heard Stephanie catch her breath and glanced over at her sister who was staring across the yard with a strange expression on her face. Celeste turned. Myles was coming back laughing; with him were Thor and Erin, hand in hand, something the girls hadn't seen in months.

Eva got up to greet Erin and Perry held out his hand to Thor. "Welcome. Come get something to eat before it's all gone."

In the confusion Stephanie and Celeste both heard Dundas, Eva's husband, say, "Don't you two ever fight? You always look like newlyweds," and the sisters looked at each other.

"Occasionally," Thor said, "but that puts spice into life." He laughed down at Erin who made a moue at him and then gave him one of her adoring looks.

"What happened to them?" Celeste whispered to Stephanie. "I thought they went off to fight."

"So did I," Stephanie whispered back.

Celeste turned her back on the crowd to wipe a tear away. "I was afraid they were going to get a divorce when we went back home."

"So was I." gulped Stephanie, and then they both looked at each other and giggled.

Impulsively, Celeste reached out and hugged Stephanie. "Gosh! It's nice to feel safe again."

Chapter XIX

Missily turned from the phone. "It sounds as if all the young people are there except for Jon and Alexis. Jean fixed a barbecue for dinner and now they're snacking."

"It's a good thing there will be plenty of activities. Otherwise they'd all go home round as a butter ball," Mikell said.

"Oh! What will we be doing?" Imogen wanted to know. She and Kitten were sitting at the dining table talking with Missily while she fixed the salad for dinner. Mikell lounged against the doorjamb watching them.

"You have a grand choice," he answered. "Swimming, hiking, climbing, fishing, playing games, concerts. Don't ask me what kind, Victoria," he added as Kitten looked up. "Missily has the brochure. Both Port Townsend and Fort Worden have things going on. And, of course, you can always come back to Seattle."

"Thank goodness we'll be near civilization this time," Kitten said. She had one elegant leg crossed over the other, sitting with a cup of coffee at her fingertips. Missily had gotten down her china cups because she knew Kitten disliked mugs.

Mikell watched his sister-in-law in amusement. She had never approved of him for Missily, he knew, but since it didn't bother Missily it didn't bother him. She did put on airs and he glanced at Missily who gave Kitten an irritated look before she went back to slicing cucumbers. "We weren't *that* far away last reunion," she said to her sister.

"Several hundred miles," Kitten responded.

"Come now, Vicky, it wasn't that far," Mikell said mildly. "Santa Fe is quite civilized, the home of well-know people in the arts. I don't think the ranch is fifty miles from there and Albuquerque is sixty miles from Santa Fe."

"It just as well have been hundreds," insisted Kitten. "We didn't go to civilization once."

"You don't consider the Thomin's civilized?" asked Missily slyly and Mikell frowned. Kitten always brought out the worst in his wife. He wished she were more relaxed and less critical.

"Missily," Kitten's voice took on the older sister's tone she used often with Missily, "you know I'm not speaking of the people but the surroundings."

"You'll never convince me big cities are more civilized. What's civilized about men hunting each other down to kill them like animals do in the wild? Except that it's not natural for human beings." Missily chopped the lettuce with angry strokes.

"Why are you chopping the lettuce? You know it should be torn," Kitten said.

"I don't either. By whose book?" Missily's voice was hard. "I like to chop mine and it's my kitchen."

Mikell moved swiftly to Missily's side and put an arm around her waist. She was trembling and as tense as a taut rubber band. "Imogen, what kind of activities do you like?" he asked and felt some of the tension leave Missily.

The front door opened and Diccon appeared. He'd gone to church that morning with Nigel but he was alone now.

"Nigel desert you?" Mikell asked.

"No, he wasn't with me after we got to church. Hello, Victoria."

She stood to greet him and accepted a kiss on her cheek (while Missily thought—men are supposed to get up for ladies not the other way around)—and he stood with his arm around her shoulders as she introduced Imogen who stood also to offer Diccon her hand.

"Glad to meet you, Imogen. I hope you enjoy your stay and our beautiful country. You're looking well, Victoria. How's Andante?"

Kitten smiled at Diccon. "Wonderful. Though she'd probably mad at me right now. She'll sulk a little when I get back before she'll be all right again."

"Sit down, Diccon. Would you like something to drink?" Missily asked.

"A tall glass of cold water," he answered, indicating to Kitten to sit and taking a chair himself.

Mikell got the water for him, then went back to lean against the cupboard next to Missily. "Does Andante always sulk?" he asked.

"No. Just when I do something out of the ordinary. Like have dinner out on a night she knows I'm usually home. The last time was in April or May when Auden was in town."

"Auden?" Missily's head came up.

"Yes. He and I usually have dinner together when he's in town."

"How's old Auden doing?" It was Mikell forestalling any unwanted remark from Missily. He could feel her antagonism.

"Fine. I asked him if he were married and he said he wasn't the marrying kind."

"He should have thought of that before he married Suz, not after," said Missily gathering the vegetables she hadn't used to put in the refrigerator.

"Suz has a way of trapping men," Kitten answer then sipped at her coffee.

"Vicky!" Mikell laughed. "No man has to be so weak he lets himself be trapped. If I didn't know you as well as I do I'd think you were jealous."

"Of Suz? Ridiculous! I wouldn't trade my life for hers any day."

Missily, who had glanced at Diccon and seen him pale and close his eyes briefly at Kitten's remark about Suz, said, "Imogen, we still haven't heard what activities you like."

Imogen looked vague a moment before she said, "Oh yes. Mr. Adamsen did ask me, didn't he?"

"Now wait a minute. If we're to call you Imogen you'll have to use out first names, too," said Mikell. "Mr. Adamsen makes me feel old."

She smiled and Missily thought. "Colorless. That's what she is. As if everything were muted. Even her smile."

"I like tennis--and concerts," she added hastily as Kitten turned her head to look at her.

"And Kitten's shadow," Missily thoughts went on, then, "I could scream at Kitten. Or do *something* so she wouldn't look so smug." She wiped off the cutting board viciously.

"Good," Diccon answered Imogen. "Missily and I'll stand you a match if you can get a partner. Maybe Myles will help out."

A car door slammed and they all looked out the window. Diccon rose to go out to where a flashy red convertible sat in the driveway but before he reached it his daughter ran to be caught close.

"Let me look at you, Daddy," she said. Her hair, so much like her mother's, lay in tangles around her shoulders. She had on some kind of loose top and short shorts and looked adorable. Cocking her head to one side she said, "You're more handsome than ever. Is that a bit of gray I see there?" She lightly touched his temple then threw her arms around his neck. "Gosh! It's good to see you!"

Diccon kissed her. "You're beautiful as ever. I'm so glad you're here. How was the trip?"

"Gorgeous. Come meet my Jon." She pulled him to the car where a young man stood who held out his hand to Diccon as they were introduced.

Missily watching from the window saw Jon smile and thought, "He *is* a handsome one."

"Is he black?" It was Kitten.

Missily shook her head slightly. "Pardon?"

"Alexis' boy friend. Is he black?"

"Her fiancé," corrected Missily and thought, "Get hold of yourself, Missily Adamsen." Aloud she said, "No. Mediterranean of some sort, I think Suz said."

"An Arab? Leave it to Alexis."

"The girls said Greek or something like that. Alexis told Celeste," said Missily.

The three outdoors had started for the house and Mikell went to open the door for them. Alexis spied him and ran ahead to be caught in her uncle's arms. "Uncles Mikell! Golly, you're so tall. I always forget you're almost as tall as Daddy."

"It's good to see you, sugar. You're looking mighty pretty," said her uncle. "Is this the man who's brave enough to take you on?"

She laughed and held out her hand to Jon. "Meet my favorite Uncle. This is Mikell and Aunt Missily is somewhere. Oh, there you are."

Missily had dried her hands and followed Mikell into the living room. Now she gave her niece a hug and held out a hand to Jon. "Welcome, Jon. All the younger set are out at Perry's. They'll be here after church. I'm fixing dinner. Are you hungry?"

"Famished," Alexis answered and Mikell smiled. Jon hadn't said a word yet.

He was dark as Celeste said, swarthy, Missily thought, with dark eyes that looked as though they missed nothing. He could have come from the Arabian nights. "Come meet Alexis' Aunt Victoria," she said to Jon who had given her a sudden smile, lighting his dark eyes.

"Is Aunt Vicky here? Oh, goody. Who else?" asked Alexis.

"Almost everyone now. The RV out there belongs to Thor and Erin." They were in the dining area of the big kitchen now.

Kitten stood to accept Alexis hug and gave her hand to Jon. "Well, young man, we shall have time to get to know you a little before Alexis marries you."

"Yes," he answered gravely, bowing over her hand in such a natural gesture of courtesy that it didn't seem out of place and it won Kitten. She turned. "Jon and Alexis, this is my friend Imogen English."

Imogen was also standing to greet the newcomers. Jon took her hand, said hello seriously, then stepped back to let Alexis greet her. As Alexis greeted Imogen, Thor and Erin drove up. Mikell sighed with relief. He'd wondered if they'd remember he'd need the car. He watched as Thor stopped Erin before she got around the car to give her a long kiss, then they came up the walk together arm in arm, laughing.

Missily sighed with relief herself because as Thor and Erin came into the living-room where she was standing she noticed that Thor's usual cheerfulness was back and lines gone from his face while the pinched look had left Erin's small face. Thor held up and A OK sign and grinned. Alexis spied them and squealed before she ran to get a hug.

"Lordy, girl, don't you ever quit growing?" Thor asked. "You look down on all your Aunts now."

"Not quite. Aunt Vicky is still taller."

Kitten stood in the kitchen doorway. When Erin saw her and crossed the room to her Kitten returned her hug, the first she'd given anyone. "Hello, Thor."

"Victoria. You're looking great," he said and bent to kiss the proffered cheek.

They ate around the round wooden oak dining table Missily treasured. Mikell had found it, before they were married, in a second-hand store and taken her apologetically to see it. She had stood looking at it silently so long he'd turned away with a deprecating remark about his ability to buy furniture when she startled him by whirling around to catch his hand, exclaiming, "But Mikell, don't you see? I love it." Looking down at her he'd seen tears in her eyes. "I saw one once at one of my friend's grandmother's house and have wanted one ever since," she'd explained, and Mikell had been overwhelmed with love for her. Now he also was quite fond of the table though he'd wanted to eat outside at their picnic table. Missily, however, had said no, Kitten would have enough picnics as it was.

"I wish you wouldn't let her get to you, Jedidah," Mikell had said then, as he took soup bowls out of the cupboard. "There aren't enough of these."

"Use the ones in the other cupboard, too."

"Okay. Sweetheart, you can't change her and you just get yourself upset."

"I know. I try not to get irritated but she's such a snob."

"Yes, she is but it's pathetic when you think of what little cause she has. I can't help but wonder if it's her way of feeling important."

"I suppose it could be. I hadn't thought of it that way." She smiled at him. "You are such a dear, Mikell. I wish I were as generous."

"Nonsense," he'd said and as she'd stood on tiptoes to kiss his cheek he'd turned his head to meet her lips instead.

After they'd eaten, Mikell and Missily, before they went on to church, took Kitten and Imogen to Rose's place where they were to stay that night. Thor and Erin were delighted to have the opportunity to be alone for a while, at least until Suz and Shaul came, while Alexis and Jon drove out to Perry's place. Stephanie had decided to go to church with Gretchen but Betsy refused to go again so she and Celeste spent the evening driving around Seattle with Jon and Alexis with Alexis in the driver's seat.

Most of them, except for Kitten and Imogen, gathered back at Mikell's and Missily's later where they ate ice cream and cookies and talked, some of them in the backyard, some in the living room. Alexis begged for an organ piece from her Uncle Mikell and after he played he summoned Myles to ask him to play. After his son complied Myles had to answer the questions over again for the guests; how long, why had he kept it a secret, what was he going to do with it? Laughing, he told them he had no particular ambition, just wanted to play organ.

Then Alexis wanted to know if Mikell was still building organs and when she learned he had one almost finished she wanted Jon to see it so they went out to the shop with Thor, Erin, and Nigel following. Diccon and Missily sat on in the darkening living room loath to turn on a light, watching the last rays of the setting sun slowly fade away.

"I like Jon," Missily said.

"Yes. I believe I do too, though it's a bit early for me to tell. He is courteous and he cares for Alexis. I hadn't realized until they came what it meant. She's been my little girl so long it's hard to think of her as an adult and belonging to another man."

"We haven't faced that yet," Missily said slowly. "I hadn't thought about it very deeply until Myles left for college. I wonder if it's true, as they say, that a daughter's a daughter all her life but a son is a son until he gets a wife."

Diccon laughed. "Probably not. It's probably partly true like most sayings. I'll lose Alexis to a certain extent. She was going to go to college and then come home to take care of me."

"Was she? That was quite a young thing to say. I don't think I ever wanted to stay home and take care of my father even though we were close. I didn't intend to marry someone like Mikell, though."

"What kind of man did you have in mind? Or was there already someone else?"

"No. I dated, of course, but they all paled into insignificance after I met Mikell. I guess I thought I'd marry someone well off financially. Not because I cared so much about money but because I had the idea that people who were intellectuals or highly intelligent, which *was* important, were wealthy or at least comfortable. I never dreamed a mind like Mikell's would reside in an organ repairer. Don't ask me why. That's so long ago I don't even remember." Missily was laughing.

"You and Mikell have a rather special marriage. I don't think there are many like yours any more."

"I don't think so either but I always think that's just because Mikell's mine and to me there isn't anyone better around."

"No," Diccon answered slowly. "I don't think people believe in working through problems. If I hadn't been so stubborn and had been willing to take a job either close to a big city or in one, maybe I would still have Suz. When I remember that children from homes where there is a divorce have that example of how to solve problems I'm afraid for my two."

"But sometimes it works just the opposite, Diccon," she said, distressed for him as she often was. Why did he seem so vulnerable? Was it because he still loved her so ungrateful, so self-centered sister? She could feel the tension in him and hurried on, "I mean, sometimes children from that kind of home are determined it won't happen again. And your two know it wasn't your doing. They know Suz left."

"Do they?" His voice was a close to bitterness that she'd ever heard it. "Missily, Suz left me but I'd been just as stubborn as she. I hope I've never let Nigel and Alexis think it was all one-sided. It never is, do you think?"

"I don't know. Sometimes it seems as if it is. But I do know that you didn't want a divorce. And so do Nigel and Alexis."

Diccon didn't answer. They sat in a companionable silence, Missily wishing there were some woman somewhere for Diccon. He was too precious to waste. A car door slammed, they heard Nigel say something and Missily thought, "Suz." She glanced over at Diccon but his face was only an outline. "About this time Mikell always suggests I put on the light. When we can no longer see each other," she added and reached over to switch on the lamp.

"Why doesn't he turn it on himself?" Diccon asked though his mind wasn't really on the conversation. He knew Suz and Shaul had driven up as surely as Missily did.

"I don't know. Too lazy I guess," she answered.

Diccon rose. "Think I'll go out back and see what's going on there, " he said and left the room, traveling his usual relaxed, unhurried way. He knew from experience that he could take his first sight of Suz, her laugh, her lovely long legs and wonderful hair, much better in a group. So far he'd not had to cope with coming upon her suddenly alone, unexpected without knowing she was in the vicinity. In a group he could stand back and watch her until his heart righted itself and he began to be able to control his breathing again. The light was on out back and the young people were talking to Thor and Erin who were sitting in the swing. Diccon could hear giggles coming from under the big, drooping willow. He ducked between the branches.

"Hi, chickens. What's up?" he asked, standing to let his eyes adjust until he could make out some of the youngest of the group: Betsy, Candace, Gretchen, and Stephanie.

"Hi, Uncle Diccon. We're telling ghost stories," Betsy said. "Come, sit by me."

"Better not. I might not sleep tonight," he answered, causing more giggles.

He could tell from the noises behind him that the rest of the group was coming out the back door. He heard Erin exclaim, "Suz! We thought you'd never get here."

And Suz's laugh and her voice. "We didn't hurry. Shaul's never been beyond the California border north so he had to see the scenery. We came up the Oregon coast."

His knees went weak so that he reached for a branch above his head while the girls scrambled to their feet and left the willow bower. Slowly he parted the willow branches. She was standing under the light, which shimmered in her hair and she hadn't cut it. It still lay beautifully around her shoulders. Would she ever age? Every year made her more beautiful. He left his shelter slowly, staying in the background, and then Alexis was beside him, linking her arm in his.

"Golly! She never looks any older. Do you suppose I'll preserve so well?"

He laughed. "Who know? Is that the right word?"

She giggled. "I don't know. But it says what I mean. That must be the jazz pianist."

Until then Diccon hadn't noticed the man who stood beside Suz, his hand linked in hers. He was young and handsome.

"Why doesn't he stand up straight?" Alexis murmured.

And Diccon had to smile. Jon stood almost ramrod straight. "Maybe because he plays the piano all the time," he said, his arm around her waist. She hadn't known, of course, but her presence was helping him regain his equilibrium even while the hurt of yet another man with Suz throbbed through him like an aching tooth.

Suz and Shaul were surrounded so that he lost sight of her and then she asked for Alexis who left Diccon to give her a kiss. "This is your new young friend?" Alexis asked Suz and Diccon waited to see how Suz would answer. There had been the slightest emphasis on young and he knew that Suz and Alexis had often fought like cats. Now Suz said genially, "Meet Shaul Kittim. Shaul, my beautiful daughter, Alexis. Where's your young man?"

The question was so natural that Diccon knew Suz had ignored Alexis' cattiness. Alexis seemed to accept it and held out a hand to Jon. Suz looked at him and smiled, "You'll keep her in order."

"Is she difficult?" he asked as to an equal in age and Alexis thought, "She's done it again," and felt a swift pang of fear. Surely she wouldn't take a man from her daughter.

"At times. But she's worth any trouble. Come, tell me about your plans."

They walked together to the picnic table followed by the young ones who'd dashed out from under the willow to give her a greeting hug. Whatever it is she has, thought Diccon, we all fall under her spell and she doesn't even try. Except Mikell, he amended. He knew well what Mikell thought of Suz. Right now he was talking music with Shaul and Diccon stood alone in the shadow, watching, praying for grace for the next week, begging for it. What he wanted more than anything was to disappear and not watch her, not feel the knife turn inside again and again. And yet in another way, he didn't want to leave. Now he slipped away to his car to drive, as he had the night before, to where he could see the Sound and watch the lights on the water. It gave him a measure of peace and helped with the pain. It wasn't as sharp, of course, as it had been when he was younger and first learned she was to marry again. But it was still there and still had to be accepted. He'd learned not to berate himself. He'd accepted the fact that he'd been young and foolish and that he could have been a more understanding husband but now he no longer beat himself with regrets. The other pain, that she wasn't his and had belonged to other men, was one he fought over and over again. He wished he could forget her, find someone else or something else so she wouldn't matter any more. He'd thought it would help not to see her but found that wasn't so. Since Nigel and Alexis had gone to college he and Suz seldom talked to each other and he hadn't seen her since the last reunion but the longing didn't leave.

Suz had seen him leave and felt a pang, which she couldn't identify. He'd always been there when she needed him with his gentleness, the wisdom he'd acquired through the years, his practical help with Alexis and Nigel. She wanted to know what he thought of Jon and how Nigel was doing. Nigel would tell her only what he wanted her to know. She knew he disapproved of her and wasn't even sure he liked her though he was always respectful, but Diccon would tell her things parents liked to know. She was beginning to wish she'd listened to her first intuition about Shaul. He was far too intense and she was more involved than she wanted to be. Right now he was talking to Mikell but they'd stopped earlier to get a motel room before coming to Missily's because he'd refused to stay with any of her people. She'd given in more because she knew her family would be uncomfortable with their sleeping together than for any other reason.

Much later, so late that few had gone over to Fort Worden, as Mikell and Missily talked over the events of the day in the dark where they lay side by side, hands clasped, she asked, "Do you like Jon?"

"Seems like a nice young man. Rather serious. I noticed my Missily got the smile and a very nice one, too," and his voice sounded content and proud.

"Mikell," Missily said after a moment's silence. "Diccon is taking it hard this year about Suz. I wonder why."

"I don't know. She's a beauty but I have a hard time being civil to her because of him. What good does outside beauty do if the inside's rotten?"

Missily turned in his arms and he felt her slight body shake with sobs. "Kell, won't any of the rest of my family ever become Christians?"

He stroked her hair, his lips against her forehead. "I don't know, Jeddie. Don't give up hope. They're still with us and we have a week ahead together. Who knows what God will do."

Chapter XX

The weather was beautiful when Missily and Mikell started for the ferry the next morning with their two daughters and Betsy and Stephanie. Since the girls wanted to ride the ferry to Whidbey Island and from there on to Port Townsend Mikell headed in that direction. It was a little past seven because Mikell had wanted to miss the rush hour traffic. Both mountain ranges were clear, the Olympics shining white in the morning light and both Mt. Rainier and Mt. Baker loomed high in the Cascade Range. Missily sighed in contentment, her hand resting on Mikell's leg.

He glanced at her and smiled, "Happy?"

"Deliciously so," she answered. "I do so love the times we spend together and you don't have to rush off to work.

He placed his hand over hers a moment for a squeeze before he put it back on the wheel. It was hard for him to imagine what it was like for Diccon who was not only alone without the one he loved but also had to watch her with another man. Mikell was not a man much given to introspection but every time he saw Diccon and Suz in the same area together he wondered, mostly, he knew, because Diccon still loved Suz. He often thought he would feel murderous in Diccon's place. If Diccon had remarried it wouldn't have been the same, but Mikell could never understand Diccon's faithfulness to Suz.

As the ferry got underway, he and Missily and the girls all climbed out of the car to go up the stairs so they could stand up front on the deck and watch the water. The trip to Whidbey Island was shorter than the one to Port Townsend. Suz and Shaul had driven on the ferry right behind them as had Alexis and Jon in his car and Nigel in his. Each had some of the youngest set with them, Nigel, the most in his big four-wheel drive.

"Look," Suz said. "Shaul, look how big Mt. Rainier looks." She pointed down the Sound.

"It's huge," he answered standing with his arm around her shoulders.

"It's unbelievable," exclaimed Jon, standing next to Shaul. "I had no idea the mountains out here were so big. I've been in the Rockies and didn't think there was anything like them anywhere else in the US except in California, Alaska and Hawaii."

"I told you so," said Alexis hanging on to his arm. "They're big from Alaska to Mexico. And maybe down farther, too. I've never thought about that before. Uncle Mikell, where's Daddy?"

Mikell, who was standing with Missily behind the others answered, "He came on over last night with some of the boys--Myles, Sean, Adam, Rex, and Martin, I think--to set up the tents."

Suz had turned as Alexis asked the question and Shaul watched her closely. "What's wrong?" She asked, since his eyes were still on her when she turned back.

"You still have a yen for him, don't you?'

"Who?"

"Alexis' Dad."

"Shaul, are you crazy?" she hissed, hoping Jon couldn't hear the conversation.

"You seem to be very interested in the answer to your daughter's question."

Suz gave him a level look, removed herself from his arm. "I've told you not to crowd me, Shaul. You don't own me. No man does and I intend to stay that way." She was speaking quite low, hoping not to be overheard. "I want to enjoy myself and I will only if you respect my wishes."

"Maybe you'd prefer that I go back home," he answered coldly.

Suz sighed and was glad the first ferry ride was over so they could all pile in the cars again. Though the second ride was longer Suz stayed in the car while Celeste and Trudy, who were with them, climbed out. Shaul got out too, then leaned down. "Aren't you coming?"

She shook her head and he sat back down in the car to take her hand, "Suz, I didn't mean anything."

"I hope not. I don't need remarks like that." She let her hand lay limp in his. "If I talk to Diccon or look at him are you going to jump to conclusions? After all Alexis is getting married soon and I want to talk to him. And I also want to ask him about Nigel. I've done it for years. After all they are our children."

"Okay, okay, so I was hasty. I'm sorry, Suz." His voice failed and he cleared his throat. "I've never met anyone like you before. You're good for me; you're relaxing. I guess I'm just unsure of you. I'd like to have come here with you as my wife."

"You never mentioned marriage before."

"No. I wasn't sure but our trip together has been great and I've been thinking about it."

"I'm not sure I want to get married again. Three times seems a bit much. And I get bored."

172

"I'm willing to risk that even if I only have you a few years."

Suz sat watching the far shore come closer. "I don't know, Shaul. I just don't know. I don't think I'm ready for that kind of a relationship yet. Give me time. I don't want to be tied down right now and I also want to be sure this time. I--It's not easy to go through a divorce. I don't want to risk that pain again."

"But, Suz, darling, there wouldn't have to be a divorce." Shaul had taken her hand again. "I'm willing to spend the rest of my life with you."

"There doesn't *have* to be but I know myself better than you do. I get bored or something else happens and the marriage doesn't last. Promise me one thing," she begged.

"What's that?" he asked, leaning over a little to try to see her face for she'd put her head down and her hair had swung forward.

"Don't talk about it any more during the reunion. Let's just enjoy ourselves. I want to be with the family. I don't want to go out for private tête-à-tête's or walks alone with you. Maybe later I'll be more sure of what I want but not now."

He started to accuse her of testing him but saw the girls approaching the car so he answered, "Whatever you say."

Port Townsend, one of the oldest cities in Washington, had, in the late nineteenth century, been a port of entry and an active trade center. There were still, on the bluff above the small business center, many Victorian style homes, restored, painted and with turrets, towers and Gothic trim. Self-guided tours could be taken and Missily had sent for maps. She knew others beside herself would like to walk through the quaint, fascinating town with the county courthouse, a building that combined Romanesque and Gothic architecture as well as elements of a fairy tale castle, plus all the beautiful homes. It was the wrong time of year for tours inside the homes but she and Mikell had come to Port Townsend with their four when they were younger and wandered the streets as well as touring some of the homes. It was not only an attraction for tourists but also a town for artists, musicians, and writers who had escaped the urban rush and moved in.

The town sits almost at land's end on Admiralty Inlet. North across the Strait of Juan de Fuca are the San Juan Islands and Vancouver Island, British Columbia. South some twenty miles as the crow flies, is Hood Canal, a natural fjord and in the Southwest loom the whitecapped Olympic Mountains. The Olympic Peninsula had long been a favorite place for Mikell and Missily to take their children. They had driven the loop more than once, walked the rain forest, hiked in Olympic National Park, backpacking and camping. When things got too hectic and Mikell began to be short tempered and impatient, Missily would quietly get things ready for a trip so they could spend a day or two in the silence of the forest among the huge Douglas fir, hemlock and Sitka spruce before going back home refreshed and rested no matter how weary they might be physically.

Now as the car left the ferry and drove through the town Suz sensed excitement in Shaul. He turned a corner, not following Mikell and when Suz pointed this out he said, "But this is marvelous. Why didn't you tell me it was like this?"

173

She laughed. "Shaul, I haven't been here for years. Not since I was a teen-ager at least and maybe longer. I hardly remember it. We should keep the others in sight."

"Don't worry. Probably anyone can tell us how to get to the Fort. What did you say the name was?"

"Worden. We can come back later. Shaul, the girls want to get settled."

Shaul frowned briefly then circled the block and went down the street they'd started up. Of course, by then the others were out of sight but he kept driving. Finally Suz, who was amused and trying not to laugh--she could hear the girls whispering in the back seat--asked, "Shaul, why don't we stop and ask how to get to the Fort? That's the third time we've gone past the court house."

"But look at it. It's fantastic!"

"Yes, I agree, but we can come back. Please, Shaul. The others may worry and come looking for us. We do have their daughters after all."

Shaul swore but he stopped while Suz rolled down the window and asked a man on the corner where the Fort was. Given directions they started out again and soon saw the sign. Trudy, who had never been to Port Townsend or Fort Worden, stood beside Celeste looking around after Shaul found the others and parked his car beside Mikell's.

"O-o-o! This is neat!" Trudy said, twirling around. "I lay awake last night trying to imagine all the different uniforms the soldiers would wear."

"What do you mean?" Celeste, whose interests were more personal, asked, not sure she cared.

"Well, this was guarding the entrance to Puget Sound when Teddy Roosevelt was President and you know how funny they dressed then. I tried to imagine what it'd be like to meet someone from then. I'm going to ask Aunt Rose what the women wore. She'll know."

"Do you call her Aunt Rose?"

Trudy looked back at Celeste. "Yes. Why not?"

"Well, she's not your aunt."

"I know but she seems like it. I've known her all my life."

"Do you like her?" Celeste began to walk slowly along the lawn that was part of the parade grounds in front of the officer's buildings. These were big wooden structures. The Commanding Officer's house sat somewhat apart, a big, three story building that was open for tours, which Missily had scheduled in the activities for the week. The other homes on Officer's Row were double, like huge duplexes, and in one of these--one with six bedrooms--Missily and Mikell and the others not camping in RV's would be staying.

Trudy followed, looking eagerly around her, her bright blond hair so light it almost looked silver in the sun, tied by blue ribbons on both sides of her face. "Of course I do," she answered. "Celeste, what a strange question."

"I suppose so. Do you think we'll meet any good-looking men?"

"We've got lots of them in the family."

"But they're family. Don't you like men?"

"Yes, I like men. You ask strange questions. Why wouldn't I?"

"I mean don't you have a boyfriend?"

174

Trudy thought a moment. "I don't know. I don't think much about that. I'm only sixteen and I'm not going to get married for years. I want to have a stable of my own. Come on, let's go look inside the place Aunt Missily and all of them are going to stay in." She took Celeste's hand and pulled her after her running toward the building where the adults had vanished.

Shaul dumped the luggage in the room he and Suz were to share. She had already started to unpack her garment bag. Missily and Rose and their mother were exploring, exclaiming over the furniture and the decor which were both in Victorian style but Suz disliked the heavy, old style and wanted to get outdoors.

"Leave that for later," Shaul said. "Let's go back downtown."

"We have plenty of time for that," Suz answered tranquilly, turning with her clothes to hang them in the closet.

"Suz, I'm going now." Shaul's voice was tight.

"Okay. I want to talk to my family. Go ahead and scout around. You can report back to me if you find anything interesting."

He caught her as she turned back from the closet. "Come with me, Suz." He began to kiss her throat, his hands caressing her back.

"Not now, darling. I haven't seen my sisters for years. Let me talk to them for a while first." She pulled back and grinned at him. "You'd be bored by that. Go find out what's what," she said, pushing back his hair, running her hand down his face.

"Okay. But you'd better be ready for a night on the town. I feel in my bones that this place is my town."

After he left Suz finished unpacking then took a shower and changed into shorts and a cool top, slipped sandals on her feet, combed her hair to tie it back with a scarf, put on some lipstick, ignoring any other make-up, and went out to see if she could find Diccon. She walked down to where the campers were but though she talked to the younger members of their party, including her son who was setting up a tent, she didn't see Diccon and she wouldn't ask for him. Just as she started back to the Officer's Row she saw him coming toward her. Her heart jumped. She'd recognize that stride anywhere. He moved so beautifully. Suz had loved to dance with him and he'd been considered the best dancer in their high school class. She used to tell him he should have become a dancer and he would twirl around with his hand over his heard. "Like this?" he'd ask and she'd giggle. Now she wondered why he was affecting her so strongly since she thought all those feelings had died years ago. The problem was that he stayed so dangerously attractive.

"Hello there," he said in that cheerful way that had first caught her attention years ago in high school. "They all busy down there?"

"Yes. Putting up tents, though some of them intend to sleep under the stars."

Diccon laughed. "Let's hope it doesn't rain. They slept that way last night and enjoyed it." They'd fallen in step with one another. "Been down to the beach?"

"No. Is it far?"

"Not at all. Want to go see it now or wait until the others come?"

175

"Let's go now," she answered. He seemed so at ease that she began to feel more natural with him though it struck her suddenly that this was the first time she'd been alone with him since she'd left him years ago. If it hadn't been Auden or Owen or another man friend with her, the children had been there or someone from her family.

They walked together, talking about the Fort, the beach and wharf and finally coming to the lighthouse at Point Wilson. They didn't go down but rather stood on the hill above among the trees where the old searchlight tower stood.

"Diccon," Suz said after they'd talked about how neat everything was around the lighthouse buildings with their red roofs, "what do you think of Jon?"

Diccon leaned against one of the trees, their tops flattened by the winds from the Strait. "I dunno. He seems decent. He certainly stands ramrod straight. I noticed that last night when--" he stopped then went on smoothly, "they were out back at Missily's talking."

Suz knew that he had changed midstream to keep from comparing Jon to Shaul. She turned to look at him. Darn! He was too good-looking to be running around loose.

"Diccon, why don't you get married?" She asked and could have bitten off her tongue but he only shrugged and smiled a little.

"Sorry," she said. "That's none of my business." She reached up to break off a clump of needles and began to make a chain. "Jon doesn't seem to relax. He's very polite and correct but so stiff."

"Well, it is a little daunting to be thrown among so many relatives at once, especially if they're your future bride's," Diccon said mildly.

Suz laughed. "I hadn't thought of that. Kind of like you're on inspection. I remember. I felt that way with Owen. His family was overwhelming. They are such *big* people. Friendly, outgoing, like Owen, but a bit hard to take all at once."

"Do you still see Owen?"

"Now? No, nor care to. He pales on one in a hurry. There's nothing beneath that hearty, friendly exterior. Not like---" Now it was her turn to stop and she didn't continue nor look at Diccon.

He watched her busy hands. How many times had she made pine needle chains to put around his neck and then hers? As if she read his thoughts she suddenly discarded the needles and walked to the brow of the hill. "Tell me about Nigel. Is he all right?"

"Yes. He's applied for a job in Washington."

"Why does he want to change?"

"He's wanted a job up here for some reason since he graduated last year."

"Does he have a girl?"

"Not so it's noticeable. He's dated girls there in Oregon, of course, but not anyone special." Diccon answered carefully. He wasn't sure Nigel would want him telling Suz about Lorna, particularly since there didn't seem to be any progress. "He's young yet. I hope he doesn't marry too young."

"Were you sorry you did?" she asked next without turning.

"Yes and no," he answered. "I might have been wiser if I hadn't been so young. I never regretted marrying you," he added quietly.

"Diccon, do you think it's healthy for Nigel to be so---religious?"

"That's the healthiest thing about him," he answered promptly and Suz did turn to look at him then.

"Why do you say that? Why did you turn that way? I can remember what you used to think about all that--junk." She substituted the last word for a less elegant one she'd started to use and thought, "If I stay around him he'll convert me."

"That was before I found there was a reason to live when I'd decided there couldn't be any."

She looked away, out across Admiralty Inlet where a ship was making it's way to the Strait bound for somewhere across the seas perhaps. "I hope Nigel finds a girl. It's lonely without someone to love." She said it wistfully, almost as though she'd forgotten he was there.

He wanted to take her in his arms and tell her he'd never stopped loving her, wanted to feel her hair blow across his face, feel her long, lovely body against his. With an exclamation he stood away from the tree he had been leaning against. "Better mosey back and see if anyone needs help," he said. "My tent's up but when Rose and Graham and Kitten and her friend and your folks arrive they can use help getting luggage in."

"I'll race you," Suz challenged impishly, but he took her up on the dare.

"I'm game," he said. She'd often beat him when they were younger but he was fit now physically in a way she wasn't and he outdistanced her so much that he turned back to wait for her. She was laughing, her hair flying, she'd lost her scarf somewhere. He might have caught her to him if he hadn't heard voices behind him and turned to see the "four monsters", as he'd dubbed them, coming toward them. Candace, Kate, Betsy, and Lynette were walking arm in arm down the road talking and giggling.

Candace left the group to run to them. "Hi, Aunt Suz! Did you see the Commanding Officer's house? Golly! I wonder how many people he had in his family."

"Don't say golly," Kate remonstrated.

"You just did. Don't be prissy," Candace retorted.

"What's prissy? You're not supposed to say that word," her cousin insisted.

"Have you seen the lighthouse?" Diccon asked to divert them.

"No. Where?" Instantly the quarrel was forgotten.

"On down the road. We just came from there. Don't go down to it. You can see it from the hill. Later we'll find out if someone will show it to us."

They took off on a run and Suz smiled at Diccon. "Magic," she said.

He grinned. "No, just a little hard won wisdom. Those two of ours had some horrific arguments."

They walked on together. "Do you think they'll do what you told them? Just view the lighthouse from the hill?"

"Yes, with Kate there. She's a conscientious little soul."

"Who is she?"

"She's the one who told Candace not to say golly."

"But who does she belong to?"

"She's Mikell's sister Eva's girl. There's a boy, too. Kent. He's as conscientious as she is and more serious. I don't know why since their parents aren't that way. Poor Kate. She'll have to learn she can't be everyone else's conscience."

"She's a pretty child," Suz said, for Kate had a head of coppery curls and beautiful skin, "but she'd be a pain to be around."

"Possibly. She seems to have enough other lovable qualities no one minds her corrections. You've lost your scarf."

Suz' hand went to her hair. "Oh well. I've plenty others. I suppose I look a mess," she said in a matter of fact way.

Diccon swallowed all the things he wanted to say. She was looking particularly beautiful. Her color was high and her eyes alive. "You look all right to me," he said. "A little wind blown but you're on vacation."

She laughed. "Auden called me a hoyden."

"Well, aren't you--at times?" he asked. "It's becoming," he added, picked up a stick from the road and gave it a whirling toss so it went quite far toward the beach.

She didn't answer. Too many memories, suppressed for years, were coming back and she didn't want to remember. If she did she would have to admit what a mess she'd made of her life and so far she'd been able to shrug it off. She was glad when they arrived back at the quarters where she was staying. There were other cars now, as Diccon had said and he remarked, "Just in time," before he sprinted across the grass to the cars.

Lunch was eaten picnic style much to Kitten's disgust. She sat fastidiously at one of the tables eating off one of the plates Genevieve Curtis, Graham's mother, had given her. Genevieve had announced she would not eat off paper plates and did anyone else want a decent plate? Kitten had accepted one gratefully along with the stainless steel knife, fork, and spoon and a glass.

Allen Metlow sat across from her watching her with a twinkle in his eye. "Anna, are you sure you didn't get the wrong baby at the hospital?"

His wife, who had been discussing the twenty-fifth anniversary celebration of Queen Elizabeth's ascension to the throne of Great Britain with Genevieve and Maren Nielsen, Thor's mother, turned startled eyes on Allen. "What on earth are you talking about?" she demanded.

"Victoria. Are you *sure* she's ours?"

"Father, really!" Kitten said.

He shrugged. "The genes certainly don't tell. Don't you ever relax?"

She gave him a look of disgust and turned back to talking to Erin who wanted to know all Kitten had been doing since they last wrote.

Allen shook his head, got up from the table taking his plate with him, and walked over to where Mikell and Diccon were talking to Jon and Alexis. "Care if I join you?"

"Not at all. I wondered how long you'd stay with the ladies," Mikell answered.

"I hope you're not discussing the Queen, too. She's fine but in England. I've heard nothing but royalty for a month. I often wonder why we ever had a revolution. People revere the royal family as if there were some sort of magic about being Queen or Prince."

"Hooray, Grampa!" Alexis said. "Jon and I got sick of listening to all that garbage."

"Don't be so hard on people," Diccon said mildly. "We all have our fantasies even if it's just to own a Mercedes Benz."

Alexis laughed then said, "But I'm not so stupid that I believe the royal family perfect because of the accident of their birth."

"Do you think others think they're perfect? I mean don't we usually like someone better if there's a skeleton in the closet somewhere and not too distantly related either?" Allen asked.

The others laughed. "Guess you're right." Alexis conceded. "But I still think there are better things to dream about."

"What's your particular fantasy?" Jon wanted to know.

She opened her eyes wide at him, bent over to put her hand on his arm. "Oh, I'll tell you sometime," she said, "in privacy," and he pulled her over for a kiss.

"Yuck! said Candace to the group sitting like she was on the grass. "Why do they always have to get mushy?"

"They're engaged," said practical Kate.

"I know that, but Mamma and Daddy don't go around acting like that and they're married."

"That's why," Kent said. "Married people are used to each other."

"Mamma and Daddy still kiss each other and--other things--when we're around," said Betsy.

"So do my parents," put in Lynette. "I think it's neat." She, like her mother, Jean, was a plain girl but had two dimples when she smiled.

"Maybe they love each other more than Uncle Mikell and Aunt Missily," suggested Kent.

"They do not!" protested Candace hotly. "I don't mean Mamma and Daddy don't do any of those things. I just mean they don't do it publicly."

"What do you call that?" Betsy asked, pointing to where Missily stood behind Mikell with her arms around his neck. As they watched she laid her head against his hair. Mikell reached up to touch her hand.

"Well, but that's not mushy," Candace said. "I don't mind that. It's kissing like Jon and Alexis do, like they were on TV or in a movie."

"I think it'd be fun to kiss a boy," said Betsy. "Besides, I've already had boys kiss me."

The others looked at her. "You have?" Kate asked. "Why?"

"Why what? Why do boys usually kiss girls?"

"But you're too young. Does your mother know?" Kate demanded.

"No. And don't you dare tell her. It's none of her business."

There was a silence. Lynette and Kate stole a look at each other and then turned their eyes back on their food.

"You're all such babies. You probably play with dolls."

"Betsy! You were playing dolls with me the other day," said Kate.

179

"Well, when in Rome, you know." Betsy waved a languid hand.

Kent looked at her in disgust. "You're showing off. I bet no boy ever kissed you. I wouldn't kiss a girl. What a dumb thing to do."

"They have so!" Betsy said as she got up. "I'm going where there're some adults. If you went somewhere besides church you might have some fun once in a while."

"What's all this?" Nigel, discouraged because Lorna was studiously ignoring him, had been wandering around forlornly when the conversation about kissing started and, amused, he'd stopped to listen.

"Betsy's nutty," volunteered Kent. "She thinks fun means kissing boys."

"She does?" Nigel looked down at Betsy who was standing glaring at the group, her lips in a pout. "I suppose it can mean that."

"At *her* age?" Kent asked scornfully.

"Well...she is a bit on the young side," Nigel agreed.

Betsy said, "I just think it's exciting that Alexis and Jon are engaged."

"So do I," agreed Nigel, "But I would think it a bit strange if you told me you were."

"I'm not that old yet," said an indignant Betsy.

"That's what we said," Kate said and the other's agreed.

"No you didn't. You said it was yucky to kiss a boy. You don't have to get engaged to every boy you kiss."

"I didn't say it was yucky to kiss," said Kate, the last of her wiener and bun held ready to pop in her mouth.

"*I* did," Candace said firmly. "At least I said, 'Yuck,' when Jon kissed Alexis."

"Don't you like to kiss girls?" Betsy asked Nigel.

"That'd be telling." He laughed, slung her over his shoulder like a bag of flour. "Where shall I deposit her?" he asked the group. "In the water?"

"Yes, yes," Kate giggled.

"Put me down!" Betsy demanded though she was giggling too.

Nigel, still laughing, swung her around while she shrieked. He looked up to find Lorna's dark eyes on him. As soon as he looked her way she turned her head to begin talking to Granny Ellen with animation.

Granny Ellen glanced at Lorna then looked over at Nigel who was still standing with a wriggling Betsy over his shoulder no longer laughing. "Nigel," she called. "Will you come here?"

He put Betsy down, kissed her cheek then ran over to Granny Ellen's chair. "At your service, Madam."

"Will you get me another glass of lemonade? And if you don't have anything more pressing to do come sit by me and keep Lorna and I company."

Nigel took her glass with a bow and ran to fill it. "Bless her. She can't know anything," he thought, "but Lorna won't be rude enough to leave now." He went back with Granny Ellen's lemonade, gave it to her with a bow and a grin and sat on the ground beside her lawn chair.

"Aren't you eating?" she asked after she thanked him.

"Finished. Hello, Lorna. Haven't had a chance to greet you yet."

"No. It's pretty hectic, isn't it?" she answered easily. "What were you doing to poor Betsy?"

He laughed. "They were arguing over whether it was yucky to kiss a boy or not. Betsy was bragging about the fact that she had already done so."

"I bet Kate didn't like that," Lorna said with a smile.

"I don't think any of the others did either. They are blessedly free of that kind of foolishness."

"So you think kissing's foolish," Granny Ellen said. Her delicate old fingers were softly stroking Nigel's dark curls.

"Now, Granny. You know that's not what I said." He grinned at her. "I just think it's refreshing not to hear the girls talking about boys all the time as if that were all there was in the world. They'll do enough of that in three or four years."

"Heavens! I hope it's more than that. I can remember how irritating the girls at school were who were so boy crazy. That's *all* they could talk about," said Lorna, her can of Coke in her hand.

"You mean they wouldn't even talk horses?" Granny Ellen asked with a twinkle in her eyes.

Lorna looked up from her plate, then laughed. "All right. Point well taken, but at least I didn't have to worry about my horse being fickle or wait for her to call me on the phone while I almost went frantic with worry that she wouldn't."

"Do you worry about that in humans?" Nigel asked.

"Not now. I mean--" Lorna was flustered. "I never did, but the girls at school had a new boy friend every week it seemed and they were always afraid he wouldn't call."

"Maybe the boys weren't the fickle ones," suggested Granny Ellen mildly, watching Nigel closely. He was smitten by Lorna, that was for sure.

"Maybe not." Lorna shrugged. "I guess my point was that I could depend on the same horse day after day, week after week and not worry about whether it would like me or not."

"That *is* a difficulty with people, I agree," said Nigel.

Lorna looked at him sharply but he was sitting cross-legged building a house out of sticks. "Have you noticed Celeste is making eyes at Adam?" he asked.

"Is she? She's a pretty girl. But they are cousins." Lorna said.

"No. No more than you and I are," Nigel glanced up at her then went on carefully piling sticks.

"Oh! That's right. Adam's my nephew. Isn't it strange? We've always done things together so that Missily's family seems like my own family."

Nigel looked up from his building. "Do I seem like a cousin to you?" he asked.

Taken off guard Lorna said, "No. Yes. Well--I was talking about the younger ones."

"I'm glad. I wouldn't want to be your cousin," he said gravely.

Lorna moved uncomfortably, glanced at Granny Ellen and saw the she had her eyes closed. She knew she took short naps but she couldn't tell whether she was asleep now or not. She wanted to leave but could think of no reason to do so, so she took a deep breath. "Nigel, I need to ask your forgiveness for being so---rude that day the colt died."

"You were upset," he replied calmly though his heart was lighter.

"But that's no excuse. I know what I said isn't true."

"You know what I remembered?" His eyes were back on his shaky house. "I remembered the time I'd seen a doe trying to get her fawn to stand up after a hunter killed it and left it to die. I stood and wept that day."

"Oh, Nigel. I hate hunters!" she said fiercely.

"I don't. There are decent ones and careless ones. There isn't anything wrong with harvesting the meat God gives us any more than there is in picking berries in the wild. I *am* angered, though, by the careless people who just shoot anything that moves without taking time to see what it is. Or just shoot for fun."

"But you don't hunt, do you?"

"No, nor fish but that's a personal choice not because I think it's wrong. I enjoy other things better."

"Like what?" Lorna turned on the bench, putting both feet up to wrap her arms around her knees. She looked quite fetching in her jeans and dark rose T-shirt, her dark hair in two braids tied at the ends with a ribbon to match her shirt.

Nigel looked up at her, glanced at Granny Ellen, then went back to putting sticks carefully on his house. "Hiking, camping, cross-country skiing, swimming. Oh, and horseback riding." He looked up suddenly and she laughed.

"You'd better add that."

"Are you going to do any this week?"

"I don't know. I don't think I will. I like my own horse best. I thought I'd go on one of the hikes, use my own legs for a change. Are you going mountain climbing?"

"Hope to. Aunt Suz says Mr. Kittam has climbed mountains all over the world so he's going."

"It won't be too hard, will it?"

"For you?"

"No. I won't climb mountains. You know that, don't you?"

"I didn't think so but I wasn't sure whether I remembered right or not. We won't go on a long hard climb. We haven't time or equipment. Probably just a day. I don't know who else is going."

"I'm glad you're not going on a difficult one. It scares me when--people climb up dangerous places. Too many people fall."

Nigel carefully laid the last stick across the top of the house. She had changed what she'd started to say. "There. Would madam like to move in?"

Lorna laughed. "No floor, sir. I don't like dirt floors."

"Never satisfied. That's a woman for you." He rose lithely to go sit in front of her on the bench, straddling it. "Maybe I'll give up the climb and come hiking with you."

"Oh, I wouldn't want you to do that. I didn't mean for you not to climb at all. I'd feel guilty if you gave it up because of what I said," though panicky was what she felt. She wasn't sure she was ready for the attention he was

182

giving her. She felt ambivalent. Part of her was excited that he should care for her, but she was still hesitant because of their age difference, though that seemed less alarming then it had before. Somehow there didn't seem to be the gap any more.

"I like these," he said, touching her braids lightly. "You look young and sweet."

She flipped them back over her shoulder. "Too young, probably but I decided we were on vacation and I'm not going to worry about my hair." She rose. "It looks as if the ladies are cleaning up so I'll go help." Then she realized she'd kicked his house and it had collapsed. "Nigel! I'm sorry. I didn't mean to be so clumsy."

He had risen, too. "No matter," he said and bent to kiss her cheek. "No floor, remember?"

She laughed up at him, standing there breathless a moment before she turned and fled.

"Nice escape," said Granny Ellen from behind Nigel.

He turned. "You weren't asleep. I thought not."

"How long have you loved her? And don't dissimulate. I'm not almost ninety for nothing."

He sat back down on the bench. "I don't know. It seems like forever."

"She told me about the day you were so sympathetic about her colt. It made quite an impression on her."

"It did?" Nigel started to add that Lorna hadn't acted as though it had then decided against it.

"I heard her apologize. I don't know why, but I do know she appreciated whatever you did. She felt embarrassed at being caught crying like that."

"Whatever for? I thought it was perfectly natural. She'd wanted that colt badly." He picked up Lorna's dishes and then gathered Granny Ellen's. "Don't you tell her how I feel, you hear? She's skittish enough as it is."

Granny Ellen smiled at him. "All right. I'll behave quite properly. You'll see."

Nigel's eyebrows went up. "I don't know whether that means what it's supposed to or not." He leaned over to kiss her cheek. "You must have been quite a handful for Grampa."

There was some scuba diving among the younger folk that afternoon. Nigel took a group down under the wharf with lights so they could see the sea life. Most of the older people sat in the lawn chairs they'd brought, relaxing in the sun. Missily, Kitten, Imogen, and Erin walked around the Fort stopping at the Centrum to find out what was going on musically. Suz and Shaul were lying on the beach in the sun with Alexis and Jon, talking lazily. They were going into town together at night to some of the places Shaul had found in his earlier foray. The men were playing horseshoes, lawn bowling, or swimming. It was all very lazy and relaxing.

Later, after the evening meal in the officer's quarters where most of them had gathered, they sat at the table talking, cups of coffee or cans of pop or beer before them. Some of the younger ones drifted outdoors to go to the beach. Imogen asked about the tennis court and Erin and Thor immediately

183

challenged her to a game. Myles offered to be Imogen's partner and they drifted out followed by Nigel and Lorna and others who wanted to watch. Nigel had managed a seat next to Lorna at the table and now walked out beside her. Granny Ellen smiled then noticed that Diccon was watching with satisfaction, also.

"He'll get her, you'll see," she said softly to Diccon who was seated on her right.

His eyes came to hers. He grinned. "You don't miss anything, do you?"

"What else is there to do with my time? Lorna talks about him frequently though I'm sure she's not aware of *how* frequently. Nor would she do so intentionally. Not right now." Granny Ellen tapped Diccon's hand. "At least that's my guess."

"It would be a good match, I think," Diccon said. "They like much of the same kind of things. She's probably the reason he's wanted to come to Washington all this time."

"Oh, Jon!" Alexis said in such a voice that Diccon and Granny Ellen turned to look down the table.

"It's true. We would have been better off staying out of World War II."

"And let Hitler go on with his final solution?" his fiancée asked.

"At least we probably wouldn't have the Jews trying to take over the Mediterranean. They'd like to own the world. They aren't any better than Hitler but everyone thinks they are because they give religious reasons," Jon said.

"I agree, " said Kitten, "They own too much as it is."

"Aren't you jumping to conclusions?" Mikell asked. "As I understand it the Israelites want their homeland back, not the world and I don't think the reasons are religious."

"So? What if all natives decided they wanted their so-called homeland? Are we to move out and give the land back to the Indians?" Jon's voice was a little belligerent.

"Jon! I thought you liked the Indians and believe like I do, that they've been badly treated," protested Alexis.

"I do but I can't see that we'd solve what our ancestors did by moving out and giving everything back. It wasn't coming here that was wrong. It was treating them as if they were idiots, not respecting their religion, customs, and culture, trying to make them white Protestants."

"He *is* young," muttered Granny Ellen and when Diccon turned to look at her she said, "He's quoting instead of thinking," and Diccon grinned. "Just a minute, young man," she said raising her voice so that all heads turned her way. "I'm a white Protestant. Just what do you find so distasteful in me?"

"But I wasn't talking about you, ma'am," Jon answered. "I was talking about the way the first people who came to our country treated the Indians."

"Have you never read how some of the Catholics treated the Indians in South and Central American and on the West Coast of our own country?" was her next question.

"Yes, of course. I guess I was talking about the people who came to the East Coast. I wouldn't make a difference between different Christian groups. They're all just as bad when it comes to trying to change people."

"Hmmm," Granny Ellen took a sip of her tea, which she always drank in the evening. Her family and those who knew her were silent, waiting eagerly for what she would say next. "Then you don't believe people should ever change?"

"No. I mean yes—that is—" He looked up appealingly at Alexis who was sitting with her chin resting on her linked hands. She just grinned. She'd had too many arguments with him and she was enjoying watching him on the receiving end. "Of course people change but they shouldn't be forced against their will."

"Never?"

"No, ma'am. It's a violence of human dignity. They can be given choices but not forced against their will."

"You mean if you had a little girl, a daughter, who decided to poke a pair of sharp scissors in her eyes she should be given the choice to do so?"

"You know—" Jon started to speak angrily then remembered he was speaking to an elderly lady. "I would think you would know a decent person would know when it's wise not to let someone do something harmful to themselves."

"Yes, I see what you mean," she said as though thinking over what Jon had said and Diccon put his napkin hastily to his mouth to hide his grin. She added, "But Jon, did you ever realize it's far more harmful to go to hell than to poke out your eye? And there may be people who care enough about you not to want you to have to experience that. But there. I won't try to force my beliefs down your throat," she went on gently and those who knew her avoided each other's eyes, trying not to smile. "No one can force another to change their beliefs no matter what method they try. Only God can do that. However, I would like to go back to this question of the Jewish people. I'm surprised to hear what you had to say, Victoria. I thought you were brought up better than that. I can't remember ever hearing Allen or Anna talk that way."

"I hope I think for myself," said Kitten primly. "If you lived back East you'd understand better."

"But, Kitten, all kinds of musicians, great ones, have been and are Jewish," said Missily at this point.

"Of course. There are always exceptions in any race."

"But Hitler wanted to get rid of all of them. He didn't make that kind of differences."

"It's kind of a mute argument anyway, isn't it?" asked Jon. "That's a lot of propaganda the U. S. put out. All that stuff about gas chambers. No one believes it any more. Not intelligent people."

There was an appalled silence around the table and Suz became aware of Shaul making strange sounds. She turned to look at him. He was livid and shaking. Just as she reached out to him he rose abruptly so that his chair crashed over, and he left the room. Suz pushed back her chair and ran after him.

"Jon, I'm afraid you're very mistaken about many things. Some can be excused because of your age. But you are our guest and I expect you to show respect to all of us just as we would like to treat you." Mikell said. He was standing, one foot on the chair, and resting an arm on his knee.

"But, Mr. Adamsen, I didn't mean any disrespect. I thought we were just having a discussion."

"Shaul Kittam may have felt quite differently about that. His parents were killed at Auschwitz—in a gas chamber. They had managed to get their children out of the country but were arrested before they could leave." Mikell's voice was quiet but Jon stared at him.

"You mean—you mean it really happened? It wasn't made up for propaganda?" Jon asked, horrified.

"It really happened."

"Jon! You've seen the pictures. Why did you...." Alexis had been crying. Now she sniffed and rubbed her face with her hands. Rose gave her a Kleenex.

"I know," he said miserably, "but Gerald told me it was all faked for—for—so we'd go to war."

"But why would you believe him?"

"I—he's my friend!" he answered angrily.

"Jon isn't the only one who's been fed that line," said Mikell, "and we all know it's not always easy to tell when historical things are facts. Only in this case there are still too many of us alive that know about it. Some of us, not here, but others are still alive who either escaped or got out of the prison camps after the war or else saw them when they went into Germany at the end of the war, not to speak of the troops."

"That's all very well and good," said Kitten in her most condescending voice. "It was a stupid and cruel method to get rid of people but that doesn't change the fact that the Jews want to run the world or that they control much of the money. And Christians encourage them."

"Oh, shut up, Kitten!" It was Rose and her sisters stared at her. "I don't care," she said stoutly. "I'm tired of hearing her. You'd think we were all idiots the way she talks. 'Back East they do an excellent job of cooking oysters. *And* the crab. It's *quite* exceptional'." Rose mimicked Kitten so closely that Missily took a hasty drink of her lemonade to hide her smile. "As though the people from the East weren't dying to try Dungeness crab and Pacific oysters *fresh*. Why you're such a snob I'll never know. You have the same blood as the rest of us and it's red and not blue." Rose snapped angrily.

Kitten rose with dignity. "I think I'll see how Imogen and Myles are faring," she said and left the room.

"Coward!" Rose said and—

"Never mind, Rosy," her father put in. "You bested her that time. Why don't we all go see how the tennis match is going? I'll have a talk with Victoria later."

Jon and Alexis lingered behind and as Alexis took his hand he went with her to the beach instead of to the tennis court. It was windy and cool but Jon didn't seem aware of it, his fine dark hair blown onto his forehead.

186

"Alexis, I didn't know. I really didn't. It doesn't make sense. Hitler was a modern man in a scientific age."

"Well, he used scientific knowledge to get rid of people, didn't he?" she asked.

He looked around at her suspiciously but her face was serious. "I don't like Jewish people but I don't think people should be treated that way. I guess that's why I get so angry with the Jews. They are treating the people over there as if they didn't matter. There should be room enough for all of them."

"I know. I can't see how anyone could ever believe science and education would fix the world. I don't think anything can. We'll probably all get blown up by a nuclear war."

He put his arms around her. "I know, baby," he whispered. "That's why I want to have as much time with you before that happens. I never thought I'd even get to meet a girl I'd love let alone marry her. If we can go together it won't be so bad."

"But what if we don't get killed? What if we only get fall out and have to suffer all the terrible things that happen? What if we are alive on that kind of planet?" she asked, clinging to him.

"I don't know. It doesn't do any good to think about it. Let's do something. Is there a place to dance in town? Let's find out." He turned her back toward the Fort and they ran hand in hand up the hill reaching the parking lot the same time that Suz and Shaul did. Suz waved but Shaul ignored them and held the car door open for Suz to get in.

"Mr. Kittam," hollered Jon. He and Alexis ran across the black top to where Suz and Shaul were. "Mr. Kittam," Jon said again, "I would like to apologize. A—a friend told me that talk about concentration camps was propaganda so we'd go into World War II. I didn't know it was true. It's—it's horrible. No one should be treated that way."

Suz let out a sigh. She'd been concerned about Alexis marrying Jon, now she felt better. Shaul eyed the young man coldly. "Let that be a lesson to you in the future. Do your own homework. That's recent history and easily proved. *And* you should be careful about talking about Jews the way you do. You could be taken for one. Or maybe you're related to Komeni."

Suz put a hand on his arm but he ignored her.

Jon flushed. "My ancestry is not Semitic," he said hotly.

"Jon, don't," Alexis begged. "We were going to find somewhere to dance. Just as well live it up while we can. If modern people can behave like Hitler who knows how long we'll be around."

Shaul's eyes shifted to hers and softened. "Follow us. I found some places to paint the town."

"Oh good! Come on, Jon."

Reluctantly he turned to go with her to his car in order to turn it so they could follow Shaul. Jon was withdrawn and taciturn at first but holding Alexis close later in a dance he began to relax.

That night, as Missily and Mikell finally found their way to their bedroom and prepared for bed, Mikell said, "Jeddie, isn't there something that Vicky would like to do? She must feel like a fish out of water."

"Yes. There are some musical events. We went to check at Centrum earlier, but she doesn't need to be so snobbish, as if we were all hillbillies or something like that."

"It may be the only way she knows how to cope. She's out of place among so many outdoorsy people and activities," he answered unloading his pockets into one of the drawers. "I like Vicky. She's a lady. At least I can't think of any other word to describe her right now."

"And what am I, pray tell?" Missily wanted to know. She was sitting on the bed in ruffled, shorty pajamas, her long dark hair in one thick French braid down her head and back. She looked young and fetching.

Mikell's head disappeared and reappeared as he pulled his shirt over his head and dropped it on a chair. He grinned at her. "Right now you look like an adorable little girl. Oh, you're a lady all right. But Vicky's got class, I guess you'd say. Now wait!" He held up his hand as she looked indignant and opened her mouth. "I like it from a distance. I definitely would *not* like to live with it every day. Give me a warm, loving, loveable woman like my Missily any day. There's only one of her in the world and she's mine." As he said this he suddenly pounced on the bed and tipped her over. "Isn't she?"

Early the next morning, in the dark, Mikell came awake. "Wha's zat?" he asked sleepily.

Missily, who'd been asleep asked, "What?"

"That noise? What is it?"

She sat up in bed. Through the open window came the sound of singing. A male voice and a female, the latter out of tune. They were singing Led Zeppelin's "Stairway to Heaven," at the top of their lungs between giggles and "Wash out!" "Don' fall" "Hel' me."

Groaning, Mikell climbed out of bed, pulled on his trousers and went out. Missily waited miserably. She hated it when Suz got drunk. When she'd been in her pre-teens, she'd been terrified of this silly, uninhibited side of her sister and stayed away from her for days after. It had made Allen furious and there would always be a long lecture the next day. Though Suz didn't often come home that way Missily would be afraid for weeks after one of her sister's binges that she'd come home from one of her numerous dates singing off tune, giggling, laughing at her father, waking every one in the house. Now she felt the same sickness, the same fear, and when Mikell came back and fell in bed beside her, he found her shaking and crying.

"Darling, what is it? They just had too much to drink."

"I know," she cried, "but I hate it. You know that. It frightens me," she went on, forgetting that Mikell hadn't been around during those agonizing young years.

"Don't worry. I think your Dad will read them the riot act tomorrow. He was livid. Sh-h-h, darling, it's all right. They won't do it again or they'll leave. We aren't the only ones who'll let them know that."

"Mikell, you're so special," Missily said between sobs. "You're so nice about Kitten when I should be and now you get out of bed because another one of my sisters is acting like a fool. I wish my family was like yours. I don't understand why some of them don't become Christians, too."

188

Mikell held her and let her cry. It was one question for which he had no answer.

Chapter XXI

In the morning those who planned to walk and camp on the beach got together to plan their trip. Mikell's parents, Gabriel and Deborah, were coming over the next day to go with them. Besides them, Mikell and Missily, Sean, Trudy, Kent and Kate were in the group planning to take the beach hike and would be gone two days. Graham and Allan and John, Graham's father, would drive them over and go back to pick them up. Anna Metlow had never liked either climbing or hiking and she and some of the other women decided to go shopping in some of the gift shops in the towns along the Strait while the others were gone.

A far bigger group would be climbing. Shaul, Diccon, Thor and his father, Alfred, would go with the young people. They hadn't decided where to climb exactly in the Olympics but would leave an itinerary behind, as would the beach hikers. They had many places from which to choose, from alpine hiking to rock and ice climbs. They decided to go in two separate groups, the ones with Shaul deciding on a more difficult climb since all had had training and experience in mountain climbing though none, they found, as often or as varied as Shaul.

He was elated, talking about moving to Port Townsend where he'd met other artists and musicians and also talked to mountain climbers. He was sure he could find work in Seattle. He'd met another Californian, Barny McClure, who'd left the Los Angeles area and headed north to settle in Port Townsend. He was also a successful jazz pianist and had offered to help Shaul get settled.

Shaul and Suz were slow to show themselves that morning but Jon and Alexis were out with some of their cousins on the beach, running races. Mikell and Missily had stopped with a map of Fort Worden outside their vacation home to decide where to hike that day. They'd found early in their marriage that if they didn't have time alone together, they began to snap at each other and argue. Somehow, spending time walking together or sitting in their back porch swing, or alone in the living room while Mikell played the organ, they were refreshed to face the world again. So they'd learned on vacations, after more than one embarrassing altercation in front of others, to take time to be alone and this time they'd decided to do it before they went camping on the beach since they'd already had several days of company, enjoyable, but wearying and they needed time out. As they stood discussing the various hiking trails in the park a man passed them stopped and turned to ask,

"Are those your youngsters on the parade ground? They're quite talented."

Mikell and Missily looked at each other and crossed the street to the parade ground. The youngsters had attracted a group of people but seemed ignorant of the fact. The four "monsters" and Kent were marching down the wide parade ground; Betsy in front twirling her baton, stepping high while in a row behind her followed Kent, Lynette, and Kate. Behind them came Candace. Her parents grinned and relaxed. Candace was evidently the bass drummer, her drum and sticks imaginary, but not her quite vocal bum, bum, bum, bum on the first beat of each measure. Kent was doing an oompah with his imaginary tuba while Lynette's clear, carrying voice sang the melody on the trumpet no one could see but she was doing such a good job of mimicking one that it almost sounded real. Kate was playing a flute, or at least that's what Missily guessed until they got further along in the piece and then she realized the child was mimicking, uncannily, the piccolo. They were doing quite well performing Susa's "Stars and Stripes".

"Mikell," Missily put her hand on his arm. He was smiling and tapping his foot in time. He turned to her.

"Hmmm?"

"Kate. She's wonderful."

"They all are," he replied.

"But that piccolo part! How does she even remember it?"

"Does Kate forget anything?" he asked with good humor.

There was applause when they finished and someone yelled "More!"

They looked at each other. Lynette alone had been startled to hear the applause. Missily wondered if she would have continued if she'd realized there was an audience. Myles and Gretchen had come up to stand behind their parents and applauded with the others.

"We don't know any others," said Lynette beginning to walk to Missily and Mikell.

"How about 'When the Saints'?" someone else yelled.

The little group were looking at each other doubtfully when they heard, "Right on," and saw Myles sprinting across the grass toward them. He grinned at Candace, "Ready?"

"Yes, Sir!" she said gleefully. "Come on, you guys. Let's do 'When the Saints'."

And Myles, who had mimicked Satchmo so often when he and Candace sang and danced together, now began, "Oh when the Saints, go marching in," and the others fell in line.

The crowd was increasing and Erin and Thor were now standing with Missily and Mikell.

Erin said, "Why doesn't he go on stage? He's marvelous."

"Horrors!" Missily grimaced.

And Erin asked, "Doesn't your religion approve?" in that sarcastic tone she used when speaking of Missily's beliefs.

Startled, Missily turned to see if Erin was serious. "Approve of what?"

"Stage. Actors and so on."

"Why would 'quote unquote' my religion not approve?"

"A lot of religious people think all actors and actresses are evil people," her sister answered.

"Hush!" Thor said. "Watch the kids, Erin. Don't pick a fight." He took the sting out of his words by swinging her in front of him and wrapping both arms around her, leaning over to kiss her cheek.

Missily slipped her arm in Mikell's with a sigh. Every time she thought she'd learned to accept as well as respect the way he felt about not demonstrating his feelings in public and saw Thor and Erin and she would wish Mikell were at least a little more that way. She was glad Erin and Thor had resolved what had been wrong between them. When the song came to an end there was more applause and yells of "More! More!"

Myles bowed, turned to his group to say, "Follow me. Let's do 'Onward Christian Soldiers'. It's just straight, four four, Betsy. Let's go."

So they followed. He marched down the line of people, veered across the lawn and proceeded down the street toward where his folks were staying. At the end of the song they all made a dash for the house and fell into chairs, laughing and panting.

"Myles, you're wonderful," said Betsy. "I didn't know you could do that. Can you do more?"

"Some. We need Gretchen and an organ though," he answered from where he was stretched out on the couch.

"Why?"

"She plays a mean organ. For Candace and I when we're goofing off."

As Mikell, Missily, Thor and Erin made their way to the house Missily said to Erin as they walked behind the men. "Erin, I didn't mean it would be horrid for Myles to go on stage. I was thinking of his reaction. He'd hate it. We used to encourage him because he's so good at that kind of thing—you should see him and Candace—but he laughs. Says it's for fun, not work."

"Well, how was I to know why you said what you did?" Erin asked shortly.

"You couldn't. That's why I explained," answered Missily calmly, then asked, "What's wrong? I'm not angry with you."

"Missily, a lot of religious people *do* think all actresses and actors are evil."

"I know they do. At least I know some Christians do. I don't know about what other religions believe. But I happen to believe being an actor or actress is like any other profession. There are just as many people who behave atrociously in real estate, law, medicine, teaching, you name it. It's not the profession or vocation. It's how one acts that's right or wrong unless you're talking about something like being a professional criminal or a prostitute or something against God's law. That kind of job is wrong in itself."

"But don't you think it's harder to be—well, religious—when you're an actor than a doctor?"

"Not really. Anyone can be religious, but I take it that you mean to be a Christian. The big difference is that it makes front-page news more often when an actor or actress commits adultery than when a doctor does. Though, of course, they don't call it that any more. There are a lot of Christians in the acting profession. I think some of them would only act in

192

what they'd call Christian films or plays. If more Christians were willing to do quality acting whether as film stars or on the stage maybe drama wouldn't be in such a sad state. Besides, that's only talking about one sin. The problem is that Christians are so prone to point out sexual sins as though they were the worst ones and forget about things like lying, gossiping, cheating, etc."

The men had gone in while the sisters loitered behind, standing in front of the house. Erin said, "Missily, I can't figure you and Mikell out at all. The church we grew up in never cared whether we danced or went to movies or all those things but neither did it hang on to the old fashioned ideas of miracles and—and all the rest like you do. I mean we were a twentieth century church not caught up in some ancient religion no one needs any more, but most people who believe like you do I call holier than thou people."

Missily reached over to straighten Erin's collar where Thor had messed it. How she loved this pretty sister of hers. "Erin, I used to think of it that way, too, but I know some of those people now and all of them aren't that way. We have people in our church who won't do any of the things most people outside of the church think all Christians stay away from. The ones called fundamentalists or conservatives or evangelicals. We used to say Bible Thumper, remember?" And as Erin nodded she went on, "But there are a lot of Christians like Mikell and I. Christians aren't all uniform like they were cut out by a cookie cutter. They're still people and they have different ideas of what's right or wrong. We happen to believe sin comes from inside and not from things like cards or movies or anything like that. It's how you use things that make it sinful, not the use itself. Unless, of course, it is expressly forbidden in the Bible.

"Some Christians think we are terribly worldly and wrong the way we believe," she went on, "and they would even disapprove of the way we rear our children. By the way, talking about children, where's Stephanie? I noticed she wasn't with Gretchen."

"She has one of her headaches," Erin answered. "I was hoping she wouldn't get one on vacation."

"What kind of headaches does she have? Or have you told me?" Missily asked as she turned toward the house.

"Migraine. We've taken her to the doctor in Albuquerque. She's supposed to watch what she eats to see what triggers them and they gave her some medicine. That helps. I hope we caught it early enough so she won't be too sick." Erin drooped a little as they climbed the stairs. "It worries me but the doctors don't seem to be. They gave her a CAT scan and whatever else they do and couldn't find anything."

Missily opened the door. "I'm glad of that but I know migraine's can be miserable."

"Missily," it was Mikell and he sounded cross. "I thought we were going on a hike."

"We are. I'm ready if you are."

"Can I go?" Candace bounced up out of the chair she'd collapsed in.

"No!" Mikell snapped and Betsy said, "I thought we were going to the museum. Daddy said he'd take us."

"Missily, you said you'd fix a lunch. Have you done that?" Mikell's voice was still cross.

"No. It won't take long." She disappeared in the direction of the kitchen.

Erin followed her. "He's certainly a cross-patch. What's eating him?"

"He'll be fine after our hike," Missily said, spreading mayonnaise on rye bread.

"One of the kids followed you once and said you do a lot of smooching."

Missily grinned. "So we have spies. I'll have to warn Mikell. And I have no idea what they meant by smooching. You know Mikell. He's not the kind to do much of that anywhere he thinks he might have an audience. I confess sometimes I'm envious of you and Thor."

"Oh well, you know I wouldn't trade Thor for anyone else. But don't worry, you were only followed once. You do realize that the rest of us wonder why you always go off alone like that." Erin was filling a thermos with iced tea to put in the backpack.

"Yes, I suppose you do. Mikell is a person who needs quiet. It's one reason, I think, that he loves his work so much. Most of it he does alone. He comes home quite cross when he's had to repair an organ with someone standing over him watching every move, talking the whole time. It isn't that he doesn't like people, it's just that he isn't the kind that can take a lot of noise and confusion. I learned that early in our marriage." She put the sandwiches in the pack and added oranges. "There. That should do. We'll be back in a couple of hours. I've signed in where we're going on the itinerary sheet, but we should be back without problems." Erin watched them start toward one of the hiking trails in the park. As she stood there Celeste came running up with Trudy. "Mamma, we need your help" she said breathlessly.

"Doing what?"

"We're going to make over Imogen."

"You're going to what?"

The girls giggled. "Make over Imogen. You know. Give her the works."

"And how're you going to do that?"

"Oh, we told her we need to practice because we were going to be beauticians someday and would she let us practice on her."

"And where do I come in?" Erin asked in amusement.

"You know what colors match. You know," Celeste said with a wave of her hand. "What goes with the different kinds of skin and hair. Remember. You taught me."

"Why don't you ask Suz?"

"Mother!" Celeste said in disgust, "You know as much as she does. Besides she says she doesn't want to risk Kit—I mean, Aunt Vicky's ire." None of the children had ever been allowed to use Victoria's nickname.

"So you did ask her first?" Erin smiled at her daughter.

"Only because she was there. We wanted both of you. We were going to ask you, too, but we don't need her. You're good enough."

Erin surveyed the girls. Celeste had done all of the talking but Trudy had been nodding her head and now she looked at Erin expectantly. "All right," Erin conceded. "Where do we find the victim?"

When Missily and Mikell came back it was to find their place transformed into a beauty salon. Candace was giving Imogen a manicure while Celeste worked with her hair. Her face was made up so that she looked completely different. Missily thought, "Why, she's almost pretty," while Mikell stared.

"What on earth?" he asked of no one in particular.

Erin came across the room. "The girls are practicing on Imogen," she said, linking her arm in his, hoping he wouldn't make any remarks and spoil things.

He frowned a moment, caught sight of Victoria glowering from the straight-backed chair while Granny Ellen sat pretending to knit but most of the time it lay idle in her hands and there was a twinkle in her eyes. She smiled at Mikell and he grinned. "Do you know where Myles is, anyone? He wanted to go with me into town to see that organ in the Presbyterian Church," he said.

"Down on the beach the last I knew," answered Celeste. "They're playing games, running races."

"Yes," said Kitten primly, "and Suz is acting like a child right along with them."

Erin turned. "What's wrong with games and races?"

"You'd think she'd begin to have some dignity at her age," answered Kitten.

"Don't be any more stupid than you have to be, Victoria," said Allan Metlow who was in one of the comfortable chairs. He had a book open but he'd been enjoying watching his granddaughters and Trudy. "Sports are as valid as a way of spending your free time, or making money, as music."

Missily slipped out the door. She had never liked it when her father and Kitten got into one of their arguments. They were both too prone to argue for the sake of the argument even when they didn't care much for the side they were defending. Her father had never liked sports but he disliked intolerance more. Missily walked down to the camping area and slipped into the Nielsen's RV going quietly back to where Stephanie was sitting against pillows reading. She smiled when she saw her aunt.

"Are you feeling better?"

"Yes. The medicine helps. My headache is gone but I feel so weak right now. Besides mother told me I couldn't go climbing tomorrow unless I stayed quiet today even if I feel fine."

Missily sat down on the side of the bed. She loved this niece of hers probably the most of all her nieces though she wouldn't have admitted it even to herself. "What're you reading?"

"*Pride and Prejudice.* I read *Sense and Sensibility* first."

"I love Jane Austin's books. I've read all of them, some more than once."

"I've read *Jane Eyre* twice already. I know that's not by Jane Austen, but remember? You send it to me for my birthday last year. Did I ever write you a thank you note?"

"Probably. I'm glad you like it."

"Aunt Missily, I—I want to ask you something. I'm glad you came. I wasn't really reading. When I get these headaches I wish I could die but I'm afraid because I don't know what happens after death. Gretchen says she's not afraid to die because she knows she'll go to heaven but I'm not even sure there is a heaven. Am I wicked not to know?" She had said it all in a rush as if she were afraid she wouldn't have the courage any other way.

Missily brushed back the lovely hair from her niece's flushed face. She felt feverish to Missily. "We can't know things we've never learned. Do you think you wouldn't be afraid if you did know what happens after a person died?"

"If I could just go to sleep forever and not wake up I wouldn't be afraid, but what if—well, Gretchen says that heaven and hell are real places. And I—I don't know that I'd want to go to heaven. I mean," she added hastily, "it doesn't sound very interesting to be like angels, but I wouldn't want to go to hell."

"Stephanie, if someone you love very much, say your father, let's say, moved a long ways away. Maybe to Norway. You've never seen Norway except in pictures but you don't know exactly what it's like. So say he moved there; wouldn't you want to go see him and live there?"

"Yes," Stephanie answered, puzzled.

"You see, that's the way it is with us. We don't know exactly what our home will be like after we leave this life. We have some word pictures but they can't describe it in a way so we really know what it will be like but the reason we want to go there is because of a person we love very much, because of Jesus Christ and what he did for us. Do you have the Bible Uncle Mikell and I gave you?"

"It—it's right here." Stephanie pulled it out from under her pillow. "I try to read it but God seems so cruel. He's always killing someone. I thought He was supposed to be loving and kind." She let the pages turn in her hand. "Daddy says it's stories like Greek and Norse myths. When I asked him about you and Uncle Mikell he said we believe whatever helps us. Some people believe in yoga and meditation, some people believe that drugs help them." She looked up at her aunt. "I told him you weren't weak people and he said no, but perhaps you felt a need to believe in a higher power. He believes he can handle things without superstition. *He* said that," she added hastily. "When I asked him if he didn't need anyone else he said yes, he needed his beautiful daughter. He was joking but I knew he was bored with the subject."

Missily reached for the Bible. "Let me tell you the story Uncle Mikell told me when I didn't believe the way I do now."

"Aunt Missily, before you start. I—I'd like to go to church but I don't know which one to go to."

"I can give you some names."

"Good. But I don't know whether I'll go. At least not until I'm older. After I leave home," she added. She'd been sitting up; now she lay back against the pillows.

"Your parents won't care if you go," Missily said.

"No, but they'll make snide remarks. And Celeste—" she broke off, her voice not quite steady.

"I'll give you the names of the churches and you can do what you like. Now, why don't you just rest and I'll tell you the story." She began where Mikell had, with the creation and as she did so she remembered how astonished she'd been that Mikell believed such things. She smiled a little as she took Stephanie's hand in hers.

Late that night Diccon wandered down to the dock alone and stood listening to the waves dash against the piles. Why, he wondered, did he continue to let himself in for the pain that seeing Suz always brought? Why did he always convince himself that this time it would be different? Every time he would decide not to come but his love for the family and the fact that his own son and daughter would be there drew him. He hadn't talked much to of either of them this time because Jon and Alexis were always going off somewhere alone while Nigel tried to stay in Lorna's vicinity as much as he could. He wondered if Suz had noticed the later. He'd seen more of her this time. She was strange, not spending much time with Shaul as she usually did the men she brought. She'd been spending far more time with the younger ones. He'd watched her run races on the beach where he'd been assigned judge, partly because he had a stopwatch, he suspected. Suz had never lost that long-legged grace that so captured his heart when she was one of the cheerleaders in high school.

He heard footsteps on the boards behind him and turned. He was standing in the shadow of the building, leaning against it, and tried to think of a way to let the other person know he was there without startling whomever it was. When the figure reached the low railing on the edge of the dock he saw it was Suz, her long hair caught back with another scarf.

"Zannie!" he whispered involuntarily and she whirled. "Sorry," he said. "I didn't mean to scare you. I wasn't sure how to let you know I was here."

"You called me—" she broke off.

He crossed the weathered, creaking boards to her side. She was looking down at the water again. He didn't know she was fighting tears. Zannie. The beloved name. He'd never liked Suz and one day he told her, "I found it—the perfect name. I'm going to call you Zannie" and had caught her to twirl her around. "My own Zannie. No one else in the world has a Zannie like my Zannie." His eyes had sparkled and she was Zannie from then on. No one else ever used the name for her, or dared. Neither Suz nor Diccon would allow it.

"I always think of you as Zannie. That's who you are to me," he said quietly, then, "Where's Shaul?"

"He went into Port Townsend. Found a place to play the piano."

"He sounds serious about moving up here. We talked some earlier today."

"Yes. He's already called a real estate agent in California about putting his place on the market."

"Will he like it here, do you think?"

"I don't know. He's a Californian. I can't imagine his liking the weather here. He has a beautiful Spanish style place outside the city overlooking the ocean, but he says he feels at home here. Diccon, does Nigel have a thing for Lorna?"

"I wondered if you'd noticed."

"Isn't she quite a bit older?"

He didn't say that was a strange question coming from her when it was obvious Shaul was years younger than Suz. "About three or four years."

"Is that all? I guess because she's Mikell's sister is seems she should be older though she doesn't look it."

"She was a caboose. She's quite a bit younger than Eva is. About ten years, I think."

"Where is Eva? Isn't she coming?"

"They're coming over Friday and Saturday. Not all on the same day. They have to take turns. Max and Molly will come only for a day as will Deborah and Gabe. They can't leave their places long.

"Didn't they come last time?"

"Some of them. I think Deborah and Gabe got someone to run the place that time and Perry and Jean took their vacation then."

"Isn't it strange?" Suz was perched on the rail now though she was looking out over the dark water. "Missily's the only one of us with many in-laws. Graham has only one sister, hasn't he?"

"I believe so." The breeze, stronger than it had been earlier, blew Suz's hair back and then onto her shoulder. He wanted to reach out, take the scarf off to run his fingers through the long tresses as he'd done so many times before. Abruptly he turned so he couldn't see her and looked across the water.

"Are you going climbing tomorrow, Diccon?" Suz asked and her voice betrayed her by wobbling. She'd always been afraid of climbing, for herself and those she loved.

"Yes. We're not going for a hard climb, though. I think we're going to camp out one night for the kids but it's not a long climb. Not many of us came prepared for much difficult climbing."

"Who else is going? I know Shaul is. He loves to climb. Is Nigel going?"

"Yes, and Thor and his father, Alexis and Jon, Myles, Gretchen—that girl climbs like a mountain goat—and Stephanie and... let me see. Some other girls." Diccon named them silently counting on his fingers, then continued. "Oh yes, Candace, Celeste and some of Mikell's nephews. I can't remember all their names. I get the boys confused and to which family they belong."

"You probably do better than I would. What about Lorna? Is she going?"

"No." Diccon turned to watch her again. "She doesn't like mountain climbing either, unless she's on a horse."

"You didn't answer my question. How does Nigel feel about her?"

"He's pretty crazy about her," Diccon answered, still not willing to betray Nigel's confidence. "So far I'm not sure she's aware of it. She still loves horses best."

"Maybe they're safer," mumbled Suz. She was feeling uncomfortable and guilty, as though she shouldn't be here with Diccon. It was irrational, she knew, but she felt she was betraying Shaul. She was also humiliated by her actions of the night before and hoped Diccon hadn't heard about it. She didn't get drunk often and she usually laughed it off but she wasn't enjoying herself as she usually did at the reunions and she was becoming more irritated with Shaul all the time though she didn't think it was his fault. Shaul wasn't behaving any differently than he ever had but Diccon....She had to quit thinking about Diccon. "I'd like to sleep in a tent for a change. It's been years since I have," she said, hunting frantically for words. Words to dispel the attraction of the man at her side. He was too religious. "I think I'll go into town tomorrow, maybe over to Seattle, and get myself a tent and a sleeping bag."

"You may try mine tonight if you wish," Diccon said.

For one wild minute she thought he was asking her to stay the night with him and her heart jumped. "What will you do?" She asked as common sense took over.

"Sleep under the stars with the boys. I've extra blankets," he answered, mentally preparing to ask Nigel for one. He had only one heavy one in his car. "I've done it many times."

"Diccon. I can't turn you out."

"Why not? It's just for tonight. No use spending money unless you know whether you still like it."

"Well, I don't know," she said hesitantly. "Where is it?"

"Down near where the girls have theirs. I'm kind of being Daddy to them. Lorna and Trudy and Kate. They've had most of the other girls there, too."

"In one tent?"

"No. They have two. But they're big ones. Kate's parents do a lot of camping so have a nice tent and so do Mikell's parents. Nigel was with me but he decided to sleep out with the others—Myles, Sean and company."

"Well..." Suz sat swinging her leg. What would she tell Shaul? Suddenly she didn't care about Shaul. "Okay. I'll try it. If I like it well enough I'll go to town tomorrow and get one."

Chapter XXII

Everyone rose early the next morning before the sun had made it above the Cascades while there was dew on everything so that the landscape sparkled in the early morning light, dewdrops spangling the grass and the multitude of spider webs. The gulls were crying and flying white in the blue sky. Not only the hikers and climbers were up preparing to leave but those who'd chose other things to do that day were up to see them off. Anna Metlow hurried from one group to the other making sure they had food and warm clothes, for the mountains and beach could both be cold, that they had first aid kits, reminding the hikers not to forget to watch the tide—there were places they would only be able to cross at low tide—and the climbers to be careful, not to take chances. They were all used to her nervous ways and answered her cheerfully except Shaul who scowled. He had no idea where Suz was and couldn't bring himself to ask. She hadn't been in their room when he got back the night before nor had she come in all night. Diccon was with the other climbers, packing and checking gear. Shaul had thought of him right away when he couldn't find Suz. He still wasn't sure of her and Diccon was an attractive man, not at all the kind a woman would desert that he could see.

Suz was standing in front of Diccon's tent brushing her hair vigorously. Alexis, who'd been out too late the night before, came out of hers and Jon's tent looking quite sleepy. "Mom! What are you doing here?" she demanded rather sharply.

Suz turned. "Hi, sleepyhead. Everyone's been up half an hour or more."

"Mom. What *are* you doing in Dad's tent?"

"I'm not in it at present but I slept in it last night," Suz said and she gave her hair several more strokes, enjoying the sight of her astonished daughter before she added, "He let me try it last night to see if I liked tenting well enough to buy one while he slept with the others under the stars." She deftly rolled her hair into a French roll and secured it. "I enjoyed it so much I'm going to Seattle today to buy one."

"Oh," Alexis said and Suz had to hide her smile. Her daughter sounded disappointed. "Oh dear! I'd better get going," she added and headed toward the others. Suz followed more leisurely, stopping to watch the sun as it shot rays high into the sky ahead of it, wishing she had her camera with her.

Shaul saw Alexis hurrying up to the group and when she was close enough he asked, "Alexis, where's Suz?"

"Down by Dad's tent," answered Alexis, her mind preoccupied with finding Jon. "She slept there last night. Jon! There you are." She ran to him leaving behind her a startled and then angry Shaul.

When Suz strolled into sight he strode over to her, took her arm roughly and pulled her away from the others. "Just what game are you trying to play with me?" he demanded.

"Shaul, you're hurting me. Let go."

"Answer me," he demanded, giving her arm a shake.

She looked at him levelly, not saying a word until he let go. "Thank you. Now will you please explain the strong arm tactics?"

"Where were you? Why weren't you in our room?" His voice was still rough and not very quiet.

Suz glanced around him at the group gathered and packing. "Don't yell. I'm not deaf. Shaul, I told you before we came that I'm my own person. I don't belong to you or any other man."

"Not even your former husband? Oh sure, I know. You're just friends," he said sarcastically. "You have to talk to him about your kids! Come off it, Suz. Your kids are grown and 'just friends' don't sleep together."

"Shaul, will you stop yelling at me. Do you want everyone to hear you?"

"I don't give a damn who hears me. I want an answer. Where were you last night?"

"Why are you asking me? You already seem to know," Suz retorted, slipped around him and went to where Nigel was hoisting a backpack on his back. She looked around for Lorna and found she was busy helping Adam with his pack. Adam looked harassed and Suz grinned. If he was anything like Nigel he would want to do his own packing. "Lorna," she called, linking her arm in Nigel's.

Lorna looked up.

"Come here, will you?" And Lorna was too polite to refuse. Behind her back Adam gave Suz a thumbs up sign and began to repack his bag. "You're not going?" Suz asked Lorna.

"No. I'm not a mountain climber and I've been on the beach hike. Granny Ellen and I are going to be lazy together."

"I'm not a mountain climber either. In fact, it frightens me. Not only for me but for these men to go," Suz said, leaning her head against her son's arm.

He slipped it around her. "No more dangerous than those highways you drive, Madre mia," he said.

"But it seems like it," said Lorna and Suz agreed.

"I'm going into Seattle and get myself a tent," she added. "I slept in Diccon's last night to try it. It's been years since I camped."

"I know you did. Dad borrowed a blanket from me. He had a heavy wool one and I had an old quilt in the car."

"Oh dear. He said he had blankets."

"He did." Nigel bent to kiss her cheek then smooth out her wrinkled brow. "Don't frown so. You'll get wrinkles," he teased. "He said he knew I had an extra one. He was quite warm. I asked."

"Aren't you going to eat breakfast before you go, Nigel?" Lorna wanted to know.

"Yes. Just trying out the pack. But we better get at it. Is Shaul ready?" he asked Suz.

"I don't know. You'll have to ask him. I'll go see if I can lend a hand getting breakfast ready." She left them, running with grace toward the buildings across the parade ground.

"She's super," Lorna said. "We had so much fun yesterday. The way everyone talked I thought—" she broke off in confusion remembering it was Nigel's mother she was talking about.

"Don't worry. I've heard it all. Probably said some of it myself. It's not easy to accept a new guy around the house every time you turn around. Alexis and I hated it. That's why we left as soon as we were old enough. She's fun but she's immoral and indolent. I know she loves Alexis and me. At least as far as she's able. But sometimes I find it hard to love her because of Dad."

"I never thought of that. It would be horrid having a new dad so often. It's—it's kind of icky," Lorna said, her small face screwed up with distaste.

Nigel laughed and reached out to run his fingers lightly down her cheek "It *was* icky."

She giggled. The word sounded strange coming from him. Nigel caught his breath and she looked up quickly. "Lorna," he said urgently but Candace came racing up.

"Time to eat. Come on. Shaul's about to leave without all of us." She pulled Nigel's hand.

"Okay, okay, young one. Isn't he going to eat?" he asked as they ran together.

Lorna stood where he left her and her hand slowly went up to touch where his fingers had rested lightly a minute ago. What had he started to say? With a sigh she walked slowly toward the building and breakfast.

After both groups were gone the rest began to talk about what they would be doing. Thor's mother, Maren Nielsen, said she was going back to bed for a while and Genevieve Curtis, Graham's mother, followed suit. Suz asked Imogen and Kitten if they wanted to go to Seattle with her.

Kitten looked at her with distaste. "No thank you," she said primly and would have walked away had not Imogen said, "Oh, Kitten, let's do. It would be fun."

Imogen, the new Imogen as Celeste and Trudy called her, had come through the girls' practice in good humor and had, in fact, asked them to teach her how to apply make-up. They had promised to go shopping with her for it and for some new clothes. She looked colorless right now but she was determined she wasn't going to give up the new look. "Maybe Suz can help me find some clothes and make-up," she said now.

"I will *not* go anywhere with that woman," said Kitten. "It's not enough for you to bring a man along to satisfy your disgusting desires," she glared at Suz. "You have to have another man, too. You slut! I'm surprised at Diccon. I thought he was a better man."

Suz slapped Kitten hard. "Shut up! You and your goody-goody ways. Who knows how many men you have back East. Or is it men?" she continued with a sidelong glance at Imogen.

Furious, Kitten started forward just as two arms went around Suz from behind her. "I thought my daughters were brought up better than to scrap in public," Allan Metlow said.

Suz relaxed against him, feeling much as she had when she was a little girl and Kitten began to act superior.

"What is all this?" he asked.

Before either of his daughters could answer Erin came up. "Hi, Suz. I hear you tried a tent last night. Thor said he found Diccon with some blankets and asked him what he was doing. He said he'd let you borrow his tent."

"He suggested it when I said I'd like to try sleeping in one again. It's been years since I camped. He told me to try his to see if I liked it before I bought one."

"Are you going to get one?"

"Yes. I'm going over to Seattle today. Want to go along? Imogen wants to do some shopping."

Kitten was watching the two of them. Then she said, "Alexis is telling everyone you slept with Diccon."

"What? " It was Allan. "Are you sure?"

"Where do you think I heard it?" his daughter answered angrily.

"Just what did she say?"

"I didn't hear her. Genevieve Curtis told me."

"And she heard it where?" He was still standing with his arms around Suz and could feel her trembling.

"I don't know. But if it isn't true why would Alexis say it?"

"Look, Kitten, you can think what you want about me," Suz interposed, "but Diccon is an honorable man and I did *not* sleep with him. I slept alone."

Kitten looked at her, her face hard, unrelenting, the red mark on her cheek where Suz had slapped her still visible. "I hope you're telling the truth. I've always liked Diccon. He was too good for you."

"Kitten! That is quite enough." Allan said sharply just as his wife hurried over to the group.

"Are you two arguing again? Kitten, you don't have your cello with you, do you? There's a group of people who are going to be playing in one of the auditoriums and the cellist is sick. I told them you play with the Philadelphia orchestra and they would like you to play with them. They said they'd find a cello."

Kitten had changed completely. "I have my cello, Mother. I'm playing a concert with a quartet in Denver after I leave here. What kind of music are they playing?"

"Come along. You'll have to ask them." Anna turned to leave with her daughter and Allan chuckled.

"She's been worried about Vicky for days. Said it isn't fair for her not to have something to do that she likes. Leave it to Anna."

"I'm going to change clothes if we're going into Seattle," Erin said. "Why don't we see if Rose wants to go."

"She's with Graham," Allan answered. "She hardly lets him out of sight since he had that operation."

"Well, I'll go change anyway."

"I will, too," said Imogen and they walked off together.

Suz turned in Allan's arms. "Daddy, what am I going to do about what Kitten said? I can't imagine Alexis telling anyone that. She knows I didn't sleep with Diccon."

"I'll scout around and find out where the story originated. We'll settle it."

"I'm serious. I don't care what they think of me. I never have. But I do care if they say things like that about Diccon."

Allan stood looking down at this wayward daughter of his who had brought so much pain into his and Anna's life yet whom he loved so much. "Why did you leave him?"

Suz looked up, startled, then hid her face against his shoulder. "Oh, Daddy. I've been such a fool. I've wasted so many years and I don't know how to change."

"Are you going to marry Shaul?"

"No. I've told him I'm not ready to be tied to anyone. I wish I knew how I could do something useful so my whole life wouldn't be a total waste."

He rocked her. "Isn't there something you'd like to do—as a volunteer, perhaps, or otherwise? Something you're interested in or find a concern?"

She shook her head still resting against him. "I don't know. I don't seem to care that much about anything. Auden said I was lazy. Maybe he's right."

"It didn't look lazy running all those races yesterday. You're good with kids. Isn't there some kind of work with them you'd like?"

"I don't know. I couldn't work with handicapped children. I—I can't stand to see them. It makes me ill and I wouldn't want to teach." She looked up, her face bleak. "I've tried and tried to think of something and then it seems easier to drift with the tide. But lately—" Diccon, she thought. If I could only be with Diccon. Sighing she stood away from her father. "Guess I'd better go change, too."

He nodded. "Don't give up. I'll look around. Maybe I can find something you'd like to do. Have a good time today. Do you have a car to drive?"

"Yes. Shaul left me his. He gave me a key yesterday morning or I probably wouldn't have one. He must have heard what Kitten did. I had no idea why he was so angry except that he's a little too possessive and I wasn't in our room when he came in last night. Thanks for the shoulder, Pops," she added kissing his cheek. Turning she ran lightly toward the house where her clothes were.

One group of the climbers came back early the next day. They had managed one of their climbs but the weather had changed and they hadn't tried a second, more difficult one.

"Visibility was getting too poor," said Diccon. "I wasn't about to risk going up higher. We could have climbed above the fog, I suppose, but both Alfred and I agreed it wiser to come back rather than risk anything.'

Allan nodded. "Good idea. No sense taking unnecessary chances. Where are the others?"

"They went on a different climb. We all talked over the possibilities and they decided on one for which they had to hike in further. We wanted to get to the climb faster."

"I wish I'd gone with them," said Candace. "I didn't want to come back yet. I wanted to climb more."

"You've plenty of time," her grandfather told her. "What are you? Eleven?"

"Grandfather! I'm thirteen, almost fourteen," Candace said indignantly.

Allan laughed, reaching out to give her a hug and Diccon, watching, wondered if anyone else noticed how much alike they looked.

The second group to show up was the beach hikers, sometime after supper, tired, still damp from the wet weather but full of the beauty and wildness of the country alongside the ocean. They'd had lovely weather the day before but a storm had blown in during the night and rain started midmorning. Now all they wanted were hot showers and clean clothes. Later they sat before one of the fireplaces drinking hot drinks and talking about the hike while the climbers told stories of their climb, most of them about Diccon, Missily noticed. He was clearly a favorite of all of them. He knew, of course, all the plants, the rocks, the mountain lore from way back and was not only interesting but had a winsome personality. She noticed that even Imogen was captured by him; she sat watching him as they all talked.

Missily said to Mikell under the conversation, eventually, "Shouldn't the rest of them be back by now?"

"I would think so. But they may have had to bivouac. Diccon says visibility was getting poor. They're all experienced climbers who know enough to camp until it clears." He reached for her hand under the blanket covering their knees. He'd said earlier he must be getting old, he still felt chilled to the bone and Suz had gotten a blanket to put over his legs. Missily had pulled it over her, too. "They might not come back until tomorrow."

"I know." She sighed. "Why didn't they all stay together?"

"I asked Diccon and he said they were going to meet and camp together if they could make it back in time but had the option of staying where they thought best so when they didn't come last night he figured their climb had taken longer than they thought it would. And he also said that since Thor and Shaul are both there and are experienced climbers we shouldn't be alarmed if they don't get back tonight."

"I suppose not, but even experienced climbers have accidents."

"I know. Let's not borrow trouble, shall we?" Mikell said gently though he wasn't easy himself and knew he wouldn't be until they were all together again. There could be some nasty weather on the mountains and he had no idea how they were fixed for food.

They went to bed late but neither one slept well. Sean had gone with them to the beach and Candace was back but that left both Myles and Gretchen on the mountains somewhere. Before six the next morning, Missily slipped quietly out of bed so as not to wake Mikell and reached for her robe, but he was already awake. "Can't sleep, Jedidah?"

"No. I thought I'd read a while."

He sat up, "I'm going to scout around and see if I can find someone who can tell me what the weather's like where they are. I'm sure they've decided to sit tight until it's safe but I'd like to know what's going on." He swung out of bed and pulled on his clothes. Before he left he took her in his arms to kiss her and found she was trembling. When he drew back to look down at her she said, "I'm scared, Mikell. What if something's happened. Myles—Gretchen...." Her voice caught and a tear slid down her cheek.

He wiped it away gently. "I know," he pulled her close feeling inadequate. "But it's better not to imagine things," he continued though he'd spent most of the night disciplining his mind not to do just that.

After he was gone she crept into the living-room to curl up in a big chair, trying to read, but she couldn't keep her mind on her book, nor relax so she gave up and went back to dress before she let herself out of the house and began to wander aimlessly about the Fort. It was so quiet. She could hear the waves on the beach and the birds were awake, the ever present gulls circling over head. The morning was so beautiful it was hard to imagine bad weather anywhere else. Missily walked down to stand, watching the water, looking across to the Islands distinct in the morning light. When she went back up toward the houses she found Erin and Suz standing out front talking. They turned as she crossed the road.

"Hear anything about our wanderers?" Suz asked.

She shook her head. "Mikell went to see if he could find out about the weather where they are."

"I don't understand why they didn't stay together," Erin said fretfully.

"Mikell says Diccon told him the other group wanted to go on a climb farther in and his group wanted to start climbing sooner. They decided to meet to camp that night unless it was too late, then they'd stay where they were. Mikell thinks they may have run into bad weather and are just waiting it out which is safer than trying to find their way back, especially if there's heavy fog or snow." Missily answered. "Did you sleep?"

"Not very much. Thor's an experienced climber but I'm still worried. I wish I'd gone with him."

"I have a feeling Mikell will report the group. There's a great rescue organization here in Washington and I know he'll want them notified if we don't hear from the others soon or at least what the weather is like."

"Missily!" cried Erin, her face pinched and white. "Why would they need rescuing? I thought it was just the weather so they camped out an extra night."

"Erin, love, I only meant if we need help there are reliable people we can call on. I didn't mean we'd need them. All of them are experienced climbers. There may have been a white out because of that storm that came in. If that's true they'll wait until they can see to leave." Missily tried to talk

206

quietly to calm her sister who was now nervously rubbing her hands together. "Mikell went to find out what the weather is like over there—or to see if someone knows. The climb they went on is on the other side where there is more rain and even snow in the higher elevations." She knew she was talking to convince herself as well as Erin, trying not to let the panic rising in her overwhelm her though her mouth was dry and her stomach in knots.

"Diccon's car is gone," Suz said suddenly.

Erin and Missily turned to look down at the parking lot then at each other. That meant that two of the men were out somewhere trying to garner information. As they stood there Diccon drove up, slammed his door and ran to his tent. Suz started running down toward the camping area, calling, "Diccon!"

He glanced her way then ducked into the tent. When he came back out he had his backpack.

"Diccon, did you find out something?" Suz asked breathlessly.

"No. You up already?"

"I couldn't sleep. What are you doing?"

"I'm going to look for them. I can't stand waiting around here."

"No!" Suz grabbed his arm. "Diccon, if something should happen to you...." her words died away as they stared at one another.

"I have to go, Zannie," he said and bent to kiss her lips gently before he went to his car.

She stood watching him drive off and thought she had never felt so alone, so afraid in all her life. As Erin and Missily came up she turned. "He's going to look for them."

"Ah!" Missily gave a sigh of relief. "Thank God."

"But, Missily, what if it's dangerous? I mean the hike? In the weather, I mean." Suz said incoherently. The terror had gripped her so strongly she was almost ill.

"Diccon? He's more used to all this than any of them. It's his living," Missily answered.

"Besides, she wouldn't be afraid," said Erin.

"Who wouldn't?" Missily asked.

"You," Erin replied sharply.

"Why not? I'm human, too. Why do you think I'm awake so early?"

"I thought you people didn't worry about things."

"If by 'you people' you mean Christians I'll have to disappoint you. We *shouldn't* worry but we do. I believe God is in control but that doesn't mean something can't happen. We don't live charmed lives. Suz, what's wrong?" Missily went to her older sister who was sobbing.

Suz didn't answer as she tried desperately to control herself, but Diccon's gentle kiss had shaken her. Memories hidden for years flooded back and the thought that something might happen to both Nigel and Diccon was more than she could handle. She tore herself out of Missily's arms and ran. Missily started to follow but Erin caught her arm.

"Let her go. She probably wants to be alone. It's funny," she mused, "I've always wondered if she ever really quit loving Diccon."

207

"How could she love him and marry someone else?" Missily demanded.

Erin, gazing out to where a ship was gliding into the Inlet said, "It's strange what one can do when they're unhappy."

"But if she stayed with Diccon she could have been happy."

Erin's eyes came back to Missily. "She hated that life. She loved the city and all the excitement. She told me so after she left Diccon. She was bored and didn't like the people they lived near."

"Why did she marry him, then? She knew what he wanted to do?"

"She thought he'd get tired of it. Missily, I never did get to thank you and Mikell for what you did for Thor and I. I think our marriage would have ended if we hadn't talked. It was all so stupid but it didn't seem so at the time."

"It never does, does it?" Missily agreed. Then she said, "Erin, I'm terrified."

Erin nodded and began to cry and they fell into each other's arms. Mikell came back a half-hour or so later to tell them he'd reported the group and searchers would be sent out.

"Oh. What do they think happened?" Erin stammered.

"No one knows yet. They had snow above 5,000 feet but the group knew enough not to climb in bad weather, I'm sure. Our two have been told not to," Mikell answered, "and I know that Thor knows that, also." He looked harassed and tired.

"Let's go get some breakfast," said Missily, striving for calmness. "Were they going to call if they found anything?" she asked as they moved toward the buildings.

"I said I'd call and check in, in about an hour."

Eventually the family collected and fixed breakfast in the camping area, staying together. Anna was remote, Rose sat beside Graham, not speaking. She didn't even offer to help with the meal and wouldn't eat until Allan talked her into it. Even the monsters were subdued and quiet, eating little, Candace asking questions no one could answer until finally Celeste said, "Shut up!" crossly. Suz hadn't come back yet and after breakfast Missily and Mikell went on a fruitless search for her. Shaul's car was still parked but she could have gone on any of the hiking trails and with over three hundred acres of Park it would be impossible to cover it all. She wasn't on the wharf, by the battery, or near the lighthouse so they gave up and went back to the gloomy group sitting at the picnic tables and on the lawn. Missily caught herself begging over and over, "Please God," and nothing else.

No one felt like doing anything and they were also doubly nervous because some of Mikell's family were coming over for the day and Max and Molly's youngest son, Rex, was one of those missing. The younger set wanted to go look for the missing ones and were told no because not only had Diccon gone but there would be an experienced rescue team looking for them. They wandered off, angry with the adults who seemed to be doing nothing.

Kitten, who had been in better spirits since she'd played in the chamber music quartet the day before, much to Anna's delight, was now subdued and had dark circles under her eyes as though she, too, hadn't slept. Imogen kept busy, helping with the meal first, cleaning up after, then going to the room where she and Kitten were staying to straighten it. She wanted to try her new make-up but felt it would be frivolous now that everyone was so anxious about the climbers.

Diccon, when he finally reached the place where he could park his station wagon and start to hike, got out, put on his backpack, in which he had two large thermoses of hot tea, and his first aid kit and he strapped on the bed roll he'd used during the night he slept out. The trail was difficult, not much used, and was overgrown so going was slow. Diccon was taking a short cut to the climbing spot, which he'd spotted when studying the map. His sense of direction had never failed him but he also had a map of the area and he knew his forests. The day was turning warm so that he was beginning to think he would have to stop and take off his jacket when he thought he saw someone ahead. Impatiently, he pushed aside the undergrowth where it had begun to take over the path until he was close enough to see that whoever it was, was sitting on the ground leaning against a tree, then he went on a run.

"Gretchen." He knelt beside the still figure. "Gretchen, it's Uncle Diccon. Darling, can you talk to me?"

She lifted her head listlessly but a flicker of life lit her eyes briefly, "Help..." she said weakly. She was soaking wet and shaking.

Diccon slung his backpack off his shoulders. "Yes, I'll help you. I've got some hot tea here," he said as he unscrewed the top off the thermos and poured part of a cup full.

"Here, drink this," he said holding her with one arm and the cup with his other hand. She gasped but took a couple of swallow.

"So cold," she said through chattering teeth.

"I know. I'm going to help you get a dry top on." Gently he took the wet shirt off her. Where was her jacket? Then he removed the wet under clothes, clenching his jaw when he saw the ugly bruises on her chest, slipping one of his sweatshirts over her head. "What is it?" he asked as she gasped again, but she didn't answer and he saw she'd bitten her lip so hard it was bleeding. "Did I hurt you?" But again she wouldn't answer. "Where's your pack?" he asked as he tried to help her get her arms in the sleeves of the sweat shirt and then she went limp and he saw that she had fainted. Quickly he got her arms into the sleeves wondering what had happened to her chest and what was giving her so much pain. He wrapped her in one of the blankets and she stirred.

"Uncle...Diccon?" she whispered.

"Yes, darling, I'm here. Can you drink some more tea? What did you do with your pack?"

"Too heavy," she answered. "Help.." her voice died out and she tried again, "help them."

"I will. Drink the rest of this. Will you just sit here? There are people coming to help. I'll go find the others."

"Dead. Maybe dead," she said and began to cry weakly.

"Drink up," he said roughly though not unkindly. "Gretchen, I need your help. You must stay here until help comes. Do you promise me?"

"Yes," she whispered.

"Good. I'll leave another cup of hot tea. Try to get it down. It'll help warm you." He rose, closed his eyes briefly. How could he leave her?

"Help...them..."

"All right, darling," he said, bent to kiss her cheek and started up the trail wondering what he would find. She looked as though she'd had a fall and there was something wrong she wouldn't talk about. Suppose, he thought suddenly, she couldn't walk. But no, she'd made it down the trail this far. She had a terrible skinned place on her face and her arms were bruised as well as her chest. What had happened? As difficult as his decision had been when he left Gretchen the next one he had to make was even more difficult. He saw her more easily than he had Gretchen because she was laying in the trail, her beautiful hair in a tangle, plastered across her face. His heart was in his mouth this time as he bent over her, felt carefully for broken bones, then picked her up and carried her to a place where he could lay her down and kneel beside her. He poured a cup of tea, felt for her pulse. It was weak but steady. "Stephanie. Stephanie, can you hear me?" he asked, thinking with another part of his mind, "What a stupid question." Aloud he said, "Stephanie, dear, look at me."

But she kept her eyes closed. It was as though she were asleep. She still had her jacket on and her clothes were dry except for her jeans, but she wasn't cold. She was burning with a fever. Diccon took off his jacket and wrapped her in it. She still had her pack in which he found extra clothes so pulled off her wet jeans and put dry ones on and wrapped the other blanket around her. She wasn't hurt like Gretchen, it didn't seem, but there was something very wrong. Picking her up he carried her back down the trail to where Gretchen still sat, eyes closed, leaning against a tree as he had left her.

"Gretchen," he said. "Look. I've got Stephanie. Can you help me? I need your help," he said hoping to rouse her that way.

She looked up at him. "What?" she whispered.

"I have my station wagon. I want to take Stephanie down there but I need you to come stay with her. Do you think you can manage? I'll find you a walking stick." He laid Stephanie down carefully and hunted up a stick. With his help Gretchen got up, gasping as she did so.

"All right?" he asked, feeling like he was torturing her.

She nodded. She would not tell him about the pain in her chest and how hard it was to breathe.

"Hold on to the stick and the tree until I get Stephanie, then hold on to me, too. We want to stay together." Diccon lifted Stephanie and agonizingly, slowly, they crept back down the trail, Diccon going sideways when it was narrow and overgrown so Gretchen could hold on to his arm. With her weight and Stephanie his arms began to cramp and he gritted his teeth to hold on to her. When they finally made it back to the station wagon, Diccon lay Stephanie down long enough to put the back seat down, put Stephanie in, lifting Gretchen in beside her, covering them both with the blankets.

"Will you be all right, love?" he asked Gretchen.

"Yes," she whispered. "Help the others."

"You're a brave girl," he told her bending to kiss her once more before he started back up the trail to where his pack was. It was agony to leave them and he prayed a rescue group would come soon. He was positive Mikell would request one but how soon he had no idea.

Mikell came into the living room late that evening where most of them had gathered. He'd gone down to the forestry department earlier and had been there most of the day. He was haggard, his face white.

"They've found them," he said into the silence. "They're..." his voice broke. Missily had crossed the room to him when he came in and now she took his hand. He looked down at her. "There's been an accident. They're not exactly sure yet what happened. It looks like they all fell."

There was a gasp and Missily said, "Mikell" entreatingly.

"I—I don't know how badly they're hurt. The girls weren't with the men. It's so confusing. They're taking them all to the hospital in Seattle. I'm going over."

"I'll go with you," Missily said. "I can't stand it here waiting, any more."

"There is one thing. Shaul, they know, was killed," he added, then, "Where's Suz?" as though he'd just realized she wasn't there.

"I don't know. She hasn't come back yet. Let's tell Erin. She's trying to take a nap on our bed. I'll go get her."

Max came across the room to Mikell. He and Molly had come from their place earlier in the day. "Missily tells me they've been gone three days."

"Yes," Mikell said. "They were going to be out two so we didn't start worrying until they didn't show up last night. They'd had a storm so that could mean they'd wait until the weather cleared. I—I didn't really expect any more than that."

"We'll go over, too. No sense staying here," Max said.

Missily came in with a jacket for Mikell. He'd been shivering when he came in. "Thank you," he said. "I think it's mostly nerves. It's not cold out. How's Erin?"

"She wasn't asleep. I haven't told her anything except you have news. I—I couldn't." Missily gray eyes were troubled.

Mikell reached over to touch her cheek. "I'll tell her. It's all right, Jeddie." And his voice was like a caress so that she felt comforted.

Erin came in looking small and anxious. "Missily said you had news."

"Yes." He took her hands in his. "There's been an accident of some kind. The rescue party has reached them and is taking them to the hospital in Seattle."

"Thor? Thor? What happened to Thor?" Erin's voice rose shrilly.

Mikell pulled her into his arms. "They're hurt. I don't know how badly. Only Shaul was killed. We're going over to the hospital. Will you come with us?"

"Thor," she whispered.

Mikell looked over Erin's head and mouthed, "Coat," and Missily left to find something for Erin to wear. "Are you coming, Kitten?" Mikell asked, still holding a whimpering Erin.

"No. I'll stay here and watch things. Please call and let us know what's going on. I'll stay by the phone."

Mikell bent to kiss her cheek. "Thanks, Vicky. I'll keep in touch." As Missily came in with one of her sweaters for Erin and helped her put it on Mikell crossed the room to Granny Ellen's chair. "Are you all right, Granny?"

"No, of course I'm not," she answered in annoyance. "Not with all of them hurt." Then she relented. "I'm sorry, Mikell. I know what you meant. We'll just have to wait for your call. God go with you."

He bent to kiss her. She smelled faintly of lilacs and her skin was petal soft. He stood a moment looking down at her. Then he whispered, "Thank you," before he turned to leave.

Erin looked exhausted and lost as Missily, with an arm around her, guided her out the door. "Stephanie," she said then. "Stephanie," and again a third time as though she couldn't get any further.

"Hold on, Erin," Mikell said. "Don't let your imagination run away. We'll get to the hospital and find out how they are." His voice was steady though his throat felt almost closed by fear. Gretchen. His Gretchen. And Myles. With determination he opened the car door for Missily and Erin. He turned as Max and Molly came out of the house.

"We'll follow you." Max said. "What about the kids?"

"I think they'll be just as well off here. They can find something to do. Candace wanted to come," Missily said. "Should we take them? Sean wanted to go, too."

"Someone can bring them later, perhaps." Mikell answered. "We don't know how long we'll have to sit in the hospital. It's better they stay here."

"How—how bad are they?" Missily finally voiced the question she'd wanted to ask earlier. The three of them were sitting together in the front seat, Erin hunched and silent.

"I don't know. They didn't give many details. Just said they'd been found and needed medical treatment. They're sending a helicopter. I could have found out more, I suppose, but I decided I'd rather go over to the hospital. We may get there not long after they do. I don't know how long it's been since they called for the copter."

When they reached the hospital after what seemed an unending ferry ride and then the drive with too much traffic, too many red lights, parked and went in they were directed to a room to wait.

Diccon drove back to Fort Worden much later, parked the car so he could run up the stairs to the house where Missily, Mikell and the others were staying. He must tell Suz about Shaul. Kitten opened to his knock.

"Diccon," she cried as he went in. "What happened? Where've you been?"

"Where's Suz?"

"I don't know. She got upset this morning, Erin said, and ran off crying. None of us can find her. Somebody's been looking off and on all day. Mr. Kittam's car's still here so she has to be somewhere in the Park."

Diccon frowned, then memory swept over him. Many times in their years together when they quarreled Suz would go off alone and he'd find her later somewhere, often curled up asleep with tear stains on her cheeks. His heart cramped now as it had done then. She'd always looked so young and lost.

"Diccon," Kitten said. "I—I'm sorry I believed what they said about you."

"What's that?" he asked dragging his mind back to the present.

"About you—about you and Suz sleeping together last night. Genevieve told me and I didn't have any reason not to believe her. I mean she isn't the kind to gossip. I don't mean..." she floundered to a stop. She suddenly realized, as face to face with Diccon she was forced to remember his integrity and honesty, if she hadn't thought Diccon would do it she wouldn't have believed what she heard.

"Told you *what*?"

"That Suz stayed the night with you in your tent. She heard Alexis tell Shaul."

"Shaul?" Diccon was suddenly alert. "Alexis told Shaul we slept together?"

"Well, no. I thought that's what she said. So did Genevieve but Allan found out she hadn't. I'm sorry. I shouldn't have believed it."

"What *did* she tell Shaul?"

Kitten became aware that Diccon's questions were short and sharp. "Why? What's the matter?"

"Do you know what Shaul said?" Diccon insisted.

"No. Genevieve said he was angry and drug Suz off to talk to her but that Suz didn't seem upset though he was glaring at her."

"Vicky, I've got to find Suz. When I do I'm going to take her over to Seattle. I'd like you to call a number." He dug into his pocket. "Here. Call them and tell them that Shaul left here angry at his girl friend. Don't tell them any details. Only that."

"I don't understand."

"I'm just guessing, but it may help understand what happened to them. It may have just been the landslide, but they were all experienced climbers and Shaul was leading, I think. He may not have been as careful as he should have been."

"Oh. I'll call." Kitten took the card.

Diccon leaned over to kiss her cheek. "You're wonderful. Sorry I can't stay. I'll tell you about things later. They're all pretty well banged up but I've got to find Zannie now," he said, reaching for the doorknob. "We'll call from the hospital."

"Mikell and Missily have already gone over," she said, "and Erin and Molly and Max. I'm not sure who else."

Diccon nodded and left. Where could she have gone? He checked the wharf, the lighthouse, the tents, both his and the one she'd bought, then stood thinking. He should have taken her with him. She could have stayed with the girls. Maybe gotten some hot tea down Stephanie. He didn't dare think of them. It hadn't taken the rescue team long to follow him up the trail but it would be a long time before he would forget finding the others. Thor and Myles were conscious, barely, but in great pain. At first, though, all he saw was a raw place on the mountain ahead and a pile of rubble—big boulders, loose rock, trees, and dirt—and stopped dead. Were the girls the only ones....? Then he saw Thor and went on a run. Thor opened his eyes as Diccon reached him and gave him a faint grin, then grimaced. His leg was twisted at an odd angle and as Diccon's practiced hands went over it he knew it was badly broken. His hand shook as he poured hot tea and helped Thor drink some.

"I'll make it. Help the others," Thor said faintly.

Diccon looked around then. It would stay with him like a nightmare for a long time. It seemed there were bodies everywhere and slowly he got up to investigate. Myles and Rex were near each other, trapped in the rubble from their waists down, Nigel was farther away and though he was free of the rubble he lay at such an odd angle Diccon's heart caught in fear. He couldn't rouse either Myles or Rex and when he got to Nigel he went down on his knees and reached for his wrist. His pulse was weak but Diccon let out the breath he'd been holding. Running his hand over Nigel he couldn't find any broken bones but found he was lying on a large rock and he carefully worked to get it out and away so he could straighten his son out. All of them had emergency blankets on but he could see no sign of packs anywhere. He looked around, counting in his head as to who should be there and remembered Shaul. It was a while before he saw, sticking out from the bottom of the rocks and dirt, a shoe on a foot and he felt sick. Turning back he went to Myles and Rex again and when the rescue team arrived they found him working desperately with a stout stick to free the two from their trap, tears running down his face.

How could he tell Suz about Shaul he wondered now as he tramped about trying to find her. Had his anger made him careless so that he wasn't careful where he climbed or was there no way to tell about the danger of the landslide? But the others were seasoned climbers, too. They wouldn't have blindly followed Shaul. He wished he hadn't told Kitten to call the rangers. Just then he saw Suz. She was standing on the battery, the night wind blowing her long hair around her. He went on a run, calling "Zannie," as he went.

She whirled around, ran down the stairs to him and he caught her tight to hold her there against him. He hadn't even admitted to himself that his fear for her and what might have happened was overshadowing the possibility that his son might not live. They had all been out in the cold and the rain for at least two days, and probably the heat the day before. All of them had the emergency blankets over them and crude shelters had been made of dead branches and sticks over Rex and Myles.

"Diccon! Oh, Diccon. I was so afraid. It's been so long. Did you find them? Are they all right?" She'd been crying—her lashes were still wet and her cheeks streaked. It had been a long, agonizing day as she fretted about her son as well as tried to fight her fear for Diccon, living over her stubbornness and grieving over what she and Diccon might have had if she'd stayed with him.

He didn't answer. He couldn't. How could he tell her that her son was probably seriously injured and that Shaul was dead? He had no idea how fond she was of the man.

"Diccon." She pulled away. "Something's wrong. What is it? It's not Nigel, is it? He's not....." She couldn't say the dreadful word.

"He's badly injured, I don't know how badly. They all are. Shaul— Zannie, Shaul was killed?"

"Killed?"

"Yes. It looked as if there was a landslide. He may have been killed instantly. We don't know. The girls seem to have gotten off lightest. I want you to come with me to Seattle to the hospital. Do you want to change your clothes?"

She looked down at her shorts. "I'd better put some slacks on. Nigel? What's wrong with him?"

"I don't know, Zannie. I think right now they need a dry warm place. That may be the worst problem. But he has some broken bones, I think, though I couldn't find any." His hands were gentle on her arms. He didn't tell her about digging frantically to free Myles and Rex, nor about Thor's twisted leg, or about taking the rock out from under Nigel. He'd done it because Nigel was his son and hadn't thought until after that he should have waited until the medics came. He pushed away the thought of Nigel's back. Nor did he tell her how he'd straightened Thor's twisted leg and applied a splint and Thor had fainted. That made it easier but he had so little to work with he'd finally left him to work on the fallen rocks and dirt over the others. "Let's go find out what we can."

She nodded though there was fear in her eyes. At the house she ran upstairs to hers and Shaul's room trying to absorb the fact he wasn't here any more. He wasn't anywhere on earth. Downstairs Diccon told those gathered there what little he knew himself.

"Mr. Kittam was killed?" Granny Ellen asked. "Oh, Diccon."

He held her hand. "I know. I have no idea how Suz feels about him."

"But Gretchen. Is Gretchen all right?" Candace was in tears. "And Myles?"

"Gretchen's not feeling very good but she walked down the trail with me to the car," said Diccon. "I don't know much, Candace." He looked up as Suz came into the room in slacks and a long-sleeved blouse. "We'll let you know as soon as we know more." He bent to kiss Granny Ellen.

Suz finished brushing her hair, stuck her brush in her purse, and deftly bound her hair back with a scarf. "Couldn't find the one that matched but who cares?"

Diccon thought of the one he'd gone back to look for, intending to give it to her and then folding it away in his jacket pocket instead. It was still where he'd left it. He hadn't been as close to or with Suz as much as he'd been this reunion since she'd left him. Usually she was too involved with the man she was with and he saw her across the room or in passing. Being with her wasn't helping his peace of mind. Though he'd never quit loving her he'd learned not to let his mind dwell on her but all the old memories and feelings were coming back and he dreaded the day they would part because he would have to fight through the pain all over again. It never occurred to him to ask her how she felt about him or if she would consider coming back to him. She didn't believe as he did for one thing, and she probably would hate where he lived now just as much as she had before though he'd built this home and it was nicer than any they'd had together.

"Diccon?"

"Hmmm?"

"You're so far away. I'm ready to go."

"I'm sorry. I was woolgathering." He gripped Granny Ellen's hand. She smiled at him to encourage him though her eyes were full of tears. He kissed her, promised again to call Kitten as soon as they knew anything and ushered Suz out the door.

As they stood on the top deck of the ferry to Seattle, traveling through the now quiet water toward the green hills and mountains, the wind blowing Diccon's dark hair down onto his forehead, taking Suz's blond waves in a playful swirl around her neck and back, Diccon told Suz what had happened when he'd found the missing group. He said it as briefly and concisely as he could. He wasn't at all sure he could stay calm if he thought about it too closely. He was terribly worried about Stephanie because she had been burning with a fever and he could not imagine what was wrong with Gretchen. Of Nigel, he refused to think.

Suz stood silent, her eyes on Diccon. His voice was steady enough but she felt the tension in him. "Are they—are they all in bad shape, Diccon?" she asked as the silence lengthened.

"That's hard to say. I would guess that they need most to be warm and dry. If they aren't suffering too much from exposure and the rain and cold, their other injuries will probably heal quickly enough." He glanced at her. "Mind you, I'm just guessing, but it's not the first time I've helped in a climbing accident. They at least were all alive, except, of course, Shaul."

She gazed ahead. "Well, if he had to go he would rather have gone that way. He told me that once; that he didn't want to get old and he hoped he could die on the mountains."

Diccon didn't reply. As far as he knew Shaul had no more faith in God than Suz had and he couldn't be quite so philosophical about his death. There *were* worse things than getting old.

"Didn't they have any of their food or clothing with them?"

"Only light packs with food for the climb and a change of clothes. They hadn't intended to stay on the mountain. I didn't have time to look for their camp but someone had put their emergency blankets over them. Probably the girls. And they all had jackets, except Gretchen."

They didn't talk much once they were off the ferry. Diccon concentrated on getting through the traffic and to the hospital. By the time they reached it there was a large group gathered in the waiting room with Mikell, Missily, Max, Molly, and Erin. Anna and Allan were there, as were Deborah and Gabriel, and to Diccon's surprise, Rose and Graham. Anna was

216

sitting with her arms around a sobbing Erin. No one could tell Diccon and Suz much. He repeated what he'd told the others, sitting beside Suz on one of the couches.

"Thor—Thor talked to you?" Erin sat up, her face blotched where her make-up had run and Anna dug in her purse for some tissue.

"Yes. He's broken a leg but he was conscious and told me to go see to the others."

"Stephanie?" was Erin's next question.

"No broken bones that I could find. Probably just needs warmth and food," he answered, his fear for Stephanie very real. He hadn't been able to rouse her. "I'm sorry I can't be more definite."

"But what happened?" Allan asked. "Could you tell?"

"It looked like a landslide to me. And it must have happened about the time they started the climb."

"But that means..." Allan began, glanced at Erin and shut his mouth.

"The rescue squad is excellent here, I understand. They went right to work." Diccon said quickly. Erin looked as if she would fall apart any moment. He looked around at the group and wished someone would come tell them something. Suz's hand crept into his and gratefully he grasped it with both hands and turned his head to give her a smile.

Chapter XXIII

The long night drug on. Some of them dozed a little only to jerk awake and nod off again. Mikell and Missily 's doctor had come in after ten.

"I'm sorry," he told them. "I've been out of town. I just got the message. A team of doctors is doing what they can. There are a lot of broken bones but that's the least of the problem. The exposure to that storm is what's gotten them down. I'll come back when I can. I can't promise you when," he'd said it all crisply, hadn't waited for questions but turned on his heel and disappeared. Missily ran after him. When she came back she had a sedative for Erin who was still sobbing off and on, shaking and pale. Mikell went to phone those at Fort Worden to tell them what the doctor said and also to say they just as well go to bed, he'd call in the morning.

Toward midnight Mikell and Graham took a stroll outdoors in the clear summer night air. Mikell felt some of his muscles relax. There were too many people, too much talking and analyzing, too many questions and guesses, too many regrets. Alfred and Diccon were both angry with themselves because they hadn't gone to look for the others when they didn't come to the camping spot that night of the first day or the morning after before they went back to Fort Worden but Diccon didn't say much. Mikell wanted to get him alone and ask him exactly what had happened but he and Suz sat side by side, her hand in his, talking very little.

Graham took out his pipe and lit it.

"You still smoking that thing?" asked Mikell, then wished he hadn't.

"No proof it hurts me," Graham said mildly. "Mikell, a man gets to thinking when he's on a hospital bed and doesn't know what will happen. And now that fine young man killed for no purpose."

It took Mikell a moment to realize that Graham was speaking of Shaul.

"I've never paid much attention to dying or what happens after but before my operation I got to wondering. The minister doesn't talk about that kind of thing. Even when I asked him when he came to see me he told me not to get morbid but to think positive thoughts. That it's been proven people who are positive get well faster."

"Didn't keep Shaul alive, did it?" Mikell asked casually as they walked slowly in step, he noticed, down the sidewalk.

"That's different. He wasn't sick."

"No. You're right. Accidents are out of our control most of the time but then so are death and sickness and health. We don't always get what we want. And when we do we don't have that much to do with it."

"Is it a fatalist you are, then?" Graham asked after puffing on his pipe in silence while they walked together.

"No. I believe God is in control of his creation."

218

"Do you believe He made the rocks fall on Myles and Gretchen?"

Mikell didn't answer immediately. When he did he said slowly, "I don't think I'd say it that way. As though He got a fiendish delight out of persecuting us. I just believe what happened wasn't a surprise to Him and even though it looks as though He was caught napping whatever happened was ordained by Him."

"That I can't believe. I don't know whether God exists or whether there is an after life but I wouldn't want to meet with that kind of God."

They walked on in silence, Graham puffing on his pipe, Mikell walking with his hands in his pockets. Then Mikell said, "The doctor's may be cutting into some of our young people."

"Why? Were they hurt that badly?" Graham stopped walking, took the pipe out of his mouth to ask.

"I don't know. I said 'may be' but if they are I trust they are doing it for a good purpose. Wouldn't you say so?"

"If it needs to be done, of course, they would. You aren't implying they'd do something—well, just to make money or something like that, are you?"

"Not at all." Mikell stood facing his brother-in-law. "It's just that we accept the fact that doctors often have to hurt us to help us and yet we think God terrible if he does the same thing."

Graham, who had been gazing back at the hospital, turned his head quickly to look at Mikell.

"Just like your cancer," went on Mikell. "Left alone, it would have caused all kinds of problems. Now you may not have any more."

"But how do you know you won't go to a worse place where God—this God you believe in—won't do worse things to make you better?"

"Because he is a covenant keeping God also. He always keeps His promises and He's promised us that, because of what Christ has done for those who believe, after this life we won't have sickness and sorrow and death because there won't be any sin or evil where we are."

They turned to retrace their steps. "It's not that I don't want to believe. It just doesn't make sense. I can't see God or any evidence of him. How can I believe in someone I don't even know exists?" Graham asked.

"But, Graham, you believe a lot of things exist you've never seen. Other countries, for example, or the atom."

"There are pictures of those places and evidence of the atom can be proved."

"The pictures could be false and scientists may decide they were all wrong and it's not atoms at all; it's something else that causes what they attribute to atoms. I don't mean that's true. I'm only trying to show that those aren't really proofs in the sense that they have the ability to be falsified."

"But I can't just make myself believe in something I don't believe," Graham protested.

"No. I agree with you there. Have you ever read the Bible?"

"How would that help? How do I know what it says is true? It's a bunch of stories anyway, just like any book like that."

219

Mikell didn't answer until, when they reached the hospital, he opened the door. "Don't let Missily hear you say that or you're in for it." He grinned. "She'll jump all over you. Besides if you've never read the Bible for yourself to see if it's true—not taken someone else's word for it—you can hardly say you've given it a fair trial, can you? Try reading it. You might be surprised."

Graham frowned and grunted in reply but he didn't argue any more.

Gretchen and Thor were the least seriously injured or affected by their accident though both were sick from their three day ordeal, without food or adequate shelter for two of those days. Thor had a badly broken leg as Diccon had thought but no more broken bones, also he had some bruises; Gretchen had three broken ribs as well as more serious bruising. She'd known she had to get help for the others some way but the pain was so bad she'd left her jacket and her pack with extra clothes behind. She and Stephanie had started out together but Stephanie was too weak and sick to walk far.

"I don't remember what happened," Gretchen told her parents weakly late the next day when they finally were allowed to see her. "I don't know why Stephanie wasn't with me when..." she stopped and frowned. "Did Uncle Diccon come or did I dream that?"

"He came, sweetheart," Missily answered. "Don't try to talk. Just rest. We'll answer your questions later. Everyone's being taken care of."

"Mr.—Mr. Kittam..." she said and began to cry.

Missily longed to hold her close but instead took her hand and looked appealingly at Mikell. He was standing on the other side of the bed and bent to kiss Gretchen. "Go to sleep, love. Get well for us. Will you?"

She nodded, "Okay, Daddy, but he—he...."

"Yes, we know. There isn't anything much to say, is there? I won't try to explain. We don't know enough about the whole picture like God does."

"I know." She closed her eyes. It seemed to be a comfort to her and not long after she drifted off to sleep.

They looked in on Myles, too, but he was sleeping. He had broken his left arm and shoulder and Mikell had said, "Oh he'll *love* that. He won't get to practice his organ for a while."

Nigel was injured the most seriously of them all. He'd had some internal injuries—they'd had to operate to stop the bleeding—and his back was badly injured though not broken. The doctors believed he would walk again but it would take time and he would have to go through therapy. He and Stephanie were both in intensive care, Stephanie with a high fever and pneumonia. Diccon and Suz were allowed to see their son for a few moments in the early morning after that long night and stood together looking down on him. His lashes lay long and dark on his now white skin and Suz remembered the day he was born and Diccon saying, "Poor kid, he has them, too," and when she asked what he'd answered "Those ridiculous long lashes. They stick." It had made her laugh because Diccon's lashes were long and he complained about them sticking often. "I love them," she'd answered.

She looked up at Diccon as she remembered this. His eyes were on Nigel, his face pale and drawn and they looked so much alike, this man and their son, that suddenly she couldn't bear the thought of all the suffering she'd caused them. She began to weep and Diccon gathered her to him to hold her.

"He'll be all right, Zannie. He's young and strong. He's a fighter, too. He'll hate lying in bed."

She nodded but couldn't stop crying so he just held her and tried not to remember standing at her bedside after she'd given birth to Nigel. How beautiful she'd looked with the baby in her arms. She'd loved him so. He wondered if she knew how her son felt about her and hoped not. Someday Nigel would have to forgive her. It wouldn't be good for him to continue to carry bitterness within him.

It was Thor who explained what happened with a blissfully happy Erin sitting beside him on the bed holding his hand while Mikell and Allan sat in the chairs available. Even the fact that Stephanie was not yet out of danger couldn't dim Erin's happiness at having Thor very much alive and fuming. "I could at least have had a reason for this damned leg," he said irritably.

"What do you mean? You do have a reason," Erin protested.

He grinned at her. "I'm no hero. I just jumped awkwardly." Then he looked past her to Allan. "Shaul started up the mountain first with Nigel behind, then Rex and Myles. The girls and I were last and going up at a different angle. We heard the most awful roar. Sounded like hundreds of jets taking off right over our heads and when I looked up I thought the whole damn mountain was coming down. I yelled at the girls to get out of the way. Stephanie ran back down, Gretchen and I ran part way, then jumped. That's when I heard my leg snap and saw Gretchen take a tumble. I think I blacked out more from the shock of the way that bone looked sticking out of my leg than the pain."

Erin shivered. "Oh, don't!"

Thor grinned. "You wanted to know."

"Not in gory detail."

"I haven't mentioned a bit of gore yet," he answered then kissed her hand in repentance. "Okay, I'll behave. It's just so damned good to be alive. I wasn't sure we weren't all going to die a slow death."

"Then Gretchen wasn't hit by the falling rocks at all?" Mikell asked, ignoring Thor's last remark.

"No. She fell pretty hard though."

"Diccon said her chest was all bruised. She doesn't remember much but she has three broken ribs."

"The hell she does! Do you know what that girl did? She and Stephanie? You would have been proud of our Stephanie, Erin. They got emergency blankets and jackets out of our pack and put them around or over us, whatever they could manage and then built a shelter over Rex and Myles. Things are a bit fuzzy. I kept going in and out, I think. Stephanie gave me the aspirin we had," Then he sobered. "Nigel. How's Nigel?"

"Not doing well. He had internal injuries and was bleeding internally," Allan answered. "He's still in intensive care."

"I wasn't sure whether he made it or not. We all knew Shaul caught it. The girls found where he'd been buried—just a foot sticking out. When I yelled names out Nigel didn't answer and the girls never really answered me about him after they found him. Myles," here Thor stopped to shake his head and smile. "I've never been fond of church music but Myles sounded pretty good, keeping the others singing, Rex and Gretchen, and Stephanie. Though Gretchen didn't do much of that. No wonder. How'd she even move with broken ribs?"

"Very painfully," said Allan dryly. "They figured Shaul was killed instantly." He didn't add that Shaul's skull had been crushed.

"I hope you never climb another mountain," said Erin. "Someone is always getting killed."

"Erin, baby, people get killed driving on the highway and falling in bathtubs but we don't stop driving or taking baths. And I bet you more people get killed on highways than on mountains." Thor gave her hand a little shake.

"I won't let Stephanie climb again," she said stubbornly. "She's suffered enough."

Instantly he was alert. "Stephanie. I thought she was all right. I *told* you. She and Gretchen helped us get covered as much as they could. Then they went to get help." He tried to sit up and fell back. "She's not hurt?"

"No bones broken," Allan said quickly. The doctor had warned them not to let Thor know how seriously ill his daughter was. "Just needs to get over being cold and wet and hungry."

"Oh," Thor sighed in relief, the color flooding back into his face.

Missily and Mikell decided not to go back to the Fort and in one of their phone calls asked Candace and Sean to pack their things. They didn't spend much time at home either. Gretchen was coming along but Myles was slow to regain any kind of strength until finally the doctors had him x-rayed again and found an injury to his spleen that was slowly seeping out blood. His parents sat next to his bed after the operation, hands clasped, not talking. Missily slept badly that night waking with nightmares that either Gretchen or Myles had been killed and sobbed in Mikell's arms.

"How do parents stand it when they lose a child?" she wailed. "Mikell, I couldn't. I'd go crazy or something."

He smoothed back her hair. "Shhh, Jeddie. I know. It shakes a person up pretty badly. You don't know how much you love them until something like this happens." He rubbed his face against her silky hair. "But I guess that's what the promise means—the one that says His grace is sufficient for us."

"I know. I should trust more. It's just that it hurts so much. Will Myles be all right now?"

"I think so. Go to sleep and we'll go see him in the morning. He may be better already." He kissed her, grateful that she was his.

Mikell talked quite a while to Kitten on the phone. She had taken over, was cooking meals, comforting the young ones and making herself indispensable. Allan and Anna went over to get their RV and when they came back to the hospital a day later they couldn't say enough about her and her ability to handle the situation.

"I didn't know she had it in her," said Anna. "She never seemed to care for anyone but herself."

"She couldn't be a Metlow and not care," Allan said, half jokingly. "How is everyone?"

" 'As well as can be expected' I'm told," said Mikell. "Nigel and Stephanie are still in intensive care. They've decided Stephanie had a virus of some kind before she started climbing. I suppose they told us what kind." Mikell rubbed his face wearily. "I can't keep it all straight. She has pneumonia—oh! You knew that. Sorry. I'm not sleeping well and now that Myles isn't doing well, I've kind of lost track."

"He's worse?" Allan asked sharply.

"No, no. It's just that I thought he wasn't hurt except for the broken bones."

Allan put his arm around Mikell's shoulder. "Let's go get some coffee. Where's Missily?"

"She's with Gretchen. I saw you from the window so came down." He smiled at Anna. "I'm not doing so hot. I thought you'd like to know how things were but I feel as though I were wrapped in a fog."

"Stephanie had a virus?" Anna asked.

"Yes. Erin said she'd had a headache the day before but she has those migraines so she thought that was what was wrong. Nigel...well, they've done all they can. They just have to wait now, they tell us."

Allan took a deep breath and turned to walk to the windows of the little room that felt like some kind of prison.

"We brought Candace with us," Anna said now. "She's downstairs. Kitten says she cries all the time."

"Where is she?"

"In the lobby. I told her I'd find out if she could come up."

"I'll go get her." Mikell said and found Candace sitting stiffly with her hands in her lap held so tightly together the knuckles were white. When she saw her father she began to cry. He reached down and gathered her to him. "Shhh, Dacey. They're going to be all right."

"B-But I-I thought they had—had hypothermia."

"People can recover from that, you know. I don't know who told you that but if it were true the doctors got them all warmed up."

"You mean M-Myles and Gretchen won't die?"

"No. Who've you been talking to?"

"No one. I was afraid to ask."

He hugged her torn between amusement and the desire to give her a little shake. "Sometimes, darling, you make life very hard for yourself. Do you want to come up and see them?"

"Do you mean I can?"

"Of course. You know enough to be quiet and not expect them to talk much. They're pretty sick yet, especially Myles. They had to operate on him yesterday, but that was to help him get better," he hastened to add though he hadn't seen his son or the doctor yet that morning.

Later that morning Missily almost ran into Lorna who was hurrying down the hall in tears. She caught her. "Lorna! What's wrong?"

223

"They won't let me see him," Lorna sobbed. "They said only family, but what if he dies and I never get to...."she gulped and choked on a sob.

"See who?" Missily asked.

"Nigel. Don't you see? I didn't know... I mean I knew he liked me but I didn't know I did him," she answered incoherently.

Missily did see and suddenly understood, remembering Nigel coming to Washington and stopping to see Lorna but not letting them know he was near. "Wait here," she said and headed for the nurses' station.

Not long after Lorna was being escorted to Nigel's room. A nurse came out just as Lorna and her nurse escort reached the room. "She can't go in there. Only family is allowed," said the other woman.

"It's his fiancée, Miss Adamsen."

"Oh, I'm sorry. I didn't know. Go right in." This was said warmly and accompanied by a smile but in her distress and fear Lorna hadn't heard either nurse. She crept slowly to stand beside the bed. It wasn't until she was in the room that she saw Suz in a chair and Diccon at a window. "Oh! I'm sorry. I-I won't stay. I-I just wanted to see him."

Diccon walked over to her. "No reason to leave. Suz and I were just going for a cup of coffee. It'll be nice to know someone who loves him is near."

Lorna looked up quickly and met Diccon's eyes. They were kind and she nodded before she turned back to look at Nigel, so white and still against the pillow, his rumpled hair dark on his forehead, the horrible tubes stuck into him. Why were there so many? What incredibly long lashes he had. She reached up to stroke the tumbled curls and a strange emotion shook her. This man might be her man. She bent her head to weep and pray, her hand still in his hair.

"Oh! Mr. Brooke, I'm so sorry I didn't let your son's fiancée in. She didn't tell me she was engaged to him, you see." It was one of the nurses who stopped Diccon and Suz in the hall.

"Quite all right," Diccon said. "Everything's fine now but keep it mum. They haven't made any announcement yet."

"I will," she promised and smiled, the first one Diccon had seen from her.

"His fiancée?" Suz asked as they took the elevator down to the cafeteria.

"Not yet but if he finds out she got in that room that way she probably will be."

"But how did the nurse know?"

"I don't know. Maybe from something Lorna said."

Suz frowned. "I don't think so otherwise she would have gotten in at first. At least from what the nurse said she didn't let Lorna in because she didn't know they were engaged and she wasn't part of the family."

"Right you are. I have no idea how she knew, unless Lorna decided she could get in that way."

They took their coffee to one of the little tables and sat down opposite each other. "Now we'll have to wait and see what develops. They should make a great couple. Lorna likes the outdoors, too."

The sentence hung in the air and Diccon wished he hadn't added it. Suz had never been an outdoor girl the way Lorna was. She loved to swim and lay in the sun but she'd never liked camping or country living. She said, "She doesn't like mountain climbing any better than I do."

Diccon looked up from his coffee into which he was stirring sugar. "It always did frighten you, didn't it, Zannie?" he asked gently.

"Yes. If I were superstitious I'd say I knew this would happen, that I felt it. But then I always did feel that way before you climbed. Diccon, is Nigel going--going to be all right?"

"I think so. He's young and healthy. It'll take time and that will irk him but I think he'll recover completely."

"But if he's in a coma...."

"He's not in a coma, darling," Diccon said, quit unconscious of the endearment which had come naturally to him but Suz caught her breath. "He's sleeping from the drugs. They keep him pretty well doped up. He's going to have a lot of pain. I thought you understood."

"I don't think I took in anything the doctor said. I'm so afraid."

"They had to operate to stop the internal bleeding and he has that to recover from as well as the effects of being out in the weather in that condition plus his back is badly injured even though there are no broken bones."

"But didn't they have to give him blood?"

"Yes. That's why he's still with us. I mean because they could give it to him. Zannie, we can be thankful for the medical knowledge the doctors have. It's one of the blessings we forget. In bygone years he would most likely have died."

"I know," she whispered. Then, "I didn't know I loved him so much. He's so like you. The first time I saw him lying there I remembered what you said when he was born."

"What's that?" he asked calmly enough though his heart had lurched.

"You said, 'Poor kid, he has them, too' and when I wanted to know what you said, 'Those ridiculous long lashes. They stick.' And I laughed because you always complained about yours."

Diccon kept his eyes on his coffee. He didn't dare look up. He wanted desperately to beg her to marry him, to never leave him again and he couldn't. She'd left him because she hadn't liked his life and he enjoyed his work, more than that it was what he was good at, what he knew. It wasn't a question of being willing to give it up for her. It was that living life as she did wasn't his kind of life and he wouldn't fit in. The friction would still be there.

"Diccon?"

"Yes?"

"Are you angry?"

His eyes did come up then. "No, of course not, Zannie. Why would I be angry?"

"I don't know. You didn't answer me so....You never did get angry very often."

"Didn't I?" he smiled. "You must have forgotten then. I had quite a temper in my younger days. I thought things had to go my way."

"But I don't remember your being that way," she protested.

"There you are." They both turned their heads. Alexis and Jon were coming toward their table. "Uncle Mikell said he thought he saw you headed this way. We met him in the lobby. Can we go up and see Nigel?" They pulled up chairs to sit on.

"For a short while. He's asleep all the time so he won't talk."

"Aunt Vicky said he's in intensive care."

"Yes. He and Stephanie. The others are still pretty sick but aren't so serious. Except Myles."

"Myles? What happened to him? I thought he only broke an arm."

"And his shoulder. Then they found he was bleeding internally—had them all scared for a while but he's recovering faster than Nigel."

"Why is he in intensive care? I don't understand what happened. Weren't they all climbing the same place?" Alexis asked nervously clasping and unclasping her purse until Jon reached over to take her hand in his, giving her a smile.

"It had to do with the angle the rocks and dirt came down, how high they were and so on. Stephanie, Gretchen and your Uncle Thor didn't get hit at all," explained her father. "Shaul took it worst, then Nigel and Myles. Rex was buried partially, too, like Myles, but he didn't get hurt so seriously. Just bruising."

"I thought Gretchen got hit."

"She jumped and fell against a tree. Only Stephanie and Rex escaped broken bones."

"Then what's wrong with her?"

"The doctors think Stephanie may have been sick before she started the hike. She has pneumonia." Diccon's voice was controlled but his jaw was set and Suz saw it move and knew he was more concerned than he seemed.

"Why didn't you know what happened, Alexis?" she asked. "Your Uncle Mikell has kept Kitten—Aunt Vicky—current."

"I know but—well, it's like a-a tomb over there and I had to get out so Jon and I drove around the Peninsula. I thought I would go crazy sitting there with everyone crying or praying or something."

"Praying?" Suz stared at her daughter.

"Well, you know Granny Ellen. She told us all to sit down and then she prayed. It's not so bad, really. She just talks to God as if he were real and heard but...you know."

Her father smiled while Suz nodded but thought, "She's as selfish and self-centered as I. Did I teach her to be that way? So uncaring?"

They gave Alexis and Jon Nigel's room number, telling them to stop at the nurse's office and let them know who they were.

"Oh yes. Lorna's up there," Suz added.

"Lorna? Lorna?" Alexis asked. "Oh, Lorna," she added before they answered, then, "Lorna? Do you mean Uncle Mikell's sister?"

"Yes."

"But why's she..." Alexis stood looking at her parents.

226

Diccon smiled. "Why would any lovely lady want to see a man she cared for?"

"But...isn't she a lot older than he?"

"No. Only three or four years," her father told her.

"Is that all? I thought... she must be a lot younger than Uncle Mikell."

"She is. Not that much older than you are in fact. Just enough so that you didn't pay attention," said Suz a bit impatiently.

"What do you mean?"

"Alexis, you've been coming to the reunions ever since you were a baby and known Lorna all your life."

"I guess I never thought of her age."

"Well, six years is quite a difference in age until you get older, at least until you are your age," Diccon agreed. "Anyway nothing official has been announced so don't jump to conclusions."

After they left he and Suz sat silently. He had gotten fresh coffee for both of them and a cinnamon roll for himself after Suz declined. He wanted desperately to watch her but he kept his eyes on the people around them or on his big roll.

"Diccon," Suz said finally, "I've been very selfish, only thinking of myself." She reached to touch his hand and he turned it to grasp hers. "I hadn't realized what it must mean to you that Nigel...that we don't know..." she broke off and he nodded in understanding. They sat like that, hands linked while they drank their coffee and he ate his roll. When he finished he finally looked at her, at the only woman he had ever loved, at the lovely hair falling over one shoulder, the clear skin tanned by the California sun, the winged brows and straight, wide mouth, all of which had once been his delight and she was startled at the pain in his eyes which she saw just a second before he stood, taking her cup.

"Shall we go back up?" he asked.

Thor was ambulatory and released not long after Rex was out. He and Erin decided she would stay until Stephanie, who was out of intensive care but still a long way from well, was able to travel and the two of them would fly home. Celeste and Betsy were to go back with Thor with Adam along to help with the driving. It had been Mikell's idea that one of the young men help since Thor couldn't drive yet and the trip was too long for Celeste to drive all the way, particularly since they were going to do it in two days and with the RV that would mean long hours because of the mountain driving. Celeste had begged for Adam with whom she'd been trying to flirt while at Fort Worden though he'd only tolerated her.

"Gosh, I'll be cooped up all day with that girl," Adam told his brother Martin one day when they were working in the orchard.

"I can think of worse fates," Martin said. "They're nice enough kids."

"Not when one is chasing you. She's flaky. I mean you can't talk about sensible things. All she talks about are TV and movie stars and herself. The only sensible girl in that family is Stephanie."

"Well, it's only for two or three days, isn't it?"

"Mr. Nielsen wants to try to make it in two days. That's over 600 miles a day. Sounds like a long trip to me."

"I wouldn't mind," said Martin. "I'd like to see that part of the country again."

"Why don't you go then? You're older anyway."

Martin laughed and punched his brother's shoulder. "Only eighteen months, you dunce. And what does that have to do with anything?"

However, Adam talked it over with his father who told Thor that he and his wife had discussed it and would rather Martin go since he'd had more driving experience and was older; Martin had just turned twenty. Thor said it didn't matter to him, he was just grateful for the help and for an extra man along. Martin took his tent and sleeping bag, leaving Adam behind who began to haunt the hospital until he got permission to visit Stephanie. He bought her a little stuffed seal from the hospital gift shop and went to her room one evening. She was sitting up in bed, propped against the pillows reading, looking quite pretty and fragile in a frilly pink bed jacket with her long hair caught in bows at each side of her head.

"Hello, Adam," she said a little shyly. She wasn't used to young men seeing her in bed.

"Brought you something," he said, handing her the gift, then watched anxiously as she opened it hoping she wouldn't think him crazy.

"Oh! He's darling!" She said. "I'll call him Pacific. How did you know I collected stuffed animals?"

"I didn't." Adam pulled up a chair and sat down. "I liked him and hoped you would. I'm glad you are getting better. You had us all scared."

"So am I," she replied, then added, "It—it's nice of you to come see me." She was puzzled. Her cousins came, which she could understand, but Adam wasn't related and none of the other Adamsen young people had come to see her except Rex who had looked in on his way home.

"It—I was afraid when you were so sick," he said looking down at his hands, which were clasped loosely in his lap. "I didn't want you to die because—because you....I didn't want you to go—to be lost," he stumbled on, not sure how to put his fears in words.

"Because I wasn't a Christian?"

His head came up. "Yes."

"I know." She laid her head back, Pacific still held in both her hands. "I have migraine headaches and before I got medicine for them I used to wish I could die because I was so sick, but I was afraid. I talked to Aunt Missily the day before we went climbing and she read to me out of the Bible and told me to read some every day out of the Bible she and Uncle Mikell gave me once." Her eyes came to his. "Then she told me a story. She said Uncle Mikell told it to her only she made fun of him, then, because she thought it was all myths. I think it's wonderful. You probably know it—all about how God made the heavens and earth and how the man and woman he made turned against him and about his forgiveness because of Christ. I asked her how she became a Christian and she told me. Adam," Stephanie's voice was shy now again, "I—I'm a Christian now, too."

"Stephanie!"

She smiled. "I asked Aunt Missily how I could be one and she explained. I knew she would. I wanted to believe but I didn't know how or what until she explained."

Adam had gotten up abruptly and walked to the window where he pulled out a handkerchief and blew his nose and wiped his face, though the tears wanted to keep coming. He heard Stephanie's voice softly behind him, unbelieving.

Adam, are you *that* glad I became a Christian?"

He turned and went back to her side, taking her hand, bending to gently kiss her cheek. "Darling girl, it's the most wonderful news I've ever had," he said.

She looked at him, wide-eyed. "But..." she said and was silent. Why should he care so much?

"It must make Aunt Missily very happy, too," he said striving for a more normal tone. "She's prayed a long time for you."

"She told me. She cried, too. She says it won't be easy for me but she'll send me books, write me, and she's given me the name of a couple of churches I can go to. Adam, I thought you liked Celeste."

"Did you?" he asked with a smile.

"She likes you."

"Celeste likes attention. By now she's probably decided Martin's more exciting. After all he's older. And he's more interesting."

Stephanie tried to look disapproving but ended up laughing. "You're probably right. I mean about Celeste."

"Would you like it if I wrote, too?" he asked. He was still holding her hand.

"Yes. Would you really write to me?"

"I would like to very much. We can encourage each other. I get discouraged at college sometimes. There's so much to learn and I don't know what I want to do when I graduate yet. You can pray for me."

"I will," she said eagerly, quite conscious of her hand in his.

Chapter XXIV

Erin, however, had a far different reaction to her daughter's sudden interest in reading the Bible. She confronted Missily one day before she went to the hospital to see Stephanie. They had just finished a lazy breakfast, talking about their childhood and Missily began to put the dishes in the dishwasher. Generally Erin left right after a quick cup of coffee in the morning and Missily thought it must be a sign of how much Stephanie had improved for Erin to take time for breakfast. She usually left about the same time as Mikell did and spent most of the day at the hospital.

"Missily," she said now, her hands with their carefully done fingernails folded on the table before her, "I don't like to have to say this but I'm quite disturbed by your trying to influence Stephanie to believe as you do. Thor and I have always believed religion a private matter and want our girls to choose for themselves whether they think they need it in their lives. We've never found a need to have, to..." she hesitated briefly before she continued, "for religion. I've always admired you and Mikell because you've never tried to force what you believe on others. I'm a bit surprised that you would stoop to do so when a child's defenses are down. It's obvious you've taken advantage of Stephanie's illness and she's quite an impressionable girl. I don't approve at all and I told her so."

Erin had said it all so smoothly that Missily suspected she'd thought it out ahead of time. "What did she say to that?" she asked, closing the dishwasher and reaching for a towel.

"What could she say except that you hadn't forced her."

Missily leaned against the kitchen cupboard. "And you don't believe her?"

"Come on, Missily. She's never heard anything like what you believe before. We're very careful the girls aren't influenced by...." Again she hesitated. "By people who are so dogmatic."

"Did it ever occur to you," asked Missily, who was beginning to feel angry with her sister, "that is just might be dogmatic to teach them the way you are?"

"But we aren't teaching them anything," Erin said patiently.

"Aren't you? What do you think religion is?" Missily came across the room to sit at the big dining room table.

"It's a belief in some higher power and a set of dogmatic rules and ways of behaving," Erin answered, still quite calmly, very in control of herself.

Missily, who had begun to shake because she had never been able to argue with any of her family except her father, asked, "And you don't think you need a higher power?"

"No. I believe man is sufficient and is growing more able everyday to run the universe."

"Then you have a religion. You believe in man and his ability."

"That's not religion, Missily. That's just common sense. I can't see how you can believe all that nonsense the way you were brought up but I won't have my girls forced to believe it."

"I thought you said you were going to let them choose what to believe."

"Yes. And I intend to guard them from fanatics. Especially from people who believe something so outdated."

"How is that letting them choose?" Missily asked, knowing she wasn't addressing the problem but too upset to think straight.

"Stephanie isn't old enough yet to make those kinds of decisions. She's always loved you and I think it's quite low of you to use that to force her to believe the trash you do." Erin's voice wasn't quite so controlled now.

"I did *not* force her." Missily's voice had risen and was shaking. "There isn't..." she broke off as the phone rang and went to the kitchen wall phone to answer. "Hello?"

"Jeddie, I left my list of appointments at home. Do you see it anywhere?"

"No," she answered and her voice wobbled as she fought tears and he said, "Something's wrong. What is it?" When she didn't answer he asked, 'Missily, what's happened. The kids?"

"They're okay."

"Is Erin still there?"

"Yes."

"Is she upsetting you?"

"Yes."

"I'll be home. I was going to have you give me the names but I'll come get my book. Don't tell her I'm coming. Hang on, darling, I'm not far away." The phone went dead.

Missily sat down again. "Mikell." She said no more but kept her hands clasped tightly in her lap. How could she keep Erin there until Mikell arrived? "I'm sorry I yelled at you," she said and swallowed. She would *not* cry. Erin had always made fun of her when she did.

"Checking in so early? Do you usually get calls this soon?" Erin asked knowing that Missily took Mikell's calls from his customers for him.

"Sometimes."

"Look, Missily. I didn't want to upset you. I thought you'd understand Thor's and my viewpoint. You wouldn't want us to tell your kids how and what to believe and make them see things our way, try to convince them you are wrong."

"You don't even know what we believe. How can you know whether you disagree or not?" asked Missily and angry tears spilled over.

"You believe the Bible is true and I disagree. I'm not alone. There are all kinds of scholars who can prove it's not true. Men who know more about that kind of thing than you do."

"How do you know they do? Because they have a string of degrees after their names? Does that make them infallible?"

"Really, Missily, I've never known you to be so irrational. That's one reason I've admired you and Mikell. You seem so sensible even though you're religious."

"And what makes you think religion makes someone senseless, stupid, and irrational?" Missily was standing behind her chair now, gripping the back of it. "Did it ever occur to you that you're the one that could be that way and not us?" She went into the kitchen and began to wash her stove, banging the burner covers around.

"Missily! What *is* wrong with you? After all Stephanie *is* my daughter and my responsibility. Or don't you think I know how to raise my own daughter?" Erin's voice was dangerously smooth.

"Not on the subject of religion. Of all the stupid ideas to think you should train your girls in manners and sports and how to dress and all the every day things and yet leave them in a vacuum when it comes to the most important area of life." She was sobbing as she talked and still slamming things around when Mikell walked in.

Instantly he went to her, removed the dishcloth and pulled her into his arms, rubbing her back. "Shhh, Jeddie, shhh. It can't be that bad." He winked at Erin, who relaxed.

Missily drew away wiping her cheeks with the back of her hands. "Yes, it can. She told me I forced Stephanie to believe what I do, that I was irrational and not sensible. She and Thor believe they should let *their* girls grow up and choose whether they want to believe anything so fanatical and dogmatic. And she said I was low to take advantage of Stephanie when she is sick and...'

"Missily," Mikell said and at the tone of his voice she stopped talking. "Go wash your face, then come back and we'll talk," he told her, recognizing approaching hysteria.

As she left Mikell swung a chair around to straddle it. "What's up?" he asked.

"I have no idea what's wrong with her. Mikell, you and Missily have never tried to force what you believe down our throats. It just seems to me to be bad taste to do so when a child is ill."

"I can appreciate your viewpoint," he answered, then paused and when Missily came in he rose, seated her, turned his chair around and sat down again. "It must look that way to you. Perhaps it would help if you could understand what did happen. You said yourself that we've never forced what we believe on you and I'm sure you know Missily well enough to know she wouldn't take advantage of Stephanie's illness to do so." Missily made a noise but he ignored her. "I don't know what Missily told you. Were you aware that Stephanie had approached her before the climb?"

"No. When? What do you mean?"

"I went to see her when she had her headache. I was just going to peek in on her to see if she was all right. She was lying in bed reading and said her headache was almost gone but you'd told her to be quiet if she wanted to go on the climb the next day." Missily told Erin though she felt resentful toward Mikell who seemed to be taking her sister's side. "She asked me what happened when someone dies because when she gets sick she wants to die but she was afraid because she didn't know what happened after."

"We've told them all that when you die you die and that's it. Why should she wonder about it?"

"Perhaps," Mikell said, "because that isn't what happens. Missily told her a story, the same story I'd told Missily years ago." He grinned at his wife. "She wasn't nearly so receptive as Stephanie. She informed me it was all myths. Erin, Stephanie was probably nearer death than you or I have ever been the other day on that mountain but when we went to see her in the hospital and she was well enough to talk, she told us that what Missily had told her had helped her not to be afraid in the way she'd always been before."

Erin didn't answer but sat looking down at her hands. She wasn't as comfortable arguing with Mikell as she was with Missily. Missily, meanwhile, had gotten up to start looking for Mikell's appointment book, going through the things on the breakfast bar, which seemed to be a catch-all for things. It wasn't there so she went to the big buffet.

"Come sit down, Missily. I'll find it later," Mikell said, catching her hand as she tried to slip past him but she pulled free and went down to their bedroom

"What is wrong with her anyway? She wouldn't even talk calmly," Erin told Mikell.

"It upset her to be told she forced Stephanie, I think, and particularly that she took advantage of Stephanie's illness. Erin, no one can make a person believe the Bible. If Stephanie accepted what Missily told her just so she wouldn't hurt her Aunt's feelings, or if she was frightened by her headaches and then experienced a peace when she was in worse trouble so that she's grabbed what Missily said for right now and she doesn't truly believe, it will show later."

Erin gave a sigh of relief. "She's young. She'll probably get over it. Thanks Mikell."

"On the other hand," he went on, "if she genuinely believes, nothing will shake her faith. Not even if you won't let her go to church or read the Bible or get in contact with other Christians. It will be hard for her but when God makes someone his own he doesn't let them go."

"You sound very confident," said Erin in irritation.

Mikell studied his sister-in-law. She was dressed casually in slacks and a blouse, her fair hair short and curled becomingly around her small face, her make-up flawless, very in control of herself as he was accustomed to her being, not at all as she'd been when they first came.

"Erin, just suppose that you're right and death ends it all. Then neither of us has anything to lose. I won't know I'm wrong that way. However, suppose I'm right and there is an after life. Not only that but there is a day of accounting coming when we will have to answer to the God who created us for what we did while here on earth. In that case I would be safe but you would have an eternity to find out how much you stand to lose. If I had to decide on that alone it seems wiser to me to believe there *is* an after life, that

I'm held responsible for how I live here on earth and I should find out what to do about it."

Erin moved restlessly. "It's getting late. I'd better get to the hospital or Stephanie will begin to worry." She rose. "I hope Missily feels better when I come back. I don't like to quarrel with her."

After she left Mikell went to look for his wife. She was standing at their bedroom window. "Missily," then since she neither turned nor looked his way he crossed to her side. "Jeddie, Erin's gone."

"All right," she said still staring out the window. "Here's your notebook. You're late for the first two appointments."

"Yes. I'd better get going. How about a kiss?"

She didn't move and turned her head so that his kiss fell on her hair. He frowned but didn't say more, just turned and left and soon Missily heard the front door slam. She stayed where she was for a while, her anger against Mikell boiling inside her. But she had work to do. Both Gretchen and Myles would be home that day and she needed to get their beds ready with clean sheets. They wouldn't have to stay in bed but would probably need to rest. Nigel was finally better also and would be moved to Mikell's folk's place when he could leave the hospital. Stephanie and Erin would fly home in a couple of days. Nigel's back wasn't completely healed and he would need physical therapy but Lorna had begged her parents to let him come to their place so he wouldn't have to stay in the hospital and she would take him back and forth for therapy. As far as Missily knew Nigel hadn't asked Lorna to marry him but at least he hadn't castigated her for her own part in getting Lorna in to see him. The whole family knew someway that there had been something said about an engagement but not where it had originated and, after all, Missily rationalized, she hadn't really said they were engaged—just kind of suggested it so Lorna could get in to see Nigel. Suz had told her that Nigel loved Lorna and she was pretty sure it was returned and a smile tugged at her mouth as she thought that her sister-in-law would also be her niece by marriage if they did marry. Wouldn't that make Nigel a brother-in-law to Mikell, too?

As she stripped Gretchen's bed and began to put the sweet smelling clean sheets on she wondered about Diccon and Suz. They had spent a great deal of time together at the hospital and Missily had seen Suz watching Diccon in a way that made her wonder if her sister would go back to California. Diccon had had to go back to work but was driving up on weekends to see his son, quieter than before, almost taciturn, not smiling much and Mikell had remarked in irritation, "What he sees in her, I'll never know. Why doesn't he just forget her and find a decent woman?"

Thor had been calling every night to see how Erin and Stephanie were and when they were coming home. Erin had told Missily that Betsy and Celeste spent the days with their next door neighbor, Cindy. Thor was determined they not be alone though he trusted Cindy's judgment on letting the girls go places with their friends and having them over. He missed Erin terribly though he didn't tell her or anyone else that he wanted her home so he would know for sure that she was his and the awful month before they left for the reunion was past. He laughed when Erin told him about Stephanie's religious ideas but Erin didn't tell that to Missily nor what he'd said.

"Leave her alone. She'll get bored with it soon enough. She's too intelligent to fall into that trap."

Missily was glad to go get Gretchen and Myles. She was still angry with Mikell and having them home took her mind off him. Candace and Sean were working and would be home after four or five. Gretchen's face was nearly healed and it looked at though it would not scar as they'd been afraid it might. Myles bruises were almost gone, too, but he told her he still had nightmares, sometimes, about all the rocks--and dirt--coming down on them and seeing Shaul hit. They talked together most of the afternoon, expecting Imogen or Kitten to come by sometime to see them. Both women were staying with Allan and Anna, as was Suz now that their week at Fort Worden was over. Kitten had canceled her Denver concert to stay until everyone was out of the hospital, astonishing her family.

Mikell was late getting home that evening so the rest of them went ahead with supper as they usually did when he was late. It didn't happen often but sometimes a job would take longer than he expected, plus he had started late that morning. Erin was eating with them, entertaining her listeners with tales of the hospital staff. Missily was picking at her food, not eating, knowing she couldn't swallow if she tried. She'd done what she'd meant never to do; let Mikell leave when she was angry with him and worse than that she had stayed angry and had let others take the messages that came in and pass them on to Mikell when he'd called late that afternoon, something she'd never done before. What if something happened to him and she never saw him again? After the accident she was terrified that someone would be taken from her, as though one accident set off a reaction. She tried to concentrate on what Erin was saying, tried to be grateful that all of her sons and daughters were at the table but as the minutes stretched her panic grew.

"Missily, you're not eating," Erin said reaching over to put her hand on Missily's which was ice cold.

"I-I don't feel like it."

"You're not still mad at me about this morning, are you?"

Missily shook her head miserably and the tears, which had been threatening, spilled over.

"Mom, he's late lots of times. It's not later than any of those other times," Myles said gently.

She'd forgotten how perceptive he was and tried to take a drink of her iced tea.

"Is that what's wrong? Erin asked. "You're worried about Mikell. Good heavens, Missily, if I worried every time Thor was late I'd be a basket case."

Missily pressed her lips together. Myles reached over with his good hand to take hers. "She doesn't usually do this, Aunt Erin. Dad's late off and on. She's used to that."

"Then what is the matter?" asked his aunt with irritation.

Missily sat starting at her plate, which swam before her eyes. Suddenly she left the table and went out the back door. Parting the willow branches, she climbed up in the tree and sat with her head against the trunk, sobbing, "God please help him to come home. Please help him to be all right," she begged.

It was a subdued group who was clearing up after dinner when Mikell did drive up. Erin was working with Sean and Candace who were going up to the hospital with her to see Stephanie and Nigel. Gretchen and Myles were playing a game of Jeopardy in the living room.

"Well, our invalids have decided to come home," Mikell said as he came in the door. "Hi, you two. Good to see you." He leaned over to kiss Gretchen. "You look pretty good, sweetheart. Sores almost gone. And Myles, you're doing okay?"

"Yes. It's good to be home, Dad."

"Sorry I was late. I got held up by an accident. Hello, Erin. You cook tonight?" he asked, going into the kitchen to unload his lunch pail.

"No, but I thought I'd help the kids clean up. They're going with me to the hospital."

"Where's Missily?"

There was a short silence then Candace said, "She went out back. She didn't eat any supper. Just sat there and cried."

"Her hand was ice cold," said Erin. "I hope she's not getting sick."

Frowning, Mikell put his thermos down and headed out the back door. He looked around but could see Missily no where. He was about to call her name when he noticed Jake was out next door and decided against it. The willow, of course, She'd always liked it there. He found her sitting in the Y of the branches her face wet, her eyes swollen from crying, her hair tumbled as though she'd been pulling and twisting it as she often did when upset. Advancing to the tree he said quietly, "Jeddie."

She'd had her eyes shut tight and jumped when he said her name. The blaze of joy in her eyes made up for the long, hard day. He hadn't dwelt on the fact of her anger but he'd remember whenever he had time to think. He held out his arms and she slid out of the tree into them. He held her tight, feeling her tremble.

"I was so afraid," she whispered. "Where were you? You didn't call."

"I know. I'm sorry, Missily, love. I was delayed by an accident. I took one of the through ways, thinking it would be faster because I was already late and then had to wait for them to clear up the accident. Someone said there were two trucks involved."

"I-I let you go to work when I was angry. I was so afraid you wouldn't come home. Then what would I do? I don't want to be angry with you."

"Darling, I wouldn't leave you," he soothed wiping her face with his hands.

"No. I mean I was afraid you'd...you'd—something had happened to you and I wouldn't be able to...." and here she broke into sobs again. It still hurt that he'd seemed so unsympathetic that morning but she was no longer angry.

236

He rocked her in his arms, whispering to her to quiet her until her sobs ceased and she was calmer. "I know, love," he said then. "I was angry with you after you wouldn't or didn't call me or talk to me as you usually do. It was a long, hard day and then I ran into all that traffic stopped and I thought, 'What if my Missily had an accident and I didn't call her or at least try to find out what was wrong this morning?' and I can tell you I sweated it out until I found it was two trucks." He tipped her face up with his hand, smiled down at her, then kissed her. After a long moment he said, "Let's go tell Erin and the kids good-bye. They're going to see Stephanie."

"Oh! I forgot. I meant to see that they got to go earlier."

"Come on, then." He smiled at her. "Everything fine now?"

"I have something I want to ask you but I'm so glad you're home," she answered. He parted the willow branches for her and they went into the house hand in hand.

"Well, are you all right now?" Erin asked Missily. She was still irritated with her.

"I'm sorry, Erin. I meant to get supper done so you could leave. Thanks for cleaning up." Missily answered.

"Yes. Well, we'll leave now. Stephanie will wonder what happened to me." Erin's voice implied that Missily could have been more thoughtful. "After all she is alone in a strange town."

"Tell Stephanie we love her. If I hadn't decided to take a different road home I would have been here sooner. Tell her I'm sorry," said Mikell holding Missily close with one arm and as Erin watched he turned to kiss her hair.

Erin was puzzled. There was more to it than she knew, she realized then, because it was so seldom she saw Mikell demonstrative with his wife. After they were gone Missily got Mikell's supper ready and some soup for herself and as they sat eating she explained what had happened that morning to upset her.

"But Missily," he held his fork and knife suspended over the meat he had been cutting. "Erin was angry and she can get so nasty. I wasn't about to have her spout off like she can—and like it sounded as though she already had. I didn't know exactly what had happened but I knew it had upset you and you didn't need her nasty tongue. Kitten always irritates you but she just puts on airs. Erin is downright nasty and mean at times and I don't like it."

"Oh," said Missily in a meek little voice. "It just seemed you were taking her side. I'm sorry."

"How could I take her side? I can tell you one thing, I'll be glad when things get back to normal. I like your sisters but I can only take so much of them before I feel like throwing things and yelling."

"Mikell!" Now Missily was laughing. She leaned over to kiss him. "I love you."

Chapter XV

Stephanie hadn't had time to wonder about her mother's whereabouts. Just after she finished her own dinner, food she was heartily tired of, longing for a home-cooked meal or a big Mac with a milk shake, she looked up as visitors came in the door. It was Imogen and Kitten, two who hadn't come before, but the third person she couldn't place at first. Then some dim memory stirred of a tall, quiet man who always took time to talk to her when she saw him occasionally. When was that? She was hardly conscious of answering Kitten's questions about how she felt and thanking Imogen for the flowers she'd brought. Then she remembered. He'd been with Aunt Suz.

"Uncle Auden!" she said, astonished, then, "I mean..."

"Don't change it," he smiled as he took her hand. "I'm glad to see you're better. Victoria told me about your ordeal. Here's something for you."

She took the box, slowly opened it and caught her breath. In it lay the most beautiful doll she'd ever seen, a collector's issue, the kind she'd often spent a long time looking at in the slick magazine to which her mother subscribed, wishing she could buy one. Made of porcelain the features were delicately molded and painted exquisitely, the hair so soft it felt real. The doll was dressed in a rich, dark red velvet, Victorian style dress. "Oh," whispered Stephanie. "Oh! Thank you."

He smiled. "Does it deserve a kiss?"

She reached up to draw his head down and kissed him shyly. "Why are you here?" she wanted to know.

"To see you,' he answered perching on the edge of the bed while both Kitten and Imogen, who had met him before when he had been East, stared. This wasn't the correct, fastidious, Auden they knew.

Kitten, who had chosen to stay at Fort Worden because that seemed easier than going to the hospital for which she had almost a phobia, had enjoyed her role as surrogate mother much more than she would have imagined, but she'd been worried sick at first. All she could think about in those early days was her nieces' and nephews' suffering while she could do nothing to help them. The first night after they'd found them she'd hardly slept and went around heavy-eyed and silent the next day. Imogen finally left with some of the younger girls to walk and talk. She'd never gone back to her former colorless way of dressing and she and Celeste seemed to have a kind of affinity. But Kitten stayed quiet and gloomy and that second night after everyone was in bed she called Auden. He was the one person she'd thought of right away because of Stephanie and the thought of talking to him grew more attractive as the day passed so night time found her dialing his number,

"Auden," she said as he answered in his usual brisk manner, "this is Victoria."

"Yes, Victoria. Isn't it a little late for you?"

"It's only about eleven. Did I wake you?"

"No. Where are you?"

"I'm in Washington State at Fort Worden. Oh, the hours would be different back East, wouldn't they? I'm up here for the reunion."

"Yes?" he said. She could tell he was irritated. She'd never called him before and she wondered if he thought....well, what did he think?

"I'm sorry to bother you, Auden, but you asked about Stephanie when I last saw you."

"I did, but I thought you would tell me my next trip East."

His tone was so cold she felt discouraged, wished she hadn't called, and almost hung up. "I would have but she went mountain climbing with some of the others." Then to her embarrassment her voice broke. Victoria never cried but now as she fought for control Auden said, suddenly alert, "Victoria? What happened? Is Stephanie hurt?"

"No, but they were gone almost three days before anyone found them and there was a storm. She is in intensive care with pneumonia."

`"But surely just being out in a storm wouldn't hurt her. She's not a delicate girl, is she?"

"No, but there was an accident." Victoria's voice still threatened to falter and fail and she took a deep breath. "One of the men was killed, Nigel is also in intensive care because he had internal injuries and lost a lot of blood. Myles has a broken shoulder, Gretchen broke some ribs and Thor has a broken leg, badly broken."

"Stephanie wasn't hurt?"

"No. She and Gretchen and Thor had just started to climb and jumped out of the way. There was a landslide. The others were in the path."

"Who was killed?" Auden's voice was sharp now.

"None of my family. A man named Shaul Kittam. Suz brought him." Victoria couldn't quite keep the scorn out of her voice.

"Kittam. Shaul Kittam the jazz pianist?"

"Yes. Did you know him?"

"Not personally but he was one of the nation's finest jazz musicians. I didn't hear it on the news."

"They just found them yesterday. No, I guess it was the day before."

"Hold on." There was a silence while Victoria sat in the chair, her face in her hand. She was still fighting tears. "Victoria?"

"Yes."

"I just checked my schedule. I can't come right away but I'll be up later. Will you be at the Fort?"

"Only until Sunday. Then I'm going to my folks. Imogen English is here with me and she'll be there, too. I'm not going to leave Seattle until everyone is all right. But you don't need to come. I-I just wanted to tell you."

"I'm aware I don't have to come, Victoria," reminding her by his tone of voice how he hated to be managed by women as he'd said many times. "I want to see Stephanie. However you never did answer my question. I asked you if Stephanie was a delicate girl?"

"No. They believe she had a virus before she went on the climb. She was sick the day before but Erin thought it was one of her migraine headaches and kept her quiet all day." She was puzzled. Why was he so interested in Stephanie?

"I want you to call me if she gets worse. I take it she's stable?"

"Yes. I guess so. I don't understand what it means to be in intensive care."

"Exactly, what it implies. They watch the patients very closely. Keep up on their condition. Who else did you say was in intensive care?"

"Nigel," she answered. "Missily says it's because they were out two nights before anyone got to them."

"Great Scott! Where was everyone? What happened to Nigel?"

Victoria suddenly remembered that Nigel had been his stepson at one time. They'd never talked about them so she had no idea what Auden thought of Suz's two. She explained again, then went into more detail about the week and about Diccon going to find the other climbers.

"He still around?" Auden asked.

"Yes. He's very steady and reliable. Not at all like the careless young man I knew years ago."

"I'll call you to let you know when I'll be in town. Do Anna and Allan still live at the same place?"

"Yes."

"Good. I know how to find it. I'll fly up and rent a car. Thank you for calling. I wish I could come right away. If Stephanie gets worse call me and I'll juggle things around so I can."

"I will. Thank you for talking to me."

"Take courage, Victoria," he answered in a gentler tone than she'd ever heard him use. "Medicine can do wonders these days."

Now he was still perched on the side of Stephanie's bed as Erin, Candace and Sean came into the room. Erin stopped short just inside the door so that Candace almost ran into her. Slowly she advanced. Auden turned as Stephanie looked past him and rose.

"Hello, Erin," he said calmly.

"Auden! What are you doing here?"

"I came to see your daughter. Victoria told me about the accident."

"Victoria? Kitten?" Erin turned to look at her sister. "Why would you..." she broke off, confused.

"He is a friend," Victoria answered in her most patronizing voice.

"Of whom?"

"Of mine."

"And of Stephanie," Auden added. "Of the family, I thought. I hardly thought that because Suz and I parted ways I was *persona non grata* to the rest of the family."

Candace had gone around to the other side of the bed and stood watching the others. She couldn't remember Auden at all.

240

"You'll have to introduce me to these young people. I don't remember which ones they are." Auden said to Victoria.

"These are Missily's two youngest," Victoria answered. "Sean and Candace."

"Oh yes, I remember. The little girl with the Ethiopian Queens' name."

"You know that?" Candace was entranced. "Hardly anybody does."

"Suz probably told him," Erin said.

"Suz did not tell me. I am capable of reading for myself," said Auden coldly. He had never liked Erin.

"Stephanie!" Candace's yelp cut off any retort Erin might have made. "Where did you get that gorgeous doll?"

"Uncle Auden gave her to me," Stephanie handed the doll to Candace.

"*Uncle* Auden?" Erin asked.

"Yes," Auden cut in before she could say more. "I asked her to call me that." Stephanie turned her head quickly to look at him. He went on, "And to write me once in a while. She can give me news of the family." He turned to Stephanie and leaned over to kiss her cheek. "Good-bye, Stephanie. You're getting too many visitors. How long do you have to stay here?"

"I'm leaving the day after tomorrow. Mother and I are flying home."

He frowned. "Are you well enough for that?"

"Yes. I've been up walking and the doctor says I'm to have a wheel chair at the airport so I won't have to walk too much."

"I won't see you again, then. Take care of yourself and I'm serious about writing. I fly into Albuquerque occasionally. Maybe I can find time to come see you."

"Oh," she said. "I'd like that and I will write."

He reached into his suit coat pocket and took out a card. "I'll write my address on the back of my business card for you," he said and taking a pen from his pocket he proceeded to do so.

"Could I have one, too?" Candace asked.

"Of course," Auden handed her a card.

"But you didn't put your address on here. I want to write to you, too."

"Get it from Stephanie," Auden answered. "You've grown quite a bit since I last saw you."

"I don't remember you at all."

"Good. I don't have to feel so guilty about not remembering you." Turning he held out a hand to Sean. "You weren't much older than Candace then. You have your mother's smile."

"So they tell me," Sean said with a grin. "I do remember you, just barely. Have you been to see Nigel?"

Victoria, who had been talking to Erin, quit in the middle of a sentence. She knew Auden had only come to see Stephanie.

He answered easily, "Not yet. I'll have to see what my partners want to do. What say, Victoria? Imogen? Shall we go visit Nigel now that we're here?"

"If you want to," Victoria answered, then to Erin," He's better, isn't he? Well enough for visitors?"

"Yes, though he can't go home yet. He's going to Mikell's folks place for a while after he gets out of here," she explained to Auden. "He has to have physical therapy for his back."

"What's his room number?" Auden asked.

Erin gave it to him and watched him leave with Victoria and Imogen. Tomorrow she would talk to Victoria. No, she'd have to call or go over tonight. But then, maybe Auden was staying at her folks' too. Candace was still talking about the doll. Auden heard her clear voice as they went down the hall.

"This must have cost a fortune. It'll go up in value, Stephanie. Be sure and save the box. Why did he give it to *you*?"

Mercenary little brat, thought Auden. Like her aunt. He wasn't looking forward to seeing Suz but he could think of no way of getting out of doing so. Stephanie he'd loved since the first time he'd seen her when she was no more than six, wished she could have been his daughter. They hadn't ruined her as he'd thought they might. She would be fourteen now, too old for dolls, maybe, but not collector's item and she might still have it when she was ninety and he a dim memory.

Nigel's room was already populated with visitors when they reached it. His bed was cranked up so that he wasn't flat on his back any more, but he wasn't sitting up either. He grinned at Victoria. "Aunt Vicky. I didn't think we'd get you up here. How nice to see you and Imogen."

Victoria went over to kiss him, smelling lovely with soft skin. Nigel had always loved her. She was a lady and he liked that.

"I'm glad you're better, Nigel. I was very frightened when you and Stephanie were so ill. Do you remember Auden?" And as she said it she thought what a stupid remark it was but Nigel just held out his hand and said easily, "Hello, Auden," though he longed to look at his father.

However, Diccon had learned years ago to hide his feelings when Suz was around and now he also held out a hand to shake Auden's. Auden shook it gravely before he said, "Hello, Suz. We came to see Stephanie and thought we'd look in on Nigel while we were in the vicinity."

Suz, who had stood looking from Victoria to Auden and back from the minute they'd first come in found herself now comparing Auden and Diccon and wondered how she could ever have thought Auden could take Diccon's place. A pang went through her when she thought of Nigel and Alexis being subjected to her vagaries, having to adjust to new men acting as fathers to them. Why did either of them even love her? Or did they?

Diccon's first reaction had been to want to protect Suz but before he'd acted on it and put a protective arm around her he remembered she wasn't his and he had no idea how she felt about Auden.

Auden turned from Suz and said, "And this young lady?"

"This is Mikell's sister, Lorna," Diccon answered.

"Lorna! I didn't recognize you either. But it's been what? Five, six, years or so since I've seen you. Stephanie I think I would have known if you put me in a room with all the younger set and asked me to name them, but otherwise I've done poorly."

Lorna managed a smile for him. She and Nigel had talked together when she came and they were alone about all kinds of things, but he'd never mentioned his feelings for her and she was beginning to think she'd imagined he cared for her in any particular way other than a friend even though she was glad for the opportunity to be with him. If she could never have him as her own she would have these hours to treasure. Now she said, "I would have known you. You haven't changed."

Auden managed to get Suz alone for a moment and said to her, "Why did you leave him, Suz? You still love him."

"I thought I was in love with you, Auden," she answered.

"No you didn't. You loved my money," he retorted.

Suz looked him straight in the eye. "No. It wasn't the money. I enjoyed what you gave me but I wanted to forget Diccon and Owen and you helped me do that."

He stared down at her before he turned away. He and Victoria and Imogen left not long after and Suz gave a sigh of relief.

"What did you ever see in him, Mom?" Nigel asked.

"I don't know. I was just asking myself the same question. Security, escape. Who knows."

Diccon sucked in his breath audibly and turned away to stroll over to the window and stare out unseeingly. Behind him he heard Suz stammer, "I-I mean...I didn't mean..." and her voice faded. "Diccon," she wanted to cry out, "I didn't meant you didn't give me security. I only meant..." and what she meant made her leave the room quickly before she broke down. She'd wanted security from the desire for Diccon and the temptation to go back to him.

"Did you know your Aunt Victoria was mother to every one after the accident?" Lorna asked into the silence.

"No." Nigel answered, glad for the change in subject. He'd been aware since he'd gotten well enough to take in his surroundings again that his father was under a terrible strain. His eyes had dark circles around them and there were lines down both sides of his mouth. Nigel's dislike for his mother hadn't abated any. "How'd that happen?"

"I don't know. She just kind of took over, Mother says. Fixed meals, watched the monsters."

"The what?"

"Oh." Lorna laughed. "Didn't you hear? That's what they were calling the youngest—the four girls: Candace, Betsy, Lynette, and Kate."

Nigel laughed, too. His father had slipped quietly our of the room and Nigel said, "Thanks, Lorna."

"For what?" Her blue eyes were startled.

"For rescuing us. Mom can get us in a fix faster than anyone I know. Poor Dad. He's about done in."

Lorna had been sitting in a chair, now she rose and came to pour him some fresh water. "Time to drink. You're not getting enough water," she said severely

He grinned. "Yes, ma'am." Obediently he drank some of the cold water. "I'll be so glad to get out of here and not feel weak as a kitten. Lorna,

243

the nurse said something the other day." He paused, studying her. She was so beautiful; her long dark hair was caught back in a clasp to fall down her back and one lock would slip over her shoulder when she leaned forward, then she would flip it back.

"Well, what did she say?" she prompted.

He looked away from her to the bottom of the bed. "She said that my fiancée was a beautiful woman and I was a lucky guy."

Lorna didn't answer.

"She meant you," Nigel added, thinking she hadn't understood.

"I know," she said. "I don't know why they think that. I-I wanted to see you and they wouldn't let anyone but family and I-I ran into Missily in the hall. I was crying and not watching where I was going. She went to talk to the nurses and they let me in after one of them told another I was your fiancée."

"Aunt Missily?"

Lorna nodded, then realizing he wasn't looked at her, said, "Yes."

He raised his eyes slowly to hers, which were candid and sweet. She didn't sound as though she minded but how could he tell her how he felt when he wasn't sure he would walk again? Though the feeling was back in his legs the pain in his back was still so severe he was on medication constantly and hadn't been out of bed yet. That was also because of what had been torn up inside him. He'd had to have a second operation and more blood and was slow to recover though he was getting better and they were talking of his getting up in a day or so even though that, too, was still uncertain. The silence stretched while they looked at each other. While Nigel still hesitated they heard voices and Missily and Mikell came in with Rose and Graham. Lorna turned away to the window as Diccon had. She had no idea what Nigel thought nor what he would have said next. He seemed almost to avoid personal subjects and she was surprised he'd even said anything. It was something she thought he hadn't known and she wished desperately that no one else had come. Then she went back to the hope she held close. He would be in her home. Surely, sometime, he would say something.

Chapter XVI

Suz was staying with Rose and Graham who were up to see Nigel at least once a day. Rose had slept little until he was out of danger and her face was drawn and tired looking. She didn't say much but Mikell had remarked to Missily that Graham's illness and now Nigel had aged Rose. Graham seemed to be doing fine and as Nigel improved she began to look and act more her old self.

The five sisters got together for lunch the day before Erin and Stephanie were to leave. It would have been hard to tell they were sisters since their coloring was so different. Victoria with her expensive and stylish clothes, her beautifully cut and styled hair was a picture of elegance and taste. Suz, in contrast, was casual in a sundress and sandals that showed her beautifully tanned skin, her hair brushed carelessly back from her face but falling down her back. Still an attractive woman, she drew the most attention as they walked in together to their table. It was a place where businessmen and women met over lunch and the men's heads turned as they walked by. Rose looked matronly even though she'd never had children, stouter than the others, her hair obviously done for her. Missily and Erin followed the others, Erin with her fair hair that caught the lights and shimmered, dressed fashionably in a well cut slack suit, was telling Missily about something at work so that her small face was animated. Missily, Mikell's love, the retiring one, had a sereneness about her. Her hair was as dark a chestnut as it had been the day Mikell first saw her and her gray eyes as lovely. She was taller than Erin so was bent a little to hear her sister over the noise in the restaurant. Missily was dressed in a rose outfit that was particularly becoming and even Victoria had approved of the way she looked.

"This has been quite a reunion," Victoria remarked as they sat waiting after ordering their meal. "Let's hope we never have a repeat."

"I second that," Erin said fervently.

"But we've gotten to see each other more at least," said Rose who always tried to find something positive in every situation. "I don't mean I like the reason for it but it's been so nice having you close. We get so far apart when we live so far away from one another."

"That's true," agreed Missily. "I'm glad we've had the time we have had together. I don't feel quite so much as though we're strangers."

"Have you felt that way, too?" asked Suz. "Sometimes it's hard to remember I have four sisters."

"I don't mean I forget," answered Missily, "just that we don't seem to write or call each other much or have much to say when we do. I feel like I know a little more what you're like and do. Except for Rose, of course, whom I have the privilege of being with often." She smiled at her older sister who reached out to give her hand an affectionate pat.

"Suz, what are you going to do now?" Victoria asked casually, sitting back as her salad came. She smiled at the waitress. "Thank you."

Suz didn't answer until their food was before them all; each had ordered salads except for Rose who was having a large bowl of vegetable soup.

"What do you mean?" she asked then.

"Won't your life change now that Mr. Kittam isn't here?"

Missily frowned. Victoria was being catty. She, herself, hadn't been aware of any kind of special closeness between Suz and Shaul. However, Suz answered easily, "Shaul and I were friends. Nothing more. He knew I had made no commitment to him. I'll go back and do what I was doing before, of course."

Missily looked up quickly from her salad, which she'd been covering with blue cheese dressing. She was surprised at the answer because she'd seen Suz watching Diccon and they'd spent so much time together. She hoped Suz hadn't turned Diccon down. He was so quiet, almost taciturn these days, making the trip from Oregon on weekends to see Nigel, not smiling much and Mikell had said to Missily in irritation, "What he sees in her I'll never know. Why doesn't he just forget her and find a decent girl?"

Missily hadn't answered, but she wasn't sure she agreed. Suz wasn't as hard as she had been and the days since Nigel's accident she had seemed almost lost without Diccon. She sighed. "I guess I'm too much of a romantic," she thought. "I wanted them to get together again. Poor Diccon." And she wished she had the courage to ask Suz how she felt about Diccon.

"Heavy thoughts, Missily?" Erin asked.

"Hmm? Oh, I guess I was thinking of Nigel and about Diccon coming all the way from Bend every weekend."

"Hasn't he been wonderful?" Rose said. "Suz, I don't think you knew a good thing when you had it."

"We all live the life that suits us best," said Victoria briskly. "Suz was not suited to a backwoods life. I knew that when she married Diccon."

Suz smiled. "I remember your telling me that. It sounded romantic then." She laughed. "It always sounded like it would be wonderful in books and in the movies. Forest Rangers were so good-looking."

"You always did have your head in the clouds," said Erin.

"Me? I thought that was Missily with all her book learning. I had two feet on the ground where the bright lights were."

The sisters laughed together though Missily thought Suz's last sentence had sounded more mocking than serious and a hard note had entered.

The next day Victoria, Imogen, Erin and Stephanie all left and three days later Suz headed back to California with a promise from Rose to keep her posted on Nigel's progress. Suz said she would fly back if there were further complications, hoped to see them all at Alexis and Jon's wedding and thanked Rose and Missily for everything. She left in Shaul's car, which she was going to take to his own place where her own was parked.

As she drove away she felt she had never done anything so difficult in all her life before. Nigel would be at Deborah's and Gabriel's in another week and Suz guessed she would soon hear of another plan for wedding bells. Though neither Lorna nor Nigel had said anything she had watched them together and seen how they watched each other when they thought no one was looking—not even the one they were watching. She had no idea why they hadn't made any decision but that was their business. To have her children thinking of marriage made her feel the loss of both of them even though both had been gone from home the last few years. Far more difficult, though, was leaving Diccon. She had grown to love him as they watched Nigel's fight for life day after day. During those quiet hours they had talked about their children's lives, of what was ahead for both of them, and Suz, drawing comfort from Diccon's steady, calm presence, talked to him of the years away from him, about Auden and Owen. She said far more than she realized about the two men though she usually talked lightly of them and in that same mocking way Missily had remarked. Diccon knew that neither man had respected her and burned with anger that they would use her so cavalierly as though they had been superior in some way. He heard her restlessness and longed to be able to give her peace or at least point her in the right direction, but she'd shied away from any mention of God's care of Nigel, had lashed out at him that a God who treated those who loved him the way he supposedly had Nigel wasn't a God she'd believe in.

Now as the miles rolled away beneath her tires traveling down I-5 she found herself in tears, turned on the radio to take her mind off Diccon but could find nothing to help. Those were the longest miles she had ever traveled. She had intended to drive straight through to Southern California, but as she stopped for a late supper that night and nodded over her meal she knew she'd have to get some sleep or she might not make it at all. She had the fleeting thought, "So what?" What reason had she to go back?

After only two or three hours of sleep she woke and, since she couldn't go back to sleep again, let herself out of the motel room quietly and started down the highway again. After she delivered Shaul's car she had no idea what she would do. Right that moment she didn't think she could go back to the world of plastic people behind masks, smiling herself, being pleasant and entertaining when she wanted to laugh or yell at someone. But when she arrived at Shaul's place she found Brett and Eleanor distraught and lost.

"Oh, Miss Suz," Eleanor said. "What will we do without him? We've been with him for years. Ever since he bought this place. When he called he sounded so happy. He said we would like it up there. And now he's gone." Her face worked and the tears rolled down her cheeks.

The three of them sat talking until late that night. Brett and Eleanor wanted to know all about the accident and about Port Townsend.

"Oh, I didn't know your son was hurt. How old is he?" Eleanor asked when Suz explained about the climb and who had been hurt.

"He's..." Suz paused. "Let's see. He's twenty-one."

"That old?" Eleanor said, then added hastily. "I mean, you don't look old enough to have a son twenty-one."

247

"Thank you," Suz said wryly, well aware that Eleanor must be doing some figuring in her head since Shaul *hadn't* been old enough to have a son that age.

"Is he going to be all right?" Eleanor asked quickly.

"I hope so. His back is still not good and he'll need quite a bit of physical therapy. But he was much better when I left. He'll stay at my brother-in-law's parent's home. They are good friends. At least he'll be there until he's able to get around and care for himself again." Then she began to describe Port Townsend for them.

"Would we like it there, do you think Miss Suz?" asked Brett.

When Shaul had first brought Suz to his house and introduced her to Brett and Eleanor he gave her name as Suz Springs but they'd began calling her Miss Suz not long after. She'd tried to get them to drop the Miss but hadn't succeeded. When she'd asked Shaul he'd just laughed. "They watch the old movies. That's the way they think things should be done. You can't change them. I gave up years ago."

So now she said, "I don't know. It's very different than here. You might not like the weather. There's not the sun we have."

"Mr. Shaul told us it was a nice, small town. I'd like a smaller place." Eleanor said wistfully. "Somewhere I could walk to town or the grocery store."

"You could do that, all right. It's a fascinating town right on the water and since their hopes of getting a railroad fell through a long time ago, it never grew much. There are a lot of Victorian homes and buildings and they give tours so you can see them. Plus it's close to the Olympic Mountains."

"Is it as pretty as he said?" Brett asked.

"I don't know what he said but it *is* in a beautiful setting, and yes, I think it's a pretty town."

"I'd like to go see it. Mr. Shaul didn't have family, you know, and Brett and I thought he should just... well, he wanted to be... to be..."

"Cremated," supplied Brett. "We thought it would be fitting to scatter his ashes up there in the mountains. And we'd like to see Port Townsend."

"There's no reason why you shouldn't. Brett, you do gardening. You could probably get a job in something along that line." Suz said. "Unless you had something else in mind."

"No. I hadn't thought of a job." His long face became quite sad. "I don't know what we'll do without him. He was all the family we had."

"Well, for a while you'll have the care of this place until everything is settled. Don't rush into anything yet. And I'll be around to help you any way you wish," Suz said, feeling needed for the first time in years.

It gave her an interest in the days that followed. She and her father had had a long talk before she left Washington but she hadn't reached any conclusion as to what she wanted to do in life. None of the things he had suggested were anything which interested her. She continued to go to the parties and write her column which was witty, informal and somewhat of a gossip column but never vicious. The parties were beginning to bore her so much that if she hadn't had Eleanor and Brett to help and be with she would most likely have done something outrageous at one of them. She disliked

248

many of the hostesses and their husbands she tried to avoid as much as possible. Suz didn't realize that her outlook on life had undergone a subtle but far-reaching change during the hours with Diccon.

Diccon's unfailing gentleness, his integrity and openness, his advice to her as well as his sympathy and compassion had broken through the hard shell she'd built around herself. She'd been startled when she understood how deeply he suffered for those he loved and it set her to wondering what it had been like for him after she'd left him in the dead of the night with his two children. She found time alone difficult because her thoughts invariably went to Diccon and she realized that she finally knew what it meant to love a man. Despair would grip her so that she began to drink more than was customary for her. Only when she spent the day and night at Shaul's place did she have a measure of peace as she helped Brett and Eleanor go through Shaul's belongings.

Things changed when the will was read. Shaul had left everything to Brett and Eleanor. They were wealthy enough not to have to work the rest of their lives. No one contested the will and Eleanor went around in a daze. "Miss Suz," she said one day, "I don't know what to think. I never knew he would do that. I mean, we're so much older. I thought we would die first."

"He made provision for that," Brett reminded her. "If we predeceased him the money was to go to the Jewish Hospital in Denver to help with the children there."

"I know," his wife said.

"Are you going to Port Townsend?" Suz asked.

"Oh! We can't do that," Eleanor answered.

"Why not?"

"Well, Mr. Shaul gave us this house. We just can't leave it." The woman's eyes filled with tears which threatened to overflow.

"But Shaul put it on the market. He would have had to make a new will and you would probably have been given his home in Port Townsend."

Eleanor's face brightened. "I never thought of that, did you Brett?"

Her husband grunted in answer. He'd tried to explain that very thing earlier but Eleanor had her mind set and wouldn't listen.

Suz helped them get things ready to move, finding markets for Shaul's considerable collection of books, his music and, on sudden inspiration, called Auden to see if he would like to buy Shaul's collection of jazz records and tapes. He came to look it over and paid a good price for them all.

"There are some treasure here," he said. "Collector's items."

"I wasn't sure but I thought there might be," Suz answered. "I'm glad I remembered you collected them, too."

"Yes. Thank you," he said as they walked out to his car together. Just before he got in he asked. "How's your family?"

"Everyone is about back to normal."

"Nigel?"

"It's slow and he gets discouraged. He's still walking with a walker." Suz looked past Auden over the valley to the ocean, fighting tears.

"Well, I hope he gets better. Thanks again," he said in that business-like tone he'd used since he'd decided she bored him.

She didn't answer, didn't watched him drive away. He hadn't ever cared much for either Alexis or Nigel. They'd disturbed his orderly life. Why he'd married her she would never know. She turned slowly back to the house, her mind on Nigel now. She called Deborah each week to check on his progress before she talked to Nigel. No word yet of any engagement between Nigel and Lorna. Suz wondered if she should have stayed and gotten an apartment so she and Nigel could have lived together at least until he was well enough to live alone. She hadn't felt he wanted her around, had been willing to go to Deborah and Gabe's place after Gabe had talked to him. Sighing she went in to help Eleanor.

That night, late on a Sunday, she opened her apartment door just as the phone began to ring. She was tired and dispirited and almost ignored it but thought if it were Alexis or Nigel she wouldn't want to miss their call so she shut the door behind her and ran to get the phone. "Hello."

"Zannie? Diccon here."

"Diccon!" She sat down in a hurry. "Is something wrong?"

"No. I just got back from Washington. Thought I'd give you a buzz. Nigel and I took a little walk today. He's managing without the walker now. Has a cane."

"Oh, Diccon. How wonderful!"

"I think so, too, but he's still pretty discouraged. The doctor's still not sure he can ever go back to work full time again."

"Why not?" Suz kicked off her sandals, stretched out on her couch, wriggling her toes.

"Nothing different. Lorna says the doctor was being careful because he didn't say he couldn't, only that they didn't know yet. She told me that later. She says Nigel wants to hurry things."

Suz laughed. "I can well imagine that. He never was a patient child."

"Zannie, we walked down to that little stream that runs through Gabe's place. Oh, you've never seen it, have you?"

"No."

"Well, there's a creek that borders their property not too far from the house. We walked down there and sat down on the bank to talk. Nigel told me what the doctor said and we discussed things he could do at home. He's good working with leather and fly tying and could make money that way if he had to. What's worrying him is asking Lorna to marry him if he can't go back to work." Diccon paused and Suz waited quietly wishing he were with her. "Zannie, I don't know whether I said the right thing or not but I told him I thought it was unfair not to let Lorna make the decision whether she wanted to put up with that kind of thing and encouraged him to talk to her. What do you think?"

Suz's heart jumped and for a moment she couldn't answer then she said, "Diccon, I don't think I'm better qualified than you are. I mean I'm— well, you're much...." she stopped. The fact that he was asking her advice stunned her.

"But he's your son, too. Besides you're a woman. You'd know better whether Lorna would want to have a husband who couldn't work."

"In the first place it isn't that he can't work, Diccon, as you pointed out. He just may have to change jobs. But I wouldn't know what Lorna would think. Some women wouldn't give a hoot whether her man brought home the bacon or not. It wouldn't make any difference to me in a case like Nigel's. But from what I saw at the hospital I would say Lorna is pretty far gone on Nigel and would be willing to have him in any shape or form."

Diccon laughed. "You're probably right. At least I feel better. All the way back home I thought I'd probably given him the wrong advice."

"No one has to take advice, you know," Suz said. "Diccon, you don't have to worry about what you tell the kids. You're one of the best father's around and they know it."

"Oh, I don't know about that. I know they might think so. I guess that's what matters. What've you been doing with yourself?"

"I'm helping sort through Shaul's things so the house can be sold. Otherwise, nothing different."

"Oh." The life went out of Diccon's voice. "Well, I'll let you go. Just thought you'd at least be interested in Nigel's progress."

"I am. Thank you for calling, Diccon."

"Good night," he said and hung up.

Suz put the receiver down slowly and sat a long time thinking of the conversation and the change in Diccon's voice after she'd mentioned Shaul. Surely he couldn't think she'd cared for Shaul. And he'd asked about her for the first time in years. It was all so unfair. She wished she'd never asked Shaul to come to the reunion. After all, if Diccon did think she cared for Shaul that was her own fault. She'd slept with him and they'd all known it. Suddenly there seemed to be sense in what she's always thought of as Puritan and self-righteous. Sighing, she finally rose and went to get ready for bed.

Though neither Eleanor nor Brett played the piano they wouldn't give up Shaul's and planned to have it shipped to their new home. Suz had tried to get them to visit Port Townsend before they decided to move up there but they were both adamant. When they finally left she stood in the driveway of Shaul's home and waved good-bye. The house was up for sale and empty. The moving van had come the day before and Suz had promised to come out in the morning to say good-bye because even though they'd spent the night in town they wanted to leave from their old home.

The despair and depression lurking around corners since she'd come back from Washington descended on Suz after they left. She was hardly sleeping at all and finally went to a doctor for some sleeping tablets. She deliberately went to one she knew handed out medicine indiscriminately. Her own doctor would have wanted to know why she wasn't sleeping and sent her to a psychiatrist. She'd tried that route once after she and Auden broke up and refused to go back. She went to the pharmacy for her pills, took them home to count. There were thirty. Slowly she put them back in the pill bottle. Thirty. It was enough to put her to sleep so she wouldn't wake again. With determination she took one pill out, put the rest away and went to get a glass or water. What stupid thoughts. Maybe she'd meet someone if she opened her eyes at the parties she was going to attend in the next week.

As the evenings wore on she knew that she could never go back to the mindless way she'd been living until one night she finally slipped out quietly by herself to drive home though the night was still young. Not one man had attracted her though there were plenty of unattached and some attached, good-looking men, who had tried to get her off in a corner. It was strange to feel so uninterested, so bored with it all. An ennui settled on her. As she put her car in the garage and went up the elevator to her floor she felt so weary it was an effort to do anything. Pulling open her drapes she stood a long time looking out over the city, thinking back over the years. Auden had changed very little. He'd always been sure she'd married him for his money even though she had plenty after her divorce from Owen, and though at first she'd been fond of him, his cynicism and inability to believe her turned that fondness into an intense dislike. A slight smile tugged at the corners of her mouth. She wondered if he thought Shaul had willed the records to her. Victoria crossed her mind then and she wondered fleetingly what his relationship to her sister was and why he'd gone all the way to Washington to see Stephanie. But it was only a fleeting thought because her mind was working to the place it had persistently traveled for days. Diccon. If only I could be with Diccon, she thought as she had over and over since the day she'd driven away from Rose's.

Now, as the lights of the city blurred before her, she became aware that she was weeping. Life had no meaning. What was there for her anyway? How did people go on day after day? She thought of the sleeping pills again and this time the thought didn't seem so repulsive. She'd received a letter from Eleanor who sounded happy and busy. She and Brett had found a little house not too far from downtown. They were both doing a lot of walking. There was a big house for sale they were thinking of buying and making into a Bed and Breakfast Inn. They needed something to do.

Diccon. Her mind went back to him. His call had been so unexpected. She wished she'd explained about helping Eleanor and Brett with Shaul's things. She would see him at Alexis and Jon's wedding and at Lorna and Nigel's since they had finally decided to get married. But would she ever hear from him again? Maybe, in connection with their two but probably not often now that they would have homes of their own. Diccon, who was more than his youth had ever promised, was still single. Would he take her back again? There had been that moment in the hospital cafeteria when she'd seen the pain in his eyes and the kiss when they knew about the accident. He'd been loving, attentive. Was that because of Nigel or did he still care for her? It was something she'd not thought about for years; she'd been too immersed in her own pleasures. She had his address though she wasn't sure how to get to his place but she could ask. What would happen if she went to see him?

The thought stayed with her and the next day the desire to see him again grew stronger. Two days later she had put everything in order including her will, made sure she could withdraw her money from the bank, told her landlord she was leaving California in a week and the apartment would be empty, told the paper she wrote for she wouldn't be writing any more but would finish out the month, got rid of everything she didn't want, keeping only what was hers and nothing she had received from either Austen or Owen or any other man, stored what she kept and couldn't take with her, left a letter with her lawyer to be opened after her death telling Nigel where she'd stored her things and decided if Diccon didn't want her she'd take the sleeping pills that she'd put away for that purpose. Then she found a room to stay in until she finished writing her columns for the month.

One bright fall morning she left the place that had been home to her for over seventeen years and headed for Oregon. Though she didn't know what was ahead she felt better than she had since before she'd met Shaul. At last she had a purpose and a goal and if that one wasn't possible she had an alternative. She left her old life with no regrets as she sped back up I-5 singing along with the radio as she went.

Chapter XXVII

Diccon, weary from the long hike that afternoon, back from a weeklong trip he'd taken with a photographer and author who was writing a book about the habitat of wild animals in the Deschutes National Forest, the area Diccon worked, had eaten and showered and now stood in front of his house. Some twelve years ago, when he'd been hired for his present job, he'd built it in the forest with tall lodgepole pine trees and grasses and shrub on land he purchased several miles outside of Bend. It was a log house and he'd done much of the work himself, some with Nigel and Alexis' help when they stayed with him in the summers. He'd bought them each a horse, had one of his own and all were still in the pasture behind the house. The house wasn't large but he'd made sure the rooms were spacious and there were three bedrooms so that both Nigel and Alexis could have their own room. In fact, both were still full of their owners' things; the arrowheads Nigel had collected as well as the fishhooks he fly-tied, his hats, his fishing equipment. Alexis' bedroom had bird eggs and nests she'd found, baskets she'd made out of pine needles, pictures of horses on the wall and the ribbons and trophies she'd won in local and state horse shows. Diccon's own bedroom was sparsely furnished. He'd never gotten rid of the bedroom set that had belonged to him and Suz though most of the rest of their furniture had been second hand and become so shabby he'd replaced it. The bedroom set had been a gift from Suz's parents and they'd picked it out together so he treasured it. There was a small padded chair and throw rugs on the floor. On one wall he had put some of the pictures Nigel and Alexis had sent him through the years which they'd drawn or painted in school and with them their school photographs, each marching up the wall. He'd chosen six of each of his favorites from those taken through the years, framed and hung them. Over his bed he had hung an enlarged picture of Suz taken when she was quite young, a new bride, laughing from her perch in the tree in the front yard of their first home.

His own front yard had been left natural. Diccon wasn't a gardener and he liked the land the way it was. There were deer in the yard often in the early morning or late evening that accepted his presence. He had fenced a small area in back for a vegetable garden, which he and Alexis and Nigel grew in the summer.

Now Diccon stood in front of the house, glad to be home in one way and yet, in another, wishing the trip could have lasted longer. He had enjoyed the young writer and while in his company he hadn't had much time to think about his problems. At night he'd been tired in a good, healthy way so that he'd gone to sleep immediately. Now, though, all that he'd fought through those many years ago had to be fought over again. There weren't the questions this time, the castigation of himself for failing Suz, the humiliation of knowing he'd lost his wife, but now all the long days and nights he'd spent at the hospital with Suz watching Nigel together were taking their toll. The loneliness was so terrible, so engulfing, the longing for her so fierce he wasn't sure he could weather it. Suz, under that hard shell she'd had so long, was different than she'd ever been. She was, of course, a mature woman, but it was more than that. Though she would not admit it, she'd been terribly hurt by Auden's snobbery and Owen's callousness and when they'd talked about Nigel and Alexis she'd broken down and cried more than once because she felt she'd failed them. Diccon knew that there was a deeper, less shallow side to Suz that her family didn't see but which he'd known in part and now it was stronger. In spite of her seemingly uncaring nature she was sensitive. But she was like a ship without a rudder, without purpose or aim. She had married young, had never developed her abilities until she was convinced she had none, nothing to offer anyone.

He wished he'd given in to his impulse and asked her to come back to him. At least he wouldn't be tormented by the question of whether she would have said yes or no. He would have known one way or the other. Walking slowly across the yard he came to a tree which was a natural bench. Once broken, possibly by a snow or wind storm, it had survived and after growing horizontally for a short while had headed back up toward the sky. It made a natural seat where Diccon and Nigel had often sat talking.

Diccon missed Nigel. He'd gotten a job in Washington. It was a desk job but right now it was all he could handle. Though his back was better he was still taking therapy and didn't always make a full day's work. He was still using the cane, limping some. It wouldn't have made any difference anyway, Diccon thought, whether he'd gotten the job or not. He still would have moved since he and Lorna were going to be married early next year. Did that add to or accentuate his loneliness? Both of his children would have their families and lives of their own to lead now.

Diccon sighed and decided to check on the garden. It was cool at night and most of his produce was harvested but he tried to remember to cover the tomato plants. He heard a car in his driveway just as he started around the side of the house and frowned. He didn't want company. He continued around the house determined to ignore whoever it was but then, being Diccon, he couldn't be rude. Someone might need directions so he turned back and started across the wide front yard. The driver had gotten out and was hidden by a tree at first and then he heard the car door slam and was where he could see. A woman turned from the car, looked at the house as she dropped the keys in her purse. Something in her movements and the color of her hair, as the evening sun touched it, caught at Diccon's heart, made it lurch and begin to race. Then he smiled grimly. He'd seen Suz in too many women lately. She was nowhere near Oregon but in Southern California and yet, when he walked closer and could see her as she turned, he stopped suddenly.

"Zannie," he whispered, unbelieving, and drew his hand across his eyes. He *must* be tired.

She saw him then and hesitated before she started slowly toward him.

255

"Zannie," he said aloud this time. "I thought you were in California."

She stopped and looked at him uncertainly. "I was. Would you rather I be there?" His voice had sounded cold. How could she know that he could hardly speak?

"No!" he said forcefully and suddenly he ran, caught her in his arms and held her fiercely against him. "I was just standing here wondering how I could ever live without you. How I could face the pain of life alone with only the remembrance of your beauty, your laugh, everything that makes you who you are," he said recklessly, not caring why she'd come, overwhelmed by his need of her. "I wasn't sure I could weather it again. Not after those days and nights...." Suddenly his voice died away. Sobriety came back and with it rationality and then he found she was holding him, her body shaken with sobs.

"My love, don't cry," he whispered, gentle now.

She raised a dear, tear-streaked face. "Diccon, can you ever forgive me for the mess I've made of your life?"

"But I forgave that a long time ago. If I hadn't been so stubborn about living out in the boonies perhaps...." He broke off aware that he had no idea why she was here and of his early gabbling.

However, she didn't move away, only said, "Diccon, is it too late..." she paused. "I haven't any right to ask this," she went on and the tears slid down her cheeks, "but would you—would you consider—at least, think about taking me back again?"

He grinned down at her as he wiped the tears away with one hand, "I think you already know the answer to that. I lost my head when I saw you." Then he grabbed her close again. "And you better mean what you say," he added fiercely, "because I'm not going to let you go again."

It was her turn to laugh though it was a shaky one and her arms crept up around his neck. "Diccon, I love you so."

And then he was kissing her and Suz, who had been kissed so many times, knew this was the first time she'd ever given a kiss with real love in her heart.

" Does this mean you want to be my wife? The wife of a country hick?" he teased gently.

"More than anything in the world. I'll live wherever you want to."

"Then come see my house, my love. See if you like where I live," he turned her around gathering her small clutch purse from the ground where she'd dropped it.

They talked far into the night. He'd taken her in, made a fire and drew up the old couch in front of it, made some hot chocolate for them to drink as they sat together. He found release in talking to her, her head on his shoulder, her hands touching him gently, caressingly, the hands he'd loved so long. The perfume of her hair filled his nose, the dear laugh and voice gave him pleasure in a way he'd not known before. The years fell away and he felt young and full of a great contentment. At her prompting he admitted the agony he'd experienced when she left, the emptiness, the long, lonely days and nights, the anger, the self-recriminations without trying to blame her. Then he told her of finding peace in the God who is not only the Creator but also the Redeemer of sinners and of how Mikell had helped and taught him.

She clung to his hand and wept. "I didn't know. We fought so much I thought you would be glad to get rid of me, find someone who loved the outdoors in the way you did. And you seemed so calm when I finally did call you about the kids."

"But you have to remember that wasn't until a year or so later. By then I could talk without anger, or at least not so you would know I was angry. I tried to find you..." he broke off. "Let's not go over all that. It's past and you're here now."

"But, Diccon, in all the years I was married to you I was so self-centered I didn't know what kind of person you were. Alexis and I have had some long conversations since then and she told me about their summers with you. I—I never would take time to listen before. She isn't sure she believes as you do. Right now she's so wrapped up in Jon that's all the further she looks. Nigel and I talked, too. Diccon, the years could have turned you bitter," and here she began to sob, great wrenching sobs so that he pulled her close to rock her in his arms.

"Sh-h-h, love. Please, Zannie. That's all in the past. A bad dream. All that matters is that you're here and we can go on from now, not look back. We both made mistakes but we've learned from them."

"But how can you ever trust me again?" she sobbed.

He looked down at her tear-streaked face, her troubled eyes, "Ah, but you've had your Vanity Fair and know it's just that and not life."

She closed her eyes and laid her head back on his shoulder. "When we were at the hospital I was so afraid for Nigel. Then I went back to California and knew there was nothing there for me. Tell me how it helped you to become—religious."

He laughed gently. "It wouldn't have helped at all if I'd just become religious. Oh, I guess it might have helped in a way, but not ultimately. It would have been rather like a Band-Aid on a festering wound, but I know what you're trying to say. I met a Person. A Person so great, so compassionate, so giving that there was nothing I could do but believe. I met Jesus Christ." He smoothed her hair back. "Not the Jesus of the movies, but the Christ of Scriptures, the Lord of the universe, the Savior of sinners, the Redeemer."

"But I don't see how that could help. I don't understand. I know what it means to redeem something—like, well, like coupons," she gave a little laugh, "but how can that have anything to do with religion?" Suz asked, fitting her hands to his. He had long slender fingers as she also had but his were longer and definitely a man's. She thought briefly of Shaul's hands and wondered that she had never noticed the strength and beauty of Diccon's before. "And how can a--a person make much difference?"

"Zannie, you know how restless you feel, how dissatisfied with life you are?"

She agreed but added, "If I'm with you that'll change."

"How do you know it will?" he asked affectionately. "You've gone through a shattering experience. How do you know what you want now will be when that's faded in time."

"But you said you trusted me."

"Darling, I do. As far as you are capable you will be faithful to me. The only problem is that not one of us knows what tomorrow will bring and what we'll face or how we'll react. If I put complete trust in any human, including myself, I can expect nothing but failure one way or another. It's humanly impossible for us to know what we'll do given the temptation or opportunity or test."

"You've stayed true to me, haven't you?"

"Yes, but I give all credit for that to my heavenly Father. I seem to be made constitutionally unable to love anyone but a lovely lady named Edita Suzanne. I almost got married again, once."

Suz sat up to look at him and she didn't like the thought of him holding another woman or kissing her. For the first time that she could remember she felt jealousy stir in her.

He smiled. "She was a nice girl, pleasant to be with, but after I went to the reunion that year and saw you again I knew it wouldn't be fair to marry her feeling as I still did about you so I never asked her." He reached over to tuck a strand of hair behind her ear. "She's happily married with children and I'm not sorry."

"But Diccon, I couldn't stand to hurt you like that again. I mean like I did when I left you."

"I know. Perhaps, though, you would feel I would be hurt more if you stayed with me. I'm just making up hypothetical situations, Zannie. I want you to see that trusting me isn't the answer. After all, I'm not immortal, not yet. I'll die some day. Becoming a Christian doesn't make life dull and uninteresting. On the contrary. Remember that time we saw a rebuilt pioneer home with those windows they had and how distorted things looked when you look through them? And then the difference when we stepped outside and could see the mountains and trees?"

"Yes, I think of it often."

His eyes came to hers in astonishment. He hadn't supposed she even thought of their life together the years she'd been gone.

"I didn't forget," she whispered. "I just tried not to remember. I—I kept busy."

He closed his eyes suddenly. "That's the way it is with us. Like the pioneer windows or looking through them," he said. He wasn't sure he could handle rationally any further revelations of her life away from him. He'd convinced himself she didn't care and through the years believed that. To know that she might never have been free of him was disturbing in a way he couldn't yet grasp. "We see things distorted," he went on with difficulty, fighting to keep his mind on what he was trying to explain. To have her next to him was so exquisite it was almost like pain. "Until we turn to our Creator we can't see them right. Life never looks the same after we come to know Him."

Suz got up to wander around the dark room while Diccon put another log on the fire. They'd been talking by firelight since the sun had disappeared and night had fallen with its velvety darkness. "Could you explain it to me?" she asked. "I know Missily and Mikell are different in some way and so are you and Nigel but I don't understand why. I mean you don't fit with any of the people I've known who call themselves Christians. Auden was a Catholic though he never went to church. But he was so cold. I tried a Catholic Church for a while after we were married because the church we were married in was so beautiful, but it all seemed so strange, so foreign. It didn't make sense and all I ever saw in Mom was a frantic effort to do a lot of good things for others. Dad, of course, wanted the business being a church member would bring him. I've had others come to me on the beach and try to force some kind of spiritual laws or something like that on me. I acted like I agreed just to make them leave. And in school the kids who went around talking about—about God *did* act as though everything fun in the world was—was—" she stopped, at loss for words.

"Evil?" Diccon asked. He had turned on the couch so he could watch her. She had gone from object to object in the room, touching them lingeringly as though she loved all his things. She stood before his bookcase now, her fingers running lightly over the backs of the books.

"Yes," she said. "That's it."

"There are all kinds of people who profess Christianity in the world. God made us all different and he doesn't take our personalities away when he makes us his. Instead He uses them for His purpose. Christians aren't a lot of robots or puppets on a string and though basically they all believe the same there are differences. Like, for instance, how we believe we should live in the world. That's why some people withdraw from the world, like the nuns and monks, or people who go to Christian schools, to church, only do business with others who say they are Christians and only have friends who also profess Christianity. Then there are those who don't seem to be much different than their neighbor who doesn't claim any kind of religious faith plus all shades in between. There are a lot of people like Mikell and Missily and Nigel and I. The importance of Christianity isn't in our differences. I don't mean that the differences don't matter, they do, but of first importance is the One who came so we could find forgiveness and rest." Diccon turned to look at the fire. It was hard to know what to say to her. She knew so little and there was so much to learn. She had lived for pleasure all her life. Did he start with the law or did he tell her about what Christ had done?

She came to sit beside him. "Diccon, is there really a heaven and a hell?"

"Yes, though I can't tell you much about either one. A lot of language in the Bible is symbolic when it tells us about them. That's not because God doesn't want us to know but because we couldn't understand if he did tell us in any other way. It's somewhat like trying to tell someone what mountains are like if they have never seen one or even a picture of one."

"I just wonder where—where—" her voice broke.

259

"Shaul is?" Diccon asked gently though his heart sank. If she had come to him because she had loved Shaul and lost him would she stay? But her next words cancelled that idea.

She nodded, the tears spilling over. "I never loved him. I didn't even know him very long and I'm not sure I even liked him. He was so intense and I never liked jazz; you know that. But he wasn't a bad person. He was rather a dear in some ways and I can't see why—well, what did he do that would deserve—punishment like that?"

He took her hand in his. "The problem is that we all deserve hell from Adam on plus none of us loves God and our neighbor perfectly because we're rotten to the core even if it doesn't show. At least not to each other. God would be just in sending us all to hell. The wonder is that He doesn't because He's also merciful." He reached for a Bible that lay on the shelf not far from him. "Let me read to you. Maybe if I do and you ask questions it will help." He opened to the Gospel of John and began to read. They progressed slowly as he explained each verse to her. It was so familiar it was hard to remember that once it had been as foreign to him as it was now to her.

His old clock struck the hour. It was the only thing that he had that had been his parents and he'd had to buy it at an auction of one of his uncles' estates. He loved it. Those short years he'd been with his parents before their sudden death in an airplane crash, had been marked by it's melodious chimes and it brought memories of love and soft arms holding him and a man's laugh. Now Suz sat up suddenly.

"Diccon, you have to work tomorrow and it's two o'clock. What time do you have to get up?"

"At five," he answered.

"But that's terrible. I have a motel room in Bend. Can we get together for dinner tomorrow?" She rose.

"Of course, but I work in the Forestry Station there so we'll have breakfast—if you'll be up to have it with me—in one of my favorite cafes. And lunch *and* dinner somewhere together. You don't think I'm going to let you out of my sight any longer than I have to, do you?" He had risen, too, and reached for her. "I'll follow you to town to see you make it safely and kiss you good-night."

"You'll do no such thing," she said, leaning back in his arms. "You need to get your rest. I'm used to traveling alone."

"Tonight has been more restful than anything I've had for a long time." He kissed her nose. "Don't argue. From now on *I* take care of you. Tomorrow we find out how soon we can get married because I'm not going to wait one minute longer than I have to."

"You're sure?" she asked anxiously.

"I'm sure," he answered before he drew her close for a long kiss.

The next morning as they sat across the table from each other in the little café where he often had breakfast, she asked, "Did you get any sleep?"

"Yes. Slept like a log, to my disgust."

"Why?"

"Because I wanted to lay there and think about you for a while."

And she had to laugh. He closed his eyes briefly. "Diccon what is it?" Her voice was sharp with concern.

He opened his eyes and reached for her hands, his eyes luminous with unshed tears. "Do you know how much I love your laugh? It has haunted me for years."

"Oh, Diccon!" she cried and the tears spilled over. She dug into her purse for a tissue. "How can you still love me?"

"Did you sleep?" he asked.

"No," she said, then withdrew her hands and sat back as the waitress put their plates before them, looking curiously at Suz. She had never seen Diccon alone with a woman before and especially not at breakfast.

After she left he said, "No. Why not?"

"There is too much to think about. When I left California to come here I didn't think I'd have the kind of welcome I've had. I *hoped* but I was almost sure I'd have to leave you and I—I intended to end it all. I put everything in order there. I wasn't going to go back at all. I wasn't going anywhere on this earth except six feet underground if you didn't want me."

"Zannie!" Diccon reached for her hand.

She turned it and grasped his. "I read the Bible you gave me last night for the rest of the night. There are some beautiful places in it. Like—well, I don't know how to pronounce it. It begins with a Ps."

"Psalms." Diccon said, then, "P-s-a-l-m-s?"

"Yes. So that's Psalms. I didn't know it was spelled that way. Is it poetry?"

"Yes, though the Hebrew poetry has a different form than ours."

"I liked to read some of that. But it's all so strange. I tried to read some of the first part but there's so much killing and cheating and lying. Aren't there any stories about nice people?"

Diccon almost strangled on his coffee and set the cup down. "Where did you read?"

"About someone called Abraham for one. Did you know he let the king in the country they were in have his wife like a mistress. I mean, I know we have wife swapping now but at least the wives get to choose and make their own decisions."

"Does that make it different?" Diccon asked in amusement.

"Well, yes, because their husbands aren't treating them like objects they own but people with minds of their own."

"In other words, modern ways of doing wrong are better than ancient ones."

"Yes. No. Diccon, what do you mean?"

"Zannie, adultery is adultery no matter what guise it comes in. Besides Sarah never became the king's mistress or concubine or whatever. God saw to that. He spoke to Abimilech in a dream to tell him who Sarah really was and before that, when Abraham did the same thing in Egypt, God sent a plague on Pharaoh and his household and Sarah was safe."

"But Abraham was—was—" before his interested gaze she hesitated.

"Darling, try to eat something. You'll feel better. Then you'd better try to get some sleep," Diccon suggested.

261

Suz looked up and there was terror in her eyes. "I can't," she whispered. "I'm afraid. When you leave I'm sure you won't come back and I want to end it all, but I read the Bible and it scares me because it doesn't make any sense."

Diccon knew that wasn't what was bothering her. It had made all too much sense, evidently, or she wouldn't have become frightened. "Wait here. I'll be right back," he said. Fearfully she watched him go to the phone. The conversation was brief and he was back at the table. "Eat, Zannie. I'm not going in to work today. That'll give us three days together to plan and talk. I want to call Mikell and Missily to come down for our wedding. Just them. I don't want anyone else. Is that all right with you?"

"Yes," she whispered and tried to drink her coffee without taking her eyes off him as though he would disappear if she didn't keep him in sight.

Since Mikell would be at work during the day they decided to put off the phone call until evening. Meanwhile they went back to Diccon's place, fixed a lunch and drove into the mountains to talk and walk and eat. By then Suz was so tired she was drooping so Diccon suggested she take a nap. He spread a blanket for her in the softest place he could find, not far from a creek, and she stretched out on it. With her hand in his she went to sleep while he sat quietly, his back against a tree, watching her. Seventeen, almost eighteen years ago she had left him. In all those long years, except at first, he had never expected her to come back. The joy at having her there filled him and he sent up a wordless thanksgiving to his God. Her lashes, always so incredibly long naturally, lay dark against her skin. She wouldn't keep that lovely tan living where he did—at least not during the winter—but she didn't want to go back to California, not even for her things with him along to help. She intended to have them shipped to Oregon now that she had a place to put them.

She'd made sure he understood they were her own belongings she'd accumulated over the years and that she had nothing that Auden or Owen or any other man had bought her. He knew she was a wealthy woman. She'd already paid for most of Nigel's college expenses and was doing the same for Alexis. It was one thing they had discussed when she was still living away from him and Nigel had started college. It was then she'd told him how she stood financially and that she wanted the money to go to Nigel and Alexis. They would have to discuss finances eventually. Diccon was not the kind to let his wife support him; he made a decent salary and had a nice home. That, at least, she was willing to accept. In fact when they'd gone through it that morning she'd surprised him by her reaction.

"Diccon, it's delightful," she'd said as they went from the living room into the combination kitchen and dining room. When they went to inspect the bedrooms she'd smilingly looked at Alexis and Nigel's things but as they reached Diccon's rooms she put her hands up to her face.

"Zannie! What is it?" Diccon encircled her waist from behind and pulled her back against him.

"The furniture," she whispered, "You kept it."

He turned her around and held her close, his lips in her hair. "I couldn't part with it," he said roughly.

"Oh, Diccon!" she wailed. "I've wasted so many of our years."

"Some day," he said, rocking her a little, "when you understand Christianity better, I'll explain to you how even our wasted years are redeemed. Nothing is lost in God's economy." He tipped her chin up and kissed her lightly on her mouth then turned her head. "Look," he said indicating the picture over the bed.

She slipped out of his arms and went to take it down, then held it close, her eyes staring off into space. "Our first home. I remember. It was such a beautiful little tree and I'd climb it to watch for you to come home, then you'd catch me as I slid out of it." Smiling, she turned to him. "Remember the time I jumped and caught you off guard and we both went down?"

He laughed with her. Suz looked down at the picture again. "I was so young," she said. "Do you still think of me that way?"

"No," he said and she looked up quickly. "I think of you as a beautiful, mature woman, but I loved the young carefree girl, too. Both a delight."

Carefully she hung the picture again then came around to where he stood. "Diccon, I won't ever be able to make up to you all those years and all the heartache, but I want to love you and show you I do in a way I probably didn't know before when I was so self-centered. I—I don't think," she said in a whisper of a voice, "that I will ever forgive myself for what I've done to you."

Diccon reached for her. "My Zannie, let's not look back on regrets. If I'd been less selfish I would have gotten a job closer to a city. I would have compromised for your sake. I didn't try to see your side. I just thought you should be the way I was. Let's go on from today and learn from what has happened."

She looked up with a smile, pulled his head down to kiss his smiling mouth.

Thinking about that now, Diccon wondered idly what it would have been like to have lived with her all the years since they'd first gotten married. They would be celebrating their twenty-seventh anniversary. It was hard to imagine what had never been. All he knew was that he felt as though he had come through some howling storm into the warmth and he was relaxed and content in a way he had not been for years. All those years of loneliness, of heartache, of soul searching, of aching for her, were over and there was peace. Her trust in him was so incredible, so different from the young, wild Suz he'd fallen in love with almost twenty-eight years ago. They'd spoken of those days but briefly. It was so long ago in some ways but in others her return made them seem just yesterday. They would talk of them in the days ahead.

They had decided to go to Seattle to get married. It would be easier for Missily and Mikell and Diccon still had some vacation time left. They'd go on up to British Columbia for their honeymoon because she'd never been there and he'd lived there before he met her and loved it. He couldn't imagine what it would be like to have her in the house, cooking his meals, waiting for him. Would she be content? Somehow he thought she would. She wasn't an ambitious person and would probably make friends easily as she always did. Someday they would be grandparents. He had to smile at the thought.

A chipmunk came close in stops and starts; curious, he ran to a rock nearby, stopped, then dashed to a fallen tree closer. Diccon watched him idly. He fed them often when he was alone. They would eat from his hand, clamber up onto his shoulder. The jays and deer also let him feed them when he had time and patience. Suz stirred now to turn over and the chipmunk scampered away. Diccon drifted off to sleep to wake sometime later stiff and aching and found Suz watching him. She sat up.

"I've been lying here trying to figure out how I could ever have left you. There is no face so dear as yours anywhere else in the world. I've never met anyone else as gentle and tender and thoughtful. I must have been crazy."

He laughed. "You forget I was a great deal younger then. I've learned some things, I hope. I was pretty self-centered, too."

She shook her head. "I don't remember it."

"You do too," he said with a grin. "What else did we fight about?"

"Oh well—but was that self-centered? After all I was willing for you to work and bring home the bacon and I married you knowing what kind of job you had."

"The only problem is that I could still do that and move closer to a larger place so you could do some of the things you like to do. Zannie," he became serious, "are you sure you'll be content out here in the boonies?"

She sat looking around her than her hazel eyes met his. "Yes. I'm sure. Whatever it was I wanted before I've gotten out of my system. I would be perfectly content to live out in the wilderness as long as you were there."

Diccon closed his eyes against sudden tears. Then he said, "When did you quit smoking? I noticed you weren't at the reunion though Shaul did."

"About six or seven years ago. I went in for my yearly check-up and they thought the x-ray showed something on my lungs. It wasn't there the next time and hasn't been since, but it scared me. I haven't smoked since. Do you have a comb?"

He handed her the one out of his pocket and watched her run it through the long dark-blond hair. "I'm glad you haven't cut it," he said.

"Oh, but I have. More than once, but I always decide I like it long best until I get tired of it again."

"I like it long. That's my Zannie."

As she handed back the comb her eyes filled with tears and she wiped them away with the back of her hand. "I'm sorry. I haven't cried like this since—since the night I left you. I cried for days afterwards."

"But why?"

"I didn't want to leave you, Diccon, but I was too stubborn to give in. I was bored. I wanted excitement and I wanted it more than I did you, but I missed you terribly. Owen and I met while I was still very much in love with you. After that I decided I was being a fool and shut you out of my mind except for when I needed you for something for the kids. I was good at that until this last reunion. Poor Shaul. He was never anything but someone to keep loneliness and—I guess—fears away. I took him to the reunion because I thought it would help me. I—I didn't want to see you. I hadn't felt that

264

way in years. I suppose I didn't want to face up to what I'd done nor to the fact that I'd lost the only really decent man who'd ever wanted me."

"But you hadn't lost me."

"I know that now."

"I wanted to ask you to come back to me and was sorely tempted to ask you but I was afraid of rejection," he said. "You were so resentful of my faith and God that I didn't think you'd want anything to do with me."

"I—I didn't understand. But I think if you'd asked me—" she stopped to think about it. "Maybe I would have said no then," she said honestly. "I knew I was drawn to you but I didn't like your religion." She moved over to kneel before him." I'm so glad I came," she said as she leaned over to kiss him.

He caught her close. "Zannie," he whispered later into her hair, "thank you for coming. To me you are still my wife even though I know that's not true."

"I got the motel in Bend because I know your convictions but what difference does it make? We're going to be married. It's not like a one night affair."

"No, it's not. I agree with you but that's a temptation I'm not going to give in to." He rose, drawing her with him, holding her close a long moment. "How about going back to the house so we can make that call? Mikell should be home by the time we get there."

As they drove down the mountains, the bright golden yellow of the fall leaves glowing among the dark conifer, the air crisp and clear, Suz said, "Diccon, you said you wanted only Mikell and Missily at the wedding but," she turned in the seat to face him, then continued, "I want Rose and Graham to come and my parents. And Nigel and Lorna. I want the world to know I'm marrying you. We ran away last time. We don't have to have a reception or anything like that. We can tell them it's to be simple. It's kind of like renewing our vows, isn't it?"

"Yes," he answered. He did want only Mikell and Missily though he couldn't have said why. "What are you doing clear over there?" he asked. "There's a seat belt in the middle, too. Come here."

She slid over next to him and cuddled close.

"That's better," he said reaching for her hand. "Now, let's talk. We can have anyone you want, darling. I don't know why I only want Mikell and Missily. I would like Lorna and Nigel to be there. It's too bad Alexis and Jon are so far away. But I am definitely not going to wait for someone to come from a distance. Do you understand, young lady?"

"Yes, sir," she said meekly, then laughed. Her head went down on his shoulder. "Diccon, you are so special. I can't see why some woman hasn't snapped you up."

"Whatever for? I'm just a usual, every day man," he said lightly though his throat was so tight he wondered that his voice sounded so normal.

"There's not anything every day about you at all."

He glanced down at her. The long lashes were dark around her eyes, fringing them in beauty. "Just wait a few weeks. Then you'll be used to me again and notice all my faults."

265

But instead of taking up the joking she said seriously, "No, Diccon, I won't. From now on you'll be a cut above every other man and I will never feel worthy of you."

His throat closed and he couldn't answer. He would never say the long years alone were worth what she was giving him but they faded in the distance before such a gift. They rode in silence, something precious and new. Suz had never before been able to enjoy just being with someone else without chattering. Diccon said, "Speaking of Alexis and Nigel, don't you think we should call them also?"

"Yes. I wanted to. I wasn't sure...." her voice faded away and she sat up. "You said you only wanted Mikell and Missily and I thought..."

"You thought what?" he prompted when she didn't continue.

"I'm not sure. It seemed you might want to keep it a secret or something until it was all over and then tell them," she said slowly.

"You mean I sounded as though I might be a bit embarrassed or ashamed and want the deed accomplished before we told anyone?"

"I'm sorry, but something like that."

He swung the car into his driveway, turned off the motor, and sat looking at her. "I'm the one who is sorry. I didn't realize what it would sound like. Anyone else you'd like to ask? I don't want this to look like an elopement, come to think of it."

"Yes," she looked at him from under her lashes.

He grinned. "Go ahead. You don't have to flirt to get what you want."

"Diccon Brooke!"

He leaned over to kiss her nose. "I remember that trick," he said. "I remember how many times you wheedled something out of me looking at me that way. Don't worry," he went on as she began to look distressed. "I loved it then and I love it now and I'm quite vulnerable."

She put her hand along the side of his face. "Just think," she said and her voice was low and unsteady, "I'll be Mrs. Diccon Brooke again."

He kissed her hand, then her mouth, hard. "Whom else did you want to ask?"

"I don't know if they'll come but there's a couple a little older than you and I. Probably nearer Mother and Dad's age. They worked for Shaul. Their names are Brett and Eleanor. When I went back down to California they were heartbroken because of what had happened to Shaul. They'd been with him for years. They were so lost that I helped them with all the things they had to do. Then when the will was read they found out that Shaul had left everything he had to them: his home, car, possessions and a considerable amount of money plus a wonderful collection of records, tapes, and music."

Diccon took the keys out of the ignition, opened his door and went around to open hers. She got out slowly. He was displeased about something. "Yes, go on," he said tersely as they walked together to the house.

"It's just that," she said, nervous because she didn't know what had made him withdraw, "I became very fond of them. They helped me weather a bad place in my life. I found I didn't want to go back to the things I'd been

266

doing; parties bored me, the men irritated me, you were on my mind day and night and I didn't know where to turn. Having them need me meant a lot."

Diccon had unlocked the front door of the house and swung it open waiting for her to proceed him into the house. When they were inside she turned to him. "Diccon, what's wrong? What did I say? I never loved Shaul. I told you that. It's just that Eleanor and Brett---"

"I understand that," he said as she paused. "Zannie, maybe it's foolish of me but I don't want to wait to marry you. It feels—as though you will disappear unless I know you are mine." He laughed apologetically. "Kind of superstitious, I know."

"But why would we have to wait because I want Eleanor and Brett to come?"

"They'd have to get here or rather Seattle and—I supposed they could get a plane right away but I don't know."

"Get a plane? Oh! I forgot to tell you that Shaul wanted to move to Port Townsend. In fact, he called a real estate agent in California from Port Townsend and had his house put on the market. Brett and Eleanor were willing to move with him and decided to anyway. They're up there now and are going to buy one of the Victorian homes and fix it up as a Bed and Breakfast."

Diccon let out a big sigh. "Oh."

Suz went to him, putting her arms around him, leaning back to look at him. "Don't do that. It scares me."

"Do what?"

"Withdraw like that." Than with a gleam in her eyes she added, "Why would you think I want to put off the marriage? If I had my way I would move in right now."

Laughing, he pulled her close, swiftly and tightly, kissing her eyes and then her mouth. "Now that's settled," he said, "I'm going to make a fire. Would you like to make some coffee or hot chocolate?"

"I'd love to," she replied and taking the picnic basket with her she went into the kitchen and began to rummage through the cupboards until she found some cocoa. When he came in she had milk heating on the stove and was cleaning out the basket.

Diccon pulled a stool out to perch on as he watched her in his kitchen with contentment and thanksgiving.

"What's settled?"

"Hmm-m?" he asked lazily.

"You said it—whatever you meant—was settled now, before you kissed me."

"Oh that. I meant who was coming to the wedding."

"Oh." She didn't say any more for a moment while she stirred the cocoa and sugar into the hot milk and Diccon said, "Zannie! I haven't had real cocoa for years."

She grinned at him. She'd remembered his passion for cocoa over hot chocolate. "Diccon, tell me why it matters whether we sleep together now instead of waiting until after the wedding."

Fleetingly he thought that her attitude toward adultery hadn't changed much. "Zannie, marriage is a covenant, a commitment made before God and others. Something stated publicly. The actual joining physically belongs to marriage—it's part and parcel and belongs to the couple after the vows have been taken. It's a precious gift given to those who are made one. If I take you now I won't be holding you any higher than I would a call girl or a prostitute. It would be lack of love, not an act of love, to treat you that way."

Thoughtfully she poured them steaming mugs of cocoa and carried them to where he was sitting. "Where do you want this?"

"Let's go sit before the fire. I don't think I have any cookies."

"That's fine. I don't need anything else."

He took the mugs from her and followed her into the living room to sit beside her on the couch before the fire. She sighed and stretched before she reached for her mug. There was a silence between them as they sipped contentedly at the hot liquid. The fire crackled and a wind was blowing in the trees outside. It felt cozy and safe, something Suz hadn't experienced for years. She reached for his hand. "I forgot how safe I always feel with you," she said. "Diccon, you weren't religious when you first married me but you waited then, too."

"I know. My grandparents had instilled it into me that a man who loves the woman he wants to marry will have the discipline to wait. They weren't Christians but they certainly had high moral standards."

She laid her head back against the couch and he watched the firelight in her hair and eyes. "My parents didn't approve of it either," she said, "but I just thought they were old fogies. If you hadn't been like you were I wouldn't have stayed a virgin like I did. I can see I have a lot to learn. Alexis told me you didn't approve of her and Jon living together but she knew, of course, I saw nothing wrong with it, especially since they are going to get married."

"I'm sure you're aware that I taught both her and Nigel while they were still young why it's wrong to have premarital and extramarital sex."

"I know. How did you do it without making them either hate me or think you're outdated? Alexis says that it's your belief and she respects you but doesn't agree."

"Yes, I am aware of that," Diccon said dryly. "People don't believe in absolutes these days.'

"How did you, Diccon?"

He turned to gaze at the flickering fire. It was just beginning to turn dark so he could still see Suz. She was watching him. "I explained that you didn't believe as I do but that that didn't make you a bad person and me a good one. I told them about sin and how it holds us slaves until we're freed and that we're responsible for our actions, that my sins were as sinful as yours, just not the same ones."

She didn't answer. It was strange to have him talk so naturally about what she'd done as sin without a judgmental attitude. That was what always puzzled her about Missily and Mikell. They had more than once made it clear that they disagreed with what she was doing and though she had

268

thought it funny at the time to do even more outrageous things she'd known even then they were not hypocritical or judgmental. She wasn't sure she understood yet why what she'd done was—sin. She hadn't slept with any other man except the one to whom she was married or with whom she was having an affair. The one thing she could accept as wrong was what she had done to Diccon. He'd loved her and she'd spurned his love and left him, taking his children with her, for purely selfish reasons. To hurt him like that because she wanted more excitement was wrong to her way of thinking. But the thought that it was his love for her that kept him from accepting her offer of herself was precious after the careless attitudes she'd known for years where it wasn't considered unusual for husbands and wives to have other lovers than their own mates. There was something wholesome and sweet about belonging to one man and being able to trust that he would belong only to her.

"You're a long ways away, sweetheart," Diccon said.

She turned her head to smile at him. "I was just thinking. You don't know how different you are than what I've lived with for years. It feels, like, well, like a fresh ocean breeze. As though I'd stepped from the murky smog onto a high mountain peak into the fresh air. It's a little breathtaking."

"Shall we make our phone calls? Nigel first, then Alexis before Missily? And who else?"

"That's enough tonight. I don't want to be on the phone all night."

Diccon rose to get the phone and bring it back. It had been sitting on the stand by the couch but Diccon had swung the couch around to face the fire. "I think the cord's long enough. We'll have to get another phone. One was enough when I was alone." He sat down again. "I'll call Nigel; you call Alexis."

"But I want to hear what he says," she protested.

He pulled her close to him. "Put your ear next to mine and quit complaining."

"Yes sir!" She grinned and kissed him. "You *have* gotten bossy."

Nigel answered, sounding rushed and breathless. "Yes?"

"Nigel? Your Dad here. How're things?"

"Pretty well. I'm rushing around. Lorna's coming over for our date. There's a play in town we want to see."

"How's your back?"

"So-so. Better probably but I can't tell. I'll be glad when I can drive again. I hate having Lorna do all the running. It worries me."

"I can understand that. I have some news for you I hope you like." He smiled at Suz. She put her head close to his as he added, "I have company. Your mother is here with me. We've decided to get married. We'd like you and Lorna to be there for the wedding."

There was a silence and Diccon said, "Nigel? You there?"

"Yes," came the answer but it didn't come through very clearly. "I—I—"

Suz whispered, "He's crying."

Diccon nodded and pulled her close. "If that's all right with you," he said to his son.

Finally Nigel managed a choked, "Dad—Dad—I haven't heard anything as wonderful since Lorna promised to marry me."

"It's okay," Diccon said to Suz. "He approves."

She took the phone. "Hello, Nigel."

"Mom, what can I say? Golly, let me get a handkerchief."

"He went to get a handkerchief," she reported. "Just wait. Alexis won't cry."

"Mom," Nigel said. "I don't know---just a minute. Lorna's here."

"Now Lorna's there," Suz told Diccon.

"Good," he said.

They hung up after excited congratulations from Lorna, and Nigel promised they would be at the wedding. Suz was wiping her eyes. "He always did cry more easily than his sister," she said.

Alexis, however, was quite stunned and didn't say anything for a moment before she asked her mother, "Mom, what kind of joke is this?"

"No joke. I'm sitting right next to your father. In fact, he has his ear to the phone, too."

"Let me talk to him."

Suz handed the phone to Diccon who said, "Well?"

"Daddy, is it really you? Really and truly?"

"Really and truly, Lexy."

"Oh!" she squealed. "Jon! Jon, come here."

There was a muffled conversation then Jon came on. "I'm sorry. Alexis is crying so hard I can't understand her," he said.

Diccon let Suz answer, leaning back to watch her.

"Jon, this is Suz," she said. "Alexis' father and I are going to get married next week. I'm not sure when."

"Tuesday, if we can," Diccon supplied.

There was further conversation before Suz hung up. "They're going to try to get a flight up. It's neat Alexis worked for the airlines this summer so knows what to do. I told them we wouldn't wait and they understood. I suppose," she said with a sidelong glance at Diccon, "they think we're living together already."

"That I will correct!" Diccon reached for the phone and despite Suz's protests he called Alexis back and told her not to get any funny ideas; that her mother was staying in a motel in Bend until they were married. His daughter laughed but he could tell she was a bit vexed.

"Was that necessary?" Suz asked.

"Who is it that doesn't like hypocrites?" he countered. "Let's call Missily."

"You love her, don't you?"

"Who?" Diccon, who had started to dial, put the receiver back down.

"Missily."

"Of course, I love her. Why shouldn't I? She's a darling." He looked puzzled.

"If she'd been free would you have married her?"

"Zannie. You're not serious, are you?" Diccon put the phone aside.

270

"Well, like you said, she's a darling. She's faithful and trustworthy and she's pretty."

"Yes she is but she's not my Zannie. She's a beloved sister but not my choice for a wife. I told you I was constitutionally unable to love anyone but you. And what's more, I don't want to."

Suz moved over onto his lap to kiss him. "Let's call. I need support," she said explaining why she had moved to his lap.

He grinned. "Me, too." Then he handed her the phone and she dialed Missily's number. When Missily answered she said, "This is Suz."

"Suz! Is something wrong?" Missily asked because her sister so seldom called.

"No. Is Mikell there?"

"Not yet but he should be any minute."

"I have some news and a request," Suz continued, hanging hard to Diccon's hand. "Mikell's not there yet," she whispered to Diccon, then into the phone she said, "Missily I'm at Diccon's place."

"Diccon's! Suz is there something wrong with him? With Nigel?"

"Both are fine. So's Alexis. And so am I. Diccon and I are going to get married and we want you and Mikell to stand up with us." She said in a rush and with a chuckle Diccon pulled her against him.

There was a silence while Missily's thoughts went in all directions, then she asked, "When?"

"Is that all you can say?" Suz asked, struggling to sit up again.

"I'm sorry. You pretty well knocked the wind out of me. I didn't even know you cared about Diccon. I mean, I thought for a while at the hospital you did and then you went to California so I thought I was wrong."

Suz turned to run her hand down the side of Diccon's face and he caught it to kiss it. "I didn't either until—oh, sometime during the reunion and then I thought it was hopeless so I left," she told her sister.

"On his side? He's never quit loving you."

"I know. He told me. I don't deserve it at all."

"Here comes Mikell," Missily said as she heard the van door slam shut.

"Don't tell him. Diccon wants to."

"You haven't told me when."

"As soon as we can next week. Tuesday, hopefully. Diccon is taking two weeks off so we're coming to Seattle tomorrow. Diccon wants Pastor---" she paused to look at him and he supplied, "Justice."

"Justice to marry us and I want your help picking out a dress. We've called Nigel and Alexis and they plan to be there with Lorna and Jon. We haven't called anyone else yet. After the wedding we're going to British Columbia so I can see where Diccon used to live. Is Mikell there?"

"Yes. Here he is." Missily handed the phone to Mikell who kissed her before he took it and said hello

"Mikell, Diccon here. Are you holding on to Missily? I have some news." Diccon said, sounding more relaxed than Suz had.

"Bad news?" Mikell asked sharply.

"No. Wonderful news. Zannie and I are getting married next week."

"Zannie? Oh. You mean Suz." Then, "You mean Suz?" Mikell asked in astonishment.

"Yes."

"But—where are you?"

"Sitting in my living room. We aren't living together yet. She has a motel room in Bend." He grinned at Suz who made a face at him.

"Diccon, do you know what you're doing?" Mikell's voice was concerned. Missily had put both arms around his waist and he encircled her with his free arm. "You know what she is. Do you want to risk another heartache?"

"The first one left last night when she came here to me," Diccon answered, still calmly. He was running his hand through Suz's hair.

"But she's not a Christian, Diccon. I know you love her but oil and water don't mix."

"Have you read Hosea lately?" Diccon asked and winked at Suz as she frowned at him.

"Hosea? But I'm not sure this is the same thing. God gave Hosea a task as a prophet."

"Why don't you ask Zannie about it?" Diccon answered and handed the phone to Suz who took it, still frowning.

"Hello?"

"Suz. Mikell here. I'm not sure about all this. You know Diccon's a Christian."

"Yes."

And as she said nothing more, Mikell stumbled on. "Well—what—that is—you—I don't—"

Suz laughed. "Mikell, I'm not going to corrupt him if that's what you mean."

"I don't mean that at all," he answered indignantly, squeezing Missily so hard she said "Ouch!" "Sorry," he told her.

"Mikell, Diccon and I have been talking about what he believes. He's been reading the Bible to me and explaining. It's so strange I have a hard time understanding but it's rather wonderful, too, and Diccon's right when he says I've always been restless for something and didn't know what it was.

"I thought at first it was Diccon until he reminded me that things can happen to him." Here she caught her breath and Diccon reached up to touch her lips lightly and smile gently. "I don't know whether I believe or not but I don't disbelieve either," she went on. "I just want to know more."

Mikell didn't say anything for so long that Suz asked, "Mikell?"

"Yes," he managed. "I'm here. Can you tell Missily what you told me?"

"If you like."

Mikell handed the phone to Missily and watched as she listened and the tears that had caught in his throat spilled over her cheeks though her face was glowing. He dried her cheeks with his hands. When she finally hung up the phone after promising her sister to shop for a dress with her Monday she looked up at her husband who was waiting with one raised eyebrow.

"Mikell, I can't believe it. Suz. She's the last person I thought might become a Christian."

"Why?" he asked. "It's sinners our Lord came to save and it's hard for self-righteous people to see their need. Wouldn't Suz, just looking at it from a human view, be the one we would think most likely to see her need?"

"You're right, of course, except that she never acted like she believed what she did was wrong. Do you suppose she's doing it to get Diccon?"

Mikell, standing straddle-legged before her, reached out to pull her against him. "I hadn't thought of that but now you said it I feel better about Diccon."

"Why?"

"Because I wasn't too different. I didn't know for sure if you were sincere either though at the time I didn't doubt it at all. I only thought of it much later when it didn't matter any more because by then I did know, but I went ahead and asked you to marry me anyway."

"Mikell," Missily said slowly as she went to check on supper, "there will be some criticism in the churches, won't there? Will Pastor Justice marry them? Not just because Suz isn't a Christian but doesn't it say somewhere in the Bible you shouldn't marry a divorced person?"

"Missily!" Mikell sat down on one of the breakfast barstools and rested his head in his hands grinning at her. "Do you have to have a such a good memory? Are you going to tell Diccon that?"

"I don't think so. I may be a coward and wrong but he sounded so happy."

"And that's a valid reason—"

She had come around and put her hand over his mouth, then leaned over to kiss him before she burst into tears.

"Hey, honey." Mikell caught her close. "It's not that bad. Let's let Pastor Justice take care of it, shall we?"

"But what if he won't marry them?" she sobbed.

"I'm afraid Diccon won't let that stop him. I think—well, I know—he sees this as a case like Hosea."

"Hosea?"

"Remember, God had him marry a woman he called a wife of harlotry who left Hosea to commit adultery and God told him to get her back. I know the commentators fight over that one but I think that's the gist. I don't think Diccon has ever thought of Suz as anything but his wife and since she has come back he believes he should receive her in forgiveness. Darling, don't cry so."

"But why is life so hard? I thought everything was great for Diccon and now this."

Mikell had to smile. "Who thought of 'this'?"

"Oh, I know," she sobbed, "but I want Diccon to be happy."

"Yes, so do I, but we don't know that he'd be happy married to Suz because she is so unpredictable. Don't borrow trouble, sweetheart. I know Diccon will talk to Pastor Justice and consider what he says. And who knows what God is doing with Suz."

Missily sniffed and raised her head from Mikell's shoulder. "I hope she's as sincere as I was. She told me they've been studying John and that it

273

was miracle enough Diccon could love her and forgive her but it was even harder to believe the one who was the Creator would do so."

"Then let's hope that means she is coming to a realization of her sinfulness. Think of what that would mean to Diccon."

"God's ways are so strange. If that accident hadn't happened she might have gone back with Shaul and married him." She laid her head against Mikell's shoulder again.

He rocked her in his arms. "I don't think so. I saw her watching Diccon at the reunion. I was surprised when she went back to California. I did think she might try for Diccon then. After all he's still a good-looking man and he has a good job."

"But Suz doesn't need money. She's a wealthy woman."

"I know but she seems to need a man and she wasn't taken with Shaul."

"I didn't *think* she was but decided I was wrong." Then she raised her head and there was a delightful smile on her lips. "Do you know what she told me?"

"No, what?" he asked though he was thinking more of how wonderful her eyes were than about her words.

"That I wasn't to get any wrong ideas because Diccon wouldn't treat her as a wife until after they were married."

Mikell grinned. "Good for Diccon. I bet she doesn't have those scruples." He freed one hand to run it through her hair then pulled her head back gently to his shoulder. "I'm glad you're mine. I picked the right Metlow girl. I could never have lived through what Diccon has," he added as he bent his head to kiss her.

Chapter XXVIII

They talked late that night. Suz had asked Missily to break the news to their parents. "I wish Erin and Kitten were still here," Missily said to Mikell. "It would be nice for all of us to be at their wedding."

"Why don't you talk it over with your folks and see what they say. If Alexis and Jon can get here in time I don't see why Kitten and Erin can't."

Missily left home the next morning early so she would catch her father before he left for work. She called first to make sure he'd be there. Since he owned his own business he often left quite early in the morning but he promised to wait for her. Anna Metlow was still in her robe, her hair brushed, but she sat sleepily at the table drinking coffee. Allan got up from his chair as Missily came in to get her a cup. "It's French Vanilla this morning," he said as he poured the fragrant coffee into one of the bone china mugs her mother used.

"Umm." Missily sat down. She glanced at her mother. "You don't look awake yet, Mother."

"I'm not. I don't see why this couldn't have been done tonight," Anna answered crossly. She was never her best in the morning.

"Now, Anna," Allan said and patted his wife's hand.

Briefly, Missily wondered if she and Mikell would get to the hand patting stage. She hoped not. "It really won't wait, Mums. Not if what I want to happen can happen. Suz and Diccon called last night. They are going to get married."

"What?" Anna set her cup down sharply.

"Great!" said Allan at the same time, then added, "That's the best news I've heard for some time."

Anna looked at him incredulously. "What makes you think it will work? Especially now that Diccon's so religious, too."

Missily smiled. Anna had never become reconciled to her daughter's acceptance of what she called Mikell's brand of religion. She considered herself a good Christian but not a fanatic. Missily had learned not only not to argue but also not to mind her mother's remarks.

"When Suz was here she was quite unhappy. Felt she's wasted her life but didn't know how to remedy it. Diccon's a good man, Anna."

"I know that but she's never liked the country. That's why she left in the first place."

"I have the feeling," Allan said, "that she got the city out of her system"

"She came back to Oregon from California for the sole purpose of seeing if Diccon would take her back," Missily said. "She told me last night that she was tired of the way she was living and looked forward to Diccon's way of life. The reason I came so early was to catch Daddy before he went to

275

work. I'd like Erin and Kitten to be here for the wedding. Do you think there's any way we can get them here?"

"Hmm." Allan rubbed his chin. "I don't know about Victoria but Erin will probably want to come. We can pay her way. Kitten can afford to pay her own."

"Allan! Why should we pay one daughter's and not the other's?" Anna asked indignantly.

"Victoria, my dear, is well off. I don't know exactly why. I think she's done some investing—Auden seems to have helped her there—and I know she owns some property. With her it will be trying to convince her to come. Erin and Thor aren't poor but they don't have a lot of ready cash handy. Let's see—it's seven-thirty. I don't suppose we can get hold of Victoria now."

"We can try," said Missily. "She usually teaches at home in the mornings in the summer."

"Good. Let's give her a ring. What's the number, Anna?" Allan was already at the phone.

Victoria answered almost immediately and Allan handed the phone to Missily. Victoria was saying, "Hello? Hello?"

"Hi, Kitten," Missily answered and glared at her father who only grinned as he sat back down and reached for his coffee. Missily perched on one of the breakfast barstools.

"Missily. You took long enough to answer." Victoria's voice was crisp.

"Yes, well your father rang your number and handed the phone to me when you answered. You can blame him."

"Dad? Is something wrong? With Mother?"

"No. At least I think she's all right. A bit stunned at the moment. I have some news and a request. Diccon and Suz called me last night. They're going to get married this coming Tuesday. We'd like you to come out for the wedding."

"I *was* right then. She *did* sleep in his tent with him," said Victoria.

"What? What are you talking about? Kitten, make sense."

"At the reunion. She was furious with me. Tried to protect him but Alexis told me they'd slept together."

"Now wait just one minute," Missily said angrily, "they aren't even sleeping together now. Suz told me."

"That sounds true to form. She wouldn't want to ruin his image. How do you know they aren't? You aren't there."

"Victoria Metlow, you're horrible?" Missily said and slammed the receiver down, angry tears in her eyes.

"Missily!" Anna said in a shocked tone. "That was very rude."

"I don't care," Missily sobbed. "I don't think anyone else can make me so mad. First she said something about Suz sleeping with Diccon in his tent and then that Suz wasn't telling the truth when she said they weren't sleeping together now."

Allan had set down his cup and now put his arms around Missily. "Hush, Missily," he said gently. "I'll call her. I shouldn't have given the phone to you. Forgive me?" He smiled down at her, taking a handkerchief out of his pocket to dry her tears then sat down on the stool next to her and dialed Kitten's number again. "Victoria, this is your father," he said. "Do you always have to jump to the worst conclusions?"

"I was doing nothing of the kind. Dad, I have a student here right now. Couldn't this wait?"

"No," Allan answered easily. "We need to get this settled now. We still have to call Erin. I thought I scotched that nonsense about the reunion. Alexis and I talked and she told me that she'd said her mother was down by her father's tent. She knew that Diccon had slept out under the stars that night. Didn't we tell you?"

"I can't remember." Victoria's voice was distant, cool. "Too many things happened after that. Why are you so ready to jump to her defense? You know what she's like."

"Yes. Probably better than you do. Vicky, the best thing that could happen to Suz is for her to be able to go back to Diccon. She and I talked quite a bit after the accident and her life was coming unraveled. I was worried because she sounded desperate. And, furthermore, I happen to know Diccon better than you do. He is an honorable man and trustworthy."

"Well, be as that may be, now I have the news I need to get back to work."

"Hold on, young lady. *You* don't dismiss me." There was an edge to Allan's voice. "We've been talking things over and we want you and Erin to come out for the wedding. Now wait before you say anything. I'll give you time to think about it, but I know you can afford it and I also know you can get away if you wish. Your mother and I would like us all to be together for Suz. We missed all her other weddings, all of us, and we'd like to see all you girls here this time. It will be simple, Missily tells me. They're to be married by Missily and Mikell's minister here in Seattle. Think about what it would mean to Suz. I'll let you go but call us tonight and let us know. I hope you make the right decision and come. Bye." He hung up and Missily knew Victoria hadn't had the time to reply.

She grinned at him. "Is that the way you handle difficult customers? Or clients, I mean?"

He leaned over to kiss her lightly. "It's the only way to handle some people. Victoria needs to feel important and in control but I won't allow my children to control me."

"How well I know," Missily said and laughed at the expression on his face.

"Allan, I do think you were a bit hard on the poor child," complained Anna. "After all Edita has never given us reason to think the best of her."

"No, but Diccon has," he replied. "Even when he was young and impetuous he was respectful and honest. Now, how about Erin, Missily? Do you want to call her?"

"Yes. I can talk to Erin without any problem." Missily dialed the number and let it ring several times. Just as she started to hang up, the phone was picked up at the other end and a sleepy voice said, "Hello?"

"Erin. It's Missily. You aren't sick, are you?"

"No. Why?"

"You sound like you were asleep."

"I was." Erin laughed. "Thor and I were up until the wee hours. We're supposed to be at the ranch at noon but we'll never make it. "What's up?"

"I have some news to relay. Diccon called last night. Diccon and Suz. They're going to get married this coming Tuesday. We're kind of hoping you'll come."

"Diccon and Suz? What do you know. I thought they were acting like they were sweet on each other but then Suz went to California. What did he do? Follow her down?"

"No." Missily smiled at her parents who were both watching her. "Suz drove up to Oregon to see Diccon."

"Golly, I'd love to come but—well, we just paid for our vacation."

"Just a minute. Daddy wants to talk to you." She handed the phone to Allan.

"Hi, baby," he said. "Are you coming to the wedding?"

"I'd love to but don't see how I can, Dad."

"We're paying your way, your mother and I. We want you all here, all you girls."

"Is Kitten coming?"

"I hope so. I told her to think it over. She's being superior. Why don't you call her and convince her to come."

"Me? Why would I be able to do that?"

"I don't know. I've just noticed you seem to get along with her. Don't let her tell you any fool story about Diccon and Suz sleeping together. They haven't and they're not."

"Well, it wouldn't be the end of the world if they were," Erin said. "Don't be so old-fashioned."

"This has nothing to do with my value system and everything to do with Diccon's. You know how I feel about gossip and particularly gossip that defames another person."

"What makes you think she'd say anything like that any way?"

"Because, my dear daughter, she already said as much to Missily."

"Oh, oh." Erin laughed. "That was the wrong person to say it to."

"Erin," Allan said crisply, "no one is the right person to say something untrue to. Are you coming?"

"I'll have to talk to Thor, Dad, and see what he says. I don't think he can get away."

"Come without him."

"Daddy, you know how I feel about that."

"Just this once, for Suz's sake won't hurt. Doesn't Thor ever go away without you?" Allan motioned to Anna for more coffee but she looked at him blankly so Missily got up to refill his cup.

"Not often. Hardly ever overnight and we've already spent quite a bit of time apart this year because of the accident."

"Well, talk it over with him and if he agrees to let you come alone don't get suspicious."

"What do you mean by that? Did Missily carry tales?"

"About what?"

"About—about Thor and I."

"No. Missily's not a talebearer. I have no idea what you mean. I just know you well enough. You always did want Thor in your back pocket and were jealous if he even looked at one of your sisters. Talk it over but don't delay. We need to get that ticket."

"Okay. I'll let you know."

Allan took his cup to the table and sat down again. "She has to talk it over with Thor. She doesn't want to come without him. Then she asked me if you'd been carrying tales. Have they been having problems, Missily?"

"Nothing serious. And I'm not a talebearer." She smiled across the table at him.

He laughed. "I am put in my place. Anna, why don't you go back to bed? You're falling asleep in your chair."

She rose. "I think I will. I didn't sleep well last night."

"You *will* stay up and write those ridiculous letters. All right." He held up his hand. "They're important. But go get some rest." As she left he shook his head. "She can never wait until the next day. She has to finish even if she stays up 'til two."

"What's she crusading for now?"

"How would I know?" He smiled and the little crinkles came in the corner of his eyes. "I gave up trying to keep track years ago. It gets so boring. I've learned to let it go in one ear and out the other."

"Oh dear. I hope Mikell doesn't do that when I talk." Missily was folding a napkin as she sat there.

"But darling, you're interesting."

Her head came up. "Daddy, why did you marry Mother?"

He looked startled a moment then picked up his cup to drain it. "I'm not sure. We just kind of drifted into it. I needed a date one night at college, she was pretty and petite; I asked her out. She amused me. She was so earnest about everything. Eventually we got married."

Missily was silent while she unfolded the napkin to smooth it out. "That doesn't sound very romantic. Didn't you love each other?"

"I suppose so. What is love? We've never had a passionate marriage but we've had a good one." He reached over to take her hand. "Romance is highly overrated in our society you know. For centuries marriages were arranged. And look what I got out of my marriage; not only a faithful wife but five lovely daughters."

"Didn't you ever want a son?"

"I don't remember. I'm not a fisherman or sportsman and I found my daughters minds receptive and intelligent enough. And now I have sons."

In the end both Victoria and Erin flew out for the wedding. Thor told Erin he couldn't leave again so soon. "But go on out. Give her a good wedding," he said. "Diccon deserves it for waiting for her all these years." Then he pulled her close and added, "But don't stay a day beyond the wedding. Come back that day, if you can." So Erin left without qualms. She knew her father was right about her feelings about Thor but she would never have said so to him.

When Suz and Diccon arrived later that day they weren't told that Victoria and Erin were coming to the wedding. Suz was to stay at her parents and Diccon would go to Gabriel's place since they had room and Nigel was there almost as much as he was in his own apartment. He still had a desk job, had had another operation on his back and was still taking therapy. It was slow and he wasn't very patient. Without Lorna to encourage him and give him an incentive—he wanted to walk without a cane at his own wedding—he wouldn't have been as disciplined about his therapy as he was. He had stayed at Gabe and Deborah's until he could walk unaided except for the cane. It was while he was still there that he'd proposed to Lorna and been eagerly accepted.

Mikell and Allan took Diccon out to buy him a new suit for the wedding while Missily and Suz shopped with Anna and Rose. Suz had wanted only Missily but bowed to the inevitable. They found a beautiful light blue dress in watered silk, calf length. Rose suggested Suz get her hair cut and styled.

"It *is* styled. By some of the best hairdressers in California in fact." Suz answered. "Rosie, Diccon likes my hair long and I'm going to wear it that way as long as I can."

"Well, you are getting a bit—mature for that kind of hairdo," said her older sister.

"Where I'm going to live no one will pay that much attention any more than they did in California. It stays long," Suz said with such finality that Rose said nothing more.

As they sat eating lunch in a café Anna brought up the subject again. "Rosemonde is right, Edita, you know. You need to get a more suitable hairstyle. That makes you look..." Anna hesitated.

"Wanton?" Suz asked silkily and Missily said, "Suz!" with a laugh.

Suz grinned. "Well, Madre mia, is that what you meant?"

"I know you are used to hobnobbing with movie celebrities but I hardly think that means you have to copy them."

"I'm not. I'm not," her daughter assured her and bit into her big hamburger.

Rose and Anna had salads while Missily had ordered a club sandwich and a chocolate malt. Anna sighed. "I don't know how you girls keep your figures the way you eat."

"I know how I keep mine," Missily said. "I still have a family. I don't know how lazy bones here does."

"Haven't you ever noticed I inherited our father's figger? We don't run to fat."

"Well!" Anna exclaimed. "I hardly think I'm fat."

Suz laughed and reached over to pat her mother's hand. "No, of course, you're not. You were wondering about keeping our figures. I was trying to explain why I keep mine. I'm certainly not petite like you."

"No," Missily thought as she followed the rest of them out after they'd eaten. "She's not petite but she's wonderful." And she watched Suz walk with that lazy grace of hers, smiling at the man who opened the door so that he stood holding it even after Missily passed him, staring at Suz. Missily smiled, trying to put into words what was so attractive about Suz and failing, as usual. It had something to do with the way she moved, with her air of unconcern as though she didn't have a care in the world, with her ready laugh.

Victoria flew in on Sunday so Mikell and Missily drove to Seatac to pick her up that afternoon. She gave Missily an unexpected hug and gave Mikell both her hands. "How's everyone? The kids. Are they well?"

"All well. Except Nigel. He's still getting treatment for his back. The doctor seems to think it just takes time and even though he'll always have back problems they won't be any worse than so many others have. Nigel just gets impatient." Mikell answered stooping to kiss her cheek.

"I'm so glad he'll be all right." She walked with her arm linked in Missily's—Kitten, who never touched anyone if she could help it. Missily was almost afraid to breathe. "I've missed all of you. I've been so wrapped up in all my doings. I didn't know how much I cared until that awful accident. Missily, do you think it's as good idea for Diccon and Suz to get married again?"

"Yes. And even more so since I've seen them together. Diccon isn't doing all the giving any more."

"Hmm. Well, I hope you're right. I like Diccon. I'd hate to see him hurt again."

Mikell unlocked the car door for them, stowed Kitten's suitcases in the trunk and came around to get into the car. "That's my concern, Vicky," he said, "but I guess Diccon is an adult and he seems willing to risk it."

Diccon and Suz, who had spent the day with Nigel and Lorna, came back to the Metlow house later that night after church to find both Kitten and Erin there. Suz stopped just inside the door so that Diccon almost stepped on her heels and put an arm around her to steady her.

Erin grinned. "Hello, lovers. We thought we'd help you get married."

Suz went on into the room fighting tears as she hugged first Erin and then Kitten. Diccon was grinning and got a hug from Erin. Kitten held out her hand to him which he took and then her other one to pull her to him for a quick kiss and hug. "It's good to see you, Victoria. And Erin. I didn't know we were so important. Thor here?"

"No. He couldn't get away but he sent his best wishes. And told me to come back the same day as the wedding if I could. I can get a late flight."

"Sit down, all of you. I've got coffee and tea and I'm sure Allan has drinks if you want one. I made a couple of pies." Anna was bustling around as she talked and hurried into the kitchen.

"Drinks, anyone?" Allan inquired.

"I'll have one," said Erin.

"I will, also." It was Suz.

"You'll have to tell me what you want. It's been a long time since I fixed you anything. Diccon?"

"Coffee's fine for me, thanks." Diccon sank onto the couch beside Suz, drawing her close with one arm. "Who called you two?" he asked.

The next morning, Kitten, Erin, and Anna cornered Suz not long after she woke. Anna called them into her sewing room, which also served as an office for her. Allan, who had taken the next two days off, was eating breakfast in the kitchen.

"Suz, we've been talking. Now please don't get angry. We're thinking of you," Anna said settling herself at her desk.

Erin was sitting cross-legged on the floor like a young girl and Kitten sat in her mother's rocker. Suz took the only other chair left, the one at the sewing table. She was mildly interested in what was on their minds but mostly she was marking time until Diccon came. They were to go to talk to the minister at eleven. Her mother's workroom held evidences of her labor—both sewing and her many letters. Though her family teased her they were secretly proud of her ability to write letters and get answers and sometimes results. She had framed some of the letters Senators or Presidents had signed plus autographed pictures of several of the Senators and Representatives and Governors of Washington and of Eisenhower, Nixon and Ford. There was a cupboard that held the material she bought plus her sewing equipment. As children the five girls had spent many hours playing in the room while their mother worked. Anna had taught them all to sew which Suz had hated with a passion and Erin had disliked almost as much.

"Edita, you're not paying a bit of attention to what I'm saying," Anna said sharply, bringing Suz back to the present.

"Sorry. I was thinking about how we used to play in this room and how you tried to teach me to sew."

"Yes, well that's not important now," Anna answered shortly. "Your life is."

"My life?" Suz looked from one to the other. "But..." she hesitated. What *had* her mother been saying? "I would think you'd all be glad. I thought you liked Diccon."

"We do," Kitten said patiently. "That isn't the point. Look, Suz, Diccon's a fine person but his life isn't any different than it was before. He still lives in the country."

"I know," said Suz in a voice that could only be called ecstatic. "Do you know how tired I am of traffic and driving freeways and houses everywhere you look and going long distances to shop, to the library, to the post office? You have no idea how wonderfully peaceful Diccon's place is. Have you seen it?"

"No," answered Erin and Kitten simultaneously while Anna said, "Yes. The house is very nice. But you have to drive some distance to get to the stores and everything."

"But not in a bee hive. Fifteen or twenty miles in a beautiful countryside. Diccon and I went down that road several times and it almost seemed deserted to me."

"Besides, what bothers us most is the fact that Diccon's as religious as Missily."

"Now, Erin," her mother protested. "There's nothing wrong with religion. It's just that Edita, you were never interested in going to church. You made fun of it even when you were a teen-ager. And Diccon goes faithfully to church. I don't have anything against that. I don't agree with his beliefs but I can't see why you bother to marry him again when you will like his life style less now than you did before."

Suz looked at her sisters and her mother. "What makes you think I can't and haven't changed?"

"You're not—religious, are you?" asked Erin with trepidation.

"No. I don't think so. But I don't think Diccon's religious. We've talked a lot and he's different. He's not trying to force anything on me; just answers the questions I have."

"But Suz he believes in such antiquated ideas. You don't parade your intellect but you're too intelligent to be taken in by something so outdated and superstitious."

"Besides, it just isn't you. Ye gods! I can't imagine you going around mouthing the junk Stephanie says now that she's gone religious on us," Erin exploded. "Thor just laughs but it gives me the creeps."

"Erin, you have been taught it is unladylike to swear like that," protested her mother. "You've picked up some bad habits. Edita, dear, we're not trying to tell you what to do, only show you that you will be making the same mistakes you've repeated three times now--marrying someone just for something different and new. Why don't you marry someone who is your kind?"

"Who is *my* kind?' Suz asked. She was beginning to get angry.

"Certainly not Diccon. Not because I have anything against him. He's just not the man you should marry," her mother said kindly.

Suz stood up. "I think *I* should be the judge of that. I thought you came to see me married because you were glad for me. I didn't know you came to gang up on me."

"Now, Suz. Don't let that temper of yours make you say foolish things," Kitten said reasonably as to a fractious child.

"Excuse me," Suz said and her voice wobbled. She made her way across the room and shut the door behind her with a sharp click.

Allan looked up as she came into the kitchen. "Oh, oh. The hen party decided they had to impart their wisdom. Never mind, Suzzie, you'll soon be away from it. Sit down and have a cup of coffee with me."

"Daddy, do you think I'm going to ruin Diccon's life, too?" Suz asked as she poured herself a cup of coffee.

"Is that what they said?"

"Not exactly." She sat down across from him. "But they're sure I won't like his life style."

"Will you?"

"Yes. No one who hasn't lived in Southern California can know the peace and quiet even up here but especially at Diccon's. Some people don't mind that life but I've had enough of it."

"Then don't let them bother you. It's your life."

"I know, but..." then she heard a car door slam, got up to look out the window and left the room on a run.

Allan turned to look out and saw Diccon catch her close and give her a hard kiss. She was talking and crying and Diccon pulled her close, rocking her in his arms. Allan wondered where his daughters had gotten their passionate natures. Rose and Victoria were more like he and Anna. He hadn't expected Missily's marriage to last nor her to love her husband so completely and yet their marriage was as stable as Thor's and Erin's. Perhaps more so. Allan couldn't help but be curious about the circumstances Erin was so anxious to cover.

"Diccon," Suz was saying, "don't go away any more. I don't want to be away from you. What do they know about me and how I feel and what you're like?"

"They?" he asked. Her whole body was trembling as he held her close.

"Mother and Erin and Kitten. Diccon, I won't ruin our marriage."

"Of course, not, darling. You and I know that and we're the ones getting married."

"I—I know but I hate it. What right have they to tell me..." she broke off and held on to him.

He waited, wondering what they'd said that had so upset her. She raised a tear-wet face. "You believe me, don't you? I *know* I love you, Diccon. I don't think I ever knew what love was before. Not this—this— Well, it's much more than a feeling. It's knowing that you're the person I want to be with the rest of my life and beyond that if possible. It's wanting to do things for you, give you love and care and it's loving to be with you whether we talk or not, like in the mountains when I slept while you waited. It's having someone to go to when you're hurt knowing they'll care more than anyone else. Diccon, I *do* know, don't I?"

"Zannie," he said gently, smiling a little at her breathless deluge of words. "Of course you know. Why do you let them upset you? Can you come with me now? Have you had breakfast? Shall we go get some?" He took a handkerchief from his pocket to dry her tears.

The door opened and Suz turned. Allan came out. "Take her somewhere for a while, Diccon. Suz, they were trying to be helpful. Try to think of it that way. We blunder so badly when we try to help sometimes, but they love you."

"My purse. I have to get it." Suz ran into the house and was back right away. She stopped to give her father a hug. "I've wasted too many years away from the most wonderful man in the world. I hope I can make up some of that," she added as she kissed Allan before she ran to get into Diccon's car. He shut her door, walked around to get in his side and held up a hand to Allan before backing out of the driveway.

"Diccon," Suz said as they drove through the morning traffic, "my family is making me want more and more to believe the way you do."

Diccon asked, carefully schooling his voice to stay steady, "What do you mean?"

"Except for Missily—and Dad," she added as an afterthought, "they all seem to be sure I'm not the kind to be like you or even to like you the way you are now; that I'll like your lifestyle less now than I did before, that I should marry someone my own kind. But you are more wonderful than ever, kinder, more sensitive. I had time with you at the hospital to judge whether I liked what you are now or not. You're gentler, is the only word I can think of. And this world has little enough of gentleness that's for sure. I found that out."

Diccon swung the car into a restaurant parking lot and switched off the ignition. He sat a moment in thought, then turned to look at her. "Hungry?"

"I guess so. What were you thinking?"

He closed his eyes briefly then leaned over to give her a lingering kiss ignoring a rude remark from someone passing the car. "My darling, I love you so. Was it so awful in California?"

She nodded, sudden tears in her eyes. "I've spent years drinking, going to parties, running around with men trying to find—to find—It sounds corny to say, but to find peace. I thought having fun was what life was all about." She put her hand to his face. "Now I know that it's one of the least important things there is without—without—Diccon, why does it sound so unreal to talk about the things that really matter?"

"Probably because most people don't think of them as real. Especially God or anything supernatural. Shall we go eat?"

She grinned. "I'm sorry. I won't keep you out here any longer. I should treat my man better than that. It's probably late for you to eat breakfast. Come on."

He kissed her hands before he got out and went around to open her door. He didn't take her back to her parents' place after they'd talked to Joshua Justice. They ate lunch with the minister and his wife and family, then left to roam the city together, going to visit the high school where they'd met, walking through the Arboretum at the University, dallying on the piers where Diccon bought her trinkets to amuse her and then they stood watching the ferry boats and the sail boats and the others on the Sound, talking with hands linked. Diccon was determined not to take her back to her family until that evening when all the family that would be at the wedding would gather at the Metlow home for dinner. He had been silent so long as they stood together watching a ship make its way out of Elliot Bay bound for the ocean and foreign ports that Suz said, "You're so quiet."

"Hmm?" He turned and his eyes focused on her. Taking her arm he began to walk back toward the parking lot where their car was. "It's about time to get back, I guess. Anna won't appreciate it if we're late." Before he unlocked the car door he cupped her face gently in his hands and turned it up. "Tomorrow," he whispered. "Tomorrow I won't have to leave you. I stood there watching the ship and thinking of all the good-byes that are said and then I remembered that tomorrow I won't have to say it to you any more. Zannie, God is very good to me." He didn't add that he'd had a panicky feeling that tomorrow wouldn't happen; that he'd wake up and find it all a dream and that he would be alone as he'd been so many years.

When they reached the Metlow house Erin greeted Suz. "Where've you been? Someone named Eleanor has been trying to get you all afternoon."

"Eleanor? Did she leave a number?"

"Yes. She's at a motel here in Seattle." Erin reached into her jean pocket to pull out a paper. Suz took it eagerly and hurried to the phone.

"I can't think why she'd be so interested," Erin commented. "The woman sounded common."

"Erin," Diccon said, "that doesn't sound like a Metlow."

Erin turned to look at him with a frown, then laughed. "But then I'm not a Metlow any more, am I? I'm a Nielsen."

"You didn't learn that kind of snobbery from Thor," Diccon said to her. "Eleanor is a friend of Zannie's from California."

"Zannie? I forgot you called her that." Then her voice softened. "Do you love her so much, Diccon?"

"Yes. And I'm looking forward to a good many years with her." He took her arm and led her away from the bustle of the dining room to the empty living room. "Erin, Zannie is a different person than she was when I first married her. She hasn't had years of love like you have. And whether she brought it on herself or not doesn't change the fact that she found life very empty. You know," he went on, indicating a chair for her then seating himself in one close to hers, "it's a little like a kid going to a fair and buying all the goodies he wants and riding all the rides then suddenly finding out that he doesn't feel so well and home sounds pretty wonderful. Zannie's had her carnival. She's ready for home."

Erin, sitting with one leg under her so she could face him, said, "You didn't know I was half in love with you when I was a kid and you came home with Suz, did you? Oh, yes I was," she added as he made a dismissal motion, half-embarrassed. "In fact if I hadn't had Thor I might have tried to get you after Suz left you. Thor's first with me, but you run a close second. I don't say that to embarrass you," she added, running her fingers through her fair hair, "but because I want you to understand why I'm concerned. I don't want her to hurt you again."

Diccon stiffened. "That is exactly the kind of thing I don't want said. You seem to forget that it is never just one person's fault when a marriage fails. There were things I could have done so that Zannie might never have left me. In fact, I can't prove it but I believe if I hadn't been so stubborn she would never have left. Erin, I love you as I do all my sisters in the Metlow family but I refuse to have you hurt her any more. It's one reason I didn't bring her back earlier and if anyone so much as whispers anything like you've just said, I'll have her pack her things and she can stay with Missily tonight."

"My goodness, Diccon. You needn't get so angry. After all she is my sister. I'm not completely blind where she is concerned." Erin laughed. "She and I have had a good many crazy talks over the years. I know how she hated your life and what she thought when Nigel turned religious. It's foolish to close your eyes and get hurt all over again."

"Don't you think it's my life? And that I'm adult enough to know what I'm doing?"

"No man—adult or not—is safe when the woman he thinks he loves starts making up to him. Especially a woman like Suz."

"Good lord, Erin! You'd think you were jealous." Erin and Diccon both jumped at the sound of Allan's voice. "I thought you and I had talked this out. What are you trying to prove anyway? It's Suz and Diccon's life. Why don't you just butt out?" The phrase was so unlike Allan that Suz, who had come in just then, giggled. Her father turned and put his arm around her shoulders. "Did you reach her?"

286

"Yes. I invited her and Brett out for dinner. I'm so glad they came over early. Erin, it ain't gonna work, you know. You just as well give up. Diccon's determined to marry me and trust me on top of that. Even the preacher couldn't shake him."

"Did he try?" Allan asked in surprise.

"Well—" Suz looked at Diccon who winked at her. "No, not really. But he wanted to make pretty darn sure I was aware of how wrong I'd been living."

"Wrong? In what way? Because you're divorced?" Erin demanded.

"No-o, not that so much as the fact that I've been going from one man to another like it didn't matter. I don't mean he liked the divorces but he made it clear that they were only the result of something more serious."

"And you let him preach at you?"

Suz looked at her sister a moment before she answered. "Do you know, it didn't sound like preaching at all. Only as if he really cared about me."

Erin shrugged. "Have it your way. Who's the old lady?'

"They are friends of mine who live in Port Townsend now. You'll like them. Wait and see."

Diccon, for one, was grateful for Eleanor and Brett when they came; it made the family quit baiting Suz. Brett didn't say much but his eyes twinkled and he enjoyed his wife. Eleanor, Suz noted with amusement, gave Diccon a straight look when he was introduced as her fiancé.

"So you're Miss Suz's man?" she asked, her bright eyes direct. After she had examined him while Diccon waited quietly she held out her hand. "Yes, I think she's chosen well."

At that he smiled and took her small, work worn hand in both his. "Thank you. She has a high regard for you and your husband."

Erin, unpredictable Erin, was charming to them both. When she heard they'd bought one of the old Victorian houses to make into a Bed and Breakfast she began to ask questions and the whole table listened as Eleanor described the lovely rambling house. Later that evening, before they all left, Kitten managed to get Missily off alone, taking her out to the back yard where Anna's roses filled the air with sweet fragrance.

"Missily, do you remember when you came to see me before you married Mikell?"

"Yes." Missily turned from the roses to look at her sister, beautifully dressed as usual, her dark hair a shining cap on her head.

"Do you remember telling me you couldn't marry Mikell because of your differences; that he was too intense about religion?"

"Did I say that? I suppose I did."

Kitten reached out to touch the velvet petals of a rose. "Dad became quite irate with Mother and Erin and I when we tried to get Suz to see the same thing. Do you suppose you could get her to see sense before it's too late? I know you don't want Diccon to go through losing her again. It would be worse the second time for him."

Missily studied Kitten who avoided her eyes. Then she said, "Suz would never listen to me any more than she would you. You know that, Vicky." Missily asked more gently than she had ever spoken to Kitten before,

"Would it bother you so much if Suz became—religious, too?" She had started to say "a Christian" but realized that Victoria thought of herself as a Christian.

Kitten's head jerked up, then she turned away. "She won't. She's not the kind. No one in any of your churches would have anything to do with her if they knew her. And they would after a while. When she tires of Diccon."

"People like that don't understand what Christianity is. I admit there are those who would act as you think they would, but not everyone would. But you see I'm not at all convinced that Suz will leave Diccon again. I think she not only loves him but she's tired of her other way of life and Diccon means security and peace."

"But Suz will hate that pious nonsense. She'll not go to church with him long." Kitten's voice was almost vicious.

"Maybe. Maybe not. But I still can't see why it bothers you so much. You live a long ways away and hardly ever see us or probably think about us. I don't mean," she hastened to add as Kitten swung around, "that you deliberately forget us. Just that your life is full and time passes."

"It's like a disease. First you, then Diccon, then Nigel and now Stephanie. Like it was catching," Kitten said in a strangled voice. "And Suz would hate it."

"Are you afraid you'll—catch it?"

"No! Why would *I*? What kind of life would that be? I'm not interested in giving up my way of life. I'm satisfied whatever Suz thinks she feels," Kitten snapped at Missily.

Missily picked one of the opening buds and laid it gently against her cheek. "Vicky, when you moved East did you find it hard to give up the way of life out here?"

"Of course not. You know I liked it from the beginning. That's how I know I wouldn't want to change my life now."

"What I was thinking was that when one becomes a Christian it's a little like your move back East. It's a new life and you don't want to go back to the old one."

"There you are. Ready to go?" Mikell came around the side of the house.

"Isn't this lovely?" Missily held out the rose bud she'd picked. "Yes, I'm ready if you and the kids are." She reached over to give Kitten a hug. "Good night. I'll see you tomorrow."

Kitten nodded, keeping her head turned away, but Missily had already felt the tears on her cheeks when she'd given her a hug. She told Mikell about their talk on the way home. "I can't understand why they're so worried about Suz and Diccon. They look like two people who love each other to me."

Mikell reached over to squeeze her hand. "My romantic Jedidah. I have my qualms, too, you know. I just have more sense than to try to convince either Diccon or Suz."

Missily's chin went up. "You just wait and see. Everything will turn out lovely. Ten years from now, fifteen, I'll make you eat your words."

Mikell chuckled. "You do that. I liked her friends from Port Townsend. I told them we'd be over when they get the place operating and stay a night."

Diccon had asked Myles to play the organ for the wedding. He and Suz walked up the aisle hand in hand to face Pastor Justice, coming in on the closing bars of "Joyful, Joyful, We Adore Thee." They had met in the narthex and Suz was gratified at the expression in Diccon's eyes when he first caught sight of her. In the lovely blue gown, carrying only roses from her mother's garden, her hair brushed and loose on her shoulders she was a beautiful bride and Diccon, in his new light gray suit a fitting groom. Missily and Mikell walked the aisle first, also holding hands, then parted to let the other couple stand between them. Kitten, once more in control of herself, watched them quietly. No one could tell from her expression what she thought and she didn't cry, nor did Anna. Rose wiped a tear away furtively but Erin, who'd decided all the fuss was foolishness, was weeping openly and Allan took out a handkerchief to blow his nose. There were quite a few there, after all. Gabriel and Deborah had come with Lorna and Nigel, all sitting with Jon and Alexis. Candace was so excited she could hardly sit still and Gretchen, to whom it was all very romantic, sat dreaming between her sister and Sean. Brett and Eleanor sat with Perry and Jean and their two while Max and Molly, their sons and Eva and her family filled another pew. After the simple and moving ceremony Diccon and Suz turned around to be presented as Mr. and Mrs. Diccon Brooke. They blinked as they saw how many had gathered to see them and he turned to look at her. She shook her head and a tear ran down her cheek. He wiped it away tenderly, bending to kiss her again, whispering, "Hello, Mrs. Brooke."

"My turn," said Mikell at his elbow and the others laughed and then the newly weds were surrounded.

Though Suz and Diccon left as soon as they could--running through a shower of rice that the children threw, turning to wave before they climbed into Suz's car and headed for Canada--the others went to Gabriel's and Deborah's for a picnic dinner and spent the rest of the day together. Later in the afternoon, Myles drove Erin and Kitten to the airport with Sean along for company. Brett and Eleanor seemed to have always been part of the group and stayed until late before they left for home, beguiling the others with stories of the dinner parties Shaul had given and other jobs they'd held, of their new project.

Mikell managed to get Joshua off by himself before he and his wife left after dinner. "I wasn't sure you'd marry them. In fact, Missily brought it up last night before I thought of it," he said as they walked slowly to the creek running rapidly downhill, not far away from where the tables and chairs had been set up.

Joshua smiled. He squatted down to pick up a stone and skip it across the rushing stream. "I did have some reservations when Diccon first called me from Oregon. We talked a long time. Diccon had been reading the Gospel of John to Suz, explaining as he went along and they spent quite a bit of time on the woman at the well. Diccon told me he believed it right for him to marry Suz but that if I didn't want to perform the ceremony he would listen to my reasons. He warned me that he'd already made up his mind, that he'd had a while to think it all over because of what happened at your reunion." Joshua stood up and stuck his hands in his pockets. "I wasn't entirely convinced until I talked to the two of them together. I believe your sister-in-law, is, if not already in, close to being part of the kingdom of God. Everything is so new to her and she has a lot of questions but she was beginning to understand what the Bible means by sin and by adultery, in particular, and why it is wrong. It seems the Spirit is already at work in her. And Diccon," Joshua stopped to clear his throat, "he's wonderful. I had no idea he had so much insight. I finally decided to treat it as I would any sin committed by a person before regeneration, forgiven in Christ. Whether that is the right decision or not, I'm not certain. It's one of those times when I know that others would be far more adamant about certain Scriptures but I'm not convinced that adultery can't be forgiven the same as any other sin. It wasn't held against David, remember, and he did marry Bathsheba. This is one of those times when I have to trust in the fact that Christ is my righteousness and if I made a mistake, then it is forgiven in Him. I really don't know whether I made the right decision or not. I'll just have to live with that but I don't want to sound as though I thought Christ being my righteousness made it right to do anything against Scripture. In fact, now you have me wondering again. I hope Diccon doesn't suffer because I made the wrong decision. After all, if a man murders someone, is put in prison then becomes a Christian he still has to reap what he sewed. He can't just be let out of prison without paying for his crime." He sighed and his shoulders slumped. He has been so impressed by Diccon but now wondered if he hadn't thought the matter through adequately.

It was quite late by the time Mikell and Missily made it to bed that night. Missily sat up in bed, chin on her knees waiting for Mikell to check on things and lock up, thinking of what Mikell had told her of his conversation with Joshua. It was hard to realize that she might have a sister who was also a believer. Tomorrow they would tell their four. Now Gretchen and Candace were in bed while Myles and Sean had gone somewhere with Max's boys.

"Smells like rain," Mikell said as he came into the room, pulling his shirt out of his trousers.

"Oh, I hope we do have some. We need it. Mikell, was I that pretty on my wedding day?" she asked dreamily, her cheek against her knees, her arm clasped around them.

Mikell pulled on his nightshirt and glanced at his wife. Her heavy hair fell in lovely waves across her shoulders and down the blanket. She had on one of her frilly summer nightgowns, a blue one this time that almost gave her gray eyes a blue shade. "Probably," he said and as her head came up he smiled down at her, "but you're more beautiful now than Suz or than you were when I first married you. I still say I married the right Metlow girl. She's not only the most intelligent and interesting of the bunch but she is far more beautiful than her sisters."

"I wouldn't trade my Mikell either. I watched you all day and never get over the fact that you're mine."

He turned out the light and opened the curtains and as he did so lightening lit up the backyard. Not much later the thunder crashed. Missily jumped out of bed to stand beside him. She loved thunderstorms, though they didn't have many of them. Mikell took her in his arms and they stood together as the rain began, breathing in the fragrance, listening to the rain on the roof and the leaves and both sighed in contentment.

www.ingramcontent.com/pod-product-compliance
Lightning Source LLC
Chambersburg PA
CBHW021331250626
47155CB00002B/679